All About Passion

STEPHANIE LAURENS

All About
Passion

AVON BOOKS
An Imprint of HarperCollinsPublishers

AVON BOOKS
An Imprint of HarperCollins*Publishers*
10 East 53rd Street
New York, New York 10022-5299

Chapter 1

London
August 1820

"*Good evening,* my lord. Your uncle has called. He's awaiting you in the library."

Gyles Frederick Rawlings, fifth Earl of Chillingworth,
paused in the act of divesting himself of his greatcoat, then
shrugged and let the heavy coat fall into his butler's waiting
hands. "Indeed?"

"I understand Lord Walpole will shortly return to Lambourn Castle. He wondered if you had any messages for the
Dowager Countess."

"In other words," Gyles murmured, resettling his cuffs,
"he wants the latest gossip and knows better than to return to
Mama and my aunt without it."

"As you say, my lord. In addition, Mr. Waring called earlier. On ascertaining that you were returning this evening, he
left word that he would hold himself ready to wait on your
lordship at your earliest convenience."

"Thank you, Irving." Gyles strolled into his front hall. Behind him, the front door quietly shut, propelled by a silent
footman. Pausing in the middle of the green-and-white tiles,

Gyles glanced back at Irving, waiting, a picture of patience in his butler's black. "Summon Waring." Gyles turned down the hall. "Send a footman with the carriage, given it's so late."

"Immediately, my lord."

Another well-trained footman opened the library door; Gyles walked in; the door closed behind him.

His uncle, Horace Walpole, was sitting on the *chaise*, legs stretched out, a half-empty brandy balloon in one hand. He cracked open one eye, then opened both and sat up. "There you are, m'boy. I was wondering if I'd have to go back newsless, and considering what would be safe to concoct."

Gyles crossed to the tantalus. "I believe I can spare your imagination. I'm expecting Waring shortly."

"That new man-of-business of yours?"

Gyles nodded. Glass in hand, he crossed to his favorite armchair and sank into its leather-cushioned comfort. "He's been looking into a small matter for me."

"Oh? Which matter?"

"Who I should marry."

Horace stared, then straightened. "Hell's bells! You're serious."

"Marriage is not a subject on which I would jest."

"Glad to hear it." Horace took a large sip of his brandy. "Henni said you'd be making a move in that direction, but I really didn't think you would—well, not yet."

Gyles hid a wry smile. Horace had been his guardian since his father's death; he'd been seven at the time of his sire's demise, so it was Horace who'd guided him through adolesence and youth. Despite that, he could still surprise Horace. His aunt Henrietta, Henni to all, was another matter—she seemed to know instinctively what he was thinking on all major issues, even though he was here in London while she resided at his principal estate in Berkshire. As for his mother, also at Lambourn Castle, he'd long been grateful that she kept her perceptions to herself. "It's not as if marriage is something I can avoid."

"There is that," Horace conceded. "Osbert as the next earl is not something any of us could stomach. Least of all Osbert."

"So Great-aunt Millicent regularly informs me." Gyles nodded at the large desk farther down the room. "That letter there—the thick one? That'll be another missive demanding I do my duty by the family, pick a suitable chit, and marry with all speed. One arrives every week without fail."

Horace pulled a face.

"And, of course, every time I cross Osbert's path, he looks at me as if I'm his only possible salvation."

"Well, you are. If you don't marry and beget an heir, he'll be for it. And Osbert in charge of the earldom is entirely too depressing a thought to contemplate." Horace drained his glass. "Still, I wouldn't have thought you'd let old Millicent and Osbert jockey you into marrying to please them."

"Perish the thought. But if you must know, and I'm sure Henni will want to, I intend to marry entirely to suit myself. I'm thirty-five, after all. Further denying the inevitable will only make the adjustment more painful—I'm set in my ways as it is." He rose and held out his hand.

Horace grimaced and gave him his glass. "Devilish business, marriage—take my word for it. Sure it isn't all these Cynsters marrying that's niggled you into taking the plunge?"

"That's where I was today—Somersham. There was a family gathering to show off all the new wives and infants. If I'd needed any demonstration of the validity of your thesis, today would have provided it."

Refilling their glasses, Gyles pushed aside the prickling presentiment evoked by his old friend Devil Cynster's latest infernal machination. "Devil and the others elected me an honorary Cynster." Turning from the tantalus, he handed Horace his glass, then resumed his seat. "I pointed out that while we might share countless characteristics, I'm not, and never will be, a Cynster."

He would not marry for love. That fate, as he'd assured Devil for years, would never be his.

Every Cynster male seemed unavoidably to succumb, jettisoning rakish careers of legendary proportions for love and the arms of one special lady. There'd been six in the group popularly known as the Bar Cynster, and now all were wed, all exclusively and unswervingly focused on their wives and growing families. If there was, within him, a spark of envy, he made sure it was buried deep. The price they'd paid was not one he could afford.

Horace snorted. "Love matches are the Cynsters' forte. Seem to be all the rage these days, but take my word for it— an arranged marriage has a lot to recommend it."

"My thoughts exactly. Earlier this summer I set Waring the task of investigating all the likely candidates to see which, if any, had dower properties that would materially add to the earldom."

"Properties?"

"If one is not marrying for love, one may as well marry for something else." And he'd wanted a reason for his choice, so whichever lady he ultimately offered for would entertain no illusions over what had made him drop his handkerchief in her lap. "My instructions were that my future countess had to be sufficiently well-bred, docile, and endowed with at least passable grace of form, deportment, and address." A lady who could stand by his side and impinge on his consciousness not at all; a well-bred cypher who would bear his children and disrupt his lifestyle minimally.

Gyles sipped. "As it happened, I had also asked Waring to trace the current ownership of the Gatting property."

Horace nodded his understanding. The Gatting property had at one time been part of the Lambourn estate. Without it, the earldom's principal estate was like a pie with a slice missing; regaining the Gatting lands had been an ambition of Gyles's father, and his father before him.

"In pursuing the owner, Waring discovered that the deed had passed to some distant Rawlings, then, on his demise, into the dowry of his daughter, presently of marriageable age. The information Waring is apparently anxious to impart concerns the daughter."

"She of marriageable age?"

Gyles inclined his head as the chime of the front door bell pealed through the house. A moment later, the library door opened.

"Mr. Waring, my lord."

"Thank you, Irving."

Waring, a heavy-set man in his early thirties, with a round face and close-cropped hair, entered. Gyles waved him to the armchair opposite. "You've met Lord Walpole. Can I offer you a drink?"

"Thank you, my lord, but no." Waring nodded to Horace, then sat, laying a leather satchel across his knees. "I knew how keen you were to pursue this matter, so I took the liberty of leaving a message . . ."

"Indeed. I take it you have news?"

"I have." Settling a pair of spectacles on his nose, Waring withdrew a sheaf of papers from his satchel. "As we'd heard, the gentleman and his household resided permanently in Italy. Apparently *both* parents, Gerrard Rawlings and his wife Katrina, perished together. Subsequently, the daughter, Francesca Hermione Rawlings, returned to England and joined the household of her uncle and guardian, Sir Charles Rawlings, in Hampshire."

"I've been trying to recall . . ." Gyles swirled his glass. "Were they—Charles and Gerrard—the sons of Francis Rawlings?"

Waring shuffled his papers, then nodded. "Indeed. Francis Rawlings was the grandfather of the lady in question."

"Francesca Hermione Rawlings." Gyles considered the name. "And the lady herself?"

"That proved easier than I'd expected. The family entertained extensively—any member of the ton passing through northern Italy would have met them. I've descriptions from Lady Kenilworth, Mrs. Foxmartin, Lady Lucas, and the Countess of Morpleth."

"What's the verdict?"

"A delightful young lady. Pleasant. Well-favored. A most amusing creature—that was old Lady Kenilworth. A young gentlewoman of excellent breeding—so said the countess."

"Who said 'well-favored'?" Horace asked.

"Actually, all of them said that, or words to the effect." Waring glanced at the written accounts, then offered them to Gyles.

Gyles took them, perused them. "If you put them together, they spell 'paragon.' " He raised his brows. "You know what they say about gift horses." He handed the reports to Horace. "What of the rest?"

"The young lady's now twenty-three years old, but there's no record nor rumor of any marriage. Indeed, the ladies I spoke with had lost sight of Miss Rawlings. Although most were familiar with the tragedy of her parents' death and were aware of her return to England, none have seen her since. That seemed strange, so I followed it up. Miss Rawlings is residing with her uncle at Rawlings Hall, near Lyndhurst, but I haven't been able to locate anyone presently in the capital who has met the lady, her guardian, or any member of the household in the past few years."

Waring looked at Gyles. "If you wish, I could send a man down to assess the situation locally. Discreetly, of course."

Gyles considered. Impatience—to have the whole business of his marriage safely dealt with and behind him—flared. "No—I'll deal with it myself." He glanced at Horace and smiled cynically. "There are *some* benefits to being head of the family."

After commending Waring for his excellent work, Gyles saw him into the front hall. Horace followed; he left on Waring's heels, stating his intention to return to Lambourn Castle the next day. The front door closed. Gyles turned and climbed the wide stairs.

Discreet elegance and the unmistakable grace of established wealth surrounded him, yet there was a coldness about his house, an emptiness that chilled. Solid and timelessly classical though it was, his home lacked human warmth. From the head of the stairs, he looked down the imposing sweep and concluded that it was, indeed, past time he found a lady to correct the fault.

Francesca Hermione Rawlings easily topped the list to be invited to undertake the task. Aside from anything else, he truly wanted the deed to the Gatting property. His list had other names on it, but no other lady matched Miss Rawlings's credentials. She might, of course, prove to be ineligible in some way; if so, he'd learn of it tomorrow.

No sense in dallying and allowing fate an opportunity to stick her finger in his pie.

He drove into Hampshire the next morning, reaching Lyndhurst in the early afternoon. He turned in under the sign of the Lyndhurst Arms. Bespeaking rooms there, he left his tiger, Maxwell, in charge of settling his greys. Hiring a good-looking chestnut hunter, he set off for Rawlings Hall.

According to the garrulous innkeeper, Gyles's distant kinsman, Sir Charles Rawlings, lived a reclusive life in the depths of the New Forest. Nevertheless, the road to the Hall was well graded, and the gates, when Gyles came to them, stood open. He rode in, the chestnut's hooves beating a regular tattoo along the graveled drive. The trees thinned, then gave way to extensive lawns surrounding a house of faded red brick, some sections gabled, others battlemented with a lone tower at one end. None of the building was new, not even Georgian. Rawlings Hall was well looked after but unostentatious.

A parterre extended from the front courtyard, separating an old stone wall from the lawns surrounding an ornamental lake. Hidden behind the wall, a garden ran alongside the house; beyond it lay a formal shrubbery.

Gyles drew rein before the front steps. Footsteps pattered. Dismounting, he handed the reins to the stable lad who came pelting up, then strode up the steps to the door and knocked.

"Good afternoon, sir. May I help you?"

Gyles considered the large butler. "The Earl of Chillingworth. I wish to see Sir Charles Rawlings."

To give him credit, the butler blinked only once. "Indeed, sir—my lord. If you will step this way, I'll advise Sir Charles of your arrival immediately."

Shown into the drawing room, Gyles prowled, his impatience fueled by an inexplicable sense of being just one step ahead of fate. Devil's fault, of course. Even being an *honorary* Cynster was tempting fate too far.

The door opened. Gyles swung around as a gentlemen entered—an older, softer, more careworn version of himself, with the same rangy build, the same chestnut brown hair. Despite the fact he had not previously met Charles Rawlings, Gyles would have instantly recognized him as a relative.

"Chillingworth? Well!" Charles blinked, taking in the resemblance, which rendered any answer to his question superfluous. He recovered quickly. "Welcome, my lord. To what do we owe this pleasure?"

Gyles smiled, and told him.

"Francesca?"

They'd repaired to the privacy of Charles's study. After seeing Gyles to a comfortable chair, Charles subsided into the one behind his desk. "I'm sorry—I don't see what interest you might have in Francesca."

"As to that, I'm not certain, but my . . . dilemma, shall we say? is common enough. As the head of the family, I'm expected to wed. In my case, it's something of a necessity, given it's most seriously necessary I beget myself an heir." Gyles paused, then asked, "Have you met Osbert Rawlings?"

"Osbert? Is he Henry's son?" When Gyles nodded, Charles's expression blanked. "Isn't he the one who wants to be a poet?"

"He did want to be a poet, yes. Now he *is* a poet, and that's infinitely worse."

"Good lord! Vague, gangly, never knows what to do with his hands?"

"That's Osbert. You can see why the family are counting on me to do my duty. To do him justice, Osbert himself is terrified I won't, and he'll have to step into my shoes."

"I can imagine. Even as a lad he had limp wool for a backbone."

"Therefore, having reached the age of thirty-five, I'm engaged in looking about for a wife."

"And you thought of Francesca?"

"Before we discuss particulars, I wish to make one point clear. I'm looking for an amenable bride willing to engage in an arranged marriage."

"An arranged . . ." Charles frowned. "You mean a marriage of convenience?"

Gyles raised his brows. "That always struck me as an oxymoron. How could marriage ever be convenient?"

Charles didn't smile. "Perhaps you'd better explain what you're seeking."

"I wish to contract an arranged marriage with a lady of suitable birth, breeding, and comportment to fill the role of my countess and provide me and the family with the heirs we require. Beyond that, and the household and formal duties pertaining to the role of Countess of Chillingworth, I would make no further demands of the lady. In return, in addition to the position itself and all things reasonably accruing to it, such as her wardrobe, her own carriage and servants, I will settle on her an allowance that will enable her to live in luxury for the rest of her days. I'm hardly a pauper after all."

"With due respect, neither is Francesca."

"So I understand. However, with the exception of the deed to the Gatting property, which I wish to return to the Lambourn estate, her various inheritances will remain hers to do with as she pleases."

Charles's brows rose. "That is indeed generous." His gaze grew distant. "I have to admit that my marriage was arranged . . ." After a moment, he refocused on Gyles. "I fear I must ask, cousin—is there any particular reason you're so insistent your marriage be an arranged one?"

"If you mean do I have a mistress of long standing whom I don't wish to set aside, or something of that nature, the answer is no." Gyles considered Charles, considered his open and honest brown eyes. "The reason I wish to keep my marriage—every aspect of it—on a businesslike footing is because I have absolutely no patience with the concept of love in marriage. It's a highly overrated circumstance—one, moreover, with which I desire no closer acquaintance. I do not wish my prospective wife to entertain any notion that I offer love, either now or in some rosy-hued future. From the first, I want her to know that love is not part of our equation. I see no benefit in raising the prospect, and will and do insist that my intent is made clear from the outset."

Charles regarded him for some time, then nodded. "It could be said that you're only being more honest than others who think the same."

Gyles made no answer.

"Very well—I now understand what you're seeking, but why consider Francesca?"

"Because of the Gatting property. It was, centuries ago, a dower property. Indeed, it was probably the reason for an arranged marriage back then—the property completes the circle of my Lambourn lands. It should never have been separated, but because it wasn't part of the entail, some misguided ancestor bequeathed it to a younger son, and that became something of a tradition . . ." Gyles frowned. "Gerrard was the elder, wasn't he? How is it you inherited this place and he inherited Gatting?"

"My father." Charles grimaced. "He fell out with Gerrard, as it happens because Gerrard refused to marry as he'd arranged. Gerrard married for love and went to Italy, while I . . ."

"Made the arranged marriage your brother refused?"

Charles nodded. "So Papa reorganized his will. Gerrard got the Gatting property, which I should have received, and I got the Hall." He smiled. "Gerrard didn't give a damn. Even after Papa died, he remained in Italy."

"Until he died. How did that happen?"

"A boating accident on Lake Lugano one night. No one knew until the next day. Both Gerrard and Katrina drowned."

"And so Francesca came to you."

"Yes. She's been with us for nearly two years."

"How would you describe her?"

"Francesca?" Charles's expression softened. "She's a wonderful girl! A breath of fresh air and a beam of sunshine in one. It's odd, but although she's quite lively, she's also restful—a contradiction, I know, but . . ." Charles looked at Gyles.

"I understand she's twenty-three. Is there some reason she hasn't married?"

"Not specifically. Prior to their deaths, Gerrard and Katrina, and Francesca, too, had discussed addressing the question of a husband more seriously, but the accident intervened. Francesca was adamant on observing the full period of mourning—she was an only child and greatly attached to her parents. So it was only a year or so ago that she started going about." Charles grimaced lightly. "For reasons with which I won't burden you, we don't entertain. Francesca attends the assemblies and the local dances under the auspices of Lady Willingdon, one of our neighbors . . ."

Charles's recital died away. Gyles raised a brow. "What?"

Charles regarded him speculatively, then seemed to come to some decision. "For the past year, Francesca has been actively looking for a husband. It was at her request I solicited the help of Lady Willingdon."

"And has she met anyone she considers suitable?"

"No. Indeed, I believe she's quite despondent over finding any suitable prospect locally."

Gyles regarded Charles steadily. "Indelicate question though it is, do you think your niece might find *me* suitable?"

Charles's brief smile was wry. "From all I've ever heard, if you wished her to find you suitable, she would. You could sweep any naive young lady off her feet."

Gyles's smile mirrored Charles's. "Unfortunately, in this case, using those particular talents might prove counterproductive. I want an amenable bride, not a besotted one."

"True."

Gyles considered Charles, then stretched out his legs and crossed his booted ankles. "Charles, I'm going to place you in an invidious position and claim the right of help you owe me as head of the family. Do you know of any reason that would argue against making Francesca Rawlings the next Countess of Chillingworth?"

"None. Absolutely none." Charles returned his regard steadily. "Francesca would fill the position to the admiration of all the family."

Gyles held his gaze a moment longer, then nodded. "Very well." He felt as if a vise had released from about his chest. "In that case, I'd like to make a formal offer for your niece's hand."

Charles blinked. "Just like that?"

"Just like that."

"Well"—Charles started to rise—"I'll send for her—"

"No." Gyles waved him back. "You forget—I wish this entire matter to be treated with the utmost formality. I want it made clear, not only by word but also by deed, that this is an arranged marriage, nothing more. Your description of your niece confirms the opinions of others—*grandes dames* of the ton richly experienced in evaluating the worth of marriageable young ladies. Everyone declares Francesca Rawlings an unexceptionable parti—I need no further assurances. In the circumstances, I see no reason to meet Miss Rawlings socially. You are her guardian—it's through you I'll apply for her hand."

Charles considered arguing; Gyles knew precisely when the realization that it would be wasted effort, and rather impertinent at that, dawned. He, after all, was the head of the family.

"Very well. If that's your wish, if you'll give me the details, I'll speak with Francesca this evening . . . I'd better write it down." Charles searched for pen and paper.

When he was ready, Gyles dictated and Charles transcribed the formal offer of a contract of marriage between the Earl of Chillingworth and Francesca Hermione Rawlings. As Charles scribbled the last of the settlements, Gyles mused, "It might be as well not to mention the relationship, distant as it is. It's not of any practical relevance. I'd prefer that the offer was specifically made as coming from the earl."

Charles shrugged. "It can't hurt. Women like titles."

"Good. If there's no further information you need from me, I'll leave you." Gyles stood.

Charles came to his feet. He opened his mouth, then hesitated. "I was going to insist you stay with us here, or at least dine . . ."

Gyles shook his head. "Another time, perhaps. I'm staying at the Lyndhurst Arms should you need to reach me." He turned to the door.

Charles yanked the bellpull, then followed. "I'll discuss this with Francesca this evening—"

"And I'll call tomorrow morning to hear her answer." Gyles paused as Charles joined him at the door. "One last impertinence. You mentioned your marriage was an arranged one—tell me, were you happy?"

Charles met his gaze. "Yes. We were."

Gyles hesitated, then inclined his head. "Then you know Francesca has nothing to fear in the arrangement I propose."

There'd been pain in Charles's eyes. Gyles knew Charles was a widower, but he hadn't anticipated that depth of feeling; Charles had clearly felt the loss of his wife keenly. A chill touched his nape. Gyles stepped into the hall. Charles followed. They shook hands, then the butler arrived. Gyles followed him back through the house.

As they neared the front hall, the butler murmured, "I'll just send the footman for your horse, my lord."

They stepped into the hall to find no footman in sight, but the green baize door at the hall's end was swinging wildly. A second later, a shrieking scullery maid raced out. She ignored Gyles and rushed for the butler.

"Oh, Mr. Bulwer, you got to come quick! There's a chook got loose in the kitchen! Cook's chasing it with a cleaver, but it won't stand still!"

The butler looked offended and guilty simultaneously. He slid a helpless glance at Gyles as the maid dragged with all her might on his sleeve. "I do apologize, my lord—I'll get help—"

Gyles laughed. "Don't worry—I'll find my way. By the sound of it, you'd better settle things in the kitchen if you want any dinner tonight."

Relief washed over Bulwer's face. "Thank you, my lord. The stable lad will have your horse ready." Before he could say more, he was dragged away. Gyles heard him scolding the maid as they went through the swinging door.

Grinning, Gyles strolled to the front door. Letting himself out, he descended the steps, then, on impulse, turned left. He strolled the parterre, admiring the trimmed hedges and conifers. On his left, the stone wall bordered the path, then a yew hedge continued the line unbroken. He turned left again at the earliest opportunity—an archway in the hedge giving onto a path through the shrubbery. He looked ahead; the stable's roof rose beyond the hedges.

Stepping through the archway, he paused. An intersecting path ran both right and left. Glancing toward the house, he discovered he could see all the way to where the stone wall he'd earlier paced along joined the corner of the house. Close by the house, a stone seat was built out from the wall.

On the seat sat a young lady.

She was reading a book lying open in her lap. The late-afternoon sun beamed down, bathing her in golden light. Fair hair the color of flax was drawn back from her face; fair skin glowed faintly pink. From this distance, he couldn't see her eyes yet the general set of her features appeared unremarkable, pleasant but not striking. Her pose, head tilted, shoulders low, suggested she was a woman easily dominated, naturally submissive.

She was not the sort of woman to stir him at all, not the sort of woman he would normally take the time to study.

She was precisely the sort of wife he was looking for. Could she be Francesca Rawlings?

As if some higher power had heard his thought, a woman's voice called, "Francesca?"

The girl looked up. She was shutting her book, gathering her shawl as the woman called again. "Francecsa? Franni?"

Rising, the girl called, "I'm here, Aunt Ester." Her voice was delicate and light.

Stepping out, she disappeared from Gyles's view.

Gyles smiled and resumed his stroll. He'd trusted Charles and Charles had not deceived him—Francesca Rawlings possessed precisely the right attributes to be his amenable bride.

The path opened onto a grassed courtyard. Gyles stepped into it—

A dervish in emerald green did her best to mow him down.

She landed against him like a force of nature—a small woman barely topping his shoulder. His first impression was of wild black hair curling riotously over her shoulders and back. The emerald green was a velvet riding habit; she was booted and carried a crop in one hand.

He caught her, steadied her—she would have fallen if he hadn't closed his arms about her.

Even before she'd caught her breath, his hands had gentled, his rakish senses avidly relaying the fact that she was abundantly curvaceous, her flesh firm yet yielding, quintessentially feminine—for him, elementally challenging. His hands spread over her back, then his arms locked, but lightly, trapping her against him. Full breasts warmed his chest, soft hips his thighs.

A strangled "Oh!" escaped her.

She looked up.

The green feather in the scrap of a cap perched atop her glossy curls brushed his cheek. Gyles barely noticed.

Her eyes were green—a green more intense than the emerald of her gown. Wide and wondering, they were darkly and thickly lashed. Her skin was flawless ivory tinged a faint gold, her lips a dusky rose, delicately curved, the lower sensuously full. Her hair was pulled back and anchored across her crown, revealing a wide forehead and the delicate arch of black brows. Curls large and small tumbled down, framing a heart-shaped face that was irresistibly piquant and utterly intriguing; Gyles was seized by a need to know what she was thinking.

Those startled green eyes met his, roved his face, then, widening even more, returned to his.

"I'm sorry. I didn't see you coming."

He felt her voice more than heard it—felt it like a caress inside, an invitation purely physical. The sound itself was . . . smoky—a sultry sound that somehow clouded his senses.

His very willing senses. Like recognized like in the blink of an eye. *Oh, yes,* the beast inside him purred. His lips curved subtly although his thoughts were anything but.

Her gaze lowered, fastened on his lips, then she swallowed. Light color rose in her cheeks. Her heavy lids lowered, hiding her eyes. She eased back in his arms. "If you would release me, sir . . ."

He didn't want to, but he did—slowly, with deliberately obvious reluctance. She'd felt more than good in his arms— she'd felt warm and intensely vital. Intensely alive.

She stepped back, color deepening as his hands brushed her hips as his arms fell from her. She shook out her skirts, refusing to meet his eyes.

"If you'll pardon me, I must go."

Without waiting for any answer, she slipped past him, then strode quickly down the path. Turning, he watched her retreat.

Her steps slowed. She stopped.

Then she whirled and looked back at him, meeting his gaze with neither consciousness nor guile. "Who are you?"

She was a gypsy in green framed by the hedges. The directness in her gaze, in her stance, was challenge incarnate.

"Chillingworth." Turning fully, he swept her a bow, his eyes never leaving hers. Straightening, he added, "And very definitely at your service."

She stared at him, then gestured vaguely. "I'm late . . ."

For all the world as if she hadn't been . . .

Their gazes held; something primitive arced between them—some promise that needed no words to be made.

Her gaze slid from his, traveling avidly, greedily over him as if she would commit him to memory; he did the same, no less hungry for the sight of her, poised to take flight.

Then she did. She whirled, snatched up her trailing habit, and fled, ducking down a side path toward the house, disappearing from his view.

Gaze locked on the empty avenue, Gyles suppressed an urge to give chase. His arousal gradually faded; he turned. The smile curving his lips was not one of amusement. Sensual anticipation was a currency he dealt in regularly; the gypsy knew well how to bargain.

He reached the stable and sent the lad to fetch the chestnut; settling to wait, it occurred to him that, at this juncture, he might be expected to be thinking about his bride-to-be. He mentally focused on the pale young lady with her book; within seconds, the image was overlaid by the more vibrant, more sensually appealing picture of the gypsy as he'd last seen her, with that age-old consideration blazoned in her eyes. Switching his attention back to the former required real effort.

Gyles inwardly laughed. That was, after all, precisely the point in marrying such a cypher—her existence would not interfere with his more carnal pursuits. In that, Francesca Rawlings had indeed proved perfect—within minutes of seeing her, his mind had been full of lascivious thoughts involving another woman.

His gypsy. Who was she? Her voice came back to him, that husky, sultry sound. There was an accent there—just discernible—vowels richer, consonants more dramatic than the English were wont to make them. The accent lent further sensual flavor to that evocative voice. He recalled the olive tinge that had turned the gypsy's skin golden; he also recalled that Francesca Rawlings had lived most of her life in Italy.

The stablelad led the big chestnut out; Gyles thanked the boy and mounted, then cantered down the drive.

Accent and coloring—the gypsy could be Italian. As for behavior, no meek, mild-mannered English young lady would ever have boldly appraised him as she had. Italian, then, either friend or companion of his bride-to-be. She was certainly no maid—not dressed as she had been—and no maid would have dared behave so forwardly, not on first or even second sight.

Reining in where the drive wound into the trees, Gyles looked back at Rawlings Hall. How best to play the cards he'd just been dealt he wasn't yet sure. Securing his amenable bride remained his primary objective; despite the carnal need she evoked, seducing the gypsy had to take second place.

He narrowed his eyes, seeing, not faded bricks but a pair of emerald eyes bright with understanding, with knowledge and speculation beyond the ken of any modest young lady.

He would have her.

Once his amenable bride declared she was willing, he'd turn to a conquest more to his taste. Savoring the prospect, he wheeled the chestnut and galloped down the drive.

Chapter 2

Francesca rushed into the house through the garden hall. Abruptly halting, she waited for her eyes to adjust to the dimmer light. Waited for her wits to stop whirling.

Gracious! She'd spent the last year privately bemoaning the lack of fire in English men, and now look what the gods had thrown at her. Even if it had taken them twelve months to find him, she wasn't about to complain.

She wasn't sure she shouldn't go down on her knees and give thanks.

The vision that evoked brought a laugh bubbling up, set the dimple in her left cheek quivering. Then her levity faded. Whoever he was, he hadn't come to see her; she might never meet him again. Yet he was a relative assuredly—she'd noted the resemblance to her father and uncle. A frown in her eyes, she headed into the house.

She'd just returned from a ride when she'd heard Ester call. Leaving the stables, she'd pelted for the house. She'd stayed out longer than usual; Ester and Charles might be worrying. Then she'd collided with the stranger.

A gentleman, definitely, and possibly titled—difficult to tell if Chillingworth was surname or title. Chillingworth. She said it in her mind, rolled it on her tongue. It had a certain ring to it, one that suited the man. Whatever else he might be—and she had a few ideas on the subject—he was the antithesis of the boring, unexciting provincial gentlemen she'd been assessing for the past year. Chillingworth, whoever he might be, was not boring.

Her pulse was still racing, her blood still up, far more so than could be accounted for by her ride. Indeed, she didn't think her racing pulse or the breathlessness that was only now easing owed anything to her ride—they'd come into being because he'd held her too close and smiled at her like a leopard eyeing his next meal—and because she'd known precisely what he'd been thinking.

His grey eyes had kindled, sparking yet darkening, and his lips had curved just so . . . because he'd been thinking wicked thoughts. Thoughts of flesh pressed to naked flesh, of silk sheets sliding and shushing as bodies moved in an ancient rhythm upon them. The brazen images formed readily in her mind.

Blushing, she banished them and strode on down the corridor. Glancing around and seeing no one, she waved a hand before her face. She didn't want to have to explain her blush to Ester.

The thought had her wondering where Ester was. Entering the central wing, she detoured to the kitchen. No Ester there. The staff had heard Ester call, but didn't know where she'd gone. Francesca pushed through the door into the front hall.

The hall was empty. Her bootheels clacked on the tiles as she crossed to the stairs. She was halfway up the first flight when the door to her uncle's study opened. Ester came out, saw her, and smiled. "There you are, dear."

Francesca reversed direction. "I'm so sorry—it was *such* a fine day I just rode and rode and forgot the time. I heard you call and came running. Is anything wrong?"

"No, indeed." A tall lady with a horsey face but the kindest of eyes, Ester smiled fondly as Francesca halted before her. Reaching out, Ester eased the frivolous riding cap from Francesca's unruly locks. "Your uncle wishes to speak with you, but contrary to there being anything wrong, I suspect you'll be very interested in what he has to say. I'll take this"—Ester spied the riding gloves and crop Francesca held in one hand and took them—"and these, upstairs for you. Go along now—he's waiting to tell you."

Ester's nod indicated the open study door. Intrigued, Francesca entered, shutting the door behind her. Charles was seated behind his desk, studying a letter. Hearing the latch click, he looked up, and beamed.

"Francesca, dear girl, come and sit down. I've just had the most amazing news."

Crossing to the chair to which he waved her, not before the desk but beside it, Francesca could see that for herself. Charles's eyes were alight, not shadowed with some unnameable worry as they so often were. Too often careworn and sad, his face now glowed with unmistakable good cheer. She sank onto the chair. "And this news concerns me?"

"It does, indeed." Swinging to face her, Charles leaned his forearms on his knees so his head was more level with hers. "My dear, I've just received an offer for your hand."

Francesca stared at him. "From whom?"

She heard the calm query and marveled that she'd managed to get it out. Her mind was streaking in a dozen different directions, her heart racing again, speculation running riot. It was a battle to remain still, to counsel herself to the prim and proper.

"From a gentleman—well, actually, he's a nobleman. The offer is from Chillingworth."

"Chillingworth?" Even to her, her voice sounded strained. She hardly dared trust her ears. The vision in her mind . . .

Charles leaned forward and took her hand. "My dear, the Earl of Chillingworth has made you a formal offer of marriage."

* * *

When Charles finished explaining it to her, in painstaking and repetitive detail, Francesca was even more astonished.

"An arranged marriage." She couldn't credit it. From another gentleman, yes—the English were so . . . phlegmatic. But from *him*—from the man who had held her in his arms and wondered what it would be like to . . . with her . . . Something was not right.

"He's adamant that you understand that." Charles's gentle, serious gaze remained fixed on her face. "My dear, I would not urge you to accept unless you felt comfortable with the arrangement, but I would be failing in my duty as your guardian if I didn't tell you that while Chillingworth's approach may appear cold, it is honest. Many men feel the same, but would cloak their offers in more fanciful guise thinking to win your romantic heart."

Francesca gestured dismissively.

Charles smiled. "I know you're not a flighty girl who would have your head turned by false protestations. Indeed, I know you well enough to be sure you would see through any disguise. Chillingworth is not the sort of man to employ one—that's not his style. He's of the first rank—his estates, as I've told you, are extensive. His offer is more than generous." Charles paused. "Is there anything more you'd like to know—any questions at all?"

Francesca had dozens, but they were not the sort her uncle could answer. Her suitor himself would have to explain. He was *not* the sort of man to countenance a bloodless, unemotional union. He had fire and passion in his veins, just as she had.

So what was this all about?

Then the truth dawned. "He spoke with you this afternoon while I was out riding?" When Charles nodded, she asked, "He's never seen me, has he? I can't recall meeting him before."

"I don't believe he's seen you . . ." Charles frowned. "Did you meet him?"

"On my way from the stables. He was . . . leaving."

"Well, then." Charles straightened, perceptibly brightening. "So . . ." His gaze had moved beyond Francesca; now he brought it back to her face. They had talked and talked; it was almost time for dinner. "He'll be back tomorrow morning to hear your answer. What should I tell him?"

That she didn't believe him.

Francesca met Charles's earnest gaze. "Tell him . . . that I need three days—seventy-two hours from this afternoon—to consider his proposal. Given the suddeness and . . . unexpected nature of his offer, I must think things over carefully. Three afternoons from now, I'll say yes or no."

Charles's brows had risen; by the time she'd finished speaking he was nodding. "An excellent notion. You may reassure yourself in your own mind, then give him—" Charles grimaced. "Give me, I suspect, your answer."

"Indeed." Francesca stood, determination rising within her. "I will discover what answer I'm comfortable with—and then he may have it."

It was nearly noon the next day when Gyles once again rode up the Rawlings Hall drive. Shown into the study, he saw Charles rounding the desk, his hand outstretched and a smile on his face. Not that he'd expected anything else. Shaking hands, he consented to sit.

Resuming his seat, Charles met his gaze. "I've spoken to Francesca at some length. She was not averse to your proposal, but she did ask for a period of time—three days—in which to consider her answer."

Gyles felt his brows rise. The request was eminently reasonable; what surprised him was that she'd made it.

Charles was regarding him with concern, unable to read his expression. "Is that a problem?"

"No." Gyles considered, then refocused on Charles.

"While I wish to settle this matter expeditiously, Miss Rawlings's request is impossible to deny. Marriage is, after all, a serious business—a point I wished to emphasize."

"Indeed. Francesca is not a flighty girl—her feet are planted firmly on the ground. She engaged to give a simple yes or no on the third afternoon from yesterday."

"Two days from today." Gyles nodded and stood. "Very well. I'll remain in the area and will call again on the afternoon of the agreed day."

Charles rose and they shook hands. "I understand," Charles said as he walked Gyles to the door, "that you saw Francesca yesterday."

Gyles halted and looked at his host. "Yes, but only briefly." She must have seen him watching her and been artful enough to give no sign.

"Nevertheless. Even a glimpse would be enough. She's a captivating young lady, don't you think?"

Gyles considered Charles. He was a softer, gentler man than himself; mild-mannered ladies were doubtless more his style. Gyles returned Charles's smile. "I believe Miss Rawlings will fill my countess's shoes admirably."

He turned to the door; Charles opened it. Bulwer was waiting to show him out. With a nod, Gyles left.

He elected to stroll to the stables as he had the day before. Ambling down the paths of the parterre, he scanned his surroundings.

He'd told Charles he had no wish to meet his bride-to-be formally. There was nothing to be gained from such an exercise as far as he could see. However, now that she'd stipulated a three-day wait . . .

It might be wise to meet the young lady who had calmly requested three days in which to consider him. Him and his exceedingly generous offer. That smacked of a resolution he found odd in a woman of Francesca Rawlings's character. No matter that he'd only glimpsed her, he was an expert at judging women. Yet he'd clearly misjudged his intended in one respect; it seemed prudent to check that she harbored no further surprises.

Fate was smiling on him—she was walking beside the lake, alone but for a bevy of spaniels. Head up, spine straight, she was striding away from him, the dogs gamboling about her feet. He set out in pursuit.

He drew near as she rounded the end of the lake. "Miss Rawlings!"

She stopped and turned. The shawl she clutched about her shoulders fluttered, its blue highlighting her pale blond hair, fine, straight, and drawn back in a loose chignon. Wafting wisps framed a sweet face, pretty rather than beautiful. Her most memorable feature was her eyes, very pale blue edged by blond lashes.

"Yes?"

She watched him approach without recognition, and just a touch of wariness. Gyles remembered that he'd insisted his offer be made in his titular name; she clearly did not connect him with the gentleman she was considering marrying. "Gyles Rawlings." He bowed, smiling as he straightened. Someone else must have seen him watching her yesterday and reported it to Charles—the woman who had called her, perhaps? "I'm a distant cousin. I wonder if I might walk a little way with you?"

She blinked, then smiled back, as mild as he'd imagined her to be. "If you're a relative, then I suppose that's all right." With a wave, she indicated the path by the lake. "I'm taking the dogs for their constitutional. I do that every day."

"There seem to be quite a number of them." All snuffling at his boots. They weren't gun dogs, but the smaller version—house dog, almost lapdog. He had a sudden thought. "Are they yours?"

"Oh, no. They just live here."

He glanced at her to see if she'd meant that as a joke. Her expression stated she hadn't. Falling into step beside her, he swiftly assessed her figure. She was of average height, her head just lower than his chin; she was slightly built, some-what lacking in curves, but passable. Passable.

"That dog there"—she pointed to one with a ragged ear—"she's the oldest. Her name is Bess."

As they continued around the lake, she continued naming dogs—for the life of him he couldn't think of any suitable conversational distraction. Every opening his normally agile mind supplied seemed inappropriate in light of her naïveté and undisguised innocence. It had been, he reflected, a long time since he'd last conversed with an innocent.

But there was nothing to find fault with in her manners or her deportment. After the seventh dog, he managed a comment, to which she replied readily. She displayed a guileless openness that was, as Charles had noted, oddly soothing. Perhaps because it was undemanding.

They reached the end of the lake and she turned toward the parterre. He was about to follow when a flash of emerald caught his eye. His gaze locked on a green-habited figure riding—streaking—across a distant glade. The trees afforded him only a brief glimpse, then she was gone. Frowning, he lengthened his stride and rejoined his intended.

"Dolly is quite good at catching rats . . ."

As they crossed the lawns, his companion continued with her canine family tree. He paced beside her but his attention had flown.

The damned gypsy had been riding fast—exceedingly fast. And the horse she'd been on—had it just been the distance and her small self that had made the beast appear so huge?

Reaching the parterre, his companion turned onto the path that led around the formal garden. He halted. "I must be on my way." Remembering why he was there, he summoned a charming smile and bowed. "Thank you for your company, my dear. I daresay we'll meet again."

She smiled ingenuously. "That would be pleasant. You are a very good listener, sir."

With a cynical nod, he left her.

He strode through the shrubbery, keeping an eye out for green-habited dervishes. None appeared. Reaching the stable, he looked in, then called a "Hoi!" Receiving no reply, he walked the long aisle, but could discover no stablelad. He found his chestnut, but could see no sign of any horse that had just been brought in. Yet the gypsy *should* have reached the stable by now; she'd been heading in this direction.

Returning to the yard, he looked around; there seemed to be no one about. Shaking his head, he turned to go in and fetch his own horse when a patter of feet heralded the stablelad. He came racing into the yard, lugging a double-panniered picnic basket—he skidded to a halt when he saw Gyles.

"Oh. Sorry, sir. Umm." The boy glanced to the side of the stable, looked at Gyles, then at the basket. "Umm . . ."

"Who's that for?" Gyles indicated the basket.

"Miss said to fetch it right away."

Miss who? Gyles nearly asked, but how many misses could there be at Rawlings Hall. "Here. Give it to me. I'll take it to her while you get my horse. Where is she?"

The lad handed over the basket; it was empty. "In the orchard." He nodded to the side of the stable.

Gyles set out, then glanced back. "If I haven't returned by the time you have the horse ready, just leave it tethered to the door. I'm sure you have other work to do."

"Aye, sir." The boy touched his forelock, then disappeared into the stable.

A slow smile curving his lips, Gyles walked into the orchard.

Pausing, he looked around; the orchard stretched for some distance, full of apple and plum trees, all laden with fruit as yet unripe. Then he saw the horse—a huge bay gelding at least seventeen hands high with a massive chest and a rump to be wary of—standing, saddled, reins trailing, chomping grass.

He started toward it and heard her voice.

"My, what a pretty boy you are."

The smoky, sultry voice oozed seduction.

"Come, let me stroke you—let me run my fingers over your head. *Ooooh,* that's a *good boy.*"

The voice continued, murmuring, cajoling, whispering terms of endearment, invitations to surrender.

Gyles's face hardened. He strode forward, scanning the long grass, looking for the vixen in green and the lad she was seducing . . .

She stopped talking; Gyles strode faster. He reached the apple tree beside which the bay stood. He searched the surrounding grass, but couldn't see a soul.

"Josh," she murmured, "have you got the basket?"

Gyles looked up. She lay stretched full length along a branch, one arm outstretched, reaching, fingers straining . . .

Her skirts had rucked up to her knees, revealing a froth of white petticoats and a tantalizing glimpse of bare leg above the tops of her boots.

Gyles felt giddy. Feelings and emotions whirled and clashed within him. He felt foolish, with unjustified anger bubbling through his veins and having no outlet; he was half-aroused and rocked by the fact that such a minor glimpse of honey-toned skin should have the power to so affect him. Added to all that was flaring concern.

The damned gypsy was a good nine feet off the ground.

"Got you!" She plucked what looked to be a large ball of fluff from among a clump of apples, then she tucked it to her ample bosom, sat, and swiveled—revealing a twin bundle of fluff in her other hand.

She saw him.

"Oh!" She rocked, then clutched both kittens in one hand, grabbing the branch just in time to keep from falling.

The kittens mewled piteously; Gyles would have traded places in a blink.

Eyes wide, skirts now trapped above her knees, she stared down at him. "What are you doing here?"

He smiled. Wolfishly. "I brought the basket. Josh is otherwise engaged."

She narrowed her eyes at him—indeed, she came very close to scowling at him. "Well, since you've brought it, you may as well be useful." She pointed to the lump of fur that had just discovered the toe of his boot. "They need to be collected and taken back indoors."

Setting down the basket, Gyles scooped up the fluffball at his feet and slipped it in. Then he scanned the immediate area; once assured he was not about to commit murder, he stepped beneath the branch and reached up. "Give them here."

That proved difficult, given she had to hold on to the branch at the same time. In the end, she placed one kitten in her lap and handed the other down, then handed the second down.

Returning to the basket, Gyles hunkered down, sliding each kitten in without letting any out. At the edge of his vision, he caught a flash of fur and pounced. Stuffing the runaway into the basket, he asked, "How many are there?"

"Nine. Here's another."

Standing, he took receipt of a ginger fluffball. He added it to the collection. "Can a cat have nine?"

"Ruggles obviously believes so."

Another came tumbling through the grass. He was insinuating it into the furry mewling pile writhing inside the basket when he heard a twig snap.

"Oh—*oh!*"

He turned just in time to take a giant step and catch her as she tumbled from the branch. She landed in his arms in a jumble of velvet skirts. He hefted her up easily, then juggled her into a more comfortable position.

It took two attempts before Francesca managed to fill her lungs. "Th-thank you." She stared at him, and wondered if there was something else she should say. He was carrying her as if she weighed no more than one of the kittens. His eyes were locked on hers; she couldn't think.

Then those grey eyes darkened, turned stormy and turbulent. His gaze shifted to her lips.

"I think," he murmured, "that I deserve a reward."

He didn't ask—he simply took. Bending his head, he set his lips to hers.

The first touch was a shock—his lips were cool, firm. They hardened, moving on hers, somehow demanding. Instinctively, she tried to appease him, her lips softening, yielding. Then she remembered that she was considering marrying him. She slid her hands up, over his chest, over his shoulders. Locking them at his nape, she kissed him back.

She sensed a fleeting hesitation, a momentary hiatus as if she'd shocked him—a heartbeat later it was wiped from her mind by a surge of fiery demand. The sudden pressure shook her. She parted her lips on a gasp—he surged in, ruthless and relentless, taking and claiming and demanding more.

For a moment, she clung, helplessly aware of her surrender, aware of being taken—driven—rapidly out of her depth. Aware of sensations streaking through her body, through her limbs, aware of her toes slowly curling. Far from frightening her, the feelings thrilled her. This was what she'd been created for—she'd known that all her life. But this was only half of it, half of the adventure, half of the apple when she wanted the whole. Without resistance, she let the wave of passion flow through her; as it ebbed, she gathered her will, then set about turning the tide.

She kissed him back passionately, and caught him—surprised him. He hadn't expected it; by the time he realized, he was trapped in the game with her—the heated duel of tongues that she'd always imagined must be. She'd never kissed any man like this, but she'd watched and imagined and wanted—she'd suspected mirroring his caresses would

work. That, she'd assumed, was how ladies learned the art—
by kissing and loving with someone who knew.

He knew.

Hot, urgent, their mouths melded, tongues tangling, sliding, caressing. Her flesh heated, her nerves tightened; sharp
excitement gripped her. Then the tenor of the kiss altered,
slowed, strengthened, until his deep, sliding, rhythmic
thrusts became the dominant theme.

She shuddered, felt something in her yield, something
open, unfurl. React. Her whole body felt glorious, buoyed,
languidly heated. Seduced.

Gyles was drowning, sinking beneath a wave of desire
more powerful than any he'd previously known. It drew him
under with the force of a tidal wave, eroding, washing away
his control.

Abruptly, he broke the kiss. Jerked his head back and
looked down at her. Clinging to his shoulders, held tight in
his arms, she blinked, struggling to reorient.

His features hardened. He muttered a curse, followed by,
"God, you're so damned *easy.*"

Her eyes widened, then her lips set. She wriggled furiously; he swung her down, set her on her feet. She pulled
away, stepped back, briskly brushing her bodice free of
leaves, then shaking and straightening her skirts.

Francesca recalled she'd been miffed at him—even before
that comment. He'd said he'd call in the morning—it must
have been *noon* before he'd deigned to arrive. She'd lain in
wait to waylay him. When he hadn't shown, she'd gone riding to calm herself. What did *noon* say of his eagerness to
win her?

As for his attitude! No wooing, no loverlike embraces—
just hot passion and bold seduction. All very well that the
latter appealed to her rather more than the former—*he*
couldn't have known that. Was he so uneager . . . or was it,
perhaps, that he was so sure she'd accept him?

And what, exactly, did he mean by her being "*easy*"?

She threw him a sharp glance as she knelt to check the kittens. "I understand you've made an offer, my lord."

Gyles stared at her back as she counted the kittens; he kept his frown from his face. If she'd heard about that . . . "I have."

Who the hell is she? Before he could ask, she said, "There's six here—we're missing three." She stood and looked about. "This house of yours—Lambourn Castle. Is it really a castle? Does it have battlements and towers and a drawbridge and moat?"

"No moat or drawbridge." Gyles glimpsed a grey kitten hiding beside a rock. He went to fetch it and it danced away. "There's a section of battlements remaining over the front entrance, and two towers at either end. And there's the gatehouse, too—that's now the Dower House."

"Dower House? Is your mother still alive?"

"Yes." He pounced on the kitten and collared it. Holding it by the scruff, he carried it to the basket.

"What does she think of your offer?"

"I haven't asked." Gyles concentrated on sliding the squirming kitten into the basket while simultaneously holding the others in. "It's nothing to do with her."

Only as he stood did he realize what he'd said. The truth, admittedly, but why the devil was he telling her? Turning to frown—openly—at her, he spied another bumbling feline heading for the end of the orchard. With a muttered curse, he strode after it.

"Do you live at Lambourn all of the year, or only for a few months?"

She asked the question as he returned, the wriggling, squirming bundle in one hand. She was cradling a ginger kitten in her hands, snuggled between her remarkable breasts. It was purring fit to rupture its eardrums.

The sight distracted him completely. Gyles watched, his mouth drying, his mind blank, as she bent at the waist and eased the kitten from its nesting place to lay it in the basket.

"Ah . . ." He blinked as she straightened. "I spend about half the year at Lambourn. I usually go to London for the Season, and then again for the autumn session of Parliament."

"Oh?" Real interest lit her green eyes. "So you take your seat in Parliament and speak?"

He shrugged as he stuffed the last of the kittens into the basket. "When there's a matter that interests me, yes, of course." He frowned. How had they got onto this topic?

Securing the basket's lids, he lifted it and straightened.

"Here." She held out the gelding's reins and reached for the basket. "You can lead Sultan. I'll take them."

Before he knew it, he was standing with the reins in his hand watching her walk up the orchard. Watching her delightfully rounded derriere sway as, the skirt of her habit draped over one arm, she negotiated the slight climb. Setting his jaw, he headed after her—then realized why she'd left him with the gelding.

It took a good minute before he could convince the brute that he really was serious about moving. Finally, the huge horse consented to amble after him as he strode after the witch. She who was interrogating him. As he closed the distance between them, he wondered what she thought she was about. One possible answer had him slowing.

She'd known of his offer. That argued that she was in Francesca Rawlings's confidence. Was it possible that, having confessed to meeting him, she was interrogating him on Francesca's behalf? Francesca certainly hadn't known who he was, but if the gypsy hadn't described him . . . it was possible.

Falling in behind her, he murmured, "So tell me, what else does Miss Rawlings wish to know?"

Francesca glanced back at him—was he making fun of her? She faced forward again. "Miss Rawlings," she said, somewhat tartly, "wishes to know if your town house in London is large."

"Reasonably. It's a relatively new acquisition, not even fifty years old, so it has all the modern conveniences."

"I expect you lead a very busy life while in London, at least during the Season."

"It can be hectic, but the entertainments tend to cluster in the evenings."

"I imagine there's quite a demand for your company."

Gyles narrowed his gaze on the back of her curly black head. Without seeing her face, he couldn't be sure, but . . . surely she wouldn't dare. "I am in demand among the ton's hostesses."

Let her make of that what she would.

"Indeed? And are there any specific commitments, to any *specific* hostesses, that you presently have?"

The brazen witch was asking if he had a mistress. Reaching the stable yard, she stepped onto the cobbles and turned—the green eyes that met his aggravated gaze held a power all their own.

Halting before her, he regarded her. After a fraught moment, he slowly and clearly stated, "Not at present." The fact that he was considering altering that situation heavily underscored the words.

Holding his gaze, Francesca found it easy not to smile. His grey eyes conveyed a meaning she wasn't sure she understood. Was he challenging her to be good enough, fascinating enough, to keep him from other ladies' beds? Was he telling her that whether he kept a mistress or not was up to her? There was a certain temptation in the thought, but she had her pride. Drawing herself up, she let her eyes flash censoriously, then haughtily nodded. "I must get these kittens inside. If you'll give Sultan to Josh . . ." Head regally high, she swept around and headed for the kitchens.

Gyles very nearly reached out and spun her back; his hands fisted as he fought the urge.

"Ruggles!" she called. A ginger-and-black tabby came

running. It stood to sniff the basket, then mewed and ran along beside her.

Gyles drew in his temper; the effort left him seething. That final look of hers had been the last straw. He'd been about to demand to be told precisely who she was and in what relation she stood to Francesca Rawlings when the damned witch had summarily dismissed him!

He couldn't recall the last time any lady had dared dismiss him, not like that.

Through narrowed eyes, he watched her disappear into the kitchen garden, crooning to the kittens and their mother. Unless he much mistook the matter, the gypsy had just put him firmly in his place.

Chapter 3

He couldn't get her out of his mind. Couldn't get the taste of her—so wildly passionate—out of his mouth, couldn't free his senses from her spell.

It was the next morning, and he was still ensnared.

Trotting through the forest, Gyles snorted disgustedly. With a little more persuasion, he could have had her under that damned apple tree. Why the fact so irritated him he couldn't decide—because seducing her had proved so easy? Or because he hadn't had the sense to press his advantage? If he had, she might not be tormenting him still, a thorn in his flesh, an itch he'd yet to scratch.

On the other hand . . .

He pushed the niggling thought aside. She didn't mean that much to him—she was simply a resistant witch issuing a blatant, flagrant challenge, and he'd never been able to turn his back on a challenge. That was all. He was not obsessed with her.

Not yet.

He let the warning slide from his mind. He was too old, too experienced to get caught. That was why he was here, organizing his marriage to a meek, mild-mannered cipher. Recalling that fact, he checked his position, then took the next bridle path toward Rawlings Hall.

He was earlier than he'd been the day before; he caught her as she was setting out from the kennels. She welcomed him with a sunny smile and a "Good morning, Mr. Rawlings. About again?"

He replied with a smile, but watched her closely. He'd assumed after yesterday and the report no doubt made by the gypsy that Francesca would have realized who he was.

If she had, she was a better actress than Sarah Siddons; no trace of awareness showed in her eyes, her expression or her attitude. With an inwardly raised brow, he accepted it. After mulling the situation over, he saw no reason to inform her of his identity—not now. He'd only fluster her.

As before, he found it easy to stroll beside her. Only when they'd reached the other side of the lake and she paused to admire a tree and ask him what sort he thought it might be, did he realize he hadn't been attending. He covered the gaffe easily—the tree was a birch; after that, he paid more attention. Only to discover that his intended was, indeed, the perfect choice for his needs. Her voice was airy and light, not smoky and sultry; it held no power to capture his thoughts. She was sweet and demure and unexciting—he spent more time looking at the spaniels than at her.

If he'd been walking with the gypsy, he'd have tripped over the spaniels.

Shaking his head—wishing he could shake all images of the witch out of it, especially the taunting visions that had kept him awake half the night—he hauled his mind back to the young lady presently by his side.

She evoked not the smallest spark of sexual interest; the contrast between her and her Italian companion could not have been more marked. She was precisely what he needed as his amenable bride—a young lady who aroused his passionate nature not at all. Doing his duty would be easy enough; siring a child or two on her would be no great feat. She might not be a beauty, but she was passable, unassuming, and likable enough. If she would accept his proposal, accept him without love, they would deal well enough together.

Meanwhile, given the gypsy and his bride were friends, it might be wise to ascertain the depth of their friendship before he seduced the gypsy. The thought of some grand emotional scene between himself and his wife because he had her friend in keeping was the closest thing to anathema he'd ever imagined, yet he doubted it would come to that. Who knew? Their friendship might even thrive; such arrangements were not unknown in the ton.

That niggling warning sounded again in his mind; this time, he paid it more heed. It would be wise to play safe with the gypsy, at least until he had his wife and his life secured as he wanted them.

The gypsy was wild and unpredictable. Until his marriage was fact, he'd steer clear of her temptation.

As before, he left his bride-to-be at the parterre. She accepted his departure with a smile, displaying no inclination to cling or demand more of his time. Entirely satisfied with his choice, Gyles headed for the stables.

Josh was waiting; he ran to get the chestnut. Gyles looked around. Then Josh was back. Gyles took his time mounting, dallying as long as he could before he cantered down the drive and turned into the lane to Lyndhurst.

He'd just decided to avoid the witch—it would be illogical to feel disappointed at not seeing her.

Then he did, and his heart leapt. She was a flash of graceful movement deep in a deserted ride. Before he'd thought, he'd loosed the chestnut's reins and was pounding after her.

She slowed at the end of the ride, debating which of two paths to take, then she heard the thud of the chestnut's hooves and glanced back.

A smile spread across her face, on a changing spectrum that traveled from welcoming to glorious. With an exuberant laugh, she flashed him a look of blatant challenge, then plunged down the nearest path.

Gyles followed.

The chestnut he was on was an excellent beast, but the grey she was riding was better. He rode heavier, too, and didn't know the paths she flung her mount down with such alacrity. But he kept doggedly on in her wake, knowing that, eventually, she'd let him catch her.

She glanced back at him as they thundered beneath the trees; he caught a glimpse of her teasing smile. The feather in her scrap of a cap waved as she bobbed and weaved, expertly shifting as the grey took each curve at speed.

Then they burst from the forest into a wide meadow bounded only by more trees. With a "Whoop!" Gyles let his reins fall and rode the big chestnut hands and knees, urging him on. They gained on the flying gypsy. Although she rode fast, he was relieved to note that she held the grey in. The massive hunter had to be one of Charles's mounts, bred for stamina and the chase. In this terrain it was the fastest and surest bet, especially as, at present, it was running with only a fraction of its accustomed weight.

The witch heard him closing; she flung a laugh over her shoulder. "More?"

She didn't wait for an answer but set the grey for another path.

They twisted and turned, then raced across another glade; exhilaration sang in his ears. It had been years since he'd felt such a tug, years since he'd surrendered so completely to the thrill of sheer speed, to the relentless pounding of his horse's hooves, to the echo in his blood.

She felt it, too, knew it, too—it was there in her sparkling eyes. They met his, sharing the moment, then she was off again.

It required no conscious decision to follow; as one they flowed through the forest. It enfolded them, held them within its green bosom as if they ran in a place out of time.

But time still ran.

Gyles had ridden from the age of three; he possessed an inner guide that sensed his horse's strength, how long they'd been flying at speed. A moment came when he checked. His mount still had some way to go; he'd only cantered to and from the Hall.

The thought focused his mind on the grey. He would have bet his matched pair that the gypsy had been flying from the moment she'd left the stable.

He started worrying.

His pulse leapt at every blind twist in the path; he caught his breath at every rough patch she flew over. Unbidden, images crowded into his mind—of her lying injured, fallen across a log, thrown on her lovely head, her neck twisted at an impossible angle—

He couldn't get the visions out of his mind.

The trees thinned. They exploded into another clearing. He called her back, but she'd already sprung the grey. Her face was alight—she threw back her head and laughed, then her gaze fixed ahead, she gathered the reins . . .

Gyles glanced ahead.

A fence, old and decrepit, overgrown with young saplings divided the field in two. She put the grey at it.

"No!"

His shout merged with the thunder of hooves—the grey's and the chestnut's. She was too far ahead for him to catch her eye. Then she was too close to the fence for him to risk distracting her.

Still yards ahead of him, the grey soared. In his heart, he prayed. The heavy hooves cleared the fence easily. The grey landed, then stumbled.

She shrieked.

Gyles lost sight of her as the beast went down, then the grey was up again—riderless.

Heart in his mouth, he altered his trajectory so he cleared the fence some yards from where she'd fallen, then he wheeled—

She was lying spread-eagled on her back in the middle of a gorse bush.

From the disgusted look on her face and the size of the gorse bush, she was unharmed.

The panic that had him by the throat did not immediately let go.

Trotting to the bush, he drew rein and looked down at her. His chest was heaving—the effort of the ride had left him feeling as if he'd run a mile.

His temper left him feeling like tearing a strip off her.

She started to smile at him, then caught the look in his narrowed eyes.

"You *witless* female!" He paused to let the fury behind the words sink in. "You *heard* me yell—why the devil didn't you stop?"

Her eyes flashed green fire; her chin set mulishly. "I heard you, but I'd be surprised if even a *sophisticated gentleman* such as yourself could have known there was a gorse bush here!"

"It wasn't the gorse that was your problem." She struggled to sit up, but the gorse wasn't that accommodating. He swung down from the chestnut's back. "Damn it—you shouldn't be riding, certainly not hell-bent as you were, if you can't pace your mount better. The grey was tired."

"He *wasn't!*" She struggled even more furiously to rise.

"Here." He held out a hand. When she hesitated, eyeing his hand and him through narrowed eyes, he added, "Either take my damned hand, or I'll leave you there for the night."

The threat was a good one—the gorse was in bloom, well endowed with spiny spikes.

With a look as haughty as any princess, she held out a

gloved hand. He grasped it and pulled—then she was on her feet before him.

"Thank you."

Her tone suggested she would rather have accepted help from a leper. Nose elevating, giving a haughty swish of her hips, she swung her heavy skirts around and turned to the grey. "He is *not* tired." Then her voice changed. "Knight . . . come on, boy."

The grey lifted his head, pricked his ears, then came ambling over.

"You can't get back in the saddle."

At the clipped, blunt words, Francesca threw a dismissive look over her shoulder. "I'm not one of your lily-livered English misses who can't mount without help."

He was silent for a moment, then replied, "Very well. Let's see how far you get."

Reaching for Knight's reins, she gathered them, using the action to camouflage another glance at her almost-betrothed. He was standing, arms crossed, watching her. He'd made no attempt to take his chestnut's reins.

His expression was stony—and calmly expectant.

Francesca stopped. She stared at him. "What?"

He took his time answering. "You fell into gorse."

"So?"

After another aggravating moment, he asked, "Don't they have gorse in Italy?"

"No." She frowned. "Not like tha—" The truth dawned; eyes widening, she stared at him, then twisted to look at the back of her skirt. It was covered in snapped-off spikes. She grabbed at her long curls, pulling them over her shoulders. They were adorned with spikes, too. "Oh, no!"

She shot him a glance that told him what she thought of him, then fell to pulling the spiny spikes from her skirt. She couldn't see; in places, she could barely reach.

"Would you like me to help?"

She looked up. He stood no more than two feet away. The

offer had been couched in a completely flat tone. There was nothing to be read in his eyes; his expression was utterly bland.

She gritted her teeth. "Please."

"Turn around."

She did, then looked over her shoulder. He hunkered down behind her and started plucking spikes from her skirt. She felt nothing more than an occasional tug. Reassured, she turned her attention to the curls tumbling down her back to her waist; she pulled and plucked, reached and stretched— he growled at her to stand still, but otherwise applied himself to her skirts in silence.

His gaze fixed on the emerald velvet, Gyles tried not to think of what it was covering. Difficult. He tried even harder not to think of the emotions that had crashed through him in the instant she'd fallen.

He had never, ever, felt like that—not over anyone or anything. For one fractured moment, he'd felt like the sun had gone out, like the light had been snuffed from his life.

It was ludicrous. He'd first met her two days ago.

He tried to tell himself it had been some sense of duty— some idea of responsibility to someone younger than himself, some loyalty to Charles in whose care the gypsy presumably was. He tried to tell himself a lot of things—he didn't believe any of them.

The repetitive task of removing the spikes gave him time to push his unwanted emotions back behind the wall from which they had sprung. He was determined to keep them there, safely locked away.

He plucked off the last spike, then rose and stretched his back. She'd finished her hair some time before and had waited in silence while he completed his task.

"Thank you."

The words were soft; she looked at him for a moment, then turned and gathered her reins.

He stepped beside her and wordlessly offered his cupped hands—he knew she'd bite her tongue rather than ask.

With a bob of her head, she placed her boot in his hands. He threw her up easily—she was *such* a lightweight. Frowning, he walked back to the chestnut and swung up to the saddle.

In silence, she led the way back to the lane.

He followed, deep in thought.

Once they reached the lane, he tapped the chestnut's flanks and moved up beside her.

Francesca was aware he was there, but kept her gaze fixed forward. The irritation she'd initially—perfectly legitimately—felt at his outburst was fading, only to be replaced by a *soupçon* of alarm. This was the man she might shortly marry.

Behind his terse words, his almost violent movements, she'd glimpsed a temper as fiery as hers. To her mind, that counted in his favor—she'd much rather deal with a fire-eater than a man with ice in his veins. It was his possible—now likely—attitude to her riding that filled her with concern. In the two years she'd lived in England, this country of reserve, riding had been her only outlet for the wildness that was an integral part of her soul.

An integral part of *her*—if she didn't release it, exercise it now and then, she'd go mad. And as a proper young lady in England, riding like the wind was the wildest activity permissible.

What if her husband—he whom she would vow to obey and who would have control over all aspects of her life—forbade her to ride? To ride wildly—for her, they were one and the same.

She could see the problem looming, yet before she fell, she hadn't imagined his enthusiasm. She hadn't forgotten their mutual exhilaration, the shared enjoyment. He'd reveled in the wildness as much as she.

The gates of the Hall appeared ahead; as they slowed,

Francesca shot him a glance. He was frowning. In a way that boded her no good.

"What?"

His gaze flicked to her, still aggravated, still stormy. "I'm considering riding in to inform Sir Charles you shouldn't be riding his hunters."

"No!"

"*Yes!*" The chestnut jibbed; ruthlessly, he steadied it. "You're an exceptional rider—I won't deny that—but you don't have the strength to manage hunters. If you must run wild, you'd do better on an Arab, a mare. Something fleet and nimble, but more responsive to your guidance. You on the grey—or that bay you rode yesterday—if the horse bolts, you won't be able to control it."

She met his gaze with muted belligerence, unwilling to be bullied. Unfortunately, in this case, she knew he was right. If one of Charles's hunters got away from her, all she'd be able to do was cling and pray. Their gazes remained locked, both gauging, assessing the shifting possibilities . . . "All right." Looking down, she gathered her reins. "I'll speak with Charles."

"Do that." His tone was just short of an order. "No more hunters." He paused, his gaze still on her face. "So you promise . . . ?"

She threw him a glance that had a warning blazoned in it. "I promise I'll talk to Charles tonight."

He nodded. "In that case, I'll leave you here."

He hesitated, then swept her a bow that was the essence of elegant grace—on horseback, a feat not to be sneered at. With a last look, he wheeled the chestnut and cantered down the lane.

Francesca considered his departing back, then, lips curving in an appreciative smile, she turned the grey down the drive.

Her would-be husband had redeemed himself. She'd expected him to make a push to forbid her to run wild, even though he'd enjoyed the wildness, too. Understood it, too, it seemed; he'd been clever enough to avoid the pitfall. Considering his tack, she noted that he'd seemed primarily concerned with her safety.

Pondering that, she trotted to the stable.

Later that night, clutching a woolen shawl about her nightgown, Francesca climbed onto her window seat and settled among the cushions.

For the past year, she'd been searching for a suitable husband, looking to make a respectable marriage. She'd been raised with that as her goal; she'd looked forward to having a husband, a home, and a family for as long as she could recall. She knew what she wanted from life. To be happy, contented, she needed a relationship much as her parents' had been—a fusion of deep passion and abiding love. Without that, her life would not be complete; it was her destiny—she'd known that for years.

Within four months of putting off her blacks, she'd realized she wasn't going to find her destiny in the neighborhood of Rawlings Hall.

When she'd first suggested going about, Charles had explained that the household remained reclusive because, appearances to the contrary, Frances, his daughter, her cousin, known to all as Franni, was in poor health and needed to remain quiet, undisturbed by society's demands.

She'd accepted the restriction without demur—not only did she owe Charles a debt of gratitude, but she'd come to love him dearly; she would never do anything to cause him distress. She was also fond of Ester, Charles's sister-in-law, Franni's dead mother's older sister. Ester had lived at the Hall for years, helping to raise Franni. Ester, too, deserved her consideration.

And then there was Franni, who was simply Franni—

sweet, a little simple, rather helpless. Despite being of an age, they were totally unalike, yet there was a mild if somewhat distant affection between them.

She'd kept her increasing despondency to herself, yet the prospect of living her life alone, buried in the forest, had eaten at her. Rawlings Hall had started to feel like a prison.

So Chillingworth's offer was a godsend, no matter the guise. An arranged marriage to a wealthy peer would release her from her isolation.

Did she want to be the Countess of Chillingworth?

What young lady would not want a position of such rank, complete with establishments and secure in funds, with an extraordinarily handsome husband to boot? Such a marriage with the prospect of a developing relationship would be an enviable offer.

That wasn't, however, what the earl had offered her.

He'd made it plain that he wished for *no* real relationship with his wife. There was no other way to interpret his stipulations. And despite the hours they'd spent together, despite the link she sensed between them, he'd given no indication of rescripting his offer.

He was a man of passion, of hot blood, not cold, yet his offer had been the ultimate in studied cold-bloodedness.

It made no sense.

Why had he, specifically he—the man who had held her too close in the shrubbery, kissed her in the orchard and ridden wild through the forest by her side—made such an *uncharacteristic* offer?

Reliving their encounters, she came to that moment in the forest when she'd lain helpless in the gorse and he'd stood over her with raw fury in his eyes. She'd reacted to it, to the words his fury had sparked. But what had caused the real man to so completely surface, to drop his guard?

Her fall had somehow breached the walls behind which he hid his emotions. She—her body, her person, even her eyes—could evoke his passion, but he was more comfortable with that, more confident of controlling it.

In the forest, he hadn't liked what she'd done. He hadn't liked her making him feel whatever it was he'd felt. That was why his tone had lashed, why his eyes had snapped.

His temper had been his reaction, so what was the emotion she'd evoked? Was it fear?

She considered the possibility, considered the fact that heated words and violent reactions often arose out of caring. Out of a fear of loss, fear for someone who was dear. Her father had argued vehemently, often irrationally, when faced with one of her mother's potentially dangerous whims. Could Chillingworth have felt the lick of that particular whip?

Given she and he had already felt the related lash of mutual passion, why not?

If he had . . .

The prospect of finding her destiny, all that she needed of life, within her marriage tantalized. It was what she'd always wanted, her ultimate goal, and it was possible—the ingredients were there. Her mother had always assured her that, when they were, she'd know.

She knew now. She and Chillingworth could be as passionate a couple as her parents had been, devoted to the end. That was what she wanted—the only prize she'd ultimately settle for—a passionate and enduring love.

Yet what if he would not?

What if the reason he was so set on a cold-blooded marriage was so entrenched he would not bend? It was a risk—a real one. He was neither malleable nor manageable; she would get only what he was willing to give.

Was she prepared to accept the risk and the possible consequences?

If she failed to gain what she needed from their marriage, then an arrangement such as Chillingworth had proposed would leave her free to fulfill her destiny, to search for the love she needed, outside of wedlock. That was not her first choice, but life had already taught her to bend to the prevailing wind and search for what she needed where she could.

With Chillingworth, or if not with him, then with some other gentleman, she would take what she needed from life.

She would accept Chillingworth tomorrow afternoon. No—she would instruct her uncle to accept him, if that was how Chillingworth wanted the scene played.

The breeze from the forest was cool. Rising from the window seat, she headed for her bed, inwardly shaking her head.

He was who he was—no matter what he said, he could not, in his heart, still be set on a loveless, cold-blooded relationship, not now he'd met her. Kissed her. He might stubbornly adhere to the role he'd scripted for himself; he might still cling to the fiction before Charles, herself— even to himself. But that *could not be* what his real self wanted.

Halting by her bed, Francesca tilted her head, considering her future—considering him. A challenge?

Lips firming, she set aside her shawl and climbed between the sheets.

The possibility was there—she felt confident of that—but to gain what she wanted from their marriage, she'd need much more than he'd offered thus far.

She'd need his heart.

Given openly, freely, without reservation.

Would he ever be willing to offer her that?

With a sigh, she closed her eyes and surrendered her destiny to the gods. In her sleepy mind, a distant fantasy took shape . . . of her streaking across the downs she'd read lay just north of his castle on a fleet-footed Arabian mare. With him by her side.

Across the forest, Gyles sat staring out at the night. A glass of brandy in one hand, the window open before his chair, he brooded on his soul—on its propensities. He didn't like what he saw; he didn't feel comfortable with the possibilities.

The gypsy was dangerous. Too dangerous to risk seducing. A wise man knew when to leave temptation alone.

He'd determined to give her a wide berth, yet the instant he'd seen her, he'd given chase. Without thought. Without hesitation.

The gypsy had his measure.

As for what he'd felt in the instant she'd fallen . . .

He'd offered for Francesca Rawlings. Tomorrow, he'd call at Rawlings Hall and receive her acceptance of his suit. He'd make arrangements to marry her—his perfect, meek, mild-mannered cipher—as swiftly as possible.

Then he would leave.

His hand clenched about the glass, then he downed the contents and stood.

He would not meet with the gypsy again.

Chapter 4

Francesca spoke with Charles as she'd promised. While sympathetic to Chillingworth's concern, he'd also been touchingly aware of her need to ride.

"I can't see why," Charles had said, "as long as you exercise reasonable caution, you shouldn't continue to ride my hunters until you marry and he can supply you with a suitable mount. After all, you've been riding through the forest for two years without mishap."

Those sentiments echoed Francesca's. Consequently, early the next morning, hours earlier than she normally rode, she was on the bay gelding heading down a bridle path miles away from her normal route between the Hall and Lyndhurst. Her mood was sunny, her heart light as she galloped along. Not a smidgen of guilt disturbed her; she'd done everything she could to spare Chillingworth.

She rode into the next glade at a clipping pace.

Mounted on his chestnut, he was riding toward her.

The first thing she felt was a sense of betrayal.

Then she saw his face—watched it harden—saw fury flare, then coalesce into something hotter. Betrayal was swamped by alarm.

Then he dug in his heels and came for her.

She fled. She didn't stop to think—rational thought had no place in her brain. When a man looked at a woman like that, then charged at her, there was only one sane reaction.

A bridle path was closer than he was—she took it, plunging the bay onto the track. The chestnut swooped in behind them. She gave the bay his head. She could feel the thud of the chestnut's hooves over the reverberation of the bay's strides and the frantic pounding of her heart. A vise locked tight about her chest, squeezing her heart into her throat. The wind of her passing whipped her hair back, tossing her curls in a tangle behind her.

Clinging to the bay's saddle, she rocketed on. She couldn't risk a glance back—didn't dare—couldn't spare the instant. At this pace, she needed all her concentration for the track before her. It twisted and turned. She could feel Chillingworth's gaze locked on her back, hot as a flame.

An icy tingle touched her nape, then slid down every nerve. Fear, but not a simple one. A primal one—primitive—as primitive as the expression that had flowed across his face in the instant before he'd come for her. Twisted within the fear was a strand of heat, but it gave her no comfort; it only added another dimension to her panic—fear of the unknown.

Her only thought was to escape. The knot in her gut swelled; her senses unfurled, whispering of surrender.

She tried to think, to plan how to lose him. The bay and the chestnut seemed well matched, but the paths were too narrow for him to draw alongside. Soon, they'd reach the next glade. Luckily, he rode much heavier than she.

The trees thinned. She slowed the bay, then sprang him into the open glade, racing flat out, bent low to the horse's withers. The chestnut stayed with her. She flicked a glance back and to the side—and nearly swallowed her heart as her eyes locked with Chillingworth's, mere feet away.

He was gaining steadily. He reached for her reins—

She swerved away. The opening of another path, to her side, closer than the one she'd been heading for, was her only possible route. She sent the bay racing down it; the chestnut thundered on his heels. What came next?

The answer appeared before she was ready, the trees ending abruptly at the edge of a narrow field. The terrain sloped down to a shallow brook, then rose steeply beyond it. Only one path led out of the glade—its opening lay directly across the field.

She flung the bay at the brook. Its hooves clattered on the smooth stones in the watercourse, the chestnut's hooves sounding an instantaneous echo. The bay attacked the upward slope, back legs churning as it hauled its considerable weight up the rise.

The top of the rise was one bound away when the chestnut drew level.

A hand whipped across her and grabbed her reins.

Gasping, she wrenched them back—the bay staggered.

A steely arm wrapped around her; it locked her, shoulder to chest, against an even harder frame. Instinctively, she struggled. The reins were hauled from her grasp.

"Be still!"

The words thundered, lashed.

She quieted.

The horses jostled, then settled, held steady with an iron hand. They sidled onto the short stretch of level ground at the top of the rise. Separated only by his booted leg, bay and chestnut coats flickered, then both horses eased, expelled long horsey sighs, and lowered their heads.

The arm around her felt like a manacle; it didn't ease. Breathing raggedly, her pulse racing, Francesca looked up.

Gyles met her wide gaze—and felt primitive, possessive fury surge. His head was reeling, his heart racing. His breathing was as tortured as hers.

Her cheeks were flushed; her lips parted. Her eyes, glittering green, fixed on his, flared with an awareness as old as time.

He took her lips in a searing kiss.

He gave no quarter. Even had she begged he would not have granted it—she was his. His to brand, his to seize, his to claim. He ravaged her mouth, demanded her surrender— when it came and she softened in his arm, he tightened his hold on her and deepened the kiss—sealed her fate and his.

She was soft, submissive—all woman. Her lips were as lush as he remembered, her mouth a cavern of wanton delight. She surrendered and opened fully to him, yielded on a sigh that was half moan, half entreaty. The sound drove him on; desire flicked, whipped. She offered her mouth in appeasement—he seized and demanded more.

Swept up on the tide, Francesca released her last hold on the bay's reins and gave herself up to his embrace. The hot tangle of their tongues commanded her full attention, her complete and absolute devotion. The arm about her, muscles rigid, tightened even more. Perched sidesaddle as she was with her legs curled between them, he was lifting her from her seat. She didn't care. All that mattered was the gloriously heady tide that raged between them. Mentally finding her feet in the torrent, she steadied, then she caught her breath from him and reached for him.

Sent her hands pushing over his shoulders, then twined her fingers in his hair; reached for him with her body, arching, pressing deeper into his crushing embrace. Reached for him with her lips, ardently returning the heated, hungry kisses—feeding his desire, satisfying hers.

Beneath it all, she reached for him with her soul, with all the passion and love she had in her—this, *this!* her heart sang, was what should be.

He claimed all she was, drank it in, took it all from her, and in the taking gave. He was far from gentle but she wanted no gentleness—she wanted fire and flame, passion and glory, desire and fulfillment. That was the promise in the hard lips that bruised hers, in his almost-brutal conquest of her mouth. She met each invasion with joy in her heart, with desire racing down her veins.

Beneath them, the horses shifted; his attention deflected for the briefest moment—she felt him transfer the tightened reins to the hand at her waist. Then his lips hardened—he tipped her back, bending her over the arm at her back. His freed hand closed about her jaw, framing her face, holding her steady for an invasion so powerful, so devastating, it left her senses reeling.

His hand left her face to close, hard, about her breast.

She reacted as if he'd set a sexual brand to her body, arching, pressing nearer. She felt that first touch all the way to her toes, a pleasure unlike any other spearing beneath her skin, then melting, spreading. Her temperature rose—her skin heated. Like a fever, yet not—like the warmth from an inner flame. A flame he stoked as his fingers firmed, caressed, then provocatively kneaded. Through the thick velvet, he found the peak of her breast, and teased it with hard flicks.

He swallowed her gasp and ruthlessly drove her on. She went willingly, eagerly, wanting all he would give her, all he would show her—wanting, ultimately, him. She put up no resistance. Instead, she focused what wit she still possessed on following his lead as swiftly as she could, on giving the response he demanded, on feeding and satisfying the hunger that was theirs—on making love with him.

Gyles knew it, sensed it—victorious triumph surged through him. She was his—she would surrender completely and take him into her body. There was nothing to stop him having her. One slight lift and she would be off her saddle, in his lap, then he could take her to the grass . . .

An image flashed across his brain—the grass was coarse, tufty, the ground rocky and uneven. The horses were near.

The vision of her as he would see her, watching her as he took her, her glorious hair lying tangled over that unforgiving ground, her body unprotected from his onslaught, uncushioned as she struggled to take him all, to meet his thrusts, her eyes widening then hazing with pain . . .

No!

His recoil was so violent it loosened the grip of his lust, the unforgiving grip of his passions. Dragging in a breath, he fought to clear his head—fought the compulsion that beat steadily in his blood. Momentarily lost, he mentally groped for his identity—the persona he showed to the world. He'd lost it—left it behind in the first glade, when he'd first seen her once again on a dangerous hunter.

His lips were still on hers, his tongue tangled with hers, his hand firm about her breast. It was a struggle to draw back from the brink, knowing he didn't have to, that she would prefer him to go on, not retreat.

When their lips parted, he shuddered, and pressed his face to her hair. *"Damn it!"* The words were a hoarse whisper. *"Why* did you run?"

"I don't know," Francesca breathed. Blindly, she lifted a hand and touched his cheek. "Instinct." That was what had made him seize, what had made her flee.

She was his—they both knew it. It all followed from that—his reaction, her response, like some predestined plot.

His hand left her breast and she felt bereft—she waited for him to lift her to his lap.

He tipped her face up and his lips closed over hers—for one instant, passion reigned supreme, the glory, the heat, the promise—then she felt him rein it back. Through his lips, through his gentling touch on her face, she sensed the war he waged to releash all that had flowed so freely. Disbelieving, she felt his arm slide, slowly, reluctantly from about her. Then his hands gripped her waist, his fingers tensed, flexed . . . instead of lifting her to him, he pressed her back into her saddle.

With an effort she felt, he dragged his lips from hers. She looked into his eyes, stormy, dark as a thundery sky. Beyond the grey, something raged. They were both breathing raggedly, quickly—both barely free of the power that had flared.

"Go!" The command was low, strained, as if forced from him. He held her gaze mercilessly. "Go home—back to the Hall. Ride but not wildly."

She stared at him, uncomprehending. Her skin was still heated, her heart still yearned. . . .

His gaze hardened. "Go! *Now!*"

The command cracked like a whip, impossible to defy. On a gasp, she grabbed her reins and wheeled—jerked from its rest, the bay took off down the slope.

She didn't get a chance to glance back until she was in the trees.

He was where she'd left him, sitting the chestnut he'd wheeled to watch her go. Head bowed, he was looking down, staring at one hand fisted on the saddlebow.

He'd been within a heartbeat of taking her.

As he stood before the window of his bedchamber at the inn and watched the sun sink behind the trees, Gyles faced that fact and all that it meant.

She'd done it again—effortlessly reached through his shield and called to all he hid behind it. And his feelings for her were so strong, so ungovernable, they had nearly driven him to do something he never normally would. Something that, in his right mind, he would never even consider. She had the power to drive him mad.

If he'd taken her to the ground, no power on earth would have stopped him from taking her—passionately, violently, regardless of the pain he would have caused her. Regardless of the fact that she was—his experienced senses were sure of it—virginal. Far from dampening his ardor, that last only heightened it. She would be his and his alone.

But she wouldn't be. She would never be his because he

would not let any woman wield such power over him. If he made her his, he'd risk becoming her slave. Surrender at that level was not in his nature.

He uttered a harsh laugh and swung into the room.

She'd stripped away every vestige of civilized behavior and laid bare the conqueror that, underneath the elegant glamor, was what he truly was. He was a direct descendant of Norman lords who'd seized whatever they'd wanted—who had simply and ruthlessly taken any woman who had captured their eye.

Yesterday, she'd triggered his protectiveness, yet today he'd chased her through the forest like a marauding, rapacious barbarian. When sane, he worried over her safety, yet the instant he'd seen her once again atop a hunter, that deeply buried part of him that had far more in common with a marauding, rapacious barbarian than with the elegant gentleman who paraded before the ton had come rampaging to the fore.

All he'd known was that she was openly flouting his decree, flagrantly disregarding his worry; all he'd known was an elemental need to impress on her that she was his—to possess her so utterly she couldn't deny it, deny him, deny his right to command her. He hadn't cared that he'd forced her to flee like a wild thing—his whole being had been concentrated on capturing her, subduing her, on making her his.

Even now, the remembered feelings—the primal force that had flowed through him and made the transformation from gentleman to conquering barbarian—rocked him.

Scared him.

He glanced at the window; the light had almost died. Crossing to the bed, he picked up his crop and the gloves he'd flung there earlier, then headed for the door.

It was time to call on Charles Rawlings and arrange the final details of his wedding.

He would leave Hampshire immediately after.

* * *

"Good evening, my lord."

Gyles turned as Charles Rawlings entered the study and shut the door.

Charles approached, concern in his eyes. "I hope nothing's amiss."

"Not at all." His elegant mask in place, Gyles shook Charles's hand. "My apologies for calling so late, but an unexpected matter intervened and prevented me from calling earlier."

"Well, no harm done." Charles waved Gyles to a chair. "Now, are you sure you wouldn't rather hear Francesca's decision from her lips . . . ?"

"Quite sure." Gyles waited while Charles sat. "What is her decision?"

"As you're no doubt expecting, she's agreed to your proposal. She's very conscious of the honor you do her—"

Gyles waved the formal words aside. "I fancy we both know where we stand. I am, of course, pleased that she's consented to become my countess. Unfortunately, I must return to Lambourn immediately, so I'd like to confirm the details of the marriage settlements—Waring, my man-of-business, will send you the contracts in the next few days—and we'll need to discuss the wedding itself."

Charles looked slightly stunned. "Well—"

"If Miss Rawlings is agreeable," Gyles ruthlessly continued, "I would prefer the wedding be held at Lambourn Castle—the chapel there is the traditional place in which our ancestors have celebrated their nuptials. It's now the end of August—four weeks will give sufficient time for the banns to be read and should allow ample time for Miss Rawlings to assemble her bride clothes."

Without pause, he switched to the details of the marriage settlements, forcing Charles to scurry to his desk and take notes.

After half an hour, he'd tied every loose end—tied himself into matrimony as tightly as he could.

"Now"—Gyles rose—"if there's nothing else, I must be on my way."

Charles had surrendered long since. "Once again, it's a most generous offer and Francesca is delighted—"

"Indeed. Please convey my respects to her. I look forward to seeing her at Lambourn two days before the wedding." Gyles headed for the door, forcing Charles to catch up with him. "My mother will coordinate the social details—I'm sure Miss Rawlings will receive a missive within a few days."

Charles opened the door and accompanied him down the corridor and into the front hall. Pausing before the front door as Bulwer hurried to open it, Gyles smiled sincerely and offered Charles his hand. "Thank you for your help. And thank you for taking such good care of your niece—I look forward to taking on that duty in four weeks' time."

The concern that had hovered in Charles's eyes lifted. He grasped Gyles's hand. "You won't regret this evening's work, you may be sure of that."

With a brief nod, Gyles strode out. The stablelad was walking his horse in the courtyard. Mounting, he raised a hand in salute to Charles, then he tapped his heels to the chestnut's flanks and cantered down the drive.

Never, Gyles vowed, would he return to Rawlings Hall.

If he'd turned around and looked at the house, he might have seen her, a shadowy figure at an upstairs window, watching him—her betrothed—ride away. He didn't.

Francesca watched until he disappeared into the trees, then, frowning, turned inside.

Something was not right.

By the time she'd reached the lane home that afternoon, she'd accepted that making love *al fresco* might not have been the way he'd wanted to celebrate their first joining. Her practical side had also pointed out that, despite her eagerness, beneath the trees might not have been the best venue to commence her career in that sphere.

So she'd accepted his decree and ridden home at nothing more than a canter. But why, after all that had passed between them, had he held to his determination not to speak with her face-to-face?

Where was the logic in that?

Immediately after lunch, she'd gone to Charles and informed him of her decision. Then she'd waited for her would-be husband to call.

And waited.

They'd been finishing dinner when he'd finally arrived.

A tap on her door had her smoothing the frown from her face. "Come in."

Charles looked in, then entered. He noticed the window open at her back. "You saw?"

She nodded. "Did he say . . . ?" She gestured. *Had he mentioned her?*

Charles smiled fondly; coming forward, he took her hands. "My dear, I'm sure everything will work out splendidly. Business kept him from calling earlier, and he must return to Lambourn immediately. He did say all that was proper."

Francesca returned Charles's smile with equal fondness. Her mind was all but spitting the word "proper." *Proper?* There was nothing "proper" about what lay between them— "proper" was certainly not what she would settle for. Not once she was his wife.

But she pressed Charles's hands and allowed him to believe all was well. Indeed, she wasn't seriously worried.

Not after their interlude today.

After experiencing what had risen between them, flowed like a raging river through them, regardless of her betrothed's insistence on the publicly cold-blooded approach, there was patently no need to worry.

A letter from Chillingworth's mother arrived three days later. The Dowager Countess, Lady Elizabeth, wrote to welcome Francesca into the family with such transparent joy and goodwill that all qualms Francesca had harbored on that front were laid to rest.

"She says the rest of the family is delighted with the news. . . ." Francesca shuffled the leaves of the lengthy letter. She was sitting on the window seat in the downstairs parlor; Franni was curled on the seat's other end, clutching a cushion, her blue eyes wide. Ester listened from a nearby chair. "And she's working on Chillingworth to allow her to extend the guest list, as the family's such a far-flung one, and there are so many branches, etcetera."

Francesca paused. That was not the first hint that Lady Elizabeth, while immensely pleased over the wedding, was not at one with her son over the details. As for the family members invited—the fact was there was only one family involved. She and Chillingworth were cousins, umpteen times removed perhaps, but that *should* make assembling the guest list easier. Shouldn't it?

Setting aside the point, she continued, "She says the castle staff are busy opening up the wings and polishing everything, and that I may rely on her to see that all is just so. She suggests I write with any requests or questions, and assures me she'll be delighted to advise in any way."

Her tone signified "the end." She refolded the letter.

Franni sighed. "It sounds wonderful! Don't you think so, Aunt Ester?"

"I do, indeed." Ester smiled. "Francesca will make a wonderful countess. But now we must think of a wedding gown."

"Oh, yes!" Franni sat bolt upright. "The gown! Why—"

"I'm going to wear my mother's wedding gown," Francesca quickly said. Franni was given to overenthusiasms which sometimes turned difficult. "Something old and borrowed, you know."

"Oh—yes." Franni frowned.

"A very nice idea," Ester said. "We must have Gilly up from the village and check that it fits."

Franni had been mumbling. Now she lifted her head. "That leaves something new and blue."

"Garters, perhaps?" Ester suggested.

Francesca nodded, grateful for the suggestion. "Can we go into Lyndhurst and buy them tomorrow?" Franni fixed huge eyes on Ester's face.

Ester glanced at Francesca. "I don't see why not."

"No, indeed. Tomorrow, then," Francesca said.

"Good, good, *good!*" Franni leapt up and flung her arms wide. The cushion went tumbling. "Tomorrow morning! Tomorrow morning!" She waltzed around the room. "We're going to get Francesca something new and blue tomorrow morning!" Reaching the open door, she waltzed through. "Papa! Did you hear? We're going . . ."

Ester smiled as Franni's voice died away. "I hope you don't mind, dear, but you know how she is."

"I don't mind at all." Shifting her gaze from the door to Ester's face, Francesca lowered her voice. "Charles told me he was worried that Franni would become querulous once she realizes I'm leaving, but she seems quite happy."

"To be truthful, dear, I don't think Franni will realize you're leaving—not coming back—until we return here without you. Things that are obvious to us often don't occur to her at all, and then she's upset by the surprise."

Francesca nodded, although she had never truly understood Franni's vagueness. "I'd intended to ask her to be bridesmaid, but Uncle Charles said no." She'd shown her letter to her uncle first, and he'd been adamant on that point.

"He said he wouldn't even like to say Franni will be at the wedding—he said she might not wish to be there."

Ester reached out and squeezed Francesca's hand. "That has nothing to do with what she feels for you. But she might become frightened at the last minute and not want to appear. As bridesmaid, that really wouldn't do."

"I suppose not. Charles suggested that I ask Lady Elizabeth's advice on who should stand with me—I don't even know if Chillingworth has sisters."

"Sisters, or close cousins of the bridegroom, given we have no one of suitable age on our side. Asking Lady Elizabeth would be wisest."

Ester rose; Francesca did, too. She glanced at the letter in her hand. "I'll write this afternoon." She smiled as she recalled Lady Elizabeth's warmth. "I have lots of questions, and she seems like the best person to ask."

Despite Charles's worry, Franni's transparent happiness over Francesca's wedding did not dim, although to everyone's relief, her expressions of joy became less extreme. Franni's temper remained sunny; engrossed though she was in the myriad preparations for her nuptials and her researches into her husband-to-be, his house and the estate, Francesca noted that with a certain happiness of her own. Charles, Ester, and Franni were now her family; she wanted them there, at her wedding, and as happy as she was.

When, four days before the wedding, they set out in the lumbering coach, Charles and Ester on one seat with Francesca and Franni facing them, Francesca was as excited as Franni and even more impatient. They would spend two days on the road, arriving at Lambourn Castle on the second day, two nights before the wedding as Chillingworth had stipulated. On that point he'd remained firm, unmoved by Lady Elizabeth's pleas for more time before the wedding to become acquainted with her future daughter-in-law.

Lady Elizabeth hadn't accepted his refusal with anything like good grace—Francesca had laughed at the diatribe the Dowager Countess had, in her next letter, heaped on her son's head. After their first exchange of letters, correspondence between Lambourn Castle and Rawlings Hall had proliferated dramatically, letters crossing and recrossing. By the time Francesca left Rawlings Hall, she was almost as eager to meet her mother-in-law-to-be as she was to see her handsome fiancé again.

The first day passed easily as the coach rocked its way north.

At noon on the second day, it started to rain.

Then it poured.

The road turned to mud. By late afternoon, the coach was crawling along. Heavy grey clouds had massed, then lowered; an unnatural twilight had descended, darkened further by the rain.

The coach rocked to a stop. Then it tilted, and they heard a splat as the coachman jumped down. He rapped on the door.

Charles opened it. "Yes?"

Barton stood in the road, the rain streaming off his oilskin, pouring off his hat. "Sorry, sir, but we're a long ways away from Lambourn and we're not going to be able to go much farther. The light's going. Even if you was willing to risk the horses, we can't see what muck we'd be driving into, so we'd bog for sure within a mile."

Charles grimaced. "Is there somewhere we can take shelter, at least until the rain stops?"

"There's an inn just up there." Barton nodded to the left. "We can see it from the box. Looks neat enough, but it's not a coaching inn. Other than that, we're miles from any town."

Charles hesitated, then nodded. "Take us to the inn. I'll have a look and see if we can stop there."

Barton shut the door. Charles sat back and looked at Francesca. "I'm sorry, my dear, but . . ."

Francesca managed a shrug. "At least we have a day's

grace. If the rain stops during the night, we'll be able to reach Lambourn tomorrow."

"Good God, yes!" Charles uttered a hollow laugh. "After all his planning, I wouldn't want to have to face Chillingworth and explain why his bride had missed the wedding."

Francesca grinned and patted Charles's knee. "It'll all come right—you'll see." For some reason, she felt confident of that.

The inn proved better than they'd hoped for, small but clean and very willing to cater to four unexpected guests and their servants. As the rain showed no sign of easing, they accepted their fate and settled in. The inn boasted three bedchambers. Charles took one, Ester another, while Francesca and Franni shared the largest with its canopied bed.

They gathered in the tap for a hearty meal, then retired to their rooms, agreeing on an early start the next morning, heartened by the prediction of the innwife's father who assured them tomorrow would dawn fine. Reassured, Francesca settled in the big bed beside Franni and snuffed out the candle.

They'd left the curtains open; moonlight streamed in, broken by the shadows thrown by nearby trees.

After spending the day dozing in the coach, neither of them was sleepy. Francesca wasn't surprised when Franni stirred, and asked, "Tell me about the castle."

She'd already told her twice, but Franni liked stories, and the idea of Francesca living in a castle appealed to her. "Very well." Francesca fixed her gaze on the dark canopy. "Lambourn Castle is centuries old. It sits on a bluff over a curve in the Lambourn River and guards the approach to the downs to the north. The village of Lambourn lies a little way along the river, tucked into the side of the downs. The castle has been modernized frequently and added on to as well, so it's now quite large, but it still has battlements and twin towers at either end. It's surrounded by a park filled with old oaks. The gatehouse is still standing and is now the Dower House.

With formal gardens overlooking the river, the castle is one of the great houses of the district."

She'd spent hours thumbing through guidebooks and books describing the country seats of peers, and she'd learned yet more from Lady Elizabeth. "Inside, the house is of the utmost elegance, and the views to the south are rated as spectacular. From the upper levels, there are also views north across Lambourn Downs. The downs are excellent for riding and are used for training racehorses."

"You'll like that," Franni murmured.

Francesca smiled. She said nothing more, only to hear Franni prompt, "And the bit of land that you have in your dowry is going to make the earl's estate look like one big pie again."

"Indeed." Franni had overheard enough to become curious, so she'd explained. "And that's the reason for arranging our marriage."

After a moment, Franni asked, "Do you think you'll like being married to your earl?"

Francesca's smile deepened. "Yes."

"Good." Franni sighed. "That's good."

Francesca closed her eyes, expecting that Franni would now settle. Her mind wandered . . . to Lambourn Downs, to riding a fleet-footed Arabian mare—

"I had a gentleman come to visit me—did I tell you?"

"Oh?" Wide-awake again, Francesca frowned. "When did he call?"

"Some weeks ago."

Francesca hadn't heard a word about any gentleman coming to visit Franni. That didn't mean some gentleman hadn't appeared. She considered her next question carefully; with Franni, one had to be specific, not general. "Was it before or after Chillingworth visited?"

She couldn't see Franni's face, but she could sense her struggling. "Sometime about then, I think."

Franni wasn't good with time; for her, one day was much

like another. Before Francesca could think of her next question, Franni wriggled around to face her. "When Chillingworth asked you to marry him, did he kiss you?"

Francesca hesitated. "I didn't meet him formally. The marriage was arranged through your father—he's my guardian."

"You mean you haven't even met Chillingworth?"

"We met informally. We discussed a few details—"

"But did he kiss you?"

Francesca hesitated some more. "Yes," she eventually replied.

"What was it like?"

The eagerness in Franni's voice was impossible to mistake. If she didn't appease it, Francesca knew she'd get precious little sleep. The kisses she'd shared with her husband-to-be remained fresh in her mind; it took only a moment to decide which interlude to describe. "He kissed me in the orchard. He stopped me from falling and claimed a kiss as a reward."

"And? What did it feel like?"

"He's very strong. Powerful. Masterful . . ." The words were enough to evoke the memory and send recollected sensation sweeping through her, sweeping her away—

"But was it nice?"

Francesca stifled a frustrated sigh. "It was better than nice."

"Good."

She felt Franni rocking herself happily and had to ask, "This gentleman who called, did he try to kiss you?"

"Oh, no. He was very proper. But he walked with me and listened to me very politely, so I expect he's thinking of making an offer."

"He called just once some weeks ago—"

"Twice. He came back after the first time. So that must mean he's taken with me, don't you think?"

Francesca didn't know what to think. "Did he tell you his name?" She felt Franni nod. "What was it, Franni?"

Franni shook her head. She had a pillow clutched to her middle, and she hugged it almost gleefully. "You have your Chillingworth, and I have my gentleman. That's nice, don't you think?"

Francesca hesitated, then reached out and patted Franni's arm. "Very nice." She knew better than to press Franni once she'd said "no." That was one word Franni never shifted from; any pressure would only provoke enormous and sometimes hysterical resistance.

To Francesca's relief, Franni settled, sighed, then snuggled deeper under the covers. A minute later, she was asleep.

Francesca lay staring up at the canopy, and wondered what to do. Had some gentleman called on Franni—or had she imagined it, a reaction to Chillingworth calling on her? That was possible. Franni didn't lie, not deliberately, but her version of the truth often diverged from reality. Like the time she swore they'd been held up by highwaymen, when all that had happened was that Squire Muckleridge had hailed them as they drove past.

What Franni said happened and what really had happened weren't necessarily the same thing. Francesca considered the little Franni had let fall—there was no way of telling if it was truth or fantasy.

Despite Franni's sometimes childlike behavior, in age there was only a month between them. In looks, in physical maturity, they were equals. By all outward appearances, Franni passed for a young gentlewoman. In the right setting with the right subject, she could converse perfectly rationally as long as her interlocutor did not switch subjects quickly or ask a question beyond Franni's ken. If her train of thought was broken, her vagueness quickly became apparent, but if it wasn't triggered, then there was nothing to disturb the image of a quiet, unassuming young lady.

Francesca knew there was something amiss with Franni, that her vagueness and retreat into childish ways was not a condition that was improving with time. Charles and Ester's care and concern underscored the truth, but Francesca had never asked, never forced either Charles or Ester to acknowledge that truth by explaining it to her.

That Franni's condition was a source of pain and sorrow to both Charles and Ester was something Francesca knew without asking; she strove to do nothing to add to that pain. So she considered carefully what Franni had said, considered whether and how much she should tell Charles.

Not Charles, she eventually decided. A gentleman might not understand a lonely girl's dreams. Francesca had dreamed enough in her time; Franni's gentleman might live only in Franni's mind.

Turning onto her side, Francesca snuggled down. Tomorrow she'd warn Ester—just in case Franni's gentleman had, in fact, been real.

Decision made, she relaxed and let her mind drift. Like a slow, inexorable tide, the emotions that had swept her earlier returned, inching up, then pooling inside, a well of impatient longing.

She'd waited for him for years; at his insistence, she'd waited four weeks more. Soon, it would be her wedding night. She'd wait no more.

Her dreams were ones of passion, of longing and love, of a love so deep, so enduring, it would never wane.

Morning came and she rose, restless, oddly breathless, more impatient than she'd ever been. She dressed and went downstairs. She joined the innwife's old father as he stood in the open doorway.

He glanced at her, then nodded outside. "Told you. It's cleared and gone. You'll get to your wedding on time, young mistress."

Chapter 5

The old man's prophecy held true, but they cut it very fine. The state of the roads as they pushed north deteriorated; the rains had been heavier here. They crossed the Lambourn River, swollen and running high, via a stone bridge; if the crossing had been a ford, they would never have made it. It was too dark to see much of Lambourn village beyond a cluster of roofs off to one side, huddling between the river and the escarpment of the downs.

The escarpment lowered over them as the road swung left, following the river, gradually rising above it. It was almost full dark when they slowed and turned between huge gateposts, their wrought-iron gates set wide. The crest in the gate on Francesca's side, illuminated briefly by the coach lamps, had a wolf's head as the principal device.

She leaned closer to the window, peering through the gloom. The Dower House had been on the coach's other side; she'd barely glimpsed it. They rattled along a well-graded drive, the horses at last picking up speed. Parkland dotted with huge oaks stretched as far as she could see.

The coach slowed. The tension that had steadily built all day knotted tight; her stomach was a hard ball pressing into her lungs, making it difficult to breathe. The coach halted. The door opened. A footman stood ready to assist them to the ground. Flickering light from flares lit the scene.

Francesca went first. The footman handed her down to a flagged forecourt. Releasing her skirts, she looked around.

Lambourn Castle, her new home, was exactly as she'd imagined it. The Palladian facade stetched away on either side. Tall windows were set into the pale stone at regular intervals, some with curtains drawn, others with lights glowing. The second story was topped by a stone frieze, which she knew hid the old battlements behind it. Directly before her, a sweep of steps led up to the imposing entrance, the pedimented porch held aloft by tall columns flanking double doors.

Those doors stood wide; warm light streamed out. Two tallish, older ladies stood silhouetted just outside the doors. Francesca gathered her skirts and climbed the steps.

One of the ladies came sweeping up the instant she reached the porch. "My dear Francesca, welcome to your new home! I'm Elizabeth, dear, Gyles's mama."

Enveloped in a scented embrace, Francesca closed her eyes against a rush of tears and returned the embrace eagerly. "I'm delighted to finally meet you, ma'am."

Releasing her, Lady Elizabeth held her away, shrewd grey eyes much like her son's quickly taking stock, then the countess's face lit. "My dear, Gyles has surprised me—I hadn't credited him with such good sense."

Francesca returned Lady Elizabeth's smile, then turned to meet the second lady, of similar age to the countess and equally elegant but with brown hair rather than the countess's pale curls.

The lady took her hand, then drew her closer to kiss her cheek. "I'm Henrietta Walpole, my dear—Gyles's paternal aunt. Gyles calls me Henni, and I'll expect you to as well. I can't tell you how glad I am to see you." Henni patted her hand, then released it. "You'll do wonderfully."

"And this," Lady Elizabeth waved to a portly gentleman emerging from the hall, "is Horace, Henni's husband."

In her letters, Lady Elizabeth had explained that Henni and Horace had lived at the Castle since Gyles's father's death. Horace had been Gyles's guardian until he'd reached his majority; Henni was his favorite aunt. Francesca had been keyed up to make a good impression, and was relieved that Henni had accepted her so readily. As Horace strolled up, she saw surprise sweep his face as he took in the sight of her.

Her breath caught in her throat. Then Horace returned his bemused gaze to her face, and smiled. Broadly.

"Well, then!" He took her hand and bussed her cheek. "You're a pretty little thing—suppose I should know better than to imagine m'nephew's taste would run in any other vein."

The comment earned him censorious looks from Lady Elizabeth and Henni, of which he remained oblivious, too engrossed in smiling at Francesca.

Smiling in return, she looked expectantly past him. There was a very correct butler standing in the doorway, but . . . no one else. The front hall stretched away, tiled floors gleaming, woodwork glowing, doors to either side, a footman here and there, but it was otherwise empty. She heard voices as Charles, Ester, and Franni climbed the steps. Lady Elizabeth's arm came around her; the countess steered her toward the welcoming warmth of the hall.

"I'm afraid, my dear, that Gyles could not be here to greet you." Lady Elizabeth had lowered her head and her voice; her words were just for Francesca. "An emergency arose on the estate late this afternoon, and Gyles had to ride out to deal with it. He'd expected to be here to meet you, and hoped to be back in time, but . . ."

Francesca glanced up in time to see Lady Elizabeth grimace. The older woman's eyes met hers, then Lady Elizabeth squeezed her hand. "I'm so sorry, my dear. It's not what any of us wanted."

Lady Elizabeth turned to greet Charles, Ester, and Franni; Francesca realized her mother-in-law-to-be was giving her a moment to absorb the unexpected blow. For a gentleman of Chillingworth's standing not to be present to greet his betrothed on her arrival for their wedding . . .

Francesca dimly heard Lady Elizabeth making her son's excuses to Charles. She forced herself to straighten her shoulders and turn to her uncle with a reassuring smile, conveying the impression that she found Chillingworth's absence disappointing but not distressing. For that she earned a grateful look from the countess. The greetings continued, then they passed into the house. Lady Elizabeth introduced Francesca to the elderly butler, Irving—"Irving the Younger is the butler at the London house—you'll meet him when you go up to town," and to a dapper little man who stood in Irving's imposing shadow.

"This is Wallace, my dear. He's Chillingworth's majordomo and has been with my son for many years. If there's anything you need, now or in the future, Wallace will arrange it."

Not much taller than she was, Wallace bowed low.

"Now!" Lady Elizabeth turned to address them all. "With your arrival being delayed and you having to sit cramped in the coach for so long, we thought we'd spare you the ordeal of having to greet all the others gathered for the wedding. Everyone's here, but we've asked them to remain apart"— she gestured into the great house, to the maze of reception rooms that doubtless lay beyond the hall—"to let you get your bearings. Time enough to meet everyone tomorrow. However, if you *do* wish to be introduced tonight, you have only to say the word. Otherwise, your rooms are ready, there's plenty of hot water, and dinner will be brought up whenever you desire."

Lady Elizabeth's gaze came to rest on Francesca. She glanced at Charles. "It has been a long few days. I would rather retire, if that's possible." Being introduced to a host of distant relatives, as well as tonnish peers and their sharp-eyed wives, without her fiancé by her side, was not an ordeal she'd come prepared to face.

Charles and Ester murmured their agreement. Franni said nothing; she was gazing wide-eyed about the hall.

"Of course! That's what we expected. You'll need your rest—tomorrow's the important day, after all, and we'll all need to be at our best." With reassurances and admonishments to ask for anything they needed, Lady Elizabeth ushered them upstairs. They parted in the gallery. Henni went with Ester and Franni; Horace strolled off with Charles. The countess, imparting inconsequential information, accompanied Francesca down corridors and through another gallery, eventually leading her into a pleasant chamber, warmed by a blazing fire, with wide windows looking north over the downs.

"I know it's only for one night, but I wanted you to have peace and quiet, and have enough space for donning your bridal gown tomorrow. Also, getting from here to the chapel, you won't have to cross Gyles's path."

Surveying the comfortable chamber, Francesca smiled. "It's lovely—thank you."

She was aware of the shrewdness behind Lady Elizabeth's gaze. "Would you rather eat or bathe first?"

"A bath, please." Francesca smiled at the little maid who darted up to help her with her coat. "I can't wait to get out of these clothes."

Lady Elizabeth gave orders; the maid bobbed and hurried out. As soon as the door shut, Lady Elizabeth sank down on the bed and grimaced at Francesca. "My dear, thank you. You're taking this awfully well. I could wring Gyles's neck, but . . ."—she lifted her hands palms up—"he *did* have to go. It was too serious to leave to his foreman."

"What happened?" Francesca sat in a chair by the hearth, grateful for the warmth of the fire.

"A bridge collapsed. Upriver a little way, but on the estate. Gyles had to go and actually see it to decide what was best to be done. The bridge is the only link to part of the estate. There are families stranded and so on—lots of decisions, small and large, for Gyles to make."

"I see." She did. She'd been trained to be a gentleman's wife; she knew about the responsibilities large estates entailed. Francesca glanced at the window. "Will he be safe riding back in the dark?"

The countess smiled. "He's been riding the downs since he could get atop a horse, and indeed, the downs are quite safe for riding, even in poor light. You needn't worry—he'll be here, safe and sound, and quite impatient to marry you come morning."

Francesca cast a shy glance at the countess. Lady Elizabeth caught it and nodded. "Oh, yes, he's been decidedly testy all day—and was exceedingly grim about having to go out and risk not being here when you arrived. Still, it will only whet his appetite for tomorrow." She rose as the maid returned with footmen carrying steaming pails.

When the bath had been readied and only the maid remained, Lady Elizabeth crossed to Francesca, who rose. The countess kissed her on both cheeks. "I'll leave you now, but if you need anything, or wish to speak with me again, whatever the hour, you only need ring and Millie here will answer, and she'll come and fetch me. Now, are you sure you have everything you need?"

Touched, Francesca nodded.

"Very well, then. Good night."

"Good night." Francesca watched Lady Elizabeth leave, then beckoned to the maid to assist her with her gown.

Once she'd bathed, she felt much more relaxed, much more forgiving; she could hardly blame him for the rain, or its effects, after all. Leaning back in the tub, she instructed Millie in unpacking her trunks and laying out all she would need for the morrow. Her eyes round with awe, Millie carefully shook out the ivory silk wedding gown.

"Ooh, ma'am, it's just *beautiful!*"

The gown had been reverently pressed and packed by the staff at Rawlings Hall; it only needed a good shake and a night hanging up to be absolutely perfect. "Leave it in the wardrobe. Everything else I need for tomorrow should be packed next."

Millie emerged from the wardrobe and shut the door with a soft sigh. "A rare sight you'll be in that, ma'am, pardon my saying so." She returned to Francesca's trunks. "I'll just get out your wedding finery, and your nightgown and brushes, and we'll move all the rest to the countess's suite tomorrow morning, if that's all right?"

Francesca nodded. A ripple of nervousness shivered over her skin. Tomorrow morning, she'd become his countess. His. The sensation behind the shiver intensified. She sat up and reached for the towel. Millie came running.

Later, wrapped in a bedgown, she sat by the fire and ate the simple but elegant dinner Millie had brought up on a tray. Then she dismissed the little maid, turned down the lamps, and thought about climbing into bed. Instead, she found herself drawn to the window, to the wide vista of the downs. The high, largely treeless plateau stretched away in gently rolling waves as far as her eyes could see. The sky was almost clear; the only remnants of yesterday's storms were the tattered clouds that streamed before the wind.

The moon was rising, sending a wash of silvery light over the scene.

The downs possessed a wild beauty that called to her— she'd suspected that would be the case. A sense of freedom, of nature unfettered, unrestrained, rose from the barren landscape.

And tempted her.

Tonight would be her last night alone—the last night she would have only herself to answer to. Tomorrow would bring her a husband, and she already knew—or could guess—his feelings about her riding wild through the night.

She wasn't sleepy. The long hours in the coach, hours of increasing tension, the disappointment, the anticlimax at finding him not here to greet her when she'd spent so many hours dreaming of how it would be—dreaming of the look in his eyes when next he saw her—had left her disaffected, more restless, more edgy than ever before.

Her riding habit was in her second trunk. She wrestled it free, then unearthed her riding boots, gloves and crop. The hat she could do without.

Ten minutes saw her dressed and booted, sliding through the huge house. She heard deep voices—she turned in the opposite direction. She found a secondary stair and took it down to the ground floor, then followed a corridor and found a parlor with French doors opening onto the terrace. Leaving the doors closed but unlocked, she headed for the stable block she'd glimpsed through the trees.

The trees were old oaks and beeches; they welcomed her into their shadows. She strode along, secure in the knowledge no one could see her from the house. The stable block proved to be interestingly large, two long stables and a coach barn built around a courtyard. She slipped into the nearest stable, and started down the aisle, gauging the nature of the horse in each box. She passed three hunters, even larger and more powerful than those she'd ridden at Rawlings Hall. Recalling Chillingworth's comments, she continued on, looking to see if he had a smaller mount—

The door at the end of the aisle opened. Light bobbed, illuminating tack stored in the room beyond, then the light danced into the aisle as two stablelads, one carrying a lantern, stepped through and pulled the door shut.

Halfway along the aisle, Francesca had no chance of regaining the stable door. The light had yet to reach her. Slipping the latch of the stall she stood beside, she eased the door open, then whisked around it and pressed it closed, then reached over and lifted the latch into place.

A quick glance over her shoulder reassured her. The horse whose stall she'd invaded was well mannered, and not large. It had turned its head to view her, but with her vision affected by the lamplight, she could see little more. But there was plenty of room for her to slide down against the stall door and wait for the stablelads to pass by.

"There she is—a beauty, ain't she?"

The light suddenly intensified; glancing up, Francesca saw the lamp appear just above her head. The stablelad rested it on the top of the stall door.

"Aye," the second lad agreed. "Smashing." The door shifted as two bodies leaned against it. Francesca held her breath and prayed they wouldn't look over and down. They were talking about the horse. She looked, and for the first time, saw.

Her eyes widened; she only just managed to suppress an appreciative sigh. The horse was more than merely beautiful. There was power and grace in every line, a living testimony to superior breeding. This was precisely the sort of horse Chillingworth had spoken of—a fleet-footed Arabian mare. Her bay coat glowed richly in the lamp light, dark mane and tail a nice contrast. The horse's eyes were large, dark, alert. Its ears were pricked.

Francesca prayed it wouldn't come to investigate her—not until the stableboys moved on.

"Heard tell the master bought her for some lady."

"Aye—that be right. The mare's hardly up to his weight, after all."

The other boy chortled. "Seems like the lady was."

Francesca glanced up—to see the lamp disappear. The stablelads pushed away from the door; the light retreated. She waited until the dark returned, then rose and peeked over the stall door just in time to see the two lads step out of the stable, taking the lantern with them.

"Thank God!"

A soft nose butted her in the back. She turned, equally eager to make friends. "Oh, but you're a gorgeous girl, aren't you?" The mare's long nose was velvet soft. Francesca ran her hands along the sleek coat, gauging by feel; her night vision had yet to return.

"He told me I should be riding an Arab mare, and he's just bought you for some lady." Returning to the horse's head, she stroked its ears. "Coincidence, do you think?"

The horse turned its head and looked at her. She looked at it. And grinned. "I don't think so." She threw her arms about the mare's neck and hugged. "He bought you for me!"

The thought sent her spirits soaring. Higher and higher, tumbling and turning. The mare was a wedding present—she would bet her life on it. Five minutes before, she'd been anything but pleased with Chillingworth, anything but sure of him. Now, however . . . she would forgive a man a great deal for such a present, and the thought behind it.

On such a horse, she could ride like the wind—and now she would be living on the edge of a wilderness made for riding wild. Suddenly, the future looked a lot more rosy. The dream that had teased her for the past several weeks—of riding Lambourn Downs on a fleet-footed Arabian mare with him by her side—was so close to coming true.

"Having bought you for me, he must expect me to ride you." She couldn't have resisted to save her soul. "Wait here. I have to find a saddle."

Gyles rode home through the dark, weary in mind rather than in body. He was damp after wrestling with wet timbers, but the summons to the wrecked bridge had been a godsend. It had saved his sanity.

He'd refused Devil's offer to ride out with him, even

though he could have used the help. His temper was worn too thin to allow him to deflect Devil's ribbing, which would have turned to probing the instant he lost his temper and snapped. Devil had known him too long to be easily avoided. And despite his protestations to the contrary, Devil was sure that, like all the Bar Cynster, he'd succumbed to Cupid and was, in reality, in love with his soon-to-be wife.

Devil would know the truth soon enough—the instant he laid eyes on Gyles's meek, mild-mannered bride.

Turning his grey onto the path across the downs, he let the reins lie loose, letting the beast plod at his own pace.

His thoughts were no faster. At least he'd managed to keep the guest list to a manageable hundred or so. He'd had to fight his mother every step of the way; she'd been writing furiously to Franscesca over the past weeks, but he was sure it wasn't at his bride's insistence his mother had pushed and prodded, trying to make the wedding into a grand occasion. That had never been a part of his plan.

It occured to him to wonder if his bride had actually arrived. The service, after all, was scheduled for eleven tomorrow morning. His impulse was to shrug. She'd either be there, or she'd arrive later and they'd marry whenever. It was of little real moment.

He was hardly an impatient bridegroom.

Once he'd gained Francesca's agreement and ridden away from Rawlings Hall, all urgency had left him. The matter was sealed, settled; she'd subsequently signed the marriage settlements. Since leaving Hampshire, he'd barely thought of his bride-to-be, only when his mother brandished a letter and made another demand. Otherwise . . .

He'd been thinking of the gypsy.

The memory of her haunted him. Every hour of every day, every hour of the long nights. She even haunted his dreams, and that was undoubtedly the worst, for in dreams there were no restrictions, no limits, and for a few brief moments after he awoke, he'd imagine . . .

Nothing he did, nothing he told himself, had diminished his obsession. His need for her was absolute and unwavering; despite knowing he'd escaped eternal enslavement by the skin of his teeth, he still dreamed . . . of her. Of having her. Of holding her, his, forever.

No other woman had affected him to this degree, driven him so close to the edge.

He was not looking forward to his wedding night. Just thinking of the gypsy was enough to arouse him, but he couldn't, it seemed, assuage his desire with any other woman. He'd thought about trying, hoping to break her spell—he hadn't managed to leave his armchair. His body might ache, but the only woman his mind would accept ease from was the gypsy. He was in a bad way, certainly not in the right mood to ease a delicate bride into harness.

But that would be on his wedding night; he'd cross that bridge when he reached it. Before then, he had to endure a wedding and wedding breakfast at which the gypsy would most likely be present, albeit swamped by a hundred other guests. He hadn't asked if any Italian friend of Francesca's was expected to be present. He hadn't dared. Any such question would have alerted his mother and aunt, and then there would have been hell to pay. It was going to be bad enough when they met his bride face-to-face.

He hadn't explained to them that his was an arranged marriage, and from what they'd let fall, Horace hadn't either. Henni and his mother would know the truth the instant they laid eyes on Francesca Rawlings. No meek, mild-mannered female had ever held his interest, and they knew it. They'd see his reasoning instantly, and disapprove mightily, but by then there'd be nothing they could do.

It was also because of them—Henni and his equally perspicacious mother—that he'd insisted on restricting the time the bridal party spent at the castle prior to the wedding. The less time for unexpected meetings with the gypsy the better. One exchange observed and they who knew him best would guess the truth there, too. He didn't want them to know. He didn't want anyone to know. He wished he could ignore that particular truth himself.

Reaching the lip of the escarpment, he drew rein and sat looking down on his home, perched above a curve in the river. Lights shone in some windows—and red pinpricks glowed about the forecourt, the doused flares which would only have been lit if the bridal party had arrived.

It dawned on him that fate had been kind. The rain had been a blessing, the bridal party delayed until the last reasonable minute to a time when he'd had a legitimate excuse not to be there to greet them—to risk meeting the gypsy under everyone's eyes. He now only had the wedding and wedding breakfast to endure—the absolute minimum time.

Twenty-four hours and he'd be a married man, tied in wedlock to a woman to whom he was indifferent. He would have secured all he'd set out to achieve—a suitable, mild, and undistracting wife to give him the heir he needed, and the Gatting property he wanted. All he needed to do was adhere to his plans for the next twenty-four hours and all he wanted would be his.

Never had he felt so disinterested in victory.

The grey whickered and shifted. Steadying him, Gyles heard the muted thud of hooves. Scanning the downward slope, he caught a flash of movement, shadow against shadow. A rider coming from the direction of the castle stables was angling up the escarpment.

He lost sight of them, then looked to his left. Rider and horse burst onto the crest a hundred yards away. For an instant, the pair was silhouetted against the rising moon, then the horse sprang forward. The rider was small but in control. Long black hair rippled down her back. The horse was the Arab he'd bought a week ago. Strength and beauty in motion, they streaked out onto the downs.

Gyles had wheeled the grey and set out in pursuit before he'd even thought. Then he did, and cursed himself for what he was doing, but made no move to draw rein. He cursed her, too. What the devil did she think she was doing taking a horse from his stables—no matter he'd bought the beast for her—without a by-your-leave and in the middle of the night!

Grimly, he thundered in her wake, not riding her down but keeping her in sight. Anger was what he wanted to feel, but after dogging him all day, his temper had evaporated. He could too easily understand her—how she would feel after being cooped up in a carriage for days, then finding the mare . . . had she guessed it was for her?

Anger would have been safer, but all he felt was a strange, wistfully compelling need—to talk to her again, see her eyes, her face, hear what she said when he told her the mare was hers—a gift so she could ride wild, but safe. The memory of her husky tones slid through his mind. As long as he didn't touch her, surely one last private meeting would be safe.

Francesca didn't hear the thud of hooves pursuing her until she slowed the mare. The horse was perfect, wondrously responsive; she sent it circling in a prancing arc, ready to streak back to the castle if the rider was no one she knew.

One glance and she recognized him. The moon was fully risen; it bathed him in silver, etching his face, leaving half in shadow. He was wearing a loose riding jacket, a pale shirt and neckcloth. The powerful muscles of his thighs were delineated by tight breeches tucked into long boots. She couldn't read his expression; his eyes she couldn't see. But as she slowed the mare, then halted and let him approach, she sensed no fury, no violent emotions, but something else. Something more careful, uncertain. Tilting her head, she studied him as he drew the huge grey to a halt before her.

It was the first time they'd met since those wild moments in the forest. From tomorrow, they'd live with each other, turbulent emotions and all. Perhaps that was why they both said nothing, but simply looked—as if trying to establish some frame of reference in which to move into this next stage of their lives.

They were both breathing just a little deeper than could be excused by their ride.

"How do you find her?" He nodded at the mare.

Francesca smiled and set the mare dancing. "She's perfect." She tried a few fancy steps—the mare performed without hesitation. "She's very obedient."

"Good." He was watching like a hawk, assuring himself that she could indeed control all that latent energy. When she halted, he turned the grey alongside. "She's yours."

She laughed delightedly. "Thank you, my lord. I overheard two stableboys—they said you'd bought her for some lady. I had to confess I hoped she was for me."

"Your wish has been granted."

She saw his lips lift and smiled gloriously. "Thank you. You could not have chosen a gift I'd treasure more." She'd thank him properly later—she had plenty of time.

"Come—we should start back."

She set the mare to pace the grey as they headed back toward the castle. From a trot they progressed to a canter, then he pushed into a gallop. She realized he was trying out the mare's paces by default. Setting herself to reassure him, she held the mare to precisely the right clip, easing back as he did when they reached the escarpment.

He led the way down; she kept the mare in the wake of the grey. They wound their way around to the stable block. She drew in a deep breath, then slowly exhaled as the paddock giving onto the back of the stable drew near.

She couldn't imagine a more soothing, reassuring way to have passed the evening before their wedding. They might not know each other well, but they had enough solid connections on which to base a marriage. Her nerves had settled. Of tomorrow and the future, she felt confident and assured.

"We need to be reasonably quiet." He dismounted before the stable door. "My head stableman lives over the coach barn, and he's very protective of his charges."

She kicked her feet free and slid down.

Gyles led the grey into the stable, turned the horse into his stall, then quickly unsaddled. The gypsy went past with the mare; he heard her crooning softly to the horse.

Leaving the grey, he strode to the mare's stall and was in time to lift the saddle from the mare's back. The gypsy rewarded him with a heart-stopping smile, then picked up a handful of straw and started brushing down the mare.

Gyles stowed her saddle and tack, then fetched his. He would have to guide her back to her room without being seen by anyone. And without touching her. He wasn't fool enough to imagine achieving that would be easy—just seeing her again, hearing her voice again, had evoked something he could only describe as a yearning. A need for her—a deep-seated emptiness that only she could fill.

But he wasn't going to let it rule him. Ruin him. As long as he didn't touch her, he'd survive.

Quickly brushing down the grey, he checked the horse's feed and water, then shut the stall and returned to the gypsy. She was finished, too, just checking the water, still crooning, softly sultry, to the mare. He was quite sure the horse would be ruined for anyone else.

The gypsy saw him. With a last pat, she left the mare and stepped into the aisle. Tense as a bowstring, Gyles shut the stall door and latched it.

"Thank you."

Her voice had changed—lowered—smoky, sultry, seductive. Gyles turned—

She stepped into him, twined her arms about his neck, stretched up against him, and kissed him.

The simple, passionate kiss slew him—slew all his good intentions, slew any chance of him escaping—or of her escaping him. His arms closed about her and he crushed her to him, bent his head, and took control of the kiss.

She tasted of wind and wildness, of the exhilaration of riding free and fast, unfettered, unrestrained. The invitation in her kiss was explicit—they spoke the same language, understood each other perfectly; there was no need for thought between them.

Arching against him, she drew him deeper, deeper into their kiss, deeper into her wonder. He held her against him and marveled at her bounty, at the promise inherent in her soft curves and supple limbs. His hands went searching; so did hers. And then she was cupping him, cradling him, fondling him—inexpertly admittedly, yet her desire was very clear. She wanted him as much as he wanted her.

That want hit Gyles with a punch that stole his breath, and shook a few of his laggard wits into place. He shifted back, to the side, intending to lean against a stall door—the one next to the mare's—and try to catch his breath. Try to break their kiss, try to ease back from her—

The stall door swung open behind him. It was the middle stall in the long row—the one the stablelads used to store fresh straw. Gyles stumbled back. The stall contained no horse—just a huge pile of loose straw. They landed in it, on it. Within seconds, they'd sunk into it.

They were cocooned in soft dryness, closed off in a dark world of their own. Gyles groaned. The sound was swallowed by their kiss. They lay trapped in each other's arms with her largely beneath him. Then he felt her hands shift, remembered where they'd been, felt her fingers grip his waist. Her hands were underneath his jacket; he felt her pluck at his shirt, fingers dancing along his waistband.

Oh, no. He lifted his head, broke the kiss—then couldn't think what to say.

"You're . . . impatient." One small hand was caressing him again. "You want me now."

A wealth of wonder and discovery laced her tone, confirming beyond doubt that she'd never known a man. It was too dark in the stall, in the well of the straw, to see her face. She could only be seeing him as a dark shadow above her. They were both operating primarily by touch. He wasn't sure if that was an advantage or not.

"I have to get you back into the house."

She hesitated, then he felt her soften and subtly shift beneath him. "I'm quite comfortable here."

Her movements, her tone, left him in no doubt as to her meaning.

His senses, his desires, were fighting to defeat the last of his reason. He let his head fall, trying to garner strength enough to break free. His forehead touched hers. He felt her hands slide—upward, over his chest, fingers splaying against the fine linen of his shirt.

How many women had touched him like that?

Hundreds.

How many others had made him ache, made him shake, with just that simple caress?

None.

Even though he knew the danger, when she tipped her face up and her lips found his, he couldn't resist, couldn't break away. She seduced him with a gentle touch and a kiss so innocent it reached his shielded heart.

"No," he breathed, and tried to draw back.

"Yes," she replied, and said no more. Her lips held his, not with any physical coercion, but with a power he was helpless to deny.

Francesca drank him in, drank in the promise of the hard body lying atop her, of his flagrant response to her. She was more than pleased; she felt like the cat about to lap the cream. He felt hot, hard; the tension in his body screamed of urgency.

His lips broke from hers, trailed her jaw, found her ear, slid lower.

"You like the mare?"

He sounded hoarse.

"She's beautiful."

His lips touched her throat and she instinctively arched, and heard his indrawn breath.

"She's got . . . excellent bloodlines. Her paces . . ."

He'd reached her collarbone and seemed to forget what he was saying; Francesca saw no reason to prompt him. She didn't want to talk, she wanted to explore passion, with him, now. She was about to send her hands wandering down his body, when he murmured, "You can take her with you when you leave."

Francesca stilled. And forced herself to think. She tried a number of interpretations, but couldn't find one that fitted. "Leave?" Puzzlement, she found, could overcome passion, at least in this instance. "Why would I leave?"

He sighed, and the warmth that had wrapped about them fled. He lifted his head and looked down at her.

"All the guests will leave shortly after the wedding, most after the wedding breakfast, the rest the next day." He paused, then continued, steel sliding beneath his tone, "No matter how close to Francesca you are, you'll leave with Charles and his party."

Francesca stared up at him—at the face that was just a shadow to her. Her mouth was open, her mind blank. For the space of four heartbeats, she couldn't say a word. Then her world stopped its crazy gyrations, slowed . . . She wet her lips. "The lady you're marrying—"

"I will not discuss her." The tension that shot through his body was quite different to the heated resilience of passion. It drove passion out, locked her out.

After a moment, she ventured, "I don't think you understand." She didn't, either, but she was starting to suspect. . . .

She felt the sigh he suppressed; his defensive tension eased a fraction. "She might be meek—a perfect cipher—but she's precisely what I need, what I *want,* as my wife."

"You want me." Francesca shifted beneath him, defying him to deny the obvious.

He sucked in a breath—she felt his glare. "I desire you—I neither want nor need you."

Her temper erupted. A hot retort burned her tongue, but she got no chance to utter it.

"I know you don't understand." The words were tight, harsh. "You've never known a man, certainly not one like me. You think you understand me, but you don't."

Oh, but she did, she did, and she was understanding more with every second that passed.

"You think because I am as I am, I would want a passionate wife, but the opposite is true. That's why I chose Francesca Rawlings as my bride. She'll fill the position of my countess perfectly—"

Francesca let him talk, let his words flow past her while her mind flitted back over the weeks since she'd first run into him in the shrubbery and rescripted every scene.

Gyles suddenly realized he was doing the very thing he'd said he wouldn't. Why, for God's sake? He didn't owe the gypsy any explanation. . . .

Except that he was rejecting her, deliberately turning his back on her and on a passionate liaison none knew better than he would burn brighter than most stars. She'd never offered herself to any other man; she wouldn't still be virginal, so untried, if she had.

He felt guilty, severely at fault, for turning her down. Ludicrous, but he felt guilty for hurting her even that much, even for her own good. He felt equally guilty that, even now, he was so obsessed with her he couldn't even form a mental picture of the woman he would marry on the morrow—a woman who was her close friend. There was guilt enough to sink his soul in this tortured situation.

He stopped speaking, then sighed. "At least she won't have brought those blasted dogs."

Silence.

She was still looking at him, staring up at him; he felt her breasts swell and ease against his chest.

A sense of unease slid down his spine. "She hasn't, has she? Brought that pack of lap spaniels?"

The silence stretched, then he felt her gaze refocus. She hadn't truly been watching him.

"No—your bride did not bring the dogs."

Every word vibrated with a determination he couldn't place. He felt her draw breath.

"She did, however, bring me."

Her hands had been resting against his chest—Francesca pushed them over his shoulders, twined them tight about his neck, yanked him down, and sealed his lips with hers.

Fury ignited her passion, fueled it, merged with it. She deliberately let go. Let the fire inside her rage unfettered. It was the only thing she could think of to hit him with, the only thing to which she knew he was not immune.

She couldn't begin to enumerate her hurts, her feelings, her rational, logical reactions, but her instinctive response she had no doubt about.

He'd pay—and in the coin that would cost him most dearly.

He went under—she knew it—sensed the moment the tide dragged him down. Sensed the moment when his will was submerged beneath a tide of need too strong to deny.

She fanned the flames, kept them racing. Their mouths were fused, tongues dueling, tangling. She didn't need to hold him anymore. Sliding her hands free, she went to reach down—his hands closed about her breasts and she arched, and forgot, for the moment, about caressing him, reveling in the sensations as he caressed her.

Between them, they opened her short jacket and blouse. Her chemise he undid with two flicks of his long fingers, then his hand was on her breast and she gasped. His lips returned to hers just in time to catch her cry as his fingers closed about one nipple. As the sharp sensation eased, heat flooded her. She struggled to breathe, struggled to cope, struggled to keep pace with him. She'd never done this before, and he was an expert; she'd seen more than most innocents could even imagine, but she'd never been the woman at the heart of the storm.

And it was a storm—of heat, of sensations too acute to express. She writhed like a wanton beneath him, and knew she was arousing him, driving him on.

So she writhed some more. Everything she could think of to do she did, every action that would further enflame him. She wasn't of a mind to accept anything less than his complete and abject surrender. To her—to their passion. To all that he'd thought to keep out of his life.

He dragged his lips from hers and ducked his head. Her fingers sank into his hair as his lips found her breast. The scalding touch of his tongue made her shudder, then he suckled, clamping a hand over her lips just in time to mute her scream.

She was panting, heated, flushed beyond belief when he finally lifted his head, shifted back, and rucked up her skirts. Hard fingers found her knee, then trailed higher, over the flickering skin along her inner thigh. He touched the soft curls at the apex of her thighs, then his fingers trailed down again.

They returned, to stroke, tease, then tangle in her curls, then one long finger slid between her thighs. She sucked in a breath. Her body tightened as he stroked, then gently probed, then his knee nudged hers, opening her farther. Warm darkness held them; her senses reached no further than him—the world beyond their cocoon of straw had vanished, fallen away. His touch was deliberate, knowing. Dragging in another breath, Francesca parted her thighs.

He cupped her, and her nerves shook. Then his hand shifted; one long finger pressed in, a little way at first, then deeper, deeper, penetrating her softness, opening her body.

Francesca arched, but he held her down, his other hand splayed across her stomach.

Gyles shuddered and closed his eyes. His fingers touched, traced, explored, his imagination supplying what he couldn't see. He was one step away from madness. He had no idea how he had got to this point, but there was only one way forward, one path to sanity.

Ruthlessly, he drove her on. Her body was fluid, liquid heat under his hands. She was passionate woman incarnate, wild and uninhibited; he had to kiss her again, had to stop her cries, had to stop the whimpers of pleasure that tore at his resolve. He could have pushed her to climax swiftly, brutally; some gentleness buried deep made him linger, made him show her the ways, made him steep her in pleasure, until, at the very last, she fractured in glory.

Her body eased beneath him; he felt the last tremors of completion fade and die. He eased his fingers from her, shutting his senses to the musky sweetness that called so elementally to his instincts. He started to ease back, was about to lift away when she turned, found his face with her hand, cradled his jaw, and kissed him.

Held him, trapped him in a web of raw need.

For him, she was the ultimate siren—her kisses lured him to destruction. He only just managed to cling—not to control, but to sufficient lucidity to know what he was doing, and what he must not do. She was still aroused, still aware, still playing havoc with his senses. He'd assumed, after her first climax, an extended one at that, she'd be limp and exhausted, unable further to oppose his plans.

He'd assumed wrong.

He filled his hands with her breasts, then ducked his head and filled his mouth with her soft flesh. He'd tried not to mark her where it would show, but God alone knew how successful he'd been. She'd recalled the need for silence; the knuckles of one hand were pressed to her lips, stifling her cries. She was also doing her best to mute those more intimate sounds he drew from her, but not succeeding.

He explored her lower body, naked now he'd pushed her habit to her waist. Her thighs, firm from riding, were a special delight; the smooth globes of her derriere, cradled possessively in his hands, made him shudder.

He ached to take her, to possess her as she wanted to be possessed, to take her with all the passion in his soul—but that way lay madness. Yet sate her he must. Sliding lower, avoiding the hands that tried to urge him over her, he gripped her hips and set his mouth to her softness.

She nearly choked on a scream. After that, she was too busy trying to catch her breath, trying to suppress her gasps, her screams. Too busy flowering for him.

When he finally let her free, let her fly to the stars and shatter, she was, this time, too exhausted to even grip his sleeve when he eventually drew away. He knelt over her and straightened her clothing by feel, enough to pass muster if they were caught. Then he stood and lifted her into his arms and walked from the stall and the stable.

As he crossed the lawns, he tried hard not to think, not of her, not of any of it—not of how he felt.

Tomorrow morning he would marry her friend, and that would be that.

His body was one giant throbbing ache. He doubted he'd get any sleep.

He could, of course, congratulate himself on avoiding the pit that others had fallen headlong into. He could pride himself on not having succumbed to his baser instincts, on having adhered to the honorable course. He'd have been consumed by guilt if he hadn't, on any number of counts, yet, deep within him he knew it wasn't guilt that had kept him from taking her. Only one power had been strong enough to save her—and him.

One simple, fundamental fear.

He knew in which wing his mother had put his bride-to-be; Henni had told him just in case he wanted to know. Thank heaven she had. He assumed his bride-to-be's companion had been housed nearby. Reaching the right corridor, he started along, then paused, lowered his lips to her ear and whispered, "Which room is yours?"

She waved weakly to the door at the end. He juggled her

and opened it. The windows were uncurtained; the moonlight streamed in, confirming the bed had been made up but was unoccupied.

He laid her gently on it.

Her fingers trailed down his sleeve, but her grip was too weak to hold him. He leaned over her, brushed her hair from her face, bent his head, and kissed her. One last time.

Then he drew back. He knew she was watching him.

"After the wedding, you'll return to Rawlings Hall."

He turned and left her.

Francesca watched him cross the room. She'd let him carry her to her bed assuming he was going to join her in it. As the door closed behind him, she lay back, shut her eyes, and felt bitterness well.

"I don't think so."

Chapter 6

"Ready to take the final momentous step?"

Gyles looked up as Devil sauntered into his private sitting room. Breakfast dishes crowded the table before him, but he'd paid them scant attention. Food was the last thing on his mind.

Wallace had come in early to wake him—he hadn't been asleep but had been grateful for the interruption. He'd spent enough hours with his thoughts. Bathing, dressing, dealing with the inevitable last-minute queries, had kept him busy until Wallace had served him breakfast, then retreated to tidy his bedchamber.

Just as well Devil had arrived.

"Come to witness the condemned man's last meal?"

"The thought had crossed my mind." Pulling up a chair, Devil sat facing him across the table and surveyed the dishes he'd disarranged rather than demolished. "Saving our appetite for later, are we?"

"Indeed." He felt his lips twitch.

"Can't say I blame you if all that's being said of your countess-to-be is true."

He hid a frown. "What's being said?"

"Just that your selection was precisely as one might expect. Your uncle was quite taken. None of the rest of us met her—they arrived after dark."

Gyles hadn't thought Horace's standards differed that much from his. Then again, his uncle was over sixty— perhaps he now favored the quiet and meek. "You'll meet her soon enough, then you can form your own opinion."

Devil reached for a pikelet. "You're not going to reiterate you're marrying for duty, not love?"

"And slay your fond hopes? I'm too polite a host."

Devil snorted.

Gyles sipped his coffee. Misleading Devil wasn't his aim, but he wasn't up to explaining. Denying the gypsy—denying his own raging needs—had sapped his energy. He should have been feeling smug, triumphant, anticipating the suc- cessful outcome of his careful plans. Instead, he felt in- wardly dead, his emotions leaden, dragging him down.

He'd done the right thing—the only thing he could have done—and yet . . . he felt as if he'd done something wrong. Committed some sin worse than any she'd tempted him to.

He couldn't shake aside that feeling; he'd been trying to for half the night. Now here he was, about to marry one woman while another dominated his thoughts. The combi- nation of wildness and innocence, wrapped in a package ripe for plunder, beribboned with a promise of uninhibited pas- sion, of unrestrained wantonness . . . the gypsy was enough to drive any man insane.

She'd shaken him as no woman ever had.

This morning, soon, he'd free himself of her. No matter how attached Francesca was to her, he'd put his foot down. The gypsy would be off his estate, and away from him, by sunset tomorrow at the latest.

He made a mental note to make sure she didn't forget her horse.

"I hestitate to mention it, but it's a little late for second thoughts."

Gyles refocused.

Devil nodded at the clock on the mantelpiece. "We'd better go."

Gyles turned, and saw it was indeed time. Concealing his ridiculous reluctance, he rose, then checked the set of his sleeves and settled his coat.

"The ring?"

He hunted in his waistcoat pocket, drew it out, and handed it to Devil.

Devil studied the ornate band. "Emeralds?"

"It's been in the family for generations. Mama happened to mention that emeralds would suit, so . . ."

His mother hadn't actually mentioned it; he'd walked into his countess's bedchamber, the one beyond his, and been hit over the head with the fact. His mother had redecorated the suite in his bride's favorite color—a vivid, intense emerald. In the adjoining sitting room, the emerald was tastefully muted by inmixing of turquoise and other colors, but in the bedchamber itself, in heavy silks and satins, the solid hue held sway. Touches of gilt and polished wood rendered the result even more decadent.

The room had sent his brows rising. He couldn't imagine his meek, mild, and very fair bride in it—she'd be overwhelmed by the color. Yet if it was her declared favorite, as his mother insisted, who was he to argue?

He nodded at the ring as Devil tucked it into his pocket. "I hope it fits." He headed for the door.

Devil fell in on his heels. "Can't you at least give me a few hints? What does this paragon look like? Dark or fair, tall or tiny—what?"

Opening the door, Gyles glanced over his shoulder. "You'll see in five minutes." He hesitated, then added, "Just remember, I did warn you I'm marrying for duty, not love."

Devil studied his eyes. "I hope you know what you're doing. Marriages have a tendency to last a long time."

"That," Gyles acknowledged, stepping into the corridor, "was one of the aspects that swayed me."

The chapel was in the oldest part of the castle. They reached it to find the guests already seated. Gyles continued around to the anteroom off the side. There, his father's cousin, Hector, Bishop of Lewes, was settling his robes.

"Ah—there you are, m'boy!" Hector smiled.

Gyles introduced Devil.

"We met last night." Hector returned Devil's nod, then held up a hand as he listened to the music coming from the chapel. "Ah-ha! That's our cue. The bride has been sighted and we must get to our places. Right, then?"

Gyles waved him on and followed, Devil at his back. Hector slowed as he entered the chapel. Gyles had to concentrate not to walk on his heels. He heard rustling, polite whisperings, but he didn't look at the guests. Hector led them to the altar. Gyles stopped where he knew he was supposed to, before the single step. Lifting his head, he squared his shoulders. Devil stopped beside him; shoulder to shoulder they faced the altar.

Gyles felt precisely nothing.

Hector climbed the step, then turned majestically to view the congregation. The music, provided by Hector's wife playing a spinet tucked away to one side, paused, then the opening chords of a bridal march sounded.

Gyles watched Hector. The prelate lifted his head, his cherubic face wearing its usual amiable expression, and looked down the aisle.

Hector's expression changed. His eyes widened, then sparkled. His cheeks pinkened. "Well!" he murmured. "My *word*!"

Gyles froze. What the devil had his meek and mild bride done?

Skirts shushed as ladies shuffled about to see. The expectant hush was shattered by whispers—excited ones. A wave of gasps and smothered exclamations rolled forward. Gyles felt Devil stiffen, fighting the impulse, then Devil turned his head and looked. And stilled.

Temper rising—surely Charles knew better than to let the girl appear in anything outre?—Gyles decided he may as well learn what everyone else already knew. Lips compressed, he turned—

His gaze swept the front pew on the other side of the aisle, the one reserved for the bride's family. An angular middle-aged woman sat smiling mistily, watching the bride approach. Beside her, pale blue eyes even wider than he remembered them, her mouth agape, staring straight at him as if she'd seen a ghost, sat . . .

His meek, mild-mannered bride.

Gyles couldn't wrench his gaze from her.

He couldn't breathe—his head was spinning.

If she was there, then who . . .

A *frisson* of awareness raced up his spine.

Slowly, stiffly, he completed his turn—confirmed with his eyes what his beleagured brain was screaming.

Even when he saw, he still couldn't believe.

Still couldn't breathe.

She was a vision to make strong men weak. A veil of fine lace edged with seed pearls was anchored across her crown, covering but not concealing the rampant lushness of her hair, black as a crow's wing against the ivory. Behind the veil, her emerald eyes glowed, vibrantly intense. From where he stood, the veil's edge hid her lips; his memory supplied their fullness.

Her gown was an old-fashioned fantasy in stiff ivory silk heavily sewn with pearls. She filled it to perfection, the low, square-cut neckline the perfect showcase for her magnificent breasts. The golden hue of her complexion, the darkness of her hair, and her vivid eyes allowed her to carry the ivory with dramatic flair; it wasn't the gown that dominated the vision.

From the fullness of her breasts, the gown narrowed to

tightly encircle her waist before spreading in heavy folds over her hips. That tiny waist invited male hands to seize, while her rich skirts evoked images of plunder.

She was a goddess designed to fill male minds with salacious imaginings, to claim their senses, snare their hearts, and trap them forever in a world of sensual longing.

And she was his.

And furious.

With him.

Gyles dragged in a breath as, with a susurration of silks, she stepped to her place beside him. He was dimly aware that to all eyes but his, she appeared a radiant bride, her lips curving in a smile of joyful happiness beneath her veil.

Only for him did her eyes flash. With a warning, and a promise.

Then she looked at Hector and smiled.

Hector nearly dropped his Bible. While he shuffled and reshuffled, trying to find his place, Gyles looked down and struggled to breathe. She was handling this better than he was, but then, she'd known who he was all along—

He hauled his mind off that track. He couldn't afford to let his temper rule him. He had to think. He tried, but felt trapped, as if he was fleeing through a maze meeting blank walls at every turn.

Devil nudged him. He lifted his head as Hector, finally ready, cleared his throat.

"We are gathered here today . . ."

He barely registered the words. In a daze, he repeated the phrases he had to say. Then she spoke, and instantly captured every last shred of his awareness.

In her sultry, smoky voice, she—Francesca Hermione Rawlings—vowed to be his wife, in sickness and in health, for better, for worse, until death should them part.

He had to stand there and let it happen.

Devil gave Hector the ring. Hector blessed it, then held out the open Bible, the ring balanced on the page.

Gyles picked it up and turned to her.

She extended her left hand. He closed his fingers about hers, so small and delicately boned. He slid the ring on her finger. It slipped down, but he had to ease it over her second knuckle. It fitted perfectly.

The ring glowed against her skin; the emeralds winked, their fire an echo of her eyes.

He looked up and caught her gaze. The fire burned brightly there.

She returned his regard, then her lips firmed. Surreptitiously she tugged, trying to free her hand.

Gyles tightened his hold.

For good or ill, she was his.

The realization swept him. A turbulent power, basic, elemental—wholly primitive—flowed through him.

"And now, by the grace vested in me, I pronounce you man and wife." Hector closed his Bible and beamed upon them. "You may now kiss the bride."

Gyles released her hand. With apparent calm, she raised her veil and set it back.

Sliding his hand around her waist, he drew her to him. She quickly looked up, eyes widening, lips parting—

He bent his head and covered her lips with his.

It should have been a gentle kiss, a mere formality.

It wasn't.

His arm tightened, locking her against him. His tongue plundered—a warning of his own. It was a kiss of claiming, one that spoke of primal rights, of promises made, vows taken, bargains made that would be kept.

After an instant's surprise, she caught her breath and kissed him back—with fire, with defiance—with unadulterated passion.

It was he who broke the kiss, aware that this was not the time or place. Their eyes met—they both remembered where they were and what they had to face. Silent agreement flashed between them. Because she was so much shorter, and he'd caught her so close, no one had witnessed the quality of their exchange.

About them, music swelled; Hector's wife had started the processional.

Francesca blinked, then glanced at Hector. She tried to draw back—Gyles tightened his hold on her.

Only to feel Hector's hand on his shoulder.

"Well! Might I be the first to congratulate the bride?"

He had to let her go; he forced himself to do it, forced himself to let Hector take her hands and buss her cheek.

Devil elbowed him in the back.

"Nice *duty*, if one can get it."

Gyles turned—only to have Devil nudge him aside.

"Stand back, Hector. It's my turn."

Their well-wishers surrounded them. Gyles stood by her side and refused to budge as the guests pressed forward, eager to greet his ravishing countess, to pump his hand and tell him what a lucky dog he was.

The ladies made straight for Francesca. Horace thumped him on the back. "A sly one, you are! All that talk of marrying for the family and property—well! Not that I blame you, mind—she's a demmed fetching piece."

"She did bring the Gatting property."

"Yes, well, I expect that influenced you mightily." Horace grinned at Francesca. "Must kiss the bride, what?" He moved on.

Gyles inwardly sighed. If not even Horace believed . . .

Francesca greeted Horace with a social grace quite at odds with what was running through her mind. Indeed, she was grateful to those who pressed near to squeeze her hand, kiss her cheek, and offer their congratulations—they provided her with an opportunity to catch her breath. Such occasions held no terrors; as her parents' only child, she'd been their social companion for years and was confidently at ease amidst fashionable crowds.

It wasn't the demands of the wedding that concerned her.

She wasn't at all sure what was going on in her husband's mind, but that was presently the least of her concerns. After he'd returned her to her bed, she hadn't been able to think. To her surprise, she'd fallen deeply asleep. She'd woken only just in time to hide the evidence of her nighttime excursion before Millie and Lady Elizabeth arrived to help her with her preparations. Ester had joined them, and assured her Franni was highly excited and looking forward to witnessing the wedding.

She hadn't known what to make of that.

On waking, her first thought had been that she should give him what he wanted—what he was expecting—and reorganize things so Franni walked up the aisle. She would give the Gatting property he was so set on acquiring to Franni . . . it was then she'd remembered the marriage settlements. They'd been signed and sealed, and it was her name, not Franni's, in all the crucial spots.

While their marriage was the crux of the arrangement, the ceremony was only part of that, the public acknowledgment of an agreement entered into. Legally, albeit contingent on their wedding taking place, the Gatting property was already his.

Both Charles and Chillingworth's man-of-business, a Mr. Waring, who'd traveled into Hampshire with the documents, had taken great pains to impress on her the inviolability of the agreement once signed.

She'd signed. She couldn't now refuse to marry him.

And she certainly could not thrust Franni into such an arena. He'd been out of his mind to think she could cope . . . which made her wonder if Chillingworth had spoken with Franni at all.

She had no idea what Franni thought. Was Chillingworth the gentleman her cousin had referred to? She'd had no chance before the ceremony to speak with Franni alone. Indeed, Franni had been innocently excited when she'd hurried off to the chapel with Ester.

When she'd walked up the aisle, she'd seen Chillingworth glance toward where Franni should have been, but with all eyes on her, she hadn't dared look herself. She'd been playing a part, and she'd had to play it well—had to make people believe she was a willing and happy bride. She'd hoped to glance Franni's way once she'd halted before the altar, perhaps as Charles stepped back—but the instant she'd reached Chillingworth's side . . .

Shaking aside the memory, she tried again to glimpse the pew where Franni had been, but Chillingworth had, thanks to the melee, ended on that side. He hadn't budged an inch since; she couldn't see past him. Neither Ester nor Franni had come to kiss her. Charles was hanging back. But he was smiling.

Frustrated, she glanced at Lady Elizabeth, who read her emotion correctly but misinterpreted the cause. Her mother-in-law clapped her hands. "It's time we moved on to the dining room. Now make way and let them go ahead, then you can greet them at the door and we can all chat and enjoy ourselves over the wedding breakfast."

Francesca cast her a grateful smile. Chillingworth's arm appeared before her, and she took it, preserving her mask of a radiant, joyful bride as they ran a gauntlet of rice all the way up the aisle.

Outside the chapel, her smile evaporated. Before she could turn to him, he grasped her hand. "This way."

She had to grab her skirts and run to keep up with his long strides. He cut down corridors, down stairs, around corners, leading her away from their guests, away from the reception rooms. At no stage did he moderate his pace. Then they were rushing down a narrow, dimly lit corridor—she thought they were on the ground floor. The door at the end was shut.

She was about to dig in her heels and demand to be told where he was taking her when, just before the door, Chillingworth stopped dead, whirled her about, and backed her against the wall.

Francesca felt the wall cool at her back, felt the heat of his body before her, around her. She sucked in a breath as he leaned closer, trapping her. She caught his gaze, held it.

Gyles was aware they were both breathing rapidly. The pulse throbbing at the base of her throat dragged at his senses, but he didn't take his gaze from her eyes.

Any other woman, and he would have exploited their sexual linkage to unnerve her, to gain the upper hand.

With her, he didn't dare.

There was too much between them, even now, even here. It was a hot breath caressing skin, something almost palpable, an awareness of sin as old as time.

They only had minutes, and he had no idea what she intended, whether she was going to play out the scene to its end, or erupt midway through.

"Franni—"

The sheer fury that lit her eyes—lit her—silenced him. Her rage was so potent he nearly stepped back.

"I am *not Franni.*"

Every carefully enunciated word slapped him.

"You're Francesca Hermione Rawlings." She'd better be, or he'd wring her neck.

She nodded. "And my cousin, Charles's daughter, is Frances Mary Rawlings. Known to all as Franni."

"Charles's *daughter?*" The fog started to clear. "Why the devil was she given such a similar name to you?"

"We were born within weeks of each other, me in Italy, Franni in Hampshire, and we were both named after our paternal grandfather."

"Francis Rawlings?"

She nodded again. "Now we have that settled, I have a few questions. Did you meet Franni when you visited Rawlings Hall?"

He hesitated. "I strolled with her twice."

She breathed in; her breasts rose. "Did you at any time say anything to lead Franni to believe you were considering offering for her?"

"No."

"No?" She widened her eyes at him. "You came to Rawlings Hall to find an amenable bride, you thought you'd found her, you walked twice with her—and you said nothing—gave no hint whatever of your intentions?"

"No." His temper was on a leash as tight as hers. "If you recall, I insisted on adhering to the most distant and rigid formality. It would have run counter to my plans to woo your cousin in even the most cursory way."

He could see she didn't know whether to believe him or not. He exhaled through his teeth. "I swear on my honor I never said or did *anything* to give her the slightest reason to imagine I had any interest whatever in her."

She hesitated, then stiffly inclined her head. "Did you see what happened to her? She wasn't in the chapel when we left, but I didn't see her leave."

He wasn't sure what was going on. "I only glimpsed her in the instant before you joined me. She recognized me and seemed shocked. There was an older lady with her."

"Ester—Charles's sister-in-law, Franni's aunt. She lives with them."

"I didn't see either of them later. They must have left when everyone was crowding around."

Francesca grimaced. "Charles didn't seem worried . . ."

Her gaze grew distant. Gyles wondered why she'd seemed so certain he'd spoken of his offer to her cousin. Did she believe he'd raised her cousin's hopes? But *she'd* known all along. . . .

He needed more time—a lot more time—to sort out who'd known what.

Voices reached them through the door.

He straightened. "Our presence is required." Catching her hand, he opened the door and walked out into the hall before the formal dining room.

"There they are!"

The crowd, having arrived and discovered them not where

they were supposed to be, turned and, en masse, smiled widely.

Francesca knew what they were thinking. Her blush only reinforced the picture created by her husband and the smirk on his too-handsome lips.

"Just a little detour to show Francesca more of her new domain."

The crowd laughed and parted for them. As she went forward at his side to lead the way into the formal dining room, to the banquet laid out in their honor, Francesca heard numerous ribald references as to with which part of her domain she'd recently become familiar.

Such comments did nothing to improve her mood, but she hid her temper, her feelings, well. Not one guest, nor any member of his family or hers, would have any inkling what seethed beneath her unremittingly joyful facade.

Chillingworth and she stood side by side, the perfect couple, and greeted their guests as they entered the room. Charles was among the first—he shook hands with Gyles, then embraced her warmly and kissed her cheek.

"I'm so happy for you, my dear."

"And I have so much to thank you for." Francesca squeezed his hands. "And Franni?"

Charles's smile faded. "I'm afraid the excitement proved too much, as we'd feared it would." He glanced at Gyles, who was listening attentively. "Franni isn't strong, and excitement can overwhelm her." Charles turned back to Francesca. "Ester's with her at the moment, but will join us later. Franni's simply a little disoriented—you know how she gets."

Francesca didn't, not really, but she couldn't talk longer with Charles. With an understanding smile, she released his hand and he moved on as the next guest took his place.

A tall, lanky gentleman, unquestionably another Rawlings, pumped Gyles's hand and beamed delightedly. "Capital, coz! Can't thank you enough! Huge load off my mind, I can tell you." Wearing an unfitted coat, a dark, drab waist-coat, and a soft, floppy cravat, the gentleman was some years younger than Chillingworth.

Gyles turned to Francesca. "Allow me to present my cousin, Osbert Rawlings. At present, Osbert's my heir."

"Only for the present—ha, ha!" Beaming, Osbert turned to her, then realized what he'd said. "Well, I mean to say— well, it's not as if . . ."

He slowly flushed beet red.

Francesca flashed a look at Chillingworth, then smiled radiantly at Osbert and took the limp hand he'd extended and left hanging in the air between them. "I'm so pleased to meet you."

Osbert blinked, swallowed, and refocused. "A great pleasure." Still holding her hand, he remained standing before her, staring, then he said, "You're quite devilishly beautiful, you know."

Francesca laughed, but not unkindly. "Thank you, but it's not my doing—I was born this way."

"Still," Osbert persisted. "Have to say—that moment in the chapel when you appeared, it was quite the most galvanizing instant." He stepped closer to Francesca as those behind jostled. "I was thinking of writing an ode—"

"Osbert." Gyles intervened, displeasure clear in his tone.

"Oh! Yes—of course." Osbert shook Francesca's hand, then released it. "I'll speak with you later."

He stepped away; others quickly took his place.

Moments later, when she had a chance, Francesca glanced at Chillingworth. "What's wrong with an ode?"

"Not odes. *Osbert's* odes." Gyles met her gaze. "Wait until you've heard one."

They continued shaking hands as the guests trooped past them. Gyles succeeded in preserving an acceptable facade, but his temper was wearing thin, his senses constantly abraded by Francesca's nearness, by every breath she took. When the last guest had moved on to find a seat, he offered her his arm. With her hand on his sleeve, he paraded her up the long room to the applause of all present. Two long tables ran the length of the room, guests seated on both sides. Across the head of those tables ran a third, at which the guests of honor sat facing the long room.

He handed Francesca to the chair beside his. His mother sat on his left, while Horace was on Francesca's right. Charles and Henni made up the table. At the other tables, the closest places were taken by Devil and Honoria, and three other peers and their wives. Beyond that, family and close connections filled the room. By tightly controlling the guest list, he'd ensured that other than Devil, Honoria, and a few close friends, society at large was not present.

Irving drew back his chair. Gyles sat, and footmen rushed forward to charge the glasses. The toasts and the feasting began.

They put on a good show. Gyles was conscious that no one guessed the truth, not even his perspicacious mother. Francesca played her part to perfection—then again, she'd been perfectly willing to marry him until she'd learned of his mistake. Even then, she hadn't been *un*willing. Furious perhaps, but it wasn't as if she hadn't secured precisely all he'd offered her.

He was the one whose carefully laid plans had been turned on their head—who had got far more than he wanted, indeed, precisely what he *hadn't* wanted, from the day.

And there wasn't a damned thing he could do about it.

As the courses came and went, he struggled to ignore the constant tug on his senses, an effort frustrated by having to play the role of pleased and proud groom. The toasts became increasingly risqué; the sincerity of the good wishes that flowed around him gradually sank through to his brain.

Most would consider him inordinately lucky. Virtually every man in the room bar only Devil would trade places with him in a blink. He was married to a fascinatingly beautiful woman, who was also, it seemed, a past master in the social arts. She was so freely charming, so effortlessly engaging—he wasn't blind to her qualities.

They were married—man and wife. He couldn't change it. All he could do was make the best of it.

And from what he'd already learned of his bride, if he wanted to rule his roost, he had better make a push to establish the rules. His rules.

He might have married her—that didn't mean he'd surrendered. Not even she could take from him that which he didn't wish to give. He was stronger, and infinitely more experienced than she. . . .

While he chatted to Charles and others across the table, he let his mind skate back over the previous night. Prior to that, there was nothing in his behavior with her she could legitimately rail at. Last night, however . . .

He would need to rebuild a few bridges other than the one that had washed away.

Francesca was talking to Honoria across the table, the fingers of her left hand draped loosely about the stem of her wineglass where it stood on the white linen between them. He reached out and insinuated his fingers between hers, twining them about hers. He felt the tiny shiver she instantly suppressed, felt primal recognition tighten his gut.

He waited.

Minutes later, the next course was set out. In the general hubbub as people were served, Francesca turned his way. She didn't try to withdraw her hand but when she met his gaze, he couldn't read her eyes.

"The mistake I made." She arched a brow, and he continued, "There was a reason. I had, still have, a very definite idea of what I want from marriage. And you—" He broke off. She watched him calmly. "You . . . and I . . ." He exhaled sharply. "I didn't mean to suggest you are not a perfectly acceptable bride."

She raised her brows haughtily; her eyes flashed. Then she smiled gloriously, leaned close, and patted his hand, sliding her fingers deftly from his, then she turned away to speak to Henni.

Gyles bit back his temper, reined in the urge to grab her hand and spin her back to face him. Those watching would have seen the exchange as delightful flirting; he could do nothing to disturb the image. Letting his lips curve, he turned to another conversation.

He bided his time. Obsessed with his problem, obsessed with her, to him the hours flew. Eventually, the banquet ended and everyone adjourned to the adjoining ballroom. A small orchestra played in an alcove at one end. The first order of the afternoon was the bridal waltz.

Francesca heard the opening bars and steeled herself. She turned to Chillingworth with a smile on her lips, an easy expression on her face. He drew her to him; they both felt the tremor that shook her as her thigh brushed his, and his instantaneous tensing. Only she felt the possessiveness in his grasp, in the hard palm at her back—only she was near enough to see the steely glint in his grey eyes. A fractional hesitation gripped them as they remembered just how many eyes were watching, and both, again, reined in their tempers. Without words, they stepped out, revolving slowly at first, cautiously on her part, then she recognized his prowess and relaxed.

He was an expert at waltzing. She was good at it herself. She had matters of far greater moment on her mind.

He swung her into the first turn, and she let herself flow with his stride. Let him draw her as close as he wished, so their thighs brushed and hips met—knowing every touch affected him as much as it affected her. She fixed her gaze on his and kept her lips curved. "I married you because I had no choice—*we* had no choice. The settlements were signed, the guests all here. While I might deplore your approach to marriage—your approach to me—I see no reason to acquaint the world or, indeed, anyone at all, with my disappointment."

She held his gaze for a moment more, then glanced aside.

She'd spent the last hour preparing that speech, mentally re-hearsing her tone. Given the tightness about her chest, the peculiar sensitivity that had affected her skin, she was pleased to have delivered it so creditably.

They'd completed one revolution of the large ballroom; she smiled as she watched other couples join them on the floor.

"Your disappointment?"

She turned back to the man in whose arms she was. His tone had been flat, disturbing. She raised a haughty brow, then, remembering the many onlookers, let the expression dissolve into one of laughing happiness.

"I wasn't aware"—the chill in his words warned her she was skating on thin ice—"that you have any justifiable cause for feeling dissatisfied with our dealings."

His expression was that of a groom thoroughly pleased with his bride, but there was an arrogant air, even there, in his mask, that she longed to shake. As for the coldness be-hind the mask, like steel doors shutting her out . . .

She shook her head on an airy laugh. "My disappointment stems from the discrepancy between what I believed—had *reason* to believe—I would in reality receive from the man, and what I am now being offered"—boldly she surveyed him, as much as she could see while held in his arms—"by the earl. Had I known of it, I would never have signed those wretched settlements, and we wouldn't now be condemned to living a lie."

Just the thought of the tangle he'd landed them in sent her temper into orbit. His hand tightened about hers; he drew her closer—she sucked in a breath and felt her breasts brush his chest. Raising her head, she met his gaze, defiance and a warning in hers. "I suggest, my lord, that we leave any dis-cussion of such matters until we are private, unless you wish to risk our afternoon's hard work."

His reserve broke—just for an instant—and she saw the prowling predator in his eyes. And wondered if they were about to indulge in their first argument, in public, in the middle of the ballroom in the middle of their wedding. The same thought occurred to him—she saw it in his eyes. The fact he hesitated, considered, before drawing back amazed her, intrigued her—and shook her confidence.

The musicians came to her aid and ended the waltz with a flourish. With a laugh and a smile, she stepped out of his arms and swept him an elaborate curtsy. He was forced to bow, then he raised her. All smiling delight, she turned from him, expecting to slip her fingers from his and part, each to talk to the many guests eager to have a word.

His fingers locked about her hand.

He stepped close, beside and behind her.

"Oh, no, my dear—our dance has just begun."

The murmured words brushed her ear; sensation streaked down her spine.

Lifting her chin, she smiled at Lord and Lady Charteris, and gave his lordship her other hand.

Beside her, Gyles suavely acknowledged Lady Charteris's greeting and exchanged nods with his lordship. He was operating wholly on long-ingrained habit, his mind, his senses focused on the woman by his side.

When it came to her, he was ruled by instinct, no matter how he wished it otherwise. She was who she was, invoked all he was, and he was powerless to rein that part of himself in, not with her beside him.

Disappointed, was she? Already? So soon?

They hadn't got to their marriage bed yet. Then they—she—would see. He might refuse to love her—he would refuse to love her. But he'd never said anything about not desiring her. Never denied he lusted after her. The fact that theirs was an arranged marriage changed that not at all.

He was looking forward to correcting her mistake.

They left Lord and Lady Charteris; Francesca turned to him. His hold on her hand kept her close; he bent his head so they were closer still. Her gaze touched his lips, paused, then she blinked and looked into his eyes. "I must speak with your aunt."

He smiled. Wolfishly. "She's across the room." Between them, he raised her hand. Holding her gaze, he lifted her wrist to his lips and pressed a kiss to the sensitive inner face.

Her eyes flared. He felt the tremor she fought to suppress.

His smile widened; he let his lids veil his eyes. "Come. I'll take you to her."

For the next twenty minutes, all went as he dictated. Under cover of their new relationship, he touched her cheek, her throat, trailed a finger up the inside of her bare arm. He felt her start, quiver, soften. Felt her nerves tighten, sensed her expectation swell. He played to it, letting his palm brush her bare shoulder, skate possessively over her back, down over her hips and the curves of her bottom.

Closed his hands about her tiny waist as he steered her through the crowd.

His touch was light, his actions that of a possessive man to his new bride. Any seeing them would have smiled indulgently. Only she knew his intention. Only she knew because he wanted her to know that, with him, the sensual game was one she couldn't win. Wouldn't win. Yet it was a game they were going to play.

No one, not Henni, not even his mother, saw through his mask, but Francesca, his beautiful, sensual bride, definitely did.

When, from behind her, he closed his hand about her upper arm, briefly guiding her through the throng, simultaneously letting his thumb caress the side of her breast, Francesca wondered just how far he would go. She decided she no longer cared. Raising her head, she glanced over her shoulder, deliberately tentative.

A light blush had risen to her cheeks; her breathing was

no longer steady. She had a very good idea how delicately, quiveringly hesitant she appeared.

He bent his head; his grip tightened, slowing her. His wayward thumb stroked deliberately, again.

She halted, tilted her head up, and turned toward him. Leaned back against him.

Her lips were suddenly just beneath his. Her hip rode against him. His eyes flared, grey turning stormy. They locked on hers. She sensed the catch in his breath. Holding his gaze, she shifted against him, against the ridge of his erection.

"My lord?" She breathed the words against his lips, and made them an outright challenge.

His eyes, stormy dark, hardened. She shifted back, tilting her head playfully, smiling—reminding him to smile, too.

He did, his lips curving easily—the light in his eyes, the tenor of that smile, sent a shiver coursing through her.

"My lady." He arched a brow but there was no question.

Battle was joined.

He drew first blood, whirling her into another waltz that ripped her breath away. She struck back with her own brand of teasing, artfully flirting with three gentlemen at once. When he ruthlessly cut short her exhibition, she smiled knowingly and watched his temper rise.

Shortly after, she discovered he had an advantage she couldn't match. He could touch her anywhere and her senses leapt. Her whole body, all of her skin, was sensitized—not just to his touch, but to his breath, to his very nearness. She was acutely aware of every little brush, every gliding, illicit caress.

He deserved his reputation—she'd seen enough, Lady Elizabeth had hinted at enough, for her to have a good idea of what it was. Only a past master could have accomplished what he did—done all he did—in the middle of a crowded ballroom. Very rarely did anyone see; only on a few occasions did she catch an understanding smirk or a too-wide smile.

For a full twenty minutes, he had her running ragged, her breathing increasingly fractured, her senses skittering wildly, trying to imagine what next he would do. Trying to anticipate so she could take evasive action. . . .

It suddenly dawned on her that that was the road to defeat. But she had so few avenues for attack.

She turned her mind to it—and discovered the outer edge of his ear was one sensitive spot. The side of his throat, too, but his cravat got in her way. His arms, his shoulders, his hips—those might have been more useful if they'd been bare. But his chest—when she let herself stumble against him, and splayed her hands across the wide muscles, she felt his breathing lock.

The exercise cost her another episode of feeling his hands too firm about her waist, but she slipped out of his hold smiling. Intently.

They continued to chat, to play chief attraction for the gathered throng, all the while pursuing their game. The necessity of concealing their increasingly physical clashes raised the stakes, heightened the challenge.

Finally, she found what she sought. His thighs—he tensed visibly when she artfully trailed her fingers down the long muscles, taut beneath his trousers.

For a fraction of a second, his mask slipped, and she glimpsed the man who had kissed her in the forest. Then he avoided her hand and spun her into the crowd. A second later she felt his hand on her hip, felt it slide lower, then close. Thanking heaven for her heavy skirts and petticoats, she stepped away with a teasing look.

Ten minutes later, she caught him again. With his back to the wall and her before him, her wide skirts hiding her hands, she spread her fingers about his thighs, then ran her hands upward—

Gyles caught her wrists in an iron grip. He found himself

staring into brilliant green eyes, widening slightly—and wondered what the hell they were doing. He didn't need her to touch him to arouse him; he was already aching. Their game—and her unexpected participation—had wound him tight.

If she touched him—

He flicked a glance at the crowd. They'd spent time with everyone, done their social duty; the event was drawing to a close. It was early evening, still light outside. The majority of guests would head home that night. Most would leave as soon as Francesca and he retired.

He looked into his bride's challenging eyes. "Let's continue this in private."

Her brows rose, then she inclined her head. "As you wish."

She straightened, then looked down when he didn't release her wrists. Gyles forced himself to do it—to uncurl his long fingers and let her go. She watched him do it, watched his fingers unfurl. He saw one brow arch, and realized she could feel it, sense it—the effort it cost him, and all that he was hiding, even from her.

"The door along the wall to our right—go out, take the first right, third left, first right. You'll come to a flight of stairs. Go up—it'll bring you out beside a gallery. A maid will be waiting to lead you to the countess's suite."

She'd glanced up again; he couldn't read her eyes. "And you?"

"I'll cut through the crowd and take a different exit. That way, we'll avoid any unnecessary fuss." He paused, then asked, "Assuming, of course, that you're not partial to fuss?"

She held his gaze for an instant, then, mask gone, inclined her head haughtily. "I'll see you upstairs."

She turned and glided away from him.

Gyles watched until she disappeared through the door, then he straightened and sauntered into the crowd to make good his own escape.

Chapter 7

"*Wallace?*"

"Yes, sir?"

"Get out. And take any staff in the wing with you."

"At once, sir."

Gyles watched the door close behind his majordomo, then started to pace, to give Wallace time to fetch Francesca's maid and depart the private wing. He suspected his first private meeting with his wife would not be a quiet one. She was as far removed from the meek and mild-mannered as it was possible to get—

He heard a door close. He paused, then crossed to the door into Francesca's bedchamber. He reached for the handle, then stopped. Had she realized the door was there—that it was a connecting door and not a cupboard?

Would she scream if he walked through?

Muttering a curse, he swung around and stalked to the corridor door.

In her luxurious emerald green bedchamber, Francesca sat before the dressing table and studiously brushed her hair, her eyes never leaving the door to her right, farther along the wall—the door that, so Millie had informed her, led to the earl's bedchamber.

Through there he would come. She was ready, waiting—

A glimmer of movement caught her eye. She looked into the mirror—and smothered a shriek! Leaping up from the stool she whirled, the silver-backed brush clutched like a weapon. *"What are you doing here?"* Her heart thumped. "How did you get in?"

Halting three feet away, he narrowed his eyes at her. To her relief, he ignored her first witless question. "Through the door. The main one."

He was wearing a robe nonchalantly belted over a pair of loose silk trousers. She forced her gaze past him to the corridor door, then looked back at him, at his face. "A gentleman would have knocked."

Gyles had thought about it. "I'm your husband. I own this house. I don't have to knock."

The look she cast him should have withered him. Instead, it had the opposite effect. With a gesture very like a flounce, she turned and set her brush down. It clicked on the tabletop.

He had long ago observed that the best courtesans perfected the contradictory art of dressing demurely yet appearing lushly sensual. His new wife was apparently a natural in that sphere—the ivory-silk nightgown that draped her curves was in no way outrageous, yet in it she epitomized every man's secret fantasy. The neckline was not low; it exposed very little of her breasts. Simplicity itself, the gown had no sleeves. Instead, a negligee of diaphanous gauze, liberally edged with lace, hazed the warm tone of her bare arms, the fall of lace at wrists, around the neckline and down the open front, tempting a man to reach, to touch, to brush aside and reach farther.

Her hair, fully out, was longer than he'd thought, the curling strands hanging down her back to her waist.

"Very well." She swung to face him. Eyes glittering, she

crossed her arms. He had to fight to keep his gaze on her face, away from the peaks of her breasts outlined beneath the taut silk.

"You may now explain how it was that you thought my cousin was the woman you were marrying."

The demand, and her tone, refocused his mind wonderfully. When he didn't immediately respond, she flung out her hands. "How *could* you have made such a mistake?"

"Very easily. I had perfectly reasonable grounds to imagine your cousin was the lady for whom I was offering."

Her eyes, her expression dared him to convince her. He mentally gritted his teeth. "The day I made my offer, I walked to the stable via the shrubbery."

She nodded exaggeratedly. "I remember that quite well."

"*Before* I met you, I saw your cousin sitting in the walled garden reading a book. I don't think she saw me."

"She often sits there."

"While I was watching, some woman called your name."

"Ester called me. I heard her and came running—"

"When Ester called, Franni reacted. She shut her book, gathered her shawl."

Francesca grimaced. "She's childish—always curious. If someone's called, she'll come to find out why. But surely, just from that, you didn't assume—"

"Ester called again. 'Francesca—Franni'—and Franni answered, 'I'm here.' Naturally, I assumed Franni was a diminutive of Francesca. I was *convinced* she was you."

She studied him. Her anger faded; worry clouded her eyes. "You said you met Franni—walked with her—twice. What did you say to her?"

He set his jaw. "I swore on my honor I said nothing—" He broke off when she waved the words aside.

"I accept that you didn't mention your offer, but Franni, as I said—you heard what Charles said—she's childish. She exaggerates wildly." Her hands gestured; her eyes willed him to understand. "What did you speak with her about?"

He frowned. "Why is it important?"

She pressed her lips together, then gave in. "Franni mentioned she had a gentleman caller, one who called twice. She interpreted his visits as meaning he would offer for her. She told me this days ago. I couldn't get her to reveal anything more—she's often secretive. And often what she's sure happened is pure fantasy."

His frowned deepened; she hurried on, "I don't even know if the man she was thinking of was you, but it might have been, and she might have . . ."

"Imagined the rest." Gyles thought back. "I introduced myself as Gyles Rawlings, a distant—" He broke off. Francesca's eyes had widened. "What?"

"I—we—Ester, Charles, and I—always spoke of you as Chillingworth. When we arrived here, your mother and the others did the same, at least in Franni's hearing. She might not have realized—"

"Who I was before the ceremony? That might explain her reaction. Sheer surprise makes more sense than her having read anything into our meetings."

"Those meetings?"

"The first time I walked with her all we spoke of was the dogs. I asked if they were hers. She said they just lived there. I later made a comment about their spots, with which she agreed. Then I left her. The next day, she was absorbed with trees. She was asking which was which." He shook his head. "I think I answered twice. Other than that, and saying goodbye, I can't recall saying anything more."

He studied Francesca's face. "If your cousin imagined anything, it was unfounded. Neither you nor I can do anything about that. You said yourself you don't know if it was me she was referring to or some other. Or no one. You don't know if that's why she reacted in the chapel as she did. It might, as Charles suggested, simply be overexcitement."

Francesca held his gaze. He was right—there was nothing

either of them could do, at least not at present. He reached for her—she whisked away.

"Your mistake over Franni is only the first bone we have between us, my lord." She caught his eye as she paced around him. "I wish to understand why, imagining you were offering for Franni, you were so . . ."—she gestured—"*intent* on me." She was sure he'd understand her allusion; the hardening of his already hard face confirmed he did. Swinging to face him, she spread her arms wide. "If you thought she was me, who did you think *I* was?"

His eyes narrowed to slate shards. His gaze flashed over her—she felt it like a touch, a brush of long fingers over her bare skin. Beneath her gown, her skin flickered. She suppressed a shiver and kept her gaze on his eyes.

"I thought"—the words were bitten off—"that you were a gypsy. Too *consciously* well endowed and far too bold to be a young lady." He took a prowling step toward her. "I thought you a bold and *eager* companion."

She tilted her head defiantly. "I know well what you were thinking, my lord." She made no effort to retreat as he prowled closer.

"I know you do. You were thinking along the same lines." He halted before her. Lifting one hand, he traced a finger along her jaw, then slid it beneath and tipped her face to his. His eyes held hers. "Can you deny it?"

Francesca let her lips curve. "No. But then *I* hadn't come directly from offering for another."

Gyles realized his misstep, but she didn't let him retreat.

"*How dare you!*" Eyes blazing, she jabbed a finger into his chest. "How *dare* you make an offer for me, and then, within minutes, think, consider, and even start *planning* on taking another woman as your mistress?"

"That other woman was *you!*"

"You didn't know that!" She jabbed him again. He took a step back and she was on him like a whirlwind. "You came after me, looking for me in the orchard—you kissed me—you almost *seduced* me!"

She was so much shorter and slighter than he, yet her fury burned like a flame. Hands, arms, her whole body was afire; she came at him, and he backed, step by step, before the sheer rage in her eyes.

"You left the woman you thought was your intended, and you deliberately sought me out to—"

"You were very ready to be seduced—"

"Of *course* I was! I knew who you were—you'd offered for me! I thought you wanted me—*me*, your intended bride!"

"I did want you—"

She cut him off with a torrent of Italian. He spoke the language fluently, but at the rate she spoke, he could make out less than one word in ten. Words like "arrogant," and something he thought approximated "swine," and one or two others gave him an idea of her tack, but not enough of the context for him to defend himself.

"Slow down—I can't understand you."

Her eyes flamed. "*You* can't understand *me*? You were set on marrying a lady you'd *deliberately* barely exchanged two words with! It's *I* who cannot understand *you*!"

She reverted to Italian, a flow of impassioned outpourings that, like a physical tide, swept them both along. Her gestures, always dramatic, became more emphatic, more violent. He continued to retreat while he struggled to find some point to seize long enough to gain his footing. She darted this way, then that, hands flinging wildly about.

He suddenly realized she'd opened the corridor door and backed him to the threshold. Grabbing the door's edge, he halted. "Francesca!"

The exclamation was designed to jerk her reins, to shake her to reality.

It only evoked another furious spate of Italian. She flung

up a hand as if to slap him—she didn't—she wouldn't have connected—it was just another histrionic gesture conveying her contempt, but he ducked back, stepped back, let go of the door.

Then he was in the corridor and she was in the doorway, hands on her hips, her breasts rising and falling, her black hair a silken jumble against the ivory of her gown. Green fire burned in her eyes.

She was so vividly, vitally, intensely beautiful, he literally couldn't breathe.

"And then," she said, reverting to English, "when you've managed to answer that, you can explain why it was, in the forest that morning, you *stopped*! And again in the stables— was it only last night? You want me, my lord, yet you don't! You didn't want me as your bride, but you thought to have me as your mistress. You thought to seduce me—then when you succeeded you *turned away*!" She flung up her hands. "How *can* you explain that?"

She paused, the silence dramatic after her tirade. Breasts heaving, she kept her eyes locked on his.

Then she drew in a long breath, drew herself up and lifted her chin. "You put it so succinctly last night. You don't want me, you don't need me—you only desire me. Not, however, sufficiently deeply to bother consummating a relationship. And now we're married. You might think on that."

She turned away. "Good night."

He swore and leaped for the door. It slammed shut in his face. The lock snibbed as his hand closed on the knob.

The oath he uttered was not a polite one. He glared at the door. He could hear Fate laughing.

He'd plotted and planned to gain a meek and mild bride.

And landed himself with a virago.

Francesca didn't waste any time staring at the locked door. She raced across the room to the door from his bedroom— only to skid to a horrified stop. The door had no lock.

She looked around, then ran to the escritoire. Lifting the chair before it, she rushed to jam it under the doorknob.

Standing back, she studied her handiwork. It looked far too flimsy for her peace of mind.

A chest of drawers stood to one side of the doorway; she stepped to its side, drew in a deep breath, and pushed with all her might. It shifted an inch. Encouraged, she tamped down her welling panic and pushed again. The other end of the chest hit the doorframe.

Muttering a curse, she hurried to that end, reached across and tried to jerk the corner free—

Hard hands closed about her waist.

She screamed with sheer shock. But she recognized the hands—they'd been flirting with her waist for the past hours. Her fright drowned beneath a wave of fresh fury. He juggled her, turned her—locked his hands about her waist and hoisted her up—up above his head.

Shocked anew, she grabbed handfuls of his hair—not to pull but to steady herself. His eyes flashed a warning—she ignored it, too busy trying to fathom how he'd got in.

"The other door—the one to your sitting room."

She looked across the room, and for the first time saw the door in the opposite wall.

"I take it you haven't admired the decor yet."

His urbane tone did nothing to calm her. Releasing one hand, she glanced down. He started walking, carrying her like some dangerous captured prize, high above his head at arm's length.

"What are you doing?" She tried to look around but couldn't. She thought he was making for the bed.

"Getting these proceedings back on track."

The steel beneath his words didn't escape her. "And what track is that?"

He stopped walking and went to look up, but couldn't— she had to release her hold on his hair. Reluctantly, she did. She tried to brace her hands on his forearms, but there was nothing she could hook her fingers in—the sleeves of his robe had fallen to his shoulders. Precariously balanced high above the floor, she was forced to put her trust in him, in his strength, to hold her steady.

Tipping back his head, he looked into her face. Not a single tremor disturbed the locked muscles of his arms—he was supporting her without effort.

She met his eyes. They were stormy, turbulent—intent.

After a moment, he spoke. "We're married. This is our wedding night."

A shiver slithered down her spine. Some age-old instinct warned her against replying, against uttering any contemptuous quip, any taunt. She needed to be on the ground, no longer his captive, to continue their battle. She waited, breathing rapidly. His gaze locked with hers, slowly, very slowly, he lowered her.

His hands were level with his chest, her hands had just touched his shoulders, her toes still a foot off the ground, when she felt his muscles bunch, his fingers grip.

He flung her back.

She fell full length in the middle of the huge bed. She caught her breath on a gasp and scrambled to sit up—

Gyles shrugged off his robe and went for her.

She clutched frantically but couldn't gain purchase on the slippery satin. He drew her back down, tangling her legs with his. When she continued to struggle, he caught her hands, trapped them both in one of his and anchored them above her head, then lifted over her and lowered his body to hers.

His weight subdued her, trapped her beneath him. Propped on his forearms, he met her gaze—wary but still furious.

Her breasts rose and fell against his chest, her body lay firm and supple beneath his. He shut his senses to her distractions. In a minute, he'd indulge, but first . . . "You were right the first time, when we first met, as to what I thought of you."

Francesca held his gaze and tried to read his eyes; their dark turbulence defeated her. His expression was graven, one she didn't recognize, yet some part of her did—some part of her responded. To the look in his eyes, to the harsh set of his lips, to the dark, gravelly rasp of his voice.

"I desired you—I still do." His glance strayed to the ripe mounds of her breasts. He sank against her; she felt his erection rigid against her thigh.

"Whenever I see you, all I can think of is being inside you." With his free hand, he traced the neckline of her gown, from her shoulder to the center front, where tiny buttons held it closed. One flick and the first button popped free. "Now we're married, I'll get to indulge that desire every day, every morning and every night."

He continued to unbutton her gown.

There was no doubt in her mind which track he was on. She dragged in a short breath. "You don't want me. You don't need me."

He raised his eyes and met hers. He inclined his head. "I don't want you. I don't need you. But *by heaven* I desire you." He slid one finger beneath her gaping gown and traced her upper breast—they both felt the quiver that raced through her. "And you desire me."

She knew what he intended, what he would do, knew she had no defense. But it was not what she wanted—not like this. "You don't want me as your wife. You didn't want to marry me."

"No." He shifted his weight, reaching for buttons lower down. "But I did."

The last button slid free; her gown gaped to her waist, the silk less sumptuous than the skin it concealed. Gyles slid his hand beneath the gown's edge, cupped her breast, and circled the peak with his thumb. "Which brings us to where we are." He met her gaze. "To this."

He circled her nipple again and felt her spine tense. Saw in her eyes, darkened and wide, the knowledge that she wouldn't—couldn't—win the prize she'd set her heart on. And understood why she'd been so disappointed. So very angry.

He bent over her. "Everything I promised, you will have."

But nothing more.

The vow hung between them, unsaid but implicit.

She'd seen past his mask and had hopes that he would not, could not, fulfill. Passion and desire he would give her, but passion and desire were not love—none knew that better than he.

He lowered his head and felt her tense. A fraught second ensued—he waited, gave her the moment to gauge the situation, to make her decision. Then she eased beneath him, accepting, all resistance flowing from her.

He closed the last inch; his lips hovered over hers, and they parted.

"I'm sorry."

He whispered the words against her lips, then covered them. He was sorry for disappointing her, sorry for his mistake. But not sorry that he had her, at last, beneath him.

She met his lips with hers, yet she made no demands. Her body lay responsive yet passive beneath his.

Last night, she'd been frantic, eager; now, sunk in the emerald satin of their marriage bed, she was, not physically reserved—her body wouldn't permit that—but mentally hesitant, reticent. Even reluctant.

Releasing her hands, he drew her into his arms, settling her against him, half beneath him, his hands skating over her face, over her curves.

He'd sworn he wouldn't woo her, and he hadn't. But now she was his, he was conscious of a primal need to win her, to overcome her reluctance to give herself, surrender all of herself to him. Too many women had arched beneath him for him not to know the difference between absolute surrender and the mere sharing of bodies for mutual pleasure. He knew which he wanted from his gypsy, from his suddenly elusive bride. So despite the fact he was aching, that his body wanted nothing more than to simply bury himself in her, to slake the lust that had been building for too long, he turned his mind and his considerable talents to a seduction he'd never imagined pursuing.

He'd never imagined seducing his wife.

He kissed her gently, slowly, deliberately drawing out the simple caress. Braced for an onslaught, for a ruthless claiming, Francesca was disarmed. But not taken in. She knew he was doing it deliberately, that for some unfathomable reason he'd decided he wanted more from her than a simple joining. He lay stretched along and alongside her, caging her, his strength palpable, in no way disguised. His expertise screamed in his every touch. He had the power to compel her—to make her body want him, to make her burn with desire.

As she kissed him back, tentatively, uncertain just where this was leading, she scanned back through the careful explanations of his requirements, his explicitly stated needs of this marriage. All he needed to do to achieve his desired ends was impregnate her.

Why, then, this?

She didn't know the answer. If she followed his lead, she shortly wouldn't be able to think, yet the temptation to learn whatever it was he would teach her, to discover whatever it was he wished of her, swelled and grew.

Tonight, she would be his wife in fact as well as name—that was indisputable. She'd thought it would be accomplished via a passionate but distant act—thought that's what he'd had in mind, the track he would unquestionably take.

It seemed she'd been wrong. There could be only one destination tonight, but the path he'd chosen was different and infinitely more appealing than the one she'd assumed he'd hurry her down.

She was, she decided, more than willing to follow his unexpected tack.

He'd been indulging her with warm, simple, reassuring kisses. Now his lips firmed, harder, more demanding. She opened her mouth to him, welcomed him in, gave him what he wanted. Shuddered when he took it. The pleasure he knew well how to press on her swept her wits aside. She let them go, let them slide away as she drew him deep and tuned her mind to passion.

His, and hers. The combination was powerful, dizzying. At this much slower pace, they had time to pause, to knowingly adjust, to better align one with the other. In the depths of her satin-draped bed, passion, desire, and need became physical realities, tangible qualities they weighed and traded and balanced between them.

They stepped out of time, and it lost all meaning. The only point of relevance was the journey they'd embarked on—nothing else mattered. Their kisses deepened, his tongue sliding over hers, tangling, enticing, caressing. Enflaming. Their exchanges grew hotter, more intimate. One hand cradling his lean cheek, she gave herself up to the spiraling heat, to the burgeoning need.

Their lips parted. They drew back to breathe, to catch their breath. Eyes met. The lamp on her dressing table still burned, casting golden light from a distance. Enough for them to see, to search each other's eyes, to take stock. To wordlessly agree that they'd explored that vista long enough and were ready to move on.

His hand had cupped her breast throughout, his fingers lying passive as they'd kissed. He withdrew his hand from beneath the silk and reached for the gown's shoulder. He pushed it aside. She met his eyes, then ducked her shoulder. He drew the gown and negligee down; she lifted her arm and slid it free, watching his face, watching the dark glow in his eyes.

He shifted back, and they repeated the exercise, freeing her other arm. He drew the gown down until she was bare to the waist. She had never been ashamed of her body, knew she had no reason to be. One hand resting on his shoulder, the other curled about his nape, she watched him look, survey— then he looked up and met her gaze.

Emotion flashed between them, quicksilver understanding. Her vulnerability. His possessiveness.

His gaze returned to her breasts and he settled beside her. She felt his gaze, felt her flesh react—instinctively, she tensed. But he only raised a hand and, exquisitely gently, brushed the underside of her breast.

He said nothing. Nor did she. Yet he seemed to understand her sudden uncertainty, born of the previous night, a conviction that if he suckled her breast, she would lose all ability to function beyond the dictates of rampant desire. He made no move to lower his head but, instead, traced, caressed and fondled her flesh, every touch a practiced pleasure.

Gradually, she relaxed. The unexpected vulnerability eased, teased away by his caresses, by the languid sea of desire that slowly enveloped her, not with a rush but with a gentle lapping. She'd expected to feel cool. Instead, her skin had flushed, lightly fevered, not yet aflame, but the embers were glowing. With the pads of his fingers, he circled her nipples but never touched, never tweaked, and in some intuitive part of her mind, she knew.

When he next met her eyes, his were very dark; she wondered what hers were like. Whatever he read in them seemed to satisfy. He bent his head, touched his lips to hers, and murmured, "Trust me."

His lips slid from hers to trace over her jaw, down her throat. He found the throbbing pulse at its base and licked, laved. Then he suckled there, and she felt heat flare. He pressed closer—

Her whole body reacted, arching. Fingers digging into his shoulder, she gasped.

He lifted his head.

Hands at his shoulders, she pushed. "Your chest."

He eased back and looked down. She ran her hands down, fingers splayed, pressing her palms to the heavy muscles. "You're so hot."

The sudden touch, skin to skin, the abrasion of the rough hair that ran across his chest, had made her nerves jerk and spasm. Silk-soft and sensitized, her skin seemed more reactive to touch than ever before.

The effect had reached her palms. She ran them over his chest, wondering at the sensations, at the heat, the resilence of muscles under taut skin, at the raspy tickle of his hair. She discovered the flat disc of his nipple and was interested to see its tip was as tightly furled as hers.

He shifted as her finger traced. "You'll get used to it."

His chest? Or the heightened tactile sensitivity?

Not in the next decade. She didn't say the words, but the thought must have flashed through her eyes.

He raised a brow at her. "Where were we?"

He lowered his head, and she gasped again, but the sensation of his chest pressed to her breasts was no longer such a shock. His mouth was warm at the base of her throat, then shifted along her collarbone, then swept over the upper curves of her breasts.

Heat flared anew, following the trail of his lips, ignited by their touch, then spreading in warm waves beneath her skin. He licked and laved until her breasts were swollen, but he consistently avoided the tightly ruched peaks. Until they pulsed with an ache she could no longer deny.

The fingers of one hand were tangled in his hair, her other hand flat against his chest, braced against the certainty of what was to come, when she felt his warm breath wash over one tight peak, then he lowered his head and took it into the scalding heat of his mouth.

She'd expected the same flash of sensation she'd felt last night, but while the jolt of pleasure was certainly there, it didn't, this time, rip her awareness away. He suckled, and flames pulsed through her, poured down her veins, pooled deep inside, but the heat was all pleasure, and she welcomed it, drank it in, wallowed in the warmth.

He encouraged her. It was as if her body had come to sensate life, could now experience more, appreciate more. He gave her the sensation and the time to enjoy it. With a grateful murmur, she relaxed in his arms, let her body flow on the tide he conjured, and thought of how to thank him. Relaxing her hands, she sent them wandering, over the outer edges of his ears, stroking his throat, spreading out to encompass the width of his shoulders, reaching around to stroke the muscles of his back.

How long they flowed with that particular tide, she had no idea. They experimented, testing, learning, seeking each other's pleasure, enjoying the other's gifting. Soft murmurs, low growls of appreciation, became their currency, a flicker of lids, a clash of eyes slowly drowning, a brush of dry lips, a tangle of hot tongues.

She was hot and restless when he drew her gown from her and slipped from her arms, his mouth a brand trailing over her skin. Over her midriff, her waist. Over her flickering stomach to the thatch of curls at its base.

She caught her breath and reached for him. "No. Please."

He raised his head, met her eyes. Over her breasts, rising and falling. Through the mad thud of her heart in her ears, she tried to think—tried to find words.

"It won't be like last time." His voice was so deep she could barely catch the words. "It won't end that way." His gaze remained locked on her eyes. "I need to taste you."

If he'd used any other word, she might have refused him, but there was a raw hunger in his eyes that was impossible to mistake. A novel sense of power, tantalizing in its newness, its unexpectedness, flowed through her.

He closed his hand about her knee, then pushed gently—

and she permitted it, let him part her thighs. She watched as he lifted over her other leg, pressing that aside, too, settling between. Then she let her head fall back, and steeled herself against madness.

But her mind wasn't, this time, overwhelmed. She was awash with passion, fevered, floating, senses heightened yet fully aware. Her body seemed no longer hers but theirs, as was his, vessels for their mutual pleasure. It no longer felt so shocking to feel his lips touch her there, to receive his kisses, to feel the hot wetness of his tongue as he traced and stroked, as he caressed, then lightly suckled. Her heart leapt, her chest seized; she swallowed her gasp, felt the tug on her nerves, the dizzying whirl of her senses.

Then felt the lap and probe of his tongue. Every touch sent her senses spiraling, nerves tightening, skin tingling. Pleasure blossomed once more, but on a different plane, one more intimate, more . . . sharing.

He entered her as the word echoed in her brain. She gasped, tensed, pressed the back of one hand to her lips to smother the cry building in her throat. She felt him look up, then his fingers locked about her wrist and he tugged.

"There's no one to hear."

Just him. And Gyles definitely wanted to hear every little murmur, every gasp, every shredded whimper. Every scream.

He was operating wholly on instinct—an instinct he didn't fully recognize or understand. He'd thought that, given he couldn't—wouldn't—give her his love, then the least he could do was love her—make love to her—as he had with no other woman. That was something he could give, something in return for what he wanted from her.

What he needed and would have from her.

Would take from her.

So he'd set himself the task of making the moment special, different, more intense. With her, not a difficult task. She was so very unlike any woman he'd known.

There was passion in her for the taking—a boundless, limitless sea of uninhibited warmth that was the ultimate prize for his baser self. The maurauding rapacious barbarian wanted nothing more than to seize and wallow—and there was a sneaking suspicion in his mind that his actions tonight were at least partly driven by the possibility that, if he dazzled her with delight, she would, later, be more amenable to letting him—the true him—wallow.

She was open and confident, and although patently innocent—witness her reaction to his chest—that had never happened to him before, and had left him curiously touched—yet she displayed an understanding, a sensual comprehension, at odds with that innocence.

After tonight, that innocence would be no more, and the odd contrast would disappear. The thought refocused his mind on the matter in hand—he looked into her eyes, then, retaining his hold on her wrist, reached with his other hand and trapped her free hand.

He drew her arms down, locked his hands about her wrists, then returned to the one and only distraction capable of slowing the marauding barbarian down.

She tasted of tart apples and some elusive spice. He heard her whimper as he licked and inwardly smiled. With his shoulders, he kept her thighs wide, wide enough for him to taste her as he wished, slowly, thoroughly.

He knew just how tight he was winding her, knew when to ease back, to lightly lap her swollen flesh until she calmed, knew when it was safe to slide into her honeyed warmth and feast.

The sounds she made were both balm and fiery prod to his ravenous rapacious self, a self only she had ever been able to provoke, but he was determined to prolong the pleasure of their joining, and not just for her.

He wanted to explore her, to discover as many of her secrets as he could, tonight. He didn't know why, only that he was driven and the goal felt right. In this arena, amidst the satin sheets, instinct ruled, and ruled him absolutely.

With her, with the way she affected him, that was how it would always be. Different. More intense. More vibrantly alive.

With her, he was himself, all of his true self, no elegant mask, no screen veiling his desires.

She writhed in his hold. He kept her there, held her there, on the cusp of delight. He felt the quivering in her thighs, felt the tension that held her.

Knew it was time.

He could almost feel the reins sliding, the leashes falling away as he released her hands, twisted around and stripped off his trousers. Kicking them aside, he turned back to her, then rose to sit back on his ankles. Hands resting on his thighs, he watched her, waited for her lashes to flicker, waited to see the green glitter of her eyes.

When he did, he held out both hands. "Come."

With his fingers, he beckoned. She stared at him, then struggled up, her tongue skating over her lips. She blinked at him, then swung around, up onto her knees, and gave him her hands. "How?"

He didn't answer, but drew her nearer.

Her gaze fell to his groin.

He released one of her hands and reached for her hip.

She closed her hand about him.

The jolt nearly stopped his heart. Eyes closing, he groaned, and felt her fingers flutter.

He groaned again and grabbed her wrist. He'd intended to draw her hand away but her fingers closed again.

"Show me how."

Her grip eased, tightened—he couldn't form the words much less say them.

"Like this?"

Her sultry voice, deepened by passion, heated by desire, burned through his brain.

He managed to nod, to force his fingers to function and direct hers. He heard her chuckle, then she leaned her head against his chest. The sensation of her hair, the silky mass of curls, tumbling down his bare chest made him shudder. She tightened her fingers again and he bit back a moan.

He showed her more than he'd intended, captured by the feel of her small hand on him, by the curiosity in her touch, the wonder and wantoness behind the deed.

"Enough." He had to stop her. Now, while he still had some semblance of control.

She let him draw her hand away, then shook off his hand. With a warm chuckle that only increased his pain, she reached for his thighs, grasping just above his knees, then ran her hands slowly upward, nearly to his groin. Her silky locks swung forward and caressed his aching flesh.

The sensation rocked him; he mentally swayed. Before he could reach for her, she leaned on his thighs and pushed away. Supple and light, she rose to her feet. Stepping lightly on the soft bedding, hands trailing his shoulders for balance, she placed her feet on either side of his spread knees, then sank down.

His hands closed about the backs of her thighs and he directed her. Held her to him, her stomach against his chest as she lowered herself against him. He supported her when she reached the point where she had to turn her feet, and change from standing to sinking down on her knees. Straddling him.

She shook her hair back, wrapped her arms about his shoulders, then set her lips to his. Her inner thighs rode across his hips; her knees hadn't yet reached the bed. She pressed against him, pressed down, letting her weight take her to him, urging him, still holding her, to guide her the last part of the way.

He did, one question coalescing in his brain even as he took charge of their kiss, took charge of their joining. He set the question aside as her slick swollen flesh met, then engulfed his throbbing erection. He eased into her, reveling in the heat, in the fascinating combination of firmness and soft-ness with which she sheathed him. She was tight, slick, scalding hot. Her weight, and her state of arousal, would have allowed him to fill her with a single sharp thrust. In-stead he went slowly, searching . . . reminding himself she rode daily, albeit sidesaddle . . .

He was deep in their kiss, half-buried in her body, when he met the resistance. The barbarian within him growled with satisfaction. He ravaged her mouth, drew her attention deep into the kiss, then, his hands locked about her hips, he lifted her just enough, then lowered her firmly, pushing deep, then deeper, rupturing the last barrier and filling her.

She pulled back from the kiss on a gasp, then made a strangled, whimpering sound and rested her forehead against his chest. She breathed deeply. Her fingers dug into his shoulders; her spine stiffened, and her body clamped hard around him, then gradually, increment by increment, eased. She was small—he wasn't. He released her hips and wrapped his arms about her, one hand sliding beneath the veil of her hair to stroke her back.

Every muscle he possessed was quivering, straining with the need to plunder the vulnerable, heated softness of her body. Yet he forced himself to wait, to bend his head and lay his cheek on her hair and simply hold her, until her pain subsided.

He felt her draw in a shuddering breath. When she tried to shift, he locked his arms about her. "No. Wait."

Her body hadn't yet softened, hadn't yet recovered from the shock. In another minute or two it would, and her ability to cope with his invasion, and the possession to come, would increase.

She was content to wait. One small hand lay, fingers spread, on his chest. He covered it with his hand, then lifted it to his lips and kissed each fingertip, drawing each into his mouth before releasing it.

He had her attention. Bending his head, he kissed her,

gently at first, then increasingly passionately as she responded, as her body softened and heated anew, reacting to
the caress of his hands, then the more intimate caress of his
body as he rocked her.

Then she started to move, and it was he who was rocked.
She'd reached up and framed his face, her forearms braced
on his chest as her tongue whispered over his with promises
of surrender, of the heated spoils of conquest. Using her
knees on the slippery satin but even more the contact of her
thighs with his, she undulated upon him. She didn't lift and
slide down as untutored ladies did. She used her whole body
in a sinuous, heart-stopping, mind-numbing, senses-stealing
movement that caressed him from rock-hard thighs to his
lips and beyond.

She captured him, his mind, his body, his senses—all
were hers to command. And command she did. He had no
idea how long he simply held her, his hands splayed, one on
her back, one below her waist, and took in all she lavished
on him. Drank as he hadn't drunk in years.

The movement started from her hips. She pressed down,
taking him all, her inner thighs, the softness of her caressing
his groin. The wave started from there and traveled her spine
in a slow, controlled roll, pressing her stomach, her waist,
then her chest, and finally her sumptumous breasts along his
body. At the last, her mouth would press to his, open and
inviting, luring him deep, then the wave would recede,
slowly falling back in an even more enticing caress as she
softened, body beckoning. And then it would start again.

His mind was reeling when he lifted his head and drew in
a shuddering breath. Shifting one hand to the back of her
head, he fisted it in her hair and drew her back so he could
look into her face.

Eyes more deeply green, more intense than any emerald
glinted up at him from under heavy lids.

"How did you know?" His question—the one for which
he could not conceive of an answer. She'd been as innocent,

as virginal, as he'd suspected, yet . . . she could love him like this—like a concubine from some sultan's seraglio, skilled and practiced in the sensual arts.

He didn't need to elaborate; her lips curved into a widening smile. "My parents."

Dumfounded, he stared at her. "They *taught* you?"

She laughed, breathlessly, yet he felt the sound go through him like a shot of the finest brandy, searing straight to his gut, then sliding and pooling lower, fuel for his fire. He released her hair and she pressed to him once more. "No. I watched." She caught his eye, her lips languidly curved. "I was an only child." Her words were little more than a whisper, her body restless on his. "When I was young, my bedroom connected to theirs. They always left the door open, so they would hear if I called. I used to wake and go in . . . sometimes they didn't . . . notice. After a while, I'd go back to my bed. I didn't understand, not until later, but I remember."

As the memories rolled through her, Francesca gave mute thanks. Without her loving parents, without their love for each other, she would never have had a chance for this. For now—for the experience of having a man like her husband at her mercy, caught by the splendor of her body, held by the promise of all she could give him. It was a heady thought, one small victory amid the defeats. One thing for which she would remember her wedding night.

Spearing her fingers through the wiry hair on his chest, she searched, then ducked her head and licked. Nipped.

His arms closed about her like the steel cage she knew they could be. He nudged her, and she lifted her head. He swooped and captured her mouth in a kiss that blazed.

One arm shifted to lock her hips to him, and she was suddenly more aware than she had been for some time of the hard, ridged strength buried inside her, of the latent power in the body she had, until then, held captive. The discovery rolled through her as he plundered her mouth, then he lifted his head, and breathed against her swollen lips, "Second act."

She'd seen it before, but never felt it. Never been the woman at center stage. Tonight, she was—all that was done was done to her, to her flesh, to her body, to her senses. Since seating himself within her, he'd barely moved, letting her use her body to caress him. That changed. His hold on her was restricting, but she could still move upon him, and did, but her reason was no longer to please him, but to assuage the hunger, the need that flowered and grew within her—the need he expertly fed.

He moved with her, within her; he now controlled their dance. As he surged deep inside her, filling her, impaling her, only to retreat and do it again, she tried to cling to sanity, and failed. The unnameable need blossomed within her—she could deny it no more than she could deny him. The slickness of her body, her movements upon him an uninhibited encouragement, she strove to appease that need. And him.

She lost her rhythm and instead found his, then he held her hips down and filled her more deeply. Each thrust seemed to push farther, to penetrate her more intimately, to touch a place he'd not touched before.

Fire consumed her. It came from him. He pressed it into her, pushed it deep until she went up in flames. All but sobbing, she clung to him, willing and wanton as her body became his, his to fill and plunder and take as he wished. No matter the times she'd witnessed the heat, the staggering, exhausting glory, it had never occurred to her that it would be like this—that it involved such a giving.

She pulled back from their kiss gasping, blind with need.

He changed his grip, bent her back over one arm, then his head swooped and she felt the scalding heat of his mouth at her breast.

He suckled fiercely and she shrieked. Her body tightened, tightened again as he suckled more, and thrust deeply, hotly, inside her.

The fire imploded.

And she was no longer there, but yet she could feel. Feel the sensations, excruciatingly sharp, that lanced through her, spreading outward from her core, tensed, coiled, incandescent, locked about him. The bright rapture subsided in waves, spreading under her skin, leaving it glowing. Like ripples on her sensual pond, they fanned out, then gradually faded, leaving her floating, at peace.

Waiting.

She wasn't capable of thinking, yet she knew. Knew there was more, that she wanted still more.

She wanted him. Not just inside her but with her.

He'd stilled, quieted; now he drew her upright and against him once more, holding her there, his hands moving over her, molding her to him.

Then his hands closed over her hips and he lifted her from him.

She made some sound—a whimper of disapproval. He answered with a harsh, very gravelly laugh.

"I want you beneath me."

He wanted to feel her supple and pliant under him as he took her. Wanted to hear every little gasp, every moan. Wanted to know she was open and willing, her ripe body his to fill. A primitive, elemental want. A driving, almost-desperate desire. Gyles laid her down on the emerald satin, following her down, spreading her thighs wide and settling between. He filled her with a single powerful thrust, watched her body rock, watched her arch as he pressed deeper still, and she tilted her hips to take him in.

She reached for him, drawing him down to her. He went readily, hungry for the sensation of her body under his. He moved within her, upon her, and she clutched, and drew his face to hers. He met her lips, met the fire still glowing within her and stoked it back to flame.

Into an inferno.

The blaze cindered every last veil, every last vestige of his civilized facade. He plunged into her, into her mouth, into her body, with a greedy, ravenous need. He wanted, he took, and she gave. He knew when she yielded, when she surrendered completely to the moment, to the flames, to the glory, and he exulted in his victory. She opened to him, wrapped him in her arms and welcomed him in, not just into her body but into that citadel he had wanted, needed, to claim.

He was poised on the crest of delirium when the depth of that need hit him like a blow. Understanding—of himself, of that urgent fundamental want—came in a blinding revelation. But nothing, not even his deepest fears, could stop him from seizing that which he'd thought for so long he'd never seek.

She climaxed beneath him and he was with her, drinking in her cry, fleetingly glorying in her completion before following her into the void.

His victory, or hers?

Sunk beside his sleeping wife in the satin sheets of her bed, Gyles wasn't sure. And wasn't sure he cared. If he could have his cake and eat it, too, why should he complain?

Despite her unexpected knowledge, despite all that had occurred, only he knew what had happened. Only he knew that she was the only woman to ever touch his barbarian core, the only woman whose surrender could sate, satisfy, and fulfill his true self.

The only woman his true self wanted.

She couldn't know, not unless he told her. Not unless he admitted the vulnerability out loud, in words.

Pigs would fly before he did.

Lifting one lid, he looked across the rumpled bed, now lit

only by moonlight. She was slumped on her side, facing him. He could make out the wild tangle of her black curls, the paler band of her forehead, the small hand nestled on the pillow between them. Under the covers, he had one arm slung possessively over her waist. He left it there.

He couldn't, in all conscience, wake her and have her again. He'd already done that once—bad form, of course, but what did a barbarian care? The memory of the way she'd turned to him, her eyes searching his in the night, then focusing on his lips, the way she'd met his kisses, then focused on him, on them, on what they would do, sent a shiver down his spine.

Closing his eye, he slumped deeper into the bed, trying to block out the scent of sated lust that hung heavily about them. Trying to ignore his arousal.

In the morning. Just because he'd surrendered on one front, didn't mean he had to let lust rule him.

Chapter 8

It was full light when he awoke and reached for her.

And realized she no longer lay beside him.

Gyles opened his eyes and stared, then groggily glared at the rumpled space where his eager new wife should have lain, warm and soft and ready to be aroused. . . .

He bit back a groan, turned onto his back, and slung one arm across his eyes. Damn the woman!

Half a minute later, he lifted his arm, lifted his head, and looked about the room.

He sat up, then thrust back the covers and stalked to the door to her sitting room. He flung the door open. The room was empty. Not even a maid to send into hysterics.

Cursing, he shut the door, crossed the room, and righted the chair his loving bride had placed before the door to his room with the fell intention of keeping him out. Memories of the argument that had given rise to that event followed him into his room.

Five minutes later, fully dressed, he was striding across the lawns to the stables, no longer so sure of his victory of the night. Time and again he'd underestimated her, misjudged the way her mind worked. He'd thought last night would have smoothed their path, but had it? Or had he sunk himself deeper in the mire?

If he had, given her temper, given her resolution, what might she do?

Reaching the stables, he went quickly down the aisle to the mare's box. The mare was in it; she lifted her head and stared him.

Gyles humphed and whirled.

"Shall I saddle up for you, m'lord?"

Jacobs, his head stableman, came trotting up from the tack room.

"Has anyone gone out this morning?" Jacobs would never imagine he was asking after his new wife.

"No, but I heard most of the visitors are gone."

"Most, yes. I wondered if her ladyship's uncle had gone out. He must be inside." Dismissing Jacobs, Gyles strode back to the house.

He tried to put himself in "her ladyship's" shoes, tried to imagine, if he were her, where he might go. To no avail—he had no idea what she might be thinking, feeling. Was she happy with their marriage, smugly content after last night? Ready to make the best of it, calmly resigned to the fact? Or was she sad, dismayed, even distraught that what she'd hoped would not be?

That he'd never in his life spent so much as a minute worrying about any woman's thoughts, much less her feelings, he shrugged aside as irrelevant. The gypsy was his wife— she was different.

He paused at the end of the yew walk to draw in a deeper breath, to ease the nonsensical fear that was closing about his chest. Hands on his hips, he tipped his head back.

And saw her.

On the battlements of the nearest tower.

He reached the house in seconds and raced through the corridors to the tower stair. By then, a sliver of sanity had punctured his fear. The gypsy was neither weak nor fragile. What exactly was he thinking?

He climbed the stairs at a normal pace, making no effort to be silent. Regardless of the fact that the battlements were quite safe, he didn't want to frighten her by suddenly appearing beside her.

One arm on the stone coping, she was leaning on the battlements, looking out over the park. She turned her head as he opened the tower room door and stepped onto the wooden walk. Far from being shocked, he had the impression she was not surprised to see him.

He was the one surprised.

He hadn't previously seen her in an ordinary gown—seen her as he would see her every day for the rest of his life. Taking in the simple voile gown, noting how it lovingly displayed her ample charms, how the soft material caressed her hips and thighs, the single flounce flirting about her ankles, he was acutely aware of the body the gown concealed. The lush body he'd enjoyed throughout the night.

Noting the black curls piled artlessly atop her head, tumbling about her ears and nape, noting how large and vivid were her eyes, how perfectly lashed, noticing anew the lushness of her lips, he wondered what he would have done, said, how he would have reacted if he'd seen her this way before he'd married her. He had to question his sanity in wedding her.

And knew he wouldn't have it any other way.

"I wondered where you were." He walked toward her, halting a yard away.

She looked back at the vista of treetops. "I came up here for the views and fresh air." After an instant, she added, "It seemed a good place to think."

He wasn't sure he wanted her to think, nor that he would like what she was thinking.

"The estate extends more to the east and west, I presume?"

"Yes. The escarpment's the northern boundary."

"And the Gatting property lies to the east?"

"Southeast." He waited, then added, "I'll take you to see it sometime, if you like."

She inclined her head, then waved to where a glimmer of silver marked the course of the river. "The bridge that washed away—was it over there?"

"Farther upriver."

"Was it wrecked?"

"Most of it's gone. The only span still standing is badly weakened. We'll have to rebuild completely, but meanwhile we've rigged a pulley system to ferry necessities across to the farms that way. I should go and inspect the progress— perhaps later today after the others have left."

She started to slowly stroll, fingers trailing the stones. He followed, equally slowly, as she circled the tower.

"How many 'others' are still here? Who are they?"

"Mostly relatives too ancient to set out immediately after a feast. They'll be leaving this afternoon. Your uncle, of course, is still here. He told me he planned to take a different route home and wanted to leave before luncheon. Devil and Honoria left last night—they asked me to explain that with their newest child so young, they felt they had to hurry back."

Devil had seen him on his way out of the ballroom and mouthed one word: *Coward*. He had, however, winked, then smoothly intercepted one of Gyles's uncles who'd been about to bend his ear, allowing him to escape unimpeded.

"Yes—Honoria told me." Francesca glanced back briefly, very briefly met his eye. "She's invited us to visit at Somersham."

"We might go later in the year. We'll certainly see them in town."

"You've known Devil a long time?"

"Since Eton."

She continued to stroll, leaving him studying her back— and wondering just what was going on. Just what tack she intended to take. Wondering why she, thus far so forthright, was being so elusive. She strolled out of the tower's shadow and onto the parapet.

"All right—I give in. What the devil are you thinking?"

She flashed him a glance. "About what?"

"Our marriage." He halted. Eventually, she did, too, still facing away from him with two yards between them. "I'm aware that, prior to yesterday, your expectations and mine were not the same."

She turned her head and looked at him. Her eyes were wide, but her glance was too brief for him to place the expression in them. Turning back to the view, she peered over the coping at the forecourt below. "That was before we were wed." Her husky tones reached him clearly, but conveyed nothing more than her words. "It would be faster, I think, if we left the past behind and considered instead what we each wish of our marriage now."

He was very ready to leave the past behind. "What we wish now?"

"Yes. So—what do you wish of me as your wife?"

She started to stroll again. He hesitated, watching her hips sway, then fell in again at her heels. Her question was reasonable, sensible. Her tack was rationality incarnate. The wooden planks were firm under his feet—so why did he feel he was walking on thin ice?

"My requirements haven't changed—I need you to fill the role of my countess, which you're patently well able to do. I need you to provide me with heirs, meaning two, so there's no chance of Osbert inheriting. Beyond that, your life will be yours to live as you wish."

She said nothing for sometime, walking slowly ahead of him, then she softly echoed, "As I wish."

He wished he could see her face, her eyes. He could tell very little from her voice, other than it wasn't as strong as usual.

"Tell me, my lord." She stopped beside the parapet and looked down.

He stopped a few feet away, watching her.

"Are you saying that, beyond the bearing of your heirs, I will not need to be faithful?"

The thought rocked him. It took him some time to formulate an answer, one he could force himself to say. "I am not encouraging you to be *un*faithful, but if, after providing me with the necessary heirs, you wish to develop liaisons, that will be entirely up to you."

"Provided I was discreet."

He thought he saw her lips lift wryly as she turned away and started strolling again. "I would expect my countess always to be discreet."

"And you? Will you always be discreet in pursuing the liaisons I assume you wish to be free to pursue?"

There were always whispers, rumors. "To the best of my ability, I am always discreet."

"But I—you expect me to always *succeed* in being discreet." Before he could answer, she continued, "Tell me, my lord, when would this mutual discretion of ours start?"

He frowned. "Once you've given me the heirs I require—"

"I do not think that is a viable option. Who knows how many girls you may sire? I may never get a chance to exercise *my* discretion, although I'm quite sure you will be exercising yours."

He wasn't about to discuss that point, and he was getting very tired of talking to her back.

"I do not think that is fair. What I propose is that we *both* agree to remain faithful until such time as we are satisfied I'm carrying your child. From that agreed date, we go our separate ways, until I'm delivered of the child. Then, once again, we return to faithfulness, and so on, until you have your heirs. Once that point is reached, we will both henceforth be free to pursue whatever liaisons and *discreet* connections we please."

He stopped walking.

He hadn't realized the barbarian was so close to his surface. He was suddenly very glad she was facing the other way. Hands clenched at his sides, he struggled to contain his reaction. It took him a good minute to suppress the reactive rage, the instinctive urge to roar *"No!"*

It took another thirty seconds before he could say, "If that's what you wish."

She heard the change, the undercurrent of violence in his voice. She halted, stiffened; her head rose. Then she spoke in a tone he had not before heard from her. "I have desires, needs, and requirements of my own that you have chosen not to fulfill within our marriage. I'm merely ensuring that while fulfilling *your* requirements, I'll be able to pursue my own goals."

Abruptly, she swung to face him, head high, her expression reflecting a determination as stubborn as his own. *"That* is my requirement of our marriage. I do not think it's one you can refuse."

Her eyes were brilliant but screened. The distance between them had grown to several yards; he was content that it was so. It took every ounce of control he possessed to remain still, to stop himself reaching for her, to stop himself . . .

When he could trust himself to move that much, he inclined his head. "Very well, madam. We have an agreement."

If his clipped tones bothered her, she gave no sign. Coolly, she inclined her head back, then turned and strolled on to the second tower's door. "I imagine breakfast will be served soon."

He had to breathe deeply before he could say, "If you wish, you may remain in our apartments." He started after her. "No one will be counting on seeing us this morning, or even today."

Opening the door, she turned as he neared. Her gaze touched his, then shifted past him. One brow arched, her expression calmly considering. Then she shook her head, turned, and stepped into the tower. "I do not think hiding is a good idea. I believe I had best start out as I mean to go on."

Holding the door, Gyles watched her cross the tower room and start down the stairs. Not once did she glance back. Stepping over the threshold, he closed the door, and followed her down the stairs.

She'd agreed to be everything he wished for in a wife. Within an hour, he'd been put on notice that she could, and would, deliver on her side of their agreement handsomely.

Why that left him so grumpy he couldn't understand. Perhaps because it meant that, once she was pregnant, coping with the practicalities of being his countess was clearly not going to challenge her enough to distract her from pursuing her own, currently unstated goals.

Not that he needed to hear them stated—he could guess what they were.

While he sat at the head of the breakfast table, coffee cup in hand, and lent a deaf ear to one of his great-uncle Mortimer's war stories, Gyles inwardly kicked himself for agreeing to anything. At the other end of the table, separated from him by sixteen interested elderly relatives, his wife serenely dispensed calm and gracious order along with cups of tea.

Francesca could feel his gaze on her, could sense his disaffection with the bargain they'd struck. It wasn't the bargain she'd wished for, but it was a bargain she'd accept. She hadn't been sure he would agree to her proposal, her alternate plan, but now he had, they both knew where they stood, and it was simply a matter of getting on with life.

And reconciling herself to second best.

"Well, my dear—or should I say 'my lady'?"

Francesca looked up to see Charles smiling down at her as he drew out the chair beside her. The distant cousin who had filled it had just departed to oversee her packing.

"Uncle." Impulsively, she stood and kissed Charles's cheek.

He beamed and patted her hand. "So, all's well with you?"

"Indeed." With a quick smile, Franceca sat. As Charles took his seat, she glanced around. "Is Ester coming down?"

"Shortly." Charles flicked out the napkin a footman handed him. "Franni's still asleep."

"Asleep?" Franni was usually up at daybreak.

"We had to dose her last night. She wouldn't quiet without it."

Franni sometimes needed laudanum when she became overwrought. Francesca nibbled her toast while Charles made his selection from the platters the footmen offered.

"Will Franni wake soon?" she asked as the last footman stepped back.

"I hope so."

"I'd like to talk to her before you leave."

Charles smiled. "Of course. I'm sure she won't want to leave without at least saying good-bye."

Good-byes weren't what Francesca had in mind, but she was distracted by Lord Walpole—Horace as he'd insisted she call him. He stopped beside her and patted her shoulder.

"My dear Francesca, you look radiant. Nothing like marriage to put a glow in a young lady's eyes, I always say."

"Sit down, Horace, and stop trying to make the girl blush." Coming up beside him, Henni poked him in the ribs, prodding him along the table. She smiled at Francesca. "Don't mind him. Old reprobates are the worst."

Francesca smiled back. Turning, she discovered she'd missed Ester's entrance. As she sank into a chair two places along from Charles, Ester caught her eye and smiled.

"Franni?" Francesca mouthed.

"Still sleeping," Ester mouthed back.

Francesca poured a cup of tea for Ester, then turned to the ancient cousin seated on her other side. Hostessly matters kept her busy for some time, then Charles laid a hand on her sleeve.

"My dear, we plan to leave in two hours—before luncheon. I hope you know I have every confidence in your abilities, and in your marriage, else I would never be retreating in such fashion. But I can see you're in good hands." His smiling nod referred not just to Chillingworth but also to Lady Elizabeth and Henni. "I feel I can leave you with a clear conscience."

"Oh, indeed." Francesca squeezed his hand. "I'm content."

"Good." Charles closed his hand over hers. "We've decided to travel on to Bath. It's possible the waters might help Franni. Given we're already on the road, so to speak, we thought to take her there."

"She seemed to enjoy riding in the coach."

"More so than I'd expected. It's an opportunity too good to miss, but I want to make a good start, so we'll be saying farewell soon."

Francesca returned the pressure of his fingers. "I'll be there to wave you on your way."

"As the Countess of Chillingworth." Releasing her hand, Charles rose.

Francesca smiled briefly; her smile faded as she glanced at the figure at the table's end. "Indeed."

Charles's words proved prophetic—"Good-bye" was all Franni was able to say. To mumble. When they helped her down the great staircase, Ester on one side, Charles on the other, Franni was still so drugged it was all she could do to focus on Francesca's face.

Any hope Francesca had of ascertaining what it was that had overset Franni was doomed.

She was forced to smile, exchange hugs and good wishes, and push her concern over what Franni might have imagined into the background. Chillingworth was there, shaking hands with Charles, charming Ester—bowing very correctly over Franni's hand. Franni smiled dazedly—there was no sign that she was in any way conscious of him other than as a handsome gentleman who was now Francesca's husband.

As they stood on the porch to wave the travelers away, Francesca caught Gyles's eye. The coachman gave his horses the office; the coach lurched, then rolled away. Flanked by Lady Elizabeth and Henni, they waved. Ester waved back. Another small white hand poked out of the other window and floppily waved, too.

"Just overexcited."

Francesca heard Gyles's murmur. "So it seems."

The rest of the company assembled for luncheon, a light meal designed for geriatric stomachs about to travel. Lady Elizabeth and Francesca had put their heads together and come up with a selection of dishes which, by the eagerness with which they were greeted, had fitted the bill.

The early afternoon was filled with departures, a steady stream of well-dressed old ladies and garrulous gentlemen passing through the front hall, picking their way past mountains of luggage and footmen struggling with trunks and bandboxes.

At four, the last carriage rumbled away. There were five of them standing on the porch when the carriage rounded the curve in the drive and disappeared from sight. Five pairs of shoulders sagged.

Gyles was the first to straighten and break formation. "I need to ride down to the bridge and check how the work's faring." His comment was general, but his gaze met Francesca's, quickly searched her face.

She nodded. "Of course." She hesitated, then added, "We'll see you at dinner."

With a nod, he went down the steps, then strode toward the stables.

Horace turned inside. "I'm going to have a nap in the library."

"I'll wake you for dinner," Henni dryly replied.

Francesca grinned, as did Lady Elizabeth. They followed the others into the hall.

"I think we deserve a soothing cup of tea." Lady Elizabeth raised a brow at Francesca.

She went to gesture to the drawing room, then caught herself. "The back parlor?"

Lady Elizabeth smiled. "Yes, dear."

Francesca glanced around. "Wallace?"

"Ma'am?" The dapper little man stepped out of the shadows.

"Tea, please. In the back parlor."

"At once, ma'am."

"And check if Lord Walpole needs anything."

"Indeed, ma'am."

Together with Lady Elizabeth and Henni, Francesca strolled to the back parlor, the room the family used when free of social company. Although elegant as were all the rooms Francesca had thus far seen, the back parlor was furnished with an eye to comfort rather than style. Some of the pieces were quite old, woodwork lovingly polished to a lustrous hue, cushions showing the indentations of age.

With identical sighs, Lady Elizabeth and Henni sank into what was clearly their accustomed chairs, then Lady Elizabeth's eyes flew wide. She started to rise. "My dear, I should have asked—"

"No, no!" Waving her back, Francesca crossed to a daybed. "This is more my style." Sitting, she swung her legs up and relaxed against the puffy pillows.

"Very wise," Henni said with a grin. "No sense in not getting what rest you can."

Francesca blushed.

Wallace brought in the tea tray and placed it on a small table before Francesca. She poured, and he handed the cups around, then she dismissed him with a smile and a gracious word. He bowed and departed.

"Hmm." Henni eyed the door through which Wallace had gone. "He's a cagey one, but I think he likes you."

Francesca said nothing, aware that gaining the approval and thus support of her large staff would be essential to maintaining a smoothly running household.

Lady Elizabeth set aside her cup. "I can't see that you'll face any difficulties. Wallace will be the hardest to win over, but if he'd taken you in aversion, we'd have seen the signs. The rest are very manageable, and Lord knows, you'll be able to cope with Ferdinand much better than I."

"Ferdinand?"

"Gyles's chef. He travels between London and Lambourn, wherever Gyles is in residence. Ferdinand's Italian, and on occasion reverts to his native tongue." Lady Elizabeth shook her head. "I can rarely keep up with him. I just let him rave until he runs down, then I start again in English wherever I left off. Speaking Italian as you do, you'll be able to deal with him directly."

Francesca leaned back. "Who else should I know about?"

"All the others are locals. You met Mrs. Cantle briefly yesterday."

Francesca nodded, remembering the very correct, black-garbed housekeeper.

"I'll take you over the house and introduce you to everyone tomorrow morning. We all need to sit and catch our breath today, but tomorrow everyone will be eager to meet you, and as we'll be leaving later in the day, we'd best set the morning aside for 'the grand tour.' "

"Leaving?" Francesca stared, first at Lady Elizabeth, then at Henni; both nodded. "If Gyles has asked—"

"No, no!" Lady Elizabeth assured her. "This is entirely my idea, dear. Gyles would never dream of giving me my marching orders."

Henni snorted. "I'd like to see him try. But we're only going to the Dower House—it's just across the park."

"You can easily visit—come anytime." Lady Elizabeth gestured. "We'll be there, like as not."

"What she means," Henni said, "is that we'd be only too happy to hear the latest, whenever you have anything you'd like to share."

Francesca smiled at the older ladies' hopeful expressions. "I'll visit often."

"Good." Lady Elizabeth sat back. Henni sipped her tea.

Francesca relaxed into the daybed's cushions, touched, somewhat relieved. Just a little comforted.

She'd been feeling a little betrayed. By Chillingworth, although she couldn't justify that, at least not in words; from the first, he'd made his position clear and, despite all her hopes, he hadn't altered his stance. Not in the least. She'd felt more betrayed by Lady Elizabeth. The Dowager Countess had seemed so kind, so . . . like-minded. She'd written so warmly, so openheartedly and with such welcome, that Francesca had, at first unconsciously, then rather too consciously, started to weave dreams.

Letting her head fall back against the cushions, she let her mind touch on that—her dream, the most central of her dreams, the dream that now would not be—for the first time since descending from the tower.

Sometime later, at the edge of her vision, she saw Lady Elizabeth stir, saw the dowager exchange a questioning, concerned look with Henni. Lifting her head, Francesca looked down and saw her knuckles white about the teacup's handle. She'd relaxed, and her mask had slipped. She eased her grip.

Lady Elizabeth cleared her throat. "My dear"—her voice was very gentle—"you seem rather . . . fragile. Is anything amiss?"

Summoning a polite smile, Francesca briefly met their worried gazes. "I'm just a bit tired." She wasn't; she was disappointed. The realization prodded. If she wanted to understand her husband . . . and neither Lady Elizabeth nor Henni deserved her prevarications. Lips firming, she looked at them. "Pray excuse me, but I feel I have to ask. Did you know Gyles wanted, still wants, a marriage of convenience?"

Henni choked, then spluttered.

Lady Elizabeth's eyes grew round, then rounder. "*What?*" she demanded, her tone rising. Then she recollected herself and in more dowagerish tones stated, "What utter nonsense. Where did you hear that?"

"From him."

Henni waved a hand to attract her sister-in-law's attention. "Horace mentioned something about that last night," she wheezed. "About Gyles organizing his marriage of convenience, and how it was all a hum."

"But that's ridiculous! Marriage of convenience, indeed!" Two spots of color flew in Lady Elizabeth's cheeks. Francesca had no doubt that had her errant son walked in at that moment, he would have been severely taken to task. Then Lady Elizabeth looked at Henni. "But you said it was all a hum?"

"*Horace* said it was a hum. Easy enough to see why he'd think so. But as to what *Gyles* thinks, I suspect Francesca would know better than Horace."

"We discussed it this morning," Francesca said. "He's adamant it be so."

Lady Elizabeth waved commandingly. "Tell me. If I've raised a son ignorant enough to go that route, I deserve to know about it."

Adhering faithfully to his words, Francesca repeated Gyles's specifications for their marriage. She omitted all mention of his mistake—that was strictly between them. Lady Elizabeth and Henni hung on her every word. When she concluded her recitation, they exchanged looks, eyes bright, lips pressed tight, then, to Francesca's amazement, they both burst out laughing.

She stared at them in astonishment.

"*Pray* excuse us, my dear," Lady Elizabeth gasped. "Rest assured, we're not laughing at you."

"Or at your situation," Henni added, mopping her eyes.

"No, indeed." With an effort, Lady Elizabeth composed herself. "It's just that . . . well, dear, the way he looks at you—"

"*Watches* you," Henni corrected.

"Indeed. Regardless of what he says, regardless of what he thinks . . ." Lady Elizabeth gestured, watching Francesca hopefully, then grimaced. "Drat the boy! How could he be so arrogantly stupid?"

"He's male." Henni finished her tea.

"True." Lady Elizabeth sighed. "They're all the same, I fear. Utterly befuddled when they find they must *deal* with a woman."

Francesca frowned. "Are you saying that, regardless of his . . . *professed* intent, that it might not be . . . ?"

"What we're saying is that there's no need to suppose he's any different. Stubborn as a mule, I'll grant you, but he'll eventually see the light. They all do, you know. No need to lose hope."

"Sleep you might lose." Henni grinned at her. "But consider it an investment. Mind you," she added, setting aside her cup, "I wouldn't try to argue with him over it. That'll only get his back up and, knowing Gyles, he'll become even more intractable."

Lady Elizabeth nodded. "Just leave him to it, and he'll come around. You'll see."

Unsettled, Francesca considered—them and their words. They undoubtedly knew her husband better than she, yet the sudden blossoming of hope from what she was forced, by the very contrast, to recognize as despair, left her uneasy. What if they were wrong?

She sank back against the daybed's cushions. "Tell me about him—about his childhood, what he was like."

"He was born and brought up here," Lady Elizabeth promptly replied. "He was a happy boy—not too good and too clever by half, but a likable, affectionate lad." From her tone, the dowager was slipping back into her memories; Francesca kept silent and followed. "He was our only child, sadly, but he was forever up to all the usual tricks—"

She listened as Lady Elizabeth painted a picture of an innocent, carefree boy Francesca had certainly not recognized in the man. Then a cloud passed over Lady Elizabeth's face, and she faltered. "Then Gerald died."

"His father?" Francesca gently prompted.

Lady Elizabeth nodded, then flashed her a teary smile. "I'm sorry, my dear, but it still affects me." Pulling a handkerchief from her sleeve, she waved it. "It was so very unexpected—"

"A riding accident." Gruffly, Henni took up the tale. "Gerald was in perfect health—no one would have imagined anything could harm him. He was out riding with Gyles when it happened. Gerald's horse stumbled badly and Gerald fell and cracked his head on a rock. He never recovered consciousness. He passed away five days later."

The room fell silent. Francesca could almost feel, across the distance of time, the shock such a death must have been, especially in the bosom of such a privileged family. After a moment, she asked, "Gyles?"

"He came riding in with the news. I can still remember his little white face—he was seven at the time. He raced in, crying, but he told us where and what had happened. . . ." Lady Elizabeth glanced at Henni. "I was so distraught, afterward . . ."

"We came at once," Henni said. "We didn't live here then, although we have ever since. I stayed with Elizabeth most of the time—it was a huge shock to us all. Gerald was so strong . . . but, well, it fell to Horace to take Gyles under his wing, which he did."

"Gyles was devasted," Lady Elizabeth continued. "He adored Gerald—they were extremely close. Gyles was Gerald's only child and heir, but more than that, they shared many pursuits—riding, shooting, that sort of thing."

"I remember," Henni said, "when we drove up in a lather, Gyles met us in the hall. He was so shocked yet contained— so obviously cut up and quivering inside. Horace stayed with him."

Lady Elizabeth sighed. "It was a dreadful time, but Gyles was never any trouble. Indeed, he was very quiet, as I remember."

"You know," Henni said, her gaze fixed in the past, "I don't believe I ever saw Gyles cry, not even at the funeral."

"He didn't," Elizabeth said. "I mentioned it to Horace after the funeral, and he said Gyles had behaved very properly, stiff upper lip and all that. Just how he should have behaved now he was Chillingworth, and head of the family and so on." She sniffed. "I would much rather he *had* cried—he was only seven, after all—but you know how men are."

"Gyles was remarkably quiet afterward, but then it was time for him to go up to Eton. That seemed to bring him out of his shell."

"Indeed." Lady Elizabeth shook out her skirt. "He fell in with Devil Cynster and that brood, and from then on, well, it really was just the usual things—going up to Oxford, then onto the town."

"And then all the rest of it." Henni gestured dismissively. "But you needn't bother your head on that score. Remarkably faithful, all the Rawlings men, no matter how they might behave before they front the altar."

"Very true," Lady Elizabeth confirmed. "Which brings us back to where we started and this nonsense of Gyles's *marriage of convenience*." She uttered the phrase with highbred contempt. "The truth, my dear, is that he might say it, he might even think he believes it, but it's so utterly contrary to his nature, he'll never be able to live the fiction for long."

Henni snorted. "I'll second that. It's going to be quite entertaining watching him trying to force himself to toe such a ridiculous line."

"Yes, but we won't, unfortunately, see it firsthand." Lady Elizabeth focused consideringly on Francesca. "This news makes me even more determined to remove to the Dower House with all possible dispatch."

Francesca returned her gaze. "Why?"

"So that the only person Gyles will share this great house with—the only companion he will have here—will be you. He needs time with you without distraction, enough to come to his senses." Lady Elizabeth stood, her grey eyes stern. "And the sooner he does that, the better."

Chapter 9

Lady Elizabeth and Henni retired for a nap before dinner. Francesca retired to her bedchamber, too, but was too restless to lie down.

Hope was welling within her; she wasn't sure it was wise to let it rise again. She had before, ignoring his specific declarations, purely on the grounds of her intuitive sense of him. He'd told her she was wrong.

She had no guarantee that his mother's and aunt's understanding of him was accurate, not now he was a man.

Yet she couldn't help hoping.

Shaking her head, she scanned her surroundings, searching for distraction. Beyond her window, she saw the stable block just visible through the trees.

Ten minutes later, she entered the stable.

"Can I help you, ma'am?"

Francesca smiled at the bowlegged man who came hurrying up. "I'm sorry, I don't know your name."

"Jacobs, ma'am." He doffed his cloth cap. "I'm head stableman here." His gaze raked the stalls. "In charge of all these beauties."

"Beauties, indeed. I'm after the mare."

"The Arab? Aye, she's a darling. The master mentioned she was yours. I'll fetch a saddle and bridle."

While he saddled the mare, Francesca crooned sweet nothings, idly stroking the mare's velvet nose. Then she was up in the saddle and trotting out. As she left the stable yard, she was conscious of Jacobs's gaze on her back, but he seemed satisfied she knew what she was doing.

She also knew where she was going.

Although it was September, the evenings were still long, long enough for a ride before dressing for dinner. Cantering toward the escarpment and the angled track that led up to the downs, Francesca surveyed the neat fields, already harvested, in which cattle had been turned loose to graze. Fields and fences, the meadows by the river, all appeared quietly prosperous. She reached the track; the mare eagerly bounded up.

"You haven't got a name, have you, my beauty?"

They burst onto the downs. The mare tossed her head. For some time, Francesca just rode, enjoying the sheer exhilaration of speed. She let her thoughts slide, left them in abeyance, and gave herself up to the moment.

She retraced her direction of two nights before, as well as she could remember it.

She saw him—and he saw her—while there was still some distance between them. She rode on, then sent the mare in a wide, wheeling arc, dropping in to pace beside his grey. He didn't slow, but kept on at an easy canter.

Their gazes touched, held, then his lifted—to her cap, with its jaunty plume. She looked ahead; a moment passed, then he did, too. By mutual consent, they rode through the last of the day in an oddly companionable silence.

As they neared the escarpment, the ground broke up. She slowed and let him lead. As he went forward, she glanced at his face, all hard angles and granite impassivity, and tried to imagine the young boy who'd seen his father thrown and left dying. Tried to imagine the panic, and the wrenching emotion in the decision to leave and ride for help. Not easy at any age, but at seven? The incident couldn't have passed and left no mark. It hadn't dulled his love of riding, but what other scars did he possess?

They started down the track, the mare behind the grey. Her gaze on his swaying shoulders, drinking in the controlled strength in every line of his large body, Francesca considered—him. Them. Their marriage.

Earlier, she'd been on the verge of casting her dream of finding enduring love within their marriage from the castle's parapet. Now . . .

The evening was drawing in. They cantered through the lengthening shadows and into the stable yard. Jacobs came running. She handed him the mare's reins, then wriggled her boots from the stirrups. Turning to slide from the saddle, she discovered Gyles already there. He reached up, closed his hands about her waist, and lifted her down.

The mare chose that moment to shift, nudging Francesca's back, pushing her into Gyles.

His grip firmed, his fingers sank deeper. His gaze shifted to her face; she sensed the sudden focusing of his attention. She lifted her head and met his gaze. Their faces were close. She read his eyes, saw desire in the grey, and was about to lift her face to invite his kiss—when hooves clinked and the horses screening them ambled away.

"I'll get them settled," Jacobs called back.

Gyles released her. "Yes. Good night."

Francesca echoed the sentiment, then glanced at Gyles. He gestured to the house; she fell in beside him. Although fully clothed, encased in heavy velvet, she felt his nearness like silk caressing naked flesh.

She lifted her head as they stepped into the yew walk. "The mare—does she have a name?"

After a moment, he answered, "I'd thought to leave that to you."

Not to his wife, but the woman he'd thought she'd been.

Francesca ignored the point, even though she knew it was echoing in his mind. "She's quite regal in her bearing—I thought perhaps Regina would suit."

"A queen." He nodded. "It fits."

Francesca glanced at his face; in the half-light his expression was unreadable. She pressed her palms together. Tight. "I do thank you for the mare." She gestured. "It was a very kind thought."

Regardless of his mistake.

They kept strolling; she felt his gaze touch her face but didn't meet it. Then he shrugged. "It seemed the least I could do if I was going to stop you riding hunters."

Charles's hunters, so he'd thought, not his.

She glanced up and their eyes met. Briefly.

She looked ahead and said nothing more.

He did the same.

The house loomed before them; he led her to a door. He held it open and she entered; he followed. Francesca stopped, enveloped in sudden gloom, unsure of where they were.

Gyles walked into her.

His strength wrapped around her as he steadied her against him—awareness flared, then raced, prickling over her skin. Heat followed.

For an instant, they stood locked together in the deepening gloom. Neither moved; neither spoke.

She knew his thoughts. Knew he knew hers.

His chest expanded as he drew in a breath, then, stiffly, he stepped back. He waved her on. "Straight ahead." His voice had deepened. "This will bring us to the stairs."

She stepped out; he fell in beside her. They strolled along the wide corridor. "Has work on the bridge progressed?"

"Reasonably." He paused, then added, "We'll need to get more lumber, bigger beams to better support the trusses. That'll take a week or so, and the ground's too sodden at present. . . ."

He kept talking as they climbed the stairs, then crossed into the wing they shared. They halted outside her door.

Their eyes met; their gazes held. Silence fell.

She wished she knew what he was thinking, what he saw when he looked at her. The only truth she could read in his eyes was that last night had in no way diminished his desire for her.

Nor her desire for him.

But last night had changed things between them in ways beyond the obvious. In subtle, fundamental, fateful ways.

They both knew it, sensed it. In a sudden instant of clarity, she realized he was as much at sea with what was now between them as she was.

He breathed in, then inclined his head and stepped away. "I'll see you at dinner."

She nodded, then drew her gaze from his and entered her room.

"No—not that gown, the one with the green stripes."

While Millie ran back to the armoire, Francesca sat before her dressing table and examined her reflection in the mirror. The steam from her bath had set her hair curling wildly. She'd worn it down for the wedding, and half up through the day. . . .

Reaching back, she gathered the mass and twisted, then groped for a handful of pins.

Returning with the required gown, Millie stopped and stared. "Oooh, ma'am—you do look smashing!"

Pins clamped between her lips, Francesca said nothing. Once her hair was secured, she stood and let Millie help her into the gown. As it sheathed her in soft silk, she suppressed a shiver.

And wondered what she was doing—very likely riding hell-bent for a fall. There was nothing to say that she could soften his heart by going to such lengths with her appearance. He was an experienced rake, used to dallying with the most beautiful of London's ladies. Her birth might be on a par with his, but by London standards she was, and would remain until proven otherwise, a provincial. Not one of the gilded circle.

Her person, however, was exceedingly attractive to male senses—that was one point on which she felt supremely confident. Her mother had raised her to appreciate and make the most of all God had given her.

And she wasn't going to relinquish her dream without a fight.

Drawing in a breath, she turned to her cheval mirror. Swiveling, she surveyed the effect of the inch-wide stripes running vertically down the gown. She'd never worn the gown before—she'd been saving it. Styled in Italy, the gown had been expertly cut to showcase her figure.

Judging by Millie's open mouth and platter-sized eyes, the gown succeeded in its purpose.

No jewelry or shawl, Francesca decided—nothing to detract from the effect. Satisfied, she headed for the door.

They foregathered in the family parlor. Lady Elizabeth's eyes lit the instant she saw her. Henni chuckled. Gyles, however, was not there to witness her entrance. He appeared in the doorway just ahead of Irving.

Francesca smiled and rose, silks softly rustling. Gyles crossed to where they were gathered before the fireplace. His gaze swiftly scanned her from head to toe—then back again. Then his eyes met hers, and she wished that Lady Elizabeth, Henni, and Horace had already transferred to the Dower House, and there was just the two of them, alone.

He concealed his reaction admirably, but his eyes gave him away. He took the hand she offered, bowed, then tucked it in the crook of his elbow. "Come." His glance gathered his mother, aunt, and uncle. "We'd better go in, or Ferdinand'll have fits."

He led her into the smaller dining room the family used

when alone. Even so, the table without any leaves could seat ten, and tradition dictated she sit at one end and he at the other. He led her to her seat. His fingers brushed the bare skin of her inner forearm as he released her; she fought to suppress a shiver, fought to keep the heat from her eyes. He hesitated; she felt his gaze touch her cheek, then sweep over the expanse of her breasts revealed by the gown, then he straightened and continued along the table. Horace had given both Henni and Elizabeth an arm; they all sat, and Irving signaled the footmen to serve.

The conversation, thanks largely to Lady Elizabeth and Henni, with Horace, all unknowing, roped in, remained general and animated, perfect cover for the wordless communication between Francesca and Gyles that persisted throughout the meal.

An unimpeded view of each other was the only benefit of their relative positions. They were too far apart to read each other's eyes, and in public, neither he nor she was willing to allow their expressions to reveal too much. Their silent discussion, albeit conducted in the presence of others, was intensely personal. Totally private.

And extremely unsettling.

By the time she laid aside her napkin and, with a smile for Irving, stood, Francesca was not at all sure she could disguise her reaction if Gyles laid his hand on her bare arm. Having denied any wish for port, he rose, as did Horace; she was conscious of Gyles prowling close behind her, his gaze on her, as they left the room.

They congregated in the corridor.

As hostess, Francesca gestured toward the family parlor, her gaze gathering the dowager and Henni, then she glanced at her husband and raised a questioning brow.

He met her gaze, and she felt heat flare, felt the tension coiled inside her increase.

Then he glanced at Horace. "The library?"

"Where else?" Horace set off in that direction.

With a nod for his mother and aunt, and a last look and an abbreviated bow for Francesca, Gyles followed.

Lady Elizabeth and Henni waited until the door to the family parlor closed behind them before they started cackling.

Francesca blushed, but could hardly deny what they'd seen.

She left them early. Glancing up from the cribbage board, they only smiled and murmured their good-nights, then went back to their game. Francesca climbed the stairs. And wondered how long she'd have to wait before Gyles quit the library and came to her.

Gyles was leaning against the connecting door to Francesca's bedchamber, his gaze fixed unseeing on the darkness beyond his windows, when he heard the main door to her room open, heard her quick step. Heard the scurrying patter as her maid rushed to help her undress. Imagined the rest.

Then the door opened and closed again. The maid's light footsteps faded away. Gyles waited, giving her a moment to collect her thoughts. . . .

He didn't want to examine his. He kept them from him as he waited. When the tick of the clock on the mantelpiece grew too mocking, he pushed away from the door, opened it, and went in.

She was standing before the long windows to one side of the bed. She half turned as he entered; through the shadows, their gazes touched.

There was no lamp burning, yet there was lingering light enough to see—the ivory-satin robe she wore, to note how, fashioned in the form of a Greco-Roman dress, it draped and concealed her body. Enough light to see the invitation in her stance, to sense the acceptance behind it.

She watched him as he neared. He let his gaze drift over her, and wondered how many such gowns she possessed, how many different facets of Aphrodite she could project.

He stopped by her side, facing her as she stood draped in satin and shadow. Their gazes met, held. There was no need for words, for reasons—the desire that flared between them was real and strong, and in this arena all the justification either of them required.

That simple—and he couldn't begin to explain how grateful he was. Didn't want to think why that was so.

He reached for her, his hands sliding over the satin to find and fasten about her waist, drawing her to him as he lowered his head. Their lips touched, brushed, then fused, but they both held the heat at bay, content to savor the approaching prospect, and all the steps along the way.

He drew back from the kiss, raised his head—and felt the sash at his waist release. She opened his robe, then pushed it back over his shoulders—he obliged and let it fall to the floor. Lips curved, she splayed her hands over his chest, touching, exploring, with a greed both overt and refined.

He would have smiled but couldn't. "Are you always so direct?"

His voice was a gravelly rumble. She glanced up, her eyes dark pools of emerald clouded by desire. "Usually."

Palms to his chest, she searched his eyes, his face. Then, hands sliding, fingers gripping, she pressed closer, her face tilted to his. "You like it."

A statement. He reached for the twin clips, one at each shoulder, that anchored her gown. "Yes."

The clips clicked and she stilled, then looked down as the gown slithered over her body to pool about her feet. She stood still and naked before him, then she angled her head and looked up at him from beneath her lashes.

He felt her glance but didn't meet it. His attention was riveted on her curves, pale skin kissed by the fading light. On the contrast provided by the wild tumble of her hair, black as a raven's wing, and the dark curls at the base of her stomach.

A contrast of color, and of textures—he lifted one long strand of hair and let it slide through his fingers. Light silk, while her skin felt more like soft satin.

The thought sent his hand reaching for her waist. He lifted his gaze to her face, found her eyes, then her lips. Recalled the luscious pliant softness of those full lips beneath his, of her body beneath his.

She came to him, offering both with a simple confidence that slew him. Enslaved him. He drew her against him and their lips met, then melded. Her hands slid sensuously upward, from his waist up over his chest, then she wound her arms about his neck and pressed herself to him.

He ravished her mouth, a prelude to the ravishment to come, to the ultimate pleasuring of their senses.

She met him and matched him and urged him on.

He let his hands roam, greedily tracing, possessing her curves, then he lifted her in his arms. Two steps had him by the bed. He laid her down, then stripped off his silk sleeping trousers and joined her. She welcomed him with open arms and a passion to match his.

They were driven, yet determined not to hurry, urgent yet unwilling to rush. Her fascination with his body was unfeigned; he let her have her way—let her press him to the bed and straddle his waist the better to skate her hands over him, then duck and glide her breasts across his chest.

He couldn't help wondering . . .

"Did that come from watching your parents?"

Her eyes found his in the warm gloom. "No—not that. That I just . . . made up."

He curled his hands about the smooth hemispheres of her bottom and kneaded. "I'll make a bargain with you—you can invent as you wish but don't tell me what you're replaying from memory."

She paused, then leaned her arms on his chest and lowered her breasts until skin met skin, bringing her face closer to his.

She studied his eyes, serious but unconcerned—curious.
"Didn't you ever watch your parents?"

"Good God, no!"

She chuckled, the smoky sound the epitome of wicked-
ness, lying naked in the dark as they were. Ducking her
head, she put out her tongue and lingeringly traced his collarbone. "You've led a sheltered life, my lord."

The touch and her purr poured heat through his veins.
Closing his hands, he shifted her hips, then held her steady
as, with his aching erection, he probed the slick swollen
flesh between her thighs.

"Despite my sheltered life—" He broke off as he found
her entrance and pressed in, past the constriction and into
her hot sheath. Her gasp feathered across his chest; he felt
the instinctive resistance of her body and stopped, waited.
"Despite my conservative background"—*despite being one
of the most successful rakes in the ton*—"I believe there are
still a few things I could teach you."

He glanced down and found her eyes. He couldn't see
their expression, yet he could sense hers, feel her simple
honesty when she murmured, "I'm very willing to learn."

Their gazes held. He could feel her heart beating, in her
breast, in the soft heat of her sheath. Grasping her hips, he
held her down and eased farther into her, inch by deliberate
inch, slowly filling her until she was full, until he was seated
deeply within her. All the while he watched her eyes,
watched them darken, cloud, until, at the last, her lids lowered and hid them.

He felt to his marrow the soft sigh that shuddered through
her, the melting of her body about his. He ducked his head
and she raised hers; their lips met, and nothing else mattered
beyond what was between them.

Beyond the passion, the desire—and the driving need that
fanned them.

It wasn't such a bad basis for a marriage.

*   *   *

"Get out!"

Francesca woke to Gyles's clipped accents. Pushing the covers from her face, she peeked out—in time to see her bedroom door closing. Bemused, she turned to Gyles, slumped large, hot, hard—and very naked—beside her. "What . . . ?"

"What's your maid's name?"

"Millie."

"You need to instruct Millie not to come to your room in the morning until you ring for her."

"Why?"

Turning his head on the pillow, he looked at her, then started softly laughing. His mirth rocked her in the bed. His expression still amused, he turned on his side and reached for her. "I take it," he said, "you never watched your parents in the mornings."

"No, of course not. Why . . ." Francesca broke off as she studied his eyes. Then she licked her lips and looked at his. "The morning?"

"Hmm," he said, and drew her against him.

"I'm sorry, ma'am, it won't happen again, I swear—"

"It's all right, Millie. It was my oversight—I should have mentioned. We'll say no more about it." Francesca hoped she wasn't blushing. She hadn't mentioned because she hadn't imagined . . . Looking away from Millie, who was still wringing her hands, she straightened her morning gown. "Now, I'm ready. Please tell Mrs. Cantle I wish to see her in the family parlor at ten."

"Yes, ma'am." Still subdued, Millie bobbed a curtsy.

Francesca headed for the door. And the breakfast parlor. Sustenance. Her mother's quite remarkable appetite in the mornings was now explained.

Gyles and Horace had breakfasted earlier, and Gyles had

gone out riding. Where he found the energy, Francesca could not guess but she was grateful not to have to endure his too-knowing grey gaze over the teacups.

Lady Elizabeth and Henni joined her. Once they were gustatorily satisfied, they retired to the family parlor. Mrs. Cantle, no taller than Francesca but rather more buxom and garbed in dull black, appeared promptly at ten o'clock.

She bobbed a curtsy, then clasped her hands. "You wished to see me, ma'am?" The question was addressed impartially, directed somewhere between Francesca and Lady Elizabeth, who was clearly nonplussed.

Francesca smiled. "I did. As Lady Elizabeth is removing to the Dower House this afternoon, she and I wish to use the morning to go over the house and review household practices. I wondered if you have time to accompany us?"

Mrs. Cantle struggled not to beam, but her eyes shone. "If we could just decide the menus, ma'am." She addressed Francesca directly. "I don't dare leave the heathen to his own devices, if you take my meaning. Needs constant reining in, he does."

The heathen had to be Ferdinand. "You have another cook here, I believe?" Francesca shot a glance at Lady Elizabeth, but it was Mrs. Cantle who answered.

"Indeed, ma'am, and that's the better half of the problem. None of us would deny Ferdinand's . . ."

"Artistry?"

"Aye—that's it. He's a right one with food, no doubt of it. But Cook, she's been with the family for years—fed the master since he was a boy, knows all his favorite dishes . . . and she and Ferdinand don't get on."

It wasn't hard to see why. Cook was the cook until Ferdinand appeared, and then she was demoted. "What is Cook's specialty?" Mrs. Cantle frowned. "What manner of food is she especially good at? Soups? Pastries?"

"Puddings, ma'am. Her lemon curd pudding is one of

the master's favorites, and her treacle tart will curl your toes."

"Very well." Francesca stood. "We'll start our tour in the kitchens. I'll speak with Ferdinand, and we'll decide the menu, and we'll see if I can help smooth matters over."

Intrigued, Lady Elizabeth joined them. Mrs. Cantle led them through the green baize door and into a warren of corridors and small rooms. They passed Irving in his pantry and paused to survey the household silver and plate.

As they continued in Mrs. Cantle's wake, Francesca turned to Lady Elizabeth. "I hadn't thought to ask—how will you manage at the Dower House? You'll need a butler, and a cook and maids—"

"It's all taken care of, dear." Lady Elizabeth touched her arm. "On an estate this size, there's always many eager for work. The Dower House has been standing ready for us this past week. Henni's maid and mine, and Horace's man, are presently ferrying the last of our belongings across the park, and, this afternoon, we'll go to our new home."

Francesca hesitated, then nodded. It was not her place, certainly not at that moment, to allude to what Lady Elizabeth would undoubtedly feel on leaving the house she had come to as a bride and managed for so many years.

Lady Elizabeth chuckled. "No—I don't regret leaving." Her voice was pitched low, for Francesca's ears only. "This house is so large, and Gyles's needs here and in London are more than I have energy to oversee properly. I'm more glad than I can say to have you here, willing and able to take on the responsibility."

Francesca met her ladyship's eyes. They were grey, like her son's, but softer. "I'll do my best to keep all running as smoothly and as well as you have."

Lady Elizabeth squeezed her arm. "My dear, if you can manage Ferdinand, you're destined to do better."

The kitchens opened before them—two huge rooms, the

first cavernous, the second only marginally less so. The first room contained an entire wall of hearth filled with brick ovens, roasting spits, and griddles suspended over huge grates. A deal table ran down the center of the room; a smaller table, presumably for staff dining, sat in an alcove. Pots and pans gleamed—from the walls, from shelves, and suspended from hooks high above. The room was warm; savory aromas filled the air. Francesca glimpsed a pantry to one side. The adjoining room apparently housed the scullery and preparation area.

The rooms were a hive of activity. The central table was piled high with vegetables. A ruddy-faced woman stood at the far end, her large hands plunged into a basin of dough.

Mrs. Cantle whispered to Francesca, "That's Cook—her name's Doherty, but we always call her Cook."

Numerous juniors—scullions and kitchen maids—darted about. Concentrating on her dough, Cook didn't look up—the scuffle of boots on the flags and the clank of pots and bowls had masked their arrival.

Despite the melee, Ferdinand was easy to spot. A slim, olive-skinned male, jet-black hair falling over his forehead as he wielded a knife in a blur of motion, he stood on the other side of the central table, issuing a stream of orders in heavily accented English to the two kitchen maids who hovered and buzzed around him like bees.

Mrs. Cantle cleared her throat. Ferdinand glanced up.

His eyes found Mrs. Cantle, then passed on to Francesca. His knife halted in mid-stroke. Ferdiand's mouth dropped open.

Because of her late arrival for her wedding, this was the first time Ferdinand had seen her. Francesca was grateful when Mrs. Cantle clapped her hands to gain the attention of all the others.

Everyone stopped. Everyone stared.

"Her ladyship has come to look over the kitchens."

Francesca smiled and moved past Mrs. Cantle. She let her

gaze travel the room, touching each face briefly, stopping at the last on Cook. She inclined her head. "You are Cook, I believe?"

The woman colored and bobbed, lifting her hands, only to plunge them back in the dough. "Ah—I'm sorry, ma'am." She desperately looked about for a cloth.

"No, no—don't let me interrupt you." Francesca peeked into the bowl. "Is that for the day's bread?"

After an instant's pause, Cook replied, "The afternoon's baking, ma'am."

"You bake twice a day?"

"Aye—it's not that much more effort, and it means all's fresh."

Francesca nodded. She heard Ferdinand shift and turned to him. "And you are Ferdinand?"

He crossed the knife over his chest and bowed. "*Bellisima*," he murmured.

Francesca asked him which part of Rome he hailed from. In Italian.

His mouth dropped open again, then he recovered and a torrent of impassioned Italian poured forth. Francesca let him rave for only a moment, then shushed him. "Now," she said, "I wish to discuss the menus for today. Mrs. Cantle—do you have pencil and paper?"

Mrs. Cantle bustled off to fetch them from her room. Ferdinand grasped the moment to rattle off his suggestions—in Italian. Francesca nodded and listened. When Mrs. Cantle returned and sat ready to write, Francesca halted Ferdinand with an upraised finger, then listed dishes she'd selected from his repertoire for the luncheon table. Then she turned to Cook. "And for tea, I'm very partial to scones."

Cook looked up, surprise in her eyes, but she nodded very readily. "Aye—I can do those for you."

Ferdinand broke in with voluble suggestions; Francesca waved him to silence. "Now, for tonight . . ." She detailed the dinner menu, making it clear that Ferdinand was in charge of the various courses, which smoothed his ruffled plumage. Then she came to the dessert course. "Puddings. I've heard of a dish—a lemon curd pudding." She looked at Cook. "Do you know it?"

Cook shot a glance at Mrs. Cantle, but nodded. "Aye."

"Good. For the present, Cook, you will be responsible for preparing the puddings for our dinners."

Ferdinand's expression was outraged. "But—" He followed with a string of Italian desserts. Francesca fixed him with a direct look, and in Italian said, "You do realize, do you not, that your master is English?"

Puzzled, Ferdinand looked at her. Continuing in Italian, Francesca said, "While you and I know of Italian dishes, it might be as well for you to extend your expertise in English puddings."

"I know nothing of these puddings."

The word "puddings" was loaded with contempt. Francesca only smiled. "If you were truly wise and wished to succeed, you would ask Cook to teach you the ways of English puddings."

Ferdinand sulked. "She does not like me, that one."

"Ah, but now you realize that her teachings may prove useful, then you could find a way—perhaps offer to show her your decorations to use on her puddings. Making sure, of course, that she realizes you understand the importance of her puddings to the overall meal. I will expect you to work with her to ensure the balance of tastes."

Ferdinand stared at her. The Italian portion of their conversation had been conducted at a rapid-fire pace and had taken less than a minute. With a serene smile, Francesca nodded approvingly. "Very good. Now—" She swept around and made for the door leading back into the house, startling Irving and a small army of footmen who had gathered to listen. Francesca nodded graciously and sailed past. "Mrs. Cantle?"

"Coming, ma'am."

Lady Elizabeth brought up the rear, struggling to hide a grin.

The rest of their tour was much less eventful, but loaded with detail. By the time they returned to the ground floor, Francesca had a staunch supporter in Mrs. Cantle. She was relieved the housekeeper had proved so easy to win over. Given the size of the house and the complexities of its management, reliable support was something she would need.

"That was very well done of you, my dear." Lady Elizabeth sank into her chair in the family parlor. Mrs. Cantle had returned to her duties; Henni was knitting in her chair, ready to hear their report. "You had Cantle in the palm of your hand from the moment you showed yourself ready to ease Cook's way. She and Cantle go back many years—they've been here from the time they were girls."

Lady Elizabeth looked across the parlor to where Francesca had settled on the daybed. "Mind you, you already had Cantle leaning your way—inviting her to accompany us from the first was a stroke of genius."

Francesca smiled. "I wanted to be sure she understood I valued her."

"You succeeded in making them all believe that."

"I also value what you and Henni have done to ease my way. It would have been much more difficult without your help."

Both older women looked startled, then blushed.

"Well, just in case you don't realize," Henni said gruffly, "we'll expect regular reports once we're ensconced at the Dower House."

"*Frequent* regular reports." Lady Elizabeth's lips thinned. "I still can't believe any son of mine would be so *idiotic* as to imagine any Rawlings could possibly make do with a"— she gestured airily—"*distant* marriage. You'll have to come and reassure me that he is, in fact, coming to his senses."

*   *   *

Would he come to his senses? That was the question that concerned Francesca. She was less worried over how long it might take. She'd married him; marriage lasted for a life-time. A few months, even a year—she was willing to wait. She'd waited until now, for him.

For a chance at making her dream a reality.

After luncheon, they all walked to the Dower House, crossing the park under the huge trees. It wasn't far, but the Dower House was not visible from the Castle, screened by the trees and a fold in the land.

After looking around the pretty Georgian house, then partaking of tea served by a maid clearly overawed by her recent promotion, Francesca and Gyles returned to the Castle, alone.

In the hall, Gyles was summoned by Wallace on a matter of estate business. He excused himself and left her; Francesca climbed the stairs to her bedchamber in unaccustomed solitude—a luxury she had not recently enjoyed. Although it was nearly time to dress for dinner, she didn't ring for Millie but grasped the moment to stand by her window and let her thoughts wander.

It didn't take much pondering to accept that any pressure on her part, any overt demand for more from him, would drive him away—at least emotionally. His defenses would lock into place, and she wouldn't be able to reach him—he was strong enough to resist her if he wished.

She would have to be patient. And hope. And try to guard her heart.

And do the only thing she could to weight the scales.

Unfortunately, that action was incompatible with guarding her heart.

Drawing in a breath, she held it, then exhaled and turned into the room. Crossing to the bellpull, she rang for Millie.

Chapter 10

A stableboy came running as Gyles trotted into the stable yard. He dismounted; the boy led the horse away. Gyles hesitated, then went into the stable. He stopped before the stall in which Regina stood placidly munching.

"Her ladyship didn't go out today."

Gyles turned to see Jacobs coming up the aisle.

"She went for a walk. Saw her heading off to the bluff."

Gyles inclined his head. There seemed little point in denying he'd been wondering where she was. He strolled back into the sunshine. It was early afternoon and very pleasant out of doors. Too pleasant to go inside to the ledgers that awaited him.

He discovered her on the bluff overlooking the bend in the river. Seated on a bench set amongst flowering shrubs with her back to the old rampart, she was gazing out over the river and fields. In her primrose day gown with a simple yellow ribbon threaded through her dark curls, she looked like a Florentine princess, pensive and far away. Untouchable. Unknowable. He paused, oddly unsure of his right to disturb her, so sunk in her thoughts and so still that sparrows hopped on the grass at her feet.

Her face was serene, composed—distant. Then she turned

her head and looked directly at him, and smiled gloriously.

She gestured. "It's so lovely here. I was admiring the view."

He studied her face, then walked the last steps to the bench. "I've been at the bridge."

"Oh?" She swept aside her skirts so he could sit. "Is it finished?"

"Almost." He sat and looked out over the land—his land, his fields, his meadows. "The new bracing should ensure we don't lose it again."

"How many families live on the estate?"

"About twenty." He pointed. "See those roofs? That's one of the villages."

She looked, then pointed east. "Is that another?"

"Yes." He glanced at her. "You must have been here for some time to spot it." The three thatched roofs were all but concealed by trees.

She lifted her face to the breeze, clearly enjoying having it ripple through her hair. "I've come here a few times. It's a perfect vantage point from which to learn the lay of the land."

He waited, his gaze on her face, but she kept her gaze on the rolling green and said no more.

"Have you had trouble with the staff?"

Her head whipped around. "No." She considered him. "Did you think I would?"

"No." He could see the subtle amusement lurking in her eyes. "But I did wonder how you were getting on."

Her smile dawned. "Very well." He lost contact with her eyes as she stood. "But I should be getting back."

Suppressing a spurt of irritation, he rose, too, and matched her stride as she climbed the sloping bank. He'd been trying for the last two days to get some indication of how she was faring, how she was coping. Whether she was happy. It wasn't a question he could ask outright, not as things were. But a week had now passed since they'd wed, and while he had no complaints, he did wonder if she was content.

She was his wife, after all, and if he was having his cake and eating it, too, thanks to her sensible acceptance of his plan, then it seemed only fair that she should at least be satisfied with her new life.

But he couldn't ask the simple question, and she stubbornly answered all his queries literally, smiling and side-stepping his point. That only made him wonder all the more.

At the top of the rise, she paused, drew in a savoring breath, then she slanted him a catlike smile. Her eyes held his as he joined her, daring him to look at her breasts, at her figure clearly outlined as the breeze plastered her gown to it.

Another of her ploys—distraction. He arched a brow, and she laughed. The husky sound spiraled through him, reminding him of the night just gone and they games they'd played.

She was an expert at distraction.

Smiling, she linked her arm through his. They started across the lawns, fallen leaves crunching under their feet, the scent of autumn in the air.

"If there *is* anything you would like—anything to do with the household or the house—I take it you know you have only to ask?"

His dry comment had her lips twitching. She inclined her head; silken black tendrils fleetingly caressed his cheek. "If I should discover anything I need, I'll remember you said so."

She glanced at him from under her lashes, a habit she had—one he'd learned. He caught her gaze, trapped it, held it. After a long moment, he slowly arched a brow.

Francesca wrenched her gaze from his and looked ahead. "If I discover a need . . . but at present, I have everything I . . . Who is this?"

Breathless, glad to have a distraction from her lie, she

gestured to the black carriage drawn up in the forecourt.

"I wondered how long it would be."

Gyles's tone had her glancing his way, this time with open puzzlement.

"The coach belongs to our nearest neighbors, the Gilmartins. I'm surprised Lady Gilmartin was prevailed upon to wait the full week."

"They weren't at the wedding?"

Gyles shook his head. Taking her hand, he led her up the steps. "They were visiting in Scotland, thank God." He glanced her way. "Prepare to be exclaimed over."

She threw him a puzzled frown, but let him open the door and hand her over the threshold—

"Ah! *There* they are! Well, my goodness!" A large, amply bosomed matron fluttering a pink-fringed shawl descended on Francesca. "*Well*, my lord." The woman threw an arch glance at Gyles. "You are a dark horse. And here all the local ladies were certain you had an aversion to matrimony! Haha!" The lady beamed at Francesca, then swooped, and brushed cheeks. "Wallace was trying to say you were indisposed, but we saw you plain as day by the bluff."

Francesca exchanged a glance with the stony-faced Wallace, then took the lady's hand in hers. "Lady Gilmartin, I take it?"

"Ah-ha!" Her ladyship twinkled at Gyles. "I see my reputation goes before me. Indeed, my dear, we live just past the village."

Grasping her ladyship's elbow, Francesca steered her toward the drawing room. Irving hurried to open the door.

Lady Gilmartin prattled on. "You must come and take tea, of course, but we thought to drop by this afternoon and welcome you to our little circle. Eldred?"

Reaching the center of the drawing room, Francesca released her ladyship and turned to see an anemic gentleman entering by Gyles's side. Next to Gyles, he looked wilted and withered. He bowed and smiled weakly; Francesca smiled back. Drawing in a bracing breath, she waved Lady Gilmartin to the *chaise*. "Please be seated. Wallace—we'll have tea."

Subsiding into an armchair, Francesca watched as Lady Gilmartin sorted her shawls.

"Now, where were we?" Her ladyship looked up. "Oh, yes—Clarissa? *Clarissa?* Where have you got to, gel?"

A pale, pudgy girl wearing an unladylike scowl flounced into the room, bobbed a curtsy to Francesca, then plopped down beside her mother on the *chaise*.

"This is my darling." Lady Gilmartin patted her daughter's knee. "Just a fraction *too young* to compete with you, my dear"—her ladyship indicated Gyles with her head—"but we have high hopes. Clarissa will be going up for the Season next year."

Francesca made the right noises and avoided her husband's eye. A second later, her gaze fixed on the slight gentleman belatedly strolling into the room. She blinked, and missed all Lady Gilmartin was saying. Her ladyship swiveled. "Ah, Lancelot. Come and make your bow."

Dark-haired, interestingly pale, quite startlingly handsome albeit in a studied way, the youth—for he was no more than that—swept the room with a disdainful glance. A glance that stopped, dead, on Francesca.

"Oh. I *say!*" The dark eyes, until then hooded by languid lids, opened wide. With considerably greater speed, Lancelot came around the *chaise* to bow with romantic abandon before Francesca. "I say!" he said again as he straightened.

"Lancelot will be coming up to town with us for the Season." Lady Gilmartin beamed. "I think I can say without fear of contradiction that we will cause quite a stir. *Quite* a stir!"

Francesca managed a polite smile, grateful that Wallace appeared with the tea tray, followed by Irving with the cake platter. While she poured and their guests sipped and devoured, she did her best to steer the conversation into more conventional straits.

Gyles kept his distance, talking quietly with Lord Gilmartin by the windows. When Francesca at last caught his eye, a very clear message in hers, he arched one brow fleetingly, then, with a resigned air, ushered Lord Gilmartin closer to his family.

The result was not felicitous. The instant she realized Gyles was near, Clarissa simpered. Then she giggled in a manner Francesca could only consider ill-bred and cast coy glances at Gyles.

Before Francesca could think how to rearrange the room and reseparate her husband and Clarissa, Lancelot stepped in front of her, blocking her view. Startled, she looked up.

"You're most *awfully* beautiful, you know."

The passionate glow in Lancelot's eyes suggested he was about to fling himself on his knees and pour out his callow heart.

"Yes, I know," she said.

He blinked. "You do?"

She nodded. She eased up, forcing him to step back so she could stand. "People—men—are always telling me that. It matters little to me, because, of course, I can't see it."

She'd used such lines before to confuse overardent gentlemen. Lancelot stood there, frowning, replaying her words in his head, trying to determine the correct response. Francesca slipped around him.

"Lady Gilmartin?"

"What?" Her ladyship started and dropped the scone she'd been eating. "Oh, yes, my dear?"

Francesca smiled charmingly. "It's such a lovely day outside, I wonder if you'd care to stroll in the Italian garden. Perhaps Clarissa could come, too?"

Clarissa scowled and turned a pugnacious countenance on her mother, who brushed crumbs from her skirt while peering shortsightedly at the long windows.

"Well, dear, I would love to, of course, but I rather think it's time we were leaving. Wouldn't want to overstay our welcome." Lady Gilmartin uttered one of her horsey laughs. Rising, she stepped close to Francesca and lowered her voice. "I know what men—lords or earls though they may be—are like, dear. *Quite* ungovernable in the early days. But it passes, you know—trust me on that." With a pat on Francesca's hand, Lady Gilmartin swept toward the door.

Francesca hurried after her, to make absolutely certain she headed the right way. Clarissa stumped after them; Lancelot, still puzzling, followed. Gyles and Lord Gilmartin brought up the rear.

With hearty cheer, Lady Gilmartin took her leave, her offspring silent at her heels. Lord Gilmartin was the last to quit the porch; he bowed over Francesca's hand.

"My dear, you're radiant, and Gyles is a lucky dog indeed to have won you." His lordship smiled, gentle and sweet, then nodded and went down the steps.

"Remember!" Lady Gilmartin called from the coach. "You're free to call anytime you feel the need of ladylike company."

Francecsa managed a smile and a nod. "What on earth," she murmured to Gyles beside her, "does she think your mother and aunt are? Social upstarts?"

He didn't reply. They raised their hands in farewell as the coach rocked away down the drive. "That was neatly done—you must tell Mama. She was always at a loss to save herself."

"It was an act of desperation." Francesca continued to smile and wave. "You should have warned me."

"There is no way adequately to warn anyone of Lady Gilmartin and her brood." An instant's pause ensued, then Gyles murmured, "You didn't think being my countess would be easy, did you?"

Francesca's smile deepened into a real one. His tone was easy, easy enough to confuse with banter—underlying it ran his real question. Meeting his eyes, she let her smile soften. "Being your countess is quite pleasurable."

One brow quirked. "Pleasurable?"

He was not holding her, yet she felt held. His eyes searched hers, then steadied. "That wasn't what I asked."

His voice was a murmur, drifting past her ear.

"Wasn't it?" She had to fight to keep her gaze from lowering to his lips.

Gyles studied her emerald eyes, wanting more yet not knowing how to ask for it. He *had* to try, to press her—

"My lord? Oh."

He turned. Wallace stood by the door which he'd just hauled open. "Yes?"

"I'm sorry, my lord, but you wished to be informed when Gallagher arrived."

"Very good—show him into the office. I'll join him in a moment."

He turned back to be met by a bright smile and a gesture suggesting they reenter the house.

Francesca led the way into the hall. "Gallagher?"

"My foreman." Gyles glanced at her. The moment had passed. "There are various matters I need to discuss with him."

"Of course." Her smile was a mask. "I must have a word with Irving." She hesitated, then added, "I suspect we'll have a visit from Mr. Gilmartin tomorrow. I wish to tell Irving to deny me."

Gyles met her gaze, then nodded. He turned away—then turned back. "If you encounter any problem—"

Her smile flashed. "I'm more than capable of managing a callow youth, my lord." She turned toward the family parlor. "Worry not."

Her words floated back to him. Gyles watched her walk away, and wondered just what it was he didn't need to worry about.

* * *

The next day dawned as crisply beautiful as the last. Gyles spent the morning riding his lands, checking with his tenants, learning what needed attention before winter. He made sure he was back at the Castle in time for luncheon, in time to spend an hour with his wife.

"It's such a glorious day!" She took her seat at his right—they'd agreed to dispense with the tradition that decreed they sit at either end of the table, too far apart to converse. "Jacobs told me about the track along the river. I followed it as far as the new bridge." She smiled at him. "It looks very sturdy."

"So I should hope." The bill for the lumber doubtless lay waiting in his study. Gyles pushed such mundane thoughts from his mind and turned instead to enjoying the meal, and the company.

He didn't charm her or tease her—for some reason, his usually ready tongue fell quiet in her presence. Light banter he could manage and did, but they were both aware it masked deeper feelings, the gloss over the undercurrents of their joint lives. She was more adept, more confident in this arena than he, so he let her steer the conversation, noting that she rarely let it stray to any topic that would touch too closely to them—to what lay between them.

"Mrs. Cantle said the plums are coming along wonderfully. Indeed, the orchard looks to be burgeoning."

He listened while she reported all the little things he'd always known happened at the Castle. He'd known as a boy, but forgotten as a man. Now, seeing them through her eyes, having her bring them once more to his attention, whisked him back to childhood—and reminded him that simple pleasures didn't cease to be as one grew older, not if one remembered to look, to see, to appreciate.

"I finally found Edwards and asked about the hedges in the Italian garden."

Gyles's lips twitched. "And did he reply?"

Edwards, the head gardener, was a dour Lancashireman who lived for his trees and took note of little else.

"He did—he agreed to trim them tomorrow."

Gyles studied the twinkle in Francesca's eye. "Did you threaten him with instant dismissal if he didn't comply?"

"Of course not!" Her grin widened. "I merely pointed out that hedges were composed of *little* trees, and they were getting so scraggly . . . well, they might need to be pulled out if they weren't clipped and given a new life."

Gyles laughed.

Then the meal was over, and it was time for them to part, yet they both lingered at the table.

Francesca glanced through the window. "It's so warm outside." She looked at Gyles. "Are you going riding again?"

He grimaced and shook his head. "No. I have to deal with the accounts, or Gallagher will be floundering. I have to work out the prices I'll accept for the harvest."

"Is there much to do?"

He pushed back his chair. "Mostly checking and entering, then some arithmetic."

She hesitated for only a heartbeat. "I could help, if you like. I used to help my parents with their accounts."

He held her gaze but she could read nothing in his eyes. Then his lips compressed, and he shook his head and rose. "No. It'll be easier if I do them."

She plastered on a bright smile—too bright, too brittle. "Well!" Pushing away from the table, she rose and led the way from the room. "I'll leave you to it, then."

He hesitated, then followed her out.

If she wasn't allowed to help with the estate's affairs, she would go and talk with his mother. Who would probably wheedle the whole story from her and then commiserate, which would make her feel better and more able to shrug the incident aside.

It was early days yet; Lady Elizabeth and Henni had warned her she'd need to be patient.

Patience was not her strong suit.

"What a dolt! He hates arithmetic—always did," was Henni's opinion.

"Actually, I think it's encouraging." Lady Elizabeth looked at Francesca. "He *thought* about it, you say?"

"For all of one second." Arms tightly crossed, Francesca paced the Dower House parlor. The walk through the park had invigorated her, and awoken her mind to a different tack. When it came to contributing to their shared lives, she had numerous options, after all. "Tell me about the family. The Rawlingses." Stopping by an armchair, she sank into it. "From all I gathered over the wedding, the clan, as it were, seems fragmented."

Henni snorted. "Fractured's more like it." She considered then added, "Mind you, there's no real reason that's so. It just happened through the years."

"People drift apart," Lady Elizabeth said.

"If no effort is made to hold them together."

Lady Elizabeth eyed her shrewdly. "Just what do you have in mind?"

"I'm not sure. I need to know more, first, but I am, after all, the . . ." She searched for the word. "Matriarch, am I not? If Gyles is the head of the family and I'm his countess, then it falls to me to draw the family together. Doesn't it?"

"I can't say I've ever heard it put so directly, but yes." Henni nodded. "If you want to expend the effort, that is. I have to tell you it won't be easy. The Rawlingses have always been a fiercely independent lot."

Francesca studied Henni, then smiled. "The men, perhaps, and the women, too, to some degree. But women are wise enough to know what strength lies in banding together, no?"

Lady Elizabeth laughed. "My dear, if you're willing to supply the energy, we'll be happy to supply the knowledge. What say you, Henni?"

"Oh, I'm all for it," Henni averred. "It's just that I've spent years in the company of male Rawlingses, so the family's disjunction seems normal. But you're quite right. We'd all be better off if we knew each other better. Why, we barely know all the names!"

"No, indeed! Do you remember that dreadful Egbert Rawlings who married that little slip of a thing—what was her name?"

Francesca listened as Lady Elizabeth and Henni climbed about the family tree, pointing to this limb, then that.

"There's a partial family tree in the old Bible in the library," Lady Elizabeth said when, exhausted, they finally sat sipping tea. "Just the principal line but it'll give you—and us—a place to start."

"I'll find it and make a copy." Placing her empty cup on the tray, Francesca stood. "I'd better get back. It's cold once the sun goes down."

She kissed their cheeks and left them, knowing they'd spend the next hour speculating on all she hadn't said. Setting that and the sprawling Rawlingses aside, she gave herself up to the simple pleasure of walking through the great park with the sun slanting through the trees, lighting drifts of leaves and sending the scent of autumn rising through the still air.

It was quiet and peaceful. Free, her mind wandered—to that other treed place she'd loved, the New Forest. From there, it was a hop and a skip to Rawlings Hall, to those living there. To Franni. Her own not-quite-happy state pricked and prodded, pushing her to consider how to reassure herself that Franni hadn't been hurt by the events leading to her marriage.

The solution, when she thought of it, was so simple.

He saw her walking through the golden splendor of the trees, through his park, coming home to him. The urge to go to her, to meet her and draw her to him was so strong, he felt it like a tug.

She'd gone to the Dower House. He'd been pacing by the

windows for the last half hour, knowing she'd return soon, knowing from which direction. He'd been trying to concentrate on his ledgers all afternoon, telling himself it would have been worse if he'd let her help. Yet she'd still inhabited his mind, flirting like a ghost in the dim corners, waiting to lure him into daydreams at the first lapse in his determination.

The ledgers were only half-done. He glanced at them, lying open on his desk.

Determination be damned—he had to get out. Stretch his legs, draw the crisp air into his lungs.

He passed Wallace in the hall. "If Gallagher calls, I've left the estimates on my desk."

"Very good, sir."

On the porch, he paused, searched—and spotted her climbing over the stile into the orchard. Descending the steps, he strode for the gap in the low stone wall that separated the Italian garden from the acre filled with old fruit trees. Most were laden with ripening fruit. The heady scents wreathed about him as he walked beneath the groaning branches.

The sun was low in the sky, its light golden. Francesca stood in one beam, surrounded by a nimbus of shimmering light. No angel but a goddess—an Aphrodite come to tame him. Her head was tilted back; she was looking up. He slowed, then realized she was talking to someone in a tree.

Edwards. Spotting his head gardener perched on a branch and wielding a saw, Gyles halted.

Francesca saw him—she glanced his way, then Edwards said something and she looked back at the tree.

Gyles walked nearer, but kept at Edwards's back. If Francesca was working her wiles on the old codger, he didn't want to be appealed to for help. Finding Edwards in the orchard was no surprise—the orchard contained trees. In all the years he'd been head gardener, getting him to acknowledge the existence of plant life smaller than a sapling had defeated Gyles, his mother, and even Wallace. If Francesca had any chance of succeeding, Gyles had no intention of queering her pitch.

He waited while she listened to a gruff explantion of why that particular limb in that particular tree needed to come off. Listened to her laugh, smile, cajole, and finally get Edwards's grudging agreement to consider the state of the flower beds before the forecourt.

The flower beds before the forecourt were empty, had been for as long as Gyles could recall. They resembled miniature barrows, mounds covering the dead remains.

Gyles shifted, impatience growing as Edwards began another long ramble. Francesca glanced his way, then looked up at Edwards—a minute later, she smiled, waved to Edwards, and started toward him.

About time, said his mind. *At last,* said his senses.

"I'm sorry." Smiling, she joined him. "He's very long-winded."

"I know. He relies on the fact to drive off anyone thinking to give him instructions."

She looped her arm through his. "Have you finished inside?" She looked down, shaking leaves from her hem.

"I was just out for a walk, to get some air." He hesitated. "Have you been to the folly?"

She lifted her head. "I didn't know there was one."

"Come. I'll show you."

He turned her toward the river, the man within ridiculously pleased to see her eyes light with the expectation of pleasure, with anticipation over spending time with him.

"Before I forget." She glanced briefly at his face. "I wanted to ask if you would mind if I invited Charles and Ester, and Franni, too, for a visit?"

Francesca looked down as she descended the steps to a flagged walk above the river, grateful for the support of Gyles's hand and the fact he was watching her steps, rather than her face.

"For how long?"

His tone suggested he didn't really care.

"A week. Perhaps a little longer."

It was the obvious solution to her worry over Franni. She would write to Charles and insist he read her invitation to Franni. She would make it clear that if Franni didn't wish to come, she'd understand.

And she would. Franni had enjoyed traveling in the coach. The only reason she'd refuse another journey would be if she had indeed been upset by Gyles marrying Francesca, having imagined that he was interested in her.

"I thought I'd write tomorrow, then they could come up in a few weeks."

Gyles considered, then nodded. "If you wish."

He didn't wish, but voicing his reasons for wanting to keep her to himself, keeping others at bay, was beyond him. And the last thing he wanted was to disturb the moment, having successfully escaped to spend some time alone with her, away from the house, away from his responsibilities, and hers, away from their servants and all other interested eyes.

Time alone with her had become precious.

"This way." He turned her sharply, to where another path joined the one they'd been following.

"Good heavens! I would have walked right past and not known this path was here."

"It was created like that. The folly's hidden, very private."

They descended a series of steps traversing the bluff. The stone steps were clear of leaves courtesy of the army of undergardeners, all more attuned to their noble employer's wishes than Edwards. The path led to a wide ledge jutting out from the bluff, much closer to the river than the top of the bluff yet still well above the flood line.

The ledge was thickly grassed. Shrubs lined its edge, while closer to the wall of the towering bluff, trees grew and leaned out, casting their shade over the path and the folly at the path's end. A solid structure built of the same grey stone as the castle, the folly filled the end of the ledge, stretching from the bluff wall to the drop to the river. It was not an open structure, but had windows and a proper door.

"It's a garden room out in the gardens." Francesca studied it as they approached along the path.

Gyles opened the door.

"Oh! How *beautiful*." Stepping up to the polished floor, Francesca looked around, then was drawn to the windows. "What a magnificent view!"

"I'd forgotten," Gyles murmured, closing the door. "I haven't been here for years."

Francesca glanced around at the comfortable furniture. "Well, someone comes here—it's aired, and there's not a speck of dust in sight."

"Mrs. Cantle. She says the walk does her good." Leaving Francesca by the windows, Gyles walked to where, beside a sofa, a tapestry frame stood, a piece of linen stretched on the hoop, silks dangling. "My mother used to spend a lot of time here."

The tapestry stirred long-buried memories; Gyles eventually recognized it as the one his mother had been working on at the time of his father's death. "It's too far for her these days."

And she wouldn't come anyway—that he now understood. Francesca had asked if he'd ever watched his parents making love—he'd denied it. But he had seen them together once. He'd been playing on the ledge and had heard their voices. He couldn't make out what they were saying, it had all been a jumble of sounds, so he'd crept closer and peeked in. They'd been here, on the sofa, in each other's arms, kissing and murmuring. He hadn't understood what they were doing, and it had interested him not at all. He'd gone back to playing and had given the incident no further thought.

His mother had loved his father deeply—he'd known that all along. Known the reason for her overwhelming sadness at his death, her withdrawal from the world at the time. He'd never questioned that love, never doubted its existence. But he'd forgotten just how strong love was—how enduring. How it held true through all the years.

Now he was here with Francesca. His wife.

A sound reached him; he turned and watched her open a window, pushing the halves wide. The back of the folly butted against the bluff, but its other walls were half window. A sill ran around the room at hip height, with windows set in panels reaching up, nearly to the ceiling.

Placing her hands on the wide sill, Francesca leaned out and looked down, then to either side. "The river's so close you can hear it murmuring."

"Can you?" Halting behind her, Gyles slid his arms around her and drew her back against him. She chuckled warmly and leaned back, tipped her head back. Gyles bent his head and set his lips to the curve of her throat. She shuddered delicately.

"The view is tantalizing."

He murmured the words against her skin, then shifted his hands to cup her breasts. His teeth grazed the taut line of her throat, then lightly nipped.

She reached back, down, sliding her hands down his thighs. "It's the *ambiance*," she whispered. "I can feel it."

It was his turn to chuckle; he knew precisely what she could feel. She pressed her head against his shoulder and her eyes found his, searched them, read them. He didn't try to hide his desire, his need, what he wanted, that minute, from her.

Her lips curved, sirenlike, and she turned in his arms, turned to him.

Her hand touched his cheek as he bent his head. They kissed, and it was sweet. Addictive enough for them to take, and give, and take again.

They didn't stop until they were breathless, both aching and wanting and eager. It was she who stepped back, drawing him with her, until her back met the ledge.

He arched a brow at her. "Here?"

She arched a brow back—pure challenge. "Here, my lord."

She'd never pretended to an innocence she didn't possess. He closed his hands about her waist and lifted her; she wriggled and got her balance. He lifted her skirts and pushed them back to her hips. She parted her thighs eagerly and he touched her, cupped her, lingeringly caressed her, then slid one long finger deeply into her.

"Oh!" She clutched his shoulder as her lids drooped in involuntary reaction.

He stroked, then reached deeper and she gasped.

"Don't you dare," she managed, but he only smiled. He stroked and probed until she was frantic. She was hot and wet; he delighted in the abandoned response of her body to his touch, to him.

Then she pushed his hand away and her fingers were at his waistband. He was fully erect, iron-hard, and very ready when her fingers found him and stroked, then closed. But they couldn't afford to let her have her way with him. He drew her hand away, pressed her knees wide, and guided himself to her entrance.

He pressed in and she gasped, tightened, then eased and wriggled. He clamped her hips between his hands and pressed deeper, then deeper still. Her body welcomed him, slick, scalding hot, yielding. She laced her fingers behind his nape and leaned back, gripping his flanks with her thighs, tilting her hips to take him all, settling herself about him.

With one final thrust he seated himself fully, embedded within her lushness. Their eyes met; all laughter was gone. She lifted one hand, laid it along his cheek, and guided his lips to hers, offering them to him.

He took them, and her, and she urged him on. Desire, passion and need filled them, caught them in a net of pleasure and bound them together, linked them ever more deeply as their bodies searched for, and found, delight.

Experienced delight. As she shattered in his arms, Francesca inwardly smiled, and waited, feeling her body surrender, unfurl and soften, feeling him plunder even more deeply. Then, with a harsh cry, he joined her, and filled her with a warmth far more pervasive than the physical. Joy, happiness—intangible but priceless.

Together they clung, together they gloried. She gloried even more that he'd come to her outside of her bedchamber. There was no possibility this was a duty-driven exercise, not that she'd seriously imagined their nightly interludes were such, but the confirmation was comforting. Encouraging.

She stroked his hair, soft against her palm, listened to his breathing ease, felt his heart slow.

Felt ridiculously exposed—vulnerable beyond belief, even with his strength surrounding her.

But if that's what it took, she was willing. More than willing to take the risk. She was committed to loving him and could not now draw back. Never would.

She'd crossed her Rubicon to put herself in his arms.

Chapter 11

They walked back through the park in the deepening twilight, his arm around her, her head on his shoulder. Neither said a word. Increasingly Gyles felt that between them there was too much to say, and no words in which to say it.

None of his experience had prepared him for this. She seemed more proficient, more attuned, yet even she was wary, careful. Even she protected her heart and screened her thoughts and feelings.

Feelings. Something he could not escape, could not deny. The unfettered joy he experienced when they loved was new. Achingly precious, wholly addictive. Despite that last, he was grateful—for the experience of loving at that level where the physical was subsumed by the ephermal and feelings were elevated to a different plane.

As they neared the house, he glanced at her face. He was grateful for all she was, for all she had brought him.

Raising his head, he looked up at his front door.

And was conscious he wanted still more.

He knew what he wanted—had known for some time. Yet how could he demand let alone claim her love if he was not willing to love her, openly and honestly, in return?

They climbed the porch steps in silence. He opened the

door; with a soft, sated smile, she stepped into the hall. He hesitated, then, face hardening, followed her into the house.

They met over the dinner table two hours later. Francesca's heart was light, her body still aglow as she took her seat beside Gyles. Irving oversaw the serving, then the staff withdrew as she and Gyles tasted the delicate soup Ferdinand had prepared.

Gyles glanced at her. "If you write a letter to Charles, Wallace will see it gets sent immediately."

"I'll write tomorrow." She wanted to get the question of what Franni felt about their marriage clarified. It was a black cloud hovering at the edge of her mental horizon; she wanted it dispersed so, when the time came, she could celebrate with an unfettered heart.

Never had she felt so confident of converting her dream to reality. Although she accepted they still had work to do in establishing the framework of their marriage, after this afternoon, she no longer harbored any doubt as to the basic structure, or the foundation on which they would build.

She knew better than to let her heart overflow, let her expectations show. Throughout the meal, she kept up a steady flow of general conversation, aware but unconcerned that Gyles made no effort, beyond that first comment, to introduce any subjects of his own.

At the end of the meal, they strolled side by side into the hall. She turned toward the family parlor.

Wallace stepped from the shadows and addressed his master. "I've left the documents from the study in the library as you requested, my lord."

Francesca turned and looked at Gyles.

He met her gaze. "You'll have to excuse me. There's some research I must do on certain parliamentary matters."

She couldn't read his eyes, could read nothing in his

bland expression. Thus far, he'd always joined her in the parlor; she would read a book while he read the London papers. A chill like a raindrop slithered down her spine. "Perhaps I could help." When he didn't immediately reply, she added, "With the research."

His face hardened. "No." After an instant's hesitation, he added, "These are not matters with which my countess need concern herself."

She couldn't breathe. She stood there, disbelieving, stopping herself from believing, stopping herself from reacting. Only when she was sure her mask was in place and would not fall, when she was sure she could speak and her voice wouldn't falter, she inclined her head. "As you wish."

Turning, she walked toward the parlor.

Gyles watched her go, aware Wallace was still standing in the shadows. Then he turned. A footman threw open the library door; he walked in. The door closed behind him.

He'd done it for her own good.

An hour later, Gyles rubbed his hands over his face, then stared at the three hefty volumes open on the desk before him, their pages lit by the desk lamp. On the blotter sat the drafts of three bills he and a number of like-minded lords had been discussing for some time. Given he'd decided to miss the autumn session, he'd volunteered to research the key points in their deliberations.

He'd done little to further their goals tonight.

Every time he started reading, the expression in Francesca's eyes, the sudden blanking of happiness from her face, rose to haunt him.

Lips compressing, he tugged one tome so the light fell better on the page. He'd done the honorable thing. He was not prepared to love her, not as she wished to be loved—it was better to make that plain now and not encourage her to extrapolate—to invent, to imagine—to dream any further.

Focusing on the tiny print, he forced himself to read.

The door opened. Gyles raised his head. Wallace materialized from the gloom.

"Excuse me, my lord, do you wish for anything further? Her ladyship's retired—she mentioned a slight headache. Do you wish tea to be brought to you here?"

A moment passed before Gyles replied, "No. Nothing further." He looked away as Wallace bowed.

"Very good, my lord. Good night."

Gyles stared unseeing across the darkened room. He heard the door shut; still he sat and stared. Then he pushed back his chair, rose, and walked to the long windows. The curtains were open; the west lawn was awash with moonlight, the orchard a sea of shifting shadows beyond.

He stood and stared; inside, a battle raged.

He didn't want to hurt her yet he had. She was his wife—*his*. His most deeply entrenched instinct was to protect her, yet how could he protect her from himself? From the fact he had an eminently sound reason for refusing to admit love into his life. That his decision was absolute, that he would not be swayed. That he'd long ago made up his mind never to take that risk again.

The consequences were too dire, the misery too great.

There seemed no other choice. Hurt her, or accept the risk of being destroyed himself.

He stood before the windows as the moon traversed the sky. When he finally turned inside, lowered the lamp wick and blew out the flame, then crossed the dark room to the door, one question—only one—echoed in his mind.

How much of a coward was he?

Four days later, Francesca cracked open the second door to the library and peeked in. The second door lay down a side corridor, out of sight of the main door and the footmen in the front hall. If they saw her approaching any door, they would instantly fling it wide—in this instance, the opposite of what she wished.

Gyles was not at his desk. It stood directly across the room. The chair behind it was empty, but books lay open, scattered across the desktop.

Francesca eased the door farther open and scanned the room. No tall figure stood by the long windows, nor yet by the shelves.

Swiftly, she entered and quietly shut the door. Moving to the nearest corner, she started along the bookshelves, scanning the titles.

Her caution had nothing to do with her search—she wasn't engaged in any reprehensible act. But she wanted to avoid any unnecessary encounter with Gyles. If he didn't want her in his life, so be it—she was too proud to beg. Since the evening he'd elected to spend his after-dinner hours separate from her, she'd ensured she made no demands on his time beyond the absolutely necessary.

He still came to her bed and her arms every night, but that was different. Neither she nor he would allow what occurred between them outside her bedchamber to interfere with what lay between them *inside* it.

On that, at least, they were as one.

She hadn't been back to the Dower House. While she would have liked to indulge in the comfort and support of her mother-in-law and aunt-in-law, the first question they would ask was how she was getting on, meaning getting on with her husband.

She didn't know how to answer, couldn't conceive how to explain or make sense of it. His rejection—how else was she to interpret it?—had been a blow, yet, stubbornly, she refused to give up hope. Not while he continued to come to her every night—not while, during the day, she would catch him watching her, a frown, not one of displeasure but of uncertainty, in his grey eyes.

No—she hadn't lost hope, but she'd learned not to prod. Henni had definitely been right about that. He was a latent tyrant; tyrants did not appreciate being dictated *to*. She had to let him find his own road, and pray it was one that led to her desired destination.

Such patience did not come easily. She *had* to distract herself. Remembering her intention to find the old Bible and copy the family tree therein, she'd asked Irving about the book; he believed the Bible, a huge old tome, was in the library. Somewhere amid the thousands of other old tomes. All Irving could recall was that it was covered in red leather with a spine nearly six inches wide.

Minutes ticked by. Half an hour elapsed as she circled the huge room. It would have taken longer, but there were few books that large on the shelves. Indeed, there was no book that large on the main shelves. Which left the shelves in the gallery.

Built over the side corridor from which she'd entered, the gallery was fully walled rather than railed. From a corner of the main room, a set of spiral stairs led up to an archway; stepping through, Francesca looked down the narrow room lined with floor-to-ceiling bookcases. All filled. Halfway down the room, a floor-to-ceiling partition, also covered in shelves, jutted across the room, dividing it roughly in half, leaving only a door-sized gap on one side.

The earl of Chillingworth possessed too many books. Ignoring the crick in her neck, Francesca circled the room, searching for an extralarge tome in red leather. The first room had no window; the only light came slanting through from the long windows in the other half of the gallery. She had to squint to check the titles of the few large red books she found.

None of them was the Bible.

Finishing with the first room, she stepped through the doorway into the other half of the gallery. Momentarily dazzled by the sunshine streaming in, she halted, blinking.

The silhouetted shape she'd thought some odd form of library ladder resolved into her husband sitting in a large wing chair with his long legs stretched out before him.

She gave a start, quelled it. "I'm sorry—I didn't know you

were here." She heard the defensive note in her voice. She turned. "Pray excuse me. I'll leave you."

"No."

She took an instant to consider his tone—absolute command laced with an underlying hesitancy—then she swung back to face him.

His expression was impassive. "You weren't in England at the time of the Peterloo Riot, were you?"

"The riot in Manchester?" He nodded; she shook her head. "We heard about it sometime after—most mentioned it as a regrettable occurrence."

"Indeed." Half-rising, he tugged a chair close to his; with the paper he held in his hand, he waved her to it. "Sit down and read this, and tell me what you think of it."

She hesitated, then crossed the small room. Sinking onto the chair, she accepted the paper, some sort of formal declaration. "What is this?"

"Read it." He sat back. "You're the nearest thing to an unbiased observer, one who only knows the facts without the emotions that, at the time and subsequently, have colored discussions in England."

She glanced at him, then dutifully read. By the time she reached the document's end, she was frowning. "This seems—well, illogical. I can't see how they can claim such things, or make such assertions."

"Precisely." He took back the paper. "This is supposed to be an argument against repealing the Corn Laws."

Francesca hesitated, then quietly asked, "Are you for, or against?"

He shot her a dark look. "For, of course. The damned bill should never have been enacted. A lot of us argued against it at the time, but it went through. Now we have to get it repealed before the country crumbles."

"You're a major landowner—aren't the Corn Laws to your advantage?"

"If the only measure used is immediate financial gain,

then yes. However, the overall effect on large estates, such as mine, or Devil's, or a whole host of others, is negative, because of the social costs."

"So your principal argument for repealing the bill is a financial one?"

"For the Lords, the financial arguments must be strong, but to my mind, the other arguments are stronger. Having legal title to their estates didn't save the French aristocracy. Those who won't see that, who refuse to see that times have changed and that the populace in general has rights, too, are denying a self-evident truth."

"Is this what you've been researching—how to repeal the Corn Laws?"

"That and a number of related issues. Reformation of the voting franchise is the key, but we're years away from getting anything passed."

"What's this idea about voting? Tell me."

"Well—"

He explained, and she questioned. A spirited discussion arose over the extent of the franchise necessary to satisfy the inherent demand from the presently unenfranchised.

Gyles was surprised to see the sun slanting low, surprised to realize they'd been talking for hours. Although her experience was foreign, she, too, had seen the need for wider suffrage, for establishing a broader common goal.

"Waterloo was the end of it—the point where everything became clear. We've been distracted with the French for over two decades and not paying enough attention at home. Now there's no war to bind us together, to keep people and government acting as one, the social fabric's starting to unravel."

"And so things must change." Francesca nodded. She'd risen and started pacing sometime before.

"Times change." Gyles watched her parade before him. "And the survivors will always be those who adapt."

That was a truism and applied in many circumstances, in many arenas.

She nodded and paced, her expression alive with intelligence and her own intrinsic energy. He couldn't escape the obvious—that with her beauty, understanding, and vitality, he couldn't have found a more suitable wife to partner and support him in the political sphere. That had been the consideration furthest from his mind in arranging his marriage, yet how very important it would indeed be. If he took her to London, she would become one of the political hostesses, socially adept, quick-witted, and manipulative—all in the best interests of their cause.

He knew she had the power to manipulate men—that she knew how just as she knew how to breathe, knew how to make love with him. But she'd never made the mistake of trying to manipulate him, not even in these last days when he would almost think her justified.

For one of her temperament, that couldn't have been easy.

Times change.

And those who wish to survive adapt.

She swished past him and turned. He reached out and curled his fingers about her wrist, locked them. Surprised, she looked down at him.

He met her eyes. "We've discussed politics enough . . . for the present. I have something else I'd like to discuss with you. Another matter on which I'd value your opinion."

His gaze locked with hers, he lifted the papers from his lap and dropped them beside his chair. Rising, he stood beside her, and with his free hand gripped the high back of the chair and pushed it around until it faced the windows. He stepped around it and sat, drew her closer, drew her down. She let him sit her across his lap, facing him.

Her neckline was cut wide and scooped but modestly filled in with diaphanous gauze, opening shirtlike from the point between her breasts to fold back in an open collar. Closing his hands about her waist, he bent his head and touched the tip of his tongue to the bare skin at the top of her cleavage, then he stroked slowly upward, nudging her head back, feeling her shudder between his hands as he set his lips like a brand to the base of her throat.

She was his, so totally, unquestioningly his, he was starting to believe he must be hers.

Within seconds the atmosphere in the small room changed from the politically charged to the intensely passionate.

Intensely erotic.

That was his idea, one she fell in with eagerly, searching his face only briefly before complying with his command to turn and face the windows. He lifted her slightly, settled her bottom on his thighs, then, sitting upright, his chest not quite touching her back, he bent his head and trailed his lips up the column of her throat from the curve of her shoulder to the sensitive spot beneath her ear. "Place your hands on the arms of the chair."

Without hesitation, she did. He glanced up, out of the window. "See that large oak—the one directly in front?"

Her head rose and she looked, then nodded.

"I want you to watch the top branches. Don't look away. Don't think of anything else. Just think of those branches." Releasing her waist, he trailed his fingertips—just the tips— up and around to tantalizingly trace her breasts. Her spine locked. "Concentrate on the branches."

She shifted slightly. "But . . . they're bare."

"Hmm. There's one or two leaves yet to fall."

He didn't touch so much as tease. One hand administering to each ripe mound, he watched from over her shoulder as he mirrored the movements of his hands, circling but never touching the tightening peaks, his fingertips whispering over the fine fabric as he enticed her body to respond, to react.

Her breasts swelled and firmed. He could see her tightly furled nipples taut beneath the restricting bodice. She shifted in his lap.

"Are you concentrating on those branches?"

"Mmm. Gyles—"

"Think of how bare they are."

How bare she wished to be; he didn't need telling, but that wasn't in his rapidly yet expertly designed script for this afternoon. Gently, he cupped her breasts, tested their firmness, then he took his palms from her. "Totally naked." Using only his fingertips, he closed them about her nipples, gently at first, then with increasing pressure. She gasped, and tilted her head back. "Totally exposed."

He squeezed, and her back bowed, then he released her and returned to his gently teasing touches.

"Keep watching the branches."

He repeated the torture—she was a very willing victim— until she was breathing rapidly, shallowly, and her skin was lightly flushed. She slumped against him, tipping her head back to look into his face.

She searched his eyes. "I want you inside me."

"I know."

"*Well?*" There was more than a hint of imperiousness in her tone.

His lips curved. "Raise up for a moment."

Her legs had remained to one side of his; bracing her weight on the chair arms, she rose just a little. He drew up the back of her skirt, lifted it and her petticoat and the back of her silk chemise to him, then slipped his hands beneath the froth of materials. Setting his palms to her naked bottom, he briefly gloried in the firm contours, satisfied to find her silky skin lightly dewed. Then, grasping her hip with one hand, he sent the other sliding between the backs of her thighs to gently cup her.

She gasped; her arms wobbled. He drew her down. She gasped again as her weight pressed her into his hand, fully exposed to his touch.

Francesca sensed the strength in his hand, felt his long fingers trace. Heart thundering, she wriggled, then shifted one leg to swing it over his and open herself to him, to his tantalizing touches.

"No. Sit as you were—demurely."

Demurely? She was finding it difficult to breathe. Both his hands were under her skirts, one splayed across her stomach, gently kneading, while the other touched her intimately, explored her.

She could feel the slickness, feel how hot and swollen she was. Her naked thighs and bottom rested on the fabric of his trousers, a constant reminder of her vulnerability.

"Keep studying the tree."

She dragged in a breath, lifted her head, and fixed her gaze on the collection of bare branches.

One finger pressed possessively into her. She clutched the chair arms, vainly bracing against the jolt. Her lungs seized. He stroked, then pressed deeper. She felt her body tense, had never been so aware of how her nerves coiled and tightened. An ache swelled inside her. She wanted more, much more.

Another finger slid in with the first. Her body reacted, eagerly, hungrily—she'd reached a point of strange detachment where she could feel, enjoy, yet also observe. He reached deeper, his bunched hand moving beneath her. Spine rigid, she shook her head wildly. "No!"

The movements of his fingers between her thighs, within her, slowed. "Demanding woman."

His tone was deep, gravelly—taunting.

Then he pressed his fingers deep inside her and held still, hand pressed to her swollen softness.

"Are you still concentrating on the branches?"

Her gaze was pointed in that direction, but she hadn't been seeing anything for some time. "Yes."

"Some are knobbly, aren't they?"

She looked, noting what he'd directed her eyes to see. She was dimly aware of him shifting, that the hand at her stomach had slid away, that behind her he was opening his trousers, releasing himself. Impulsively, she let go of one chair arm and groped behind her.

He slapped her hand away.

"You're supposed to be concentrating on branches. Knobbly ones. Something nice and thick and smooth."

There was only one nice, thick, smooth and knobbly object in her mind, and it had nothing to do with trees. Family trees, perhaps, not physical ones. The reason she'd come to the library floated through her mind, and out. She looked at the tree, forced herself to see it.

His hand returned, slipping under her skirts to curve possessively over her bare stomach. "Look at the tree. Concentrate on the branches."

She didn't understand but did as he asked, forced her mind as well as her eyes to focus on the naked branches, finding a thick, knobbly protrusion—concentrating on that.

He lifted her slightly, shifting her back, sliding his body beneath hers. Then he eased her down.

And she suddenly learned why she was looking at branches.

His fingers withdrew from her but remained between her thighs, guiding his erection. He entered her slowly, deliberately, drawing her to him, filling her relentlessly until he was fully seated within her, and she was fully impaled upon him.

And she'd felt every inch, every tiniest, most minute sensation, amplified by the fact that, with her mind and senses distracted, the anticipated had become the unexpected. He'd ensured her nerves were highly sensitized, sure to react intensely to the penetration. And they had. Eyes closing, she let her head fall back against his shoulder, sank her fingers deep into the arms of the chair. That slow claiming had been, not a shock, but a moment in which her sensual defenses had been down. She'd felt more. Experienced the illicit intimacy of their joining to the fullest.

There was more to come.

He closed his arms about her, his body curled around her, his head bowed beside hers. With his lips at her throat, he undulated slowly beneath her.

It was a different kind of dance. Eyes closed, concentrating on something other than branches, she used her grip on the chair arms to shift upon him. The chair was too wide and her arms now too weak to lift herself, but that, it seemed, was not required in a chair. Not the way he managed it.

She surrendered to his managing, to letting him dictate the pace and tone of their dance. Her senses were wide-open, more receptive than usual; she was more focused on their bodies merging than she'd thus far been. Embracing the experience gladly, she relaxed, released the chair arms and wrapped her arms about his.

He murmured his approval and gathered her deeper into his embrace; she felt his pleasure in his slow, rigidly paced probing of her body.

Gyles skillfully steered her up to and through a long, extended climax, stretched out so she was floating before it ended, and continued floating for long after. He seized the moments to savor her more fully, to enjoy the bounty of her body closing so hotly about his.

He wondered how long he'd last—how long his control would endure the sweet heat, the luscious, scalding silken firmness that sheathed him. Leaning back, he urged her to lie back in his arms. Thus positioned, he could prolong their joining for a considerable time. He intended to reap all he could from the interlude. Give her, show her, all he could. She lay relaxed, boneless, against him, only the faint trace of concentration between her brows attesting to her awareness. He continued to move beneath her, wallowing in the hot slickness and the pleasure her body lavished on him.

"Do I still need to look at the branches?"

"You can if you like."

Leaving his right hand splayed across her stomach, he retrieved his left, shaking it free of her skirts. He started once more to lightly trace her breasts.

She made a murmurous sound of pleasure. He didn't think she was watching the trees.

Sometime later she asked, "Does it go on like this to the end, or is there more?"

Her tone was merely curious—a pupil inquiring of her mentor. He understood what she was asking. "No—there's more."

The next stage, the next level of sensation. They were both floating on a plane of elevated awareness, where their ability to feel was amplified but in a way that didn't evoke the usual urgency, leaving them free to enjoy, to prolong the intimacy and appreciate it more deeply.

He changed his teasing to more explicit caresses, until he was kneading her breasts, squeezing nipples tight and aching once more. Her breathing was ragged, her hips squirming. Then she angled her shoulders and tipped her head back; he bent his head and kissed her, let her kiss him.

Tongues tangled. Out of nowhere, desire rose and swamped them. Raced through them.

She ground her hips against him, taking him more deeply, luring him to thrust and set her free. He stubbornly kept to his rhythm, drawing out the moment ruthlessly.

Until their kiss turned frantic, incendiary.

Under her skirts, he shifted his right hand, sliding one finger down through her curls to the spot where she ached and throbbed. He circled the tight bud, and she gasped.

He set his finger lightly on the swollen bud, let it ride there as he filled her once, twice, still to the same, maddeningly slow rhythm. Then he slowed still further, let her sense what was to come, then he pressed down, firmly, evenly, and thrust deeply inside her.

She fractured like glass. He drank her scream, then drove more deeply into her. She gasped, clung, her ebbing strength leaving her open and vulnerable, unable to do anything other than feel as he held her down and thrust more deeply, then deeper still, pushing her on.

With another scream, she shattered again as he felt his own release sweep through him. He held her locked to him as he spilled his seed deep in her womb, felt her body go lax about him, all tension released, open and willing and welcoming. Wanting and accepting.

Chest heaving, he slumped back in the chair and gathered her to him.

"Remind me"—he had to pause to catch his breath—"to teach you about flowers."

Her fingers trailed down his arm. "Do they differ significantly from trees?"

"To appreciate flowers properly, you have to be standing."

They lay there, still joined, and let the minutes tick by, neither willing to move, to disturb the moment. To cut short the deep peace that intimacy brought them.

Gyles stroked her head, fingers tangling with the long, trailing curls spilling from her topknot.

He hadn't bargained for this—not for any of it. Not for her passion, not for her intelligence—not for her love.

That precious something she was determined to give him, that part of him desperately wanted to claim. But . . . he was unsure he could pay her price. He knew what it was, what she wanted in return, and did not, even now, after four days of considering, know if he could give it to her.

She was a chance he wasn't sure he could take, yet he knew he would never get a better one. Meet a woman more compelling, one more deserving of his trust.

Honesty, sincerity—an inherent integrity. The passionate wanton who set him alight and his beautiful, assured countess were one and the same. Neither role was assumed; both were different facets of her true character. That was why people responded to her so readily—there was no falseness in her.

Understanding her, learning more of her, knowing more of her, had become an obsession just as much as possessing her physically had been. Still was.

He sensed the soft huff of her breathing, continued to stroke her hair. Continued to stare out of the window.

The barbarian within him wanted to give her what she wanted, and claim in return all she was offering him. Or, at the very least, try. The careful, rational gentleman vowed even trying was too risky. What if he succeeded? How would he cope then?

Yet denying her was beyond him—he, and she, had just proved it. A wise man holding to the arguments he'd espoused would have kept his distance other than in the bedroom.

He hadn't. He couldn't. He would have to try a different tack. At the very least, he could search for a compromise, if such a thing was to be found. That much he owed her.

Owed himself, perhaps.

Chapter 12

"*Would you like* to go riding this morning?"

Francesca looked down the breakfast table. "Riding?"

Gyles set down his coffee cup. "I offered to show you the Gatting property. I'm riding that way this morning. We could amble through the village on our way back."

"I'd like that." Francesca glanced at her gown. "But I'll need to change."

"No rush. I have to meet with Gallagher first—why don't you join us in the study when you're ready?"

She struggled not to blink, not to let her amazement show. "Yes, of course." She forced herself to sip her tea calmly, and wait until he left and had had time to reach his study before pelting up the stairs.

"Millie?" Rushing into her room, she spied the little maid by one wardrobe. "My riding habit. Quickly."

Shedding her gown, she scrambled into the velvet skirt. "Would I like to ride—*huh!*" He'd avoided asking her until now. Join him in his study? She knew where it was but hadn't set foot inside the room—she hadn't wanted to intrude uninvited into his private space.

Standing before her mirror, she fastened the short jacket

and fluffed out her lace jabot. Then she glanced upward. "Thank you, Lord."

There was nothing worse than loving someone, and having no idea whether they would *allow* themselves to love you in return.

Bootheels tapping, she went quickly down the stairs and strode to his study, her gloves in one hand, her crop swishing, her cap's emerald plume jauntily dancing above one eye. A footman scurried past to open the door for her. She smiled sunnily and swept over the threshold.

Gyles was sitting behind the desk, Gallagher in a chair before it. Gallagher rose and bowed. Gyles had looked up; he smiled easily. "We're almost finished. Why don't you sit down—I'll be ready to leave in a moment."

Francesca followed the direction of his wave and saw a comfortable chair angled in a corner. She went over and sat down, then listened. They were discussing the tenant cottages. She made mental notes for later; she was too wise to evince any overt interest. Not yet. Time enough once he'd invited her opinion; just because he'd asked her to go riding about the estate didn't mean he was ready to let her further into that area of his life.

The estate itself was an arena he could legitimately keep to himself. Many of his standing did, but she hoped he'd allow her to become involved in more than a peripheral way. Large estates were complicated to run—the prospect fascinated her, not the questions of income, output and how many bags of grain each field yielded, but the people, the community spirit, the combined energies that drove any successful group effort. On an estate such as Lambourn, that spirit was reminiscent of that of a large, sprawling family, the prosperity of all interdependent on everyone performing their allotted tasks.

Her view might be naive, but from all he'd revealed of his ideas on the voting franchise, she suspected their opinions would be largely compatible. At the moment, however, she was biding her time.

And idly scanning the room.

Like the library, the study's walls were lined with book-cases, in this instance housing, not books, but ledgers. Surveying the serried ranks, she was prepared to wager that accounts predating the establishment of the earldom would be found among them. She swung her gaze over the regimented rows, then stopped, staring at the one shelf that contained books. Old books, including one in red leather with a spine at least six inches wide.

She rose and crossed to the shelf. The book was, indeed, the old Bible she'd sought.

Behind her, a chair scraped. She turned as Gallagher bowed to Gyles, then bowed to her. "My lady. I hope you enjoy your ride."

Francesca smiled. "Thank you. I'm sure I will."

Her gaze shifted to her husband on the words; he arched a brow at her, then came around the desk as Gallagher quit the room.

"Shall we go?"

Francesca swung back to the bookcase. "This Bible—may I borrow it? Your mother mentioned there's a family tree in the front."

"There is. By all means." He pulled the heavy book out for her; his gaze drifted down her velvet skirts to her boots. "Why don't I give this to Irving, and he can take it up to your sitting room?"

She smiled and slipped a hand through his arm, as eager as he to saddle up and be gone. "What a very good idea."

Ten minutes later, they were in the saddle and off. Gyles led the way up to the escarpment, then, side by side, they flew before the wind.

Francesca flicked a glance along her shoulder. Gyles caught it—with her eyes, she flashed a challenge, then looked ahead and urged Regina on. The mare lengthened her stride, steady and sure. And fast.

The grey thundered alongside, keeping pace. The wind whipped Francesca's hair back in black streamers. Fresh and clear, the air rushed to meet them. With hands and knees, she urged the mare faster.

Stride for stride, pace for pace, they streaked across the downs. The crisp coolness of the morning enveloped them. They raced, neither intending to lose yet not thinking of winning. The exhilaration of the moment was prize enough, the speed, the thrill, the thunder. They were locked in the moment, in the movement, horses and riders merging into one entity, the pounding of hooves echoed by the pounding of their hearts.

"Slow here!"

Francesca obeyed instantly, easing back in concert as Gyles slowed the grey from gallop to canter, and finally to a walk. The escarpment was less steep there. Gyles reined in where a track led down. Francesca halted beside him.

His chest was rising and falling, as were her breasts. Their eyes met; they both grinned, ridiculously pleased. Francesca shook back her unruly curls and looked around, conscious that Gyles's gaze lingered on her face, then traveled over her with a proprietorial air.

She glanced back at him, eyes widening, questioning.

His lips quirked. Reaching out, he tugged the plume on her cap. "Come on." He clicked his reins, and the grey stepped onto the track. "Or we'll never leave."

Francesca grinned and set the mare in his wake.

They ambled down through gently rolling hills. Beyond lay fields reduced to stubble, hay stacked ready to be fetched away, the corn sheaves already gathered in.

"Is this still your land?"

"Down to the river and beyond." He pointed to the east, then around in an arc to the south until he was pointing back toward the castle. "That's the shape, with the escarpment the north boundary. Like an elongated oval."

"And the Gatting property?"

"On the other side of the river. Come on."

They followed a lane between two lush meadows, then clattered across a stone bridge. Gyles shifted the grey to a canter. Francesca kept pace. The lane rounded a bend. An old house came into view, set back in the fields, a narrow drive leading to it.

Gyles drew rein at the mouth of the drive. He nodded at the house. "Gatting. It was originally a manor house, but it's been razed and added to over the centuries—there's little of the original left."

Francesca studied it. "Were there tenants in it?"

"Still are. They're related to some of my tenants, and I knew their worth. There was no reason for them to leave." Gyles turned the grey down the lane. "Come up to this rise. You'll be able to see the whole property."

Francesca nudged the mare and followed. On the rise, she halted beside him. "Charles told me the tale of how Gatting came to be and how I came to inherit it." She rested her hands on the saddle bow. "Show me the land."

He pointed out the boundaries. It didn't seem that important a property, not compared to the rest of the estate. She said so, and he explained. They rode across the fields as he elaborated on the management strategies he currently employed. "Without Gatting, managing the acreage on this side of the river was a perennial headache."

She glanced at him. "One our marriage has relieved?"

He met her eyes. "One it's relieved."

They rode on in complete harmony, heading west through the fields. Eventually, they reached another lane, and Gyles turned back toward the river. "This'll take us to the top of the village."

Another narrow bridge got them across the Lambourn. They rode past orchards enclosed by stone walls. A square-towered church loomed directly ahead, perched above the village and surrounded by a graveyard. They came upon a cottage, neat behind a white fence; the lane turned sharply

beyond it, just before the church's lych-gate. Gyles halted at the turn and waited until Francesca came alongside. He gestured ahead. "Lambourn village."

The street dipped, then gradually rose. Beyond the point where the village ended and the houses ceased, the street joined the main road the coach had taken on her wedding eve, carrying her to the Castle farther on.

Buildings clustered on either side of the street. The houses ran the gamut from workers' cottages, abutting one another in a row, to more prosperous free-standing cottages with strips of garden between stoop and gate. In the middle of the street, a number of shops proclaimed their existence via brightly painted boards hanging over the narrow pavements. The signs of two inns, one this side of the shops, the other just past them, were the biggest.

"I hadn't realized the village was so large."

Gyles jiggled his reins; the grey stepped out. "There's a fair number of people on the estate and more in the village and on adjoining estates—enough to support a market day."

"And two inns." Francesca considered the first as they passed it. The sign identified it as the Black Bull.

"It's nearly time for lunch." Gyles glanced at her. "We can leave the horses at the Red Pigeon and I'll show you around the village, then we can lunch at the inn."

She hid her surprise. "That would be pleasant."

The Red Pigeon was a large coaching inn. Handing their reins to a freckle-faced lad, Gyles escorted Francesca through the heavy front door into the large hall.

"Harris?"

A round, bald head popped out from a door; it was followed by a rotund body clothed in black and white, with a white apron tied about the hips. Harris hurried forward.

"My lord! What a pleasure to see you."

The innkeeper's gaze fastened on Francesca.

"My dear, allow me to introduce Harris—his family have owned the Red Pigeon for as long as there have been Rawl-

ingses at Lambourn. The story goes that the first Harris served under arms to one of our ancestors and on retirement took to innkeeping. Harris, this is Lady Francesca, my countess."

Harris beamed and bowed very low. "It's a rare pleasure, my lady, to welcome you to this house."

Francesca smiled as he straightened.

"We left our horses with your Tommy." Gyles noted the interested stares of all those in the open tap. "I'm going to show Lady Francesca about, then we thought to take luncheon here. A private parlor, I think."

"Of course, my lord. The garden parlor, perhaps. It has a nice view over the roses to the orchards and river."

Gyles raised a brow at Francesca.

"That sounds splendid," she said.

Gyles retook her arm. "We'll be back in an hour."

"I'll have everything ready, my lord."

Outside, Gyles steered Francesca along the pavement to the shops. The first was a bakery.

"What a glorious smell!" Francesca paused to peer through the steamy window. A second later, a round, ruddy-faced woman appeared on the steps, wiping floury hands on a voluminous apron.

Gyles nodded. "Mrs. Duckett." The woman bobbed a curtsy and mumbled a "m'lord," her gaze fixed on Francesca. Gyles hid a wry smile. "Allow me to make you known to Lady Francesca, my countess."

Mrs. Duckett sank into her best curtsy. "My lady! Welcome to Lambourn village."

Francesca smiled and with her usual ease acknowledged the greeting and inquired after Mrs. Duckett's enterprise. Mrs. Duckett was only too happy to show her ladyship all.

Thus it went as they progressed up the street, then crossed and returned on the other side. The outing was, Gyles discovered, an unexpected education.

He'd expected that the shopkeepers would be eager to greet his countess; he hadn't realized she would be so interested—transparently sincerely—in them, in the village it-self. But she was. Her interest rang clearly in her questions, in her bright eyes and focused attention.

He found his mind following hers, seeing things through her eyes. And was surprised by what he saw. Yet that was only part of the revelation. He knew and was known to everyone here; despite that familiarity, whenever he appeared he was usually the center of attention. Not today. Which left him in the position of some ghostly observer watching Francesca's entrance on this familar scene, viewing her effect on it, on all the familiar characters.

She drew them to her like moths to a flame. Her confidence, her assuredness . . . he tried to pinpoint what her principal attraction was. He watched as she parted from the milliner, saw her smile, saw the milliner's delighted response.

Saw something he recognized. Francesca's belief in happiness, an unshakable conviction that happiness existed, that it was there for the claiming regardless of one's station in life, regardless of whatever it was that happiness meant to each one.

That conviction hung over her like a cloak, touching all about her.

She turned to him, her smile brilliant, lighting her eyes. He took the hand she held out to him, hesitated, then carried it to his lips. Her eyes widened in surprise.

"Come. It's time for lunch." With a nod to the delighted milliner, he handed Francesca from the shop.

"She seemed to have very good quality wares." Francesca glanced back at the delicate lace in the window.

Gyles guided her firmly along. "Mama and Henni both use her services on occasion."

"Hmm. Perhaps—"

"Chillingworth!"

They halted, turned; Francesca saw a middle-aged lady and gentleman crossing the street toward them.

"Sir Henry and Lady Middlesham," Gyles murmured.

"Not like the Gilmartins," was all he had time to add before the Middleshams reached them.

The introductions were made. Lady Middlesham was a comfortable woman with twinkling eyes while Sir Henry was a solid country sort, content to bow over her hand, tell her she was "a pretty little thing," then turn to Gyles with some question about the river.

"You'll have to excuse them," Lady Middlesham told her. "Our lands lie to the north and west of the Castle, on the other side of the river farther upstream. They both have an abiding interest in the fish stocks."

"Gyles fishes?"

"Oh, indeed. You should ask him to take you in summer. It's quite relaxing, doing nothing but watching them play with their rods and lines."

Francesca laughed. "I must try it sometime."

"Indeed, and we'd be pleased if you would call at the Manor sometime, too." Lady Middlesham pulled a face. "I suppose, theoretically, we should call on you first, but I always get confused with such formalities." She squeezed Francesca's hand. "Now that we've met, let's not stand on ceremony. If you have time, do call in, and next time we're passing the Castle, we'll make a point of looking in. Elizabeth and Henni are at the Dower House, I believe?"

As she and Lady Middlesham chatted, already comfortable, Francesca noted that Gyles and Sir Henry, although not close in age, were likewise comfortable in each other's company. The idea of taking her first social steps blossomed in her mind.

"Countess!"

Francesca turned, as did the others. They beheld a figure, all in black, mounted on a prancing black steed.

Lancelot Gilmartin bowed extravagantly; his horse danced nervously, nearly bumping Lady Middlesham.

"Here! I say!" Sir Henry drew his wife to safety. "Watch what you're doing there."

Lancelot looked down his nose at Sir Henry, then focused his dark gaze on Francesca. "I wanted to thank you for your hospitality. I wondered if, later this afternoon, you might like to ride on the downs. I could show you Seven Barrows. The mounds have an eerie atmosphere. Quite romantic."

Francesca was very aware of Gyles by her side, aware of the restraint he was exercising. She smiled coolly at Lancelot. "Thank you, but no." With a wave she drew Lancelot's attention to the presence beside her. "We've been out all morning riding the downs—I'll have much to catch up with this afternoon. Please convey my regards to your mother and father, and my thanks for their visit."

A scowl marred Lancelot's too-handsome features. Faced with a wall of trenchant respectability, he was forced to accept her dismissal. He didn't do it with good grace. "Some other time, then."

Nodding curtly, he dug in his heels—his horse reared, then all but bolted up the street.

"Insolent puppy!" Sir Henry glowered after Lancelot's rapidly dwindling figure.

Francesca took Gyles's arm. "One can only hope he'll grow up soon and leave such ungraciousness behind."

The comment answered the questions that had been about to bloom in the Middleshams' minds. Allowed them to dismiss Lancelot as the mere nuisance he was. Lady Middlesham pressed her hand as they made their farewells; Sir Henry smiled and expressed a wish they would meet again soon.

They parted from the Middleshams and headed for the Red Pigeon. Francesca squeezed Gyles's arm. "Lancelot is a spoilt boy, of no interest to me and no consequence to you."

Gyles slanted her a glance, grey eyes hard, then ushered her into the inn.

Harris came rushing to conduct them to the parlor he'd prepared. Francesca was pleased to approve both the parlor and the fare the innkeeper and his buxom daughter efficiently set before them. Then Harris and the girl withdrew, leaving them in comfort, well supplied with viands and wine.

The food was as delicious as it looked; Francesca was free with her praise. Glancing up, she noticed the amusement in Gyles's eyes, noted his not entirely straight lips. "What is it?"

He hesitated, then said, "I was just imagining you at a dinner party in London. You'll create a panic."

"Why?"

"It's not common practice for ladies of the ton to evince such . . . *desire* over food."

She opened her eyes wide. "If one has to eat, one may as well enjoy it."

He laughed and inclined his head. "Indeed."

The table could have sat four; they faced each other over it. It was easy to converse, and they were free of all ears. As they sampled the various meats and pastries, Francesca asked about the estate in general, encouraged when Gyles answered readily, with no hint of reluctance. They discussed the past year, the trials and successes, and the harvest presently being gathered in.

Then Harris returned to remove the dishes; setting a platter piled with fresh fruits between them, he beamed benignly and left them in peace.

Selecting a grape, Francesca asked, "The families on the estate—are they primarily long-term tenants?"

"Mostly long-standing." Watching the grape disappear, Gyles leaned back in his chair. "In fact, I can't think of any who aren't."

"So they're used to all the"—another grape was selected—"local traditions."

"I suppose so."

She studied the grape, turning it in her fingers. "What traditions are there? You mentioned a market."

"The market's held every month—I suppose it's a tradition. Everyone would certainly be upset if it was stopped."

"And what else?" She looked up. "Perhaps the church sponsors some gathering?"

Gyles met her wide eyes. "It would be a easier if you simply told me what it is you want to know."

She held his gaze, then popped the grape into her mouth and wrinkled her nose at him. "I wasn't *that* transparent."

He watched as her jaw worked, squishing the grape, watched her swallow, and didn't answer.

Folding her hands on the table, she fixed him with an earnest look. "Your mother mentioned there used to be a Harvest Festival—not the church celebration, although at much the same time—but a fete day at the Castle."

Although he kept his expression impassive, she must have seen his reaction in his eyes; she quickly said, "I know it hasn't been held for years—"

"Not since my father died."

"True—but your father died more than twenty years ago."

He couldn't now argue that most of his tenants wouldn't recall the event.

"You're the earl, and now I'm your countess. It's a new generation, a new era. The purpose of the Festival was, as I understand it, to thank the estate workers for their efforts throughout the year, through the sowing, husbanding, and reaping." She tilted her head, her eyes steady on his. "You're a caring landlord—you look after your tenants. Surely, now I'm here, it's right—appropriate—that we should again host the Festival."

She was right, yet it took some time to accustom his mind to the idea—of holding the Festival again, of he himself being the host. In all his memories, that was a position his father had filled. After his death, there had never been any question—not that he could recall—of continuing with the Festival, despite the fact it was, indeed, a very old tradition.

Times changed. And sometimes adapting meant resurrecting past ways.

She'd been wise enough to say no more, to push no further. Instead, she sat patiently, her gaze on his face, awaiting his decision. He knew perfectly well if he refused she would argue, although perhaps not immediately. His lips lifted spontaneously as he recalled her earlier comment. Transparent? She was as easy to read as the wind.

Hope kindled in her eyes at his half smile; he let his lips relax into a more definite one. "Very well. If you wish to play the role of my countess to the hilt—"

He broke off. Their eyes met, held; all levity evaporated. Then, deliberately, he inclined his head and continued, his voice even, "I see no reason to dissuade you." After an instant's pause, he added, "I won't stand in your way."

She understood what he was saying—all he was saying. After a moment, she stood and came around the table. She stopped by his side, turned, and sank gracefully onto his lap. "And will you play your part, too?"

His gaze remained steady. "In the Festival, yes."

For the rest, he could make no promises.

She studied his eyes, her own unreadable, then she smiled, her usual, warm, gloriously radiant smile. "Thank you."

Raising her hands, she framed his face, then leaned forward and kissed him, deliberately, sensuously yet without heat.

From beneath lowered lids, he watched her, and felt his hunger stir. Felt the barbarian rise, but for once, his appetite wasn't lust, not even desire.

Something else. Something more.

He kissed her back, and she returned the pleasure, and it was simply that—a shared moment of physical touching, caressing.

It had no purpose beyond that—the exchange of a gentle touch.

Eventually, she drew back and he let her. She smiled, happy and pleased. "So, how should we spread the news? It's only a few weeks away. Whom should we tell?"

"Harris." Gyles urged her to her feet and she rose. He stood, claimed her hand, then led her to the door. "We invite the whole village as well as the tenants, and in Lambourn, there's no better way of making a general announcement than by telling Harris."

So they told Harris, and Gyles and she were now committed to the Harvest Festival. The next day, Francesca received a letter from Charles accepting her invitation to visit at the Castle. Franni, he reported, was absolutely delighted at the prospect of visiting there again.

Francesca didn't know what to make of that. Perhaps, after all, Gyles had been right, and Franni's reaction at their wedding had simply been due to overexcitement. That suggested that Franni's gentleman was either someone else, or a figment of her imagination. Francesca could see no way of deciding, not until Franni, and Charles and Ester, arrived.

Putting the matter aside, she threw herself into preparations, both for the Harvest Festival and for her uncle's visit. She made lists, and lists of lists. One of the items on her list for today was dealing with the rejuvenation of the flower beds before the forecourt.

"It is simply unacceptable." Together with Edwards, she stood in the drive one hundred yards from the house, facing the forecourt and the empty, leaf-strewn beds along its nearest edge. "That is not an appealing vista and no fit introduction to the house."

"Mmm."

Dour and glum, Edwards stood, a great hulk beside her, and scowled at the offending mounds.

Arms folded, Francesca turned to him. "You're the head gardener. What are your suggestions?"

He glanced sideways at her, then cleared his throat.

"Flowers won't do aught. Not there. Needs trees, it does."

"Trees." Francesca glanced at the huge oaks surrounding them. "More trees."

"Aye. Pencil pines is what I'm thinking."

"Pencil pines?"

"Aye. See—" Rooting around in the leaves, Edwards found a stick. With one boot, he cleared a space on the ground. "If you see this as the house—just the front, like—as we can see it from here." He drew a rectangle to represent the house. "Then if we put three pines in each side, like this." With the stick, he drew in six pines, three on either side of the gap where the drive joined the forecourt, all in a line along the forecourt's front edge. "And stagger them in size, with the outermost the tallest, and the two flanking the drive the smallest, then—well, you can see."

He stepped back, gesturing to his sketch. Francesca bent over to study it. Slowly, she straightened, looked at the house, then back down at the sketch. "That's really quite good, Edwards."

She stepped back, narrowing her eyes, trying to imagine it. "Yes," she nodded decisively. "But there's one thing missing."

"Eh?"

"Come with me." She walked back along the drive almost to the empty beds. Stopping, she scuffed back leaves along the drive's edge, uncovering stone. "This is the base for a carved stone trough—there's a similar base on the other side of the drive. Lady Elizabeth remembers the troughs filled with flowers on her wedding day, but they were removed at some point."

"Aye, well—I doubt we'd be able to get such things now. Takes a mite of effort to do such work."

"Oh, there's no need for new ones. The troughs are at the far end of the orchard, almost overgrown, but I'm sure they can be dug out."

"Mmm." Edwards's frown returned.

"There're also two matching troughs, smaller ones, that

should sit on the top steps of the porch. They're presently in the field behind the stable."

"Used for horse troughs, they be."

"Indeed, but Jacobs is quite sure his charges do not need anything so fancy." Francesca met Edwards's eyes, over-hung and half-obscured by his shaggy brows. "I'll make a bargain with you. I will allow you to put in the six trees, rather than plant the *entire beds* with flowers, provided you oversee the disinterring of those troughs—all four of them—and their cleaning and replacement in their proper positions. I've heard young Johnny likes planting and tending flowers, so, under your instruction, he can fill the troughs and plant the appropriate bulbs—I want tulips and daffodils, followed by other flowers as the seasons progress. I don't know what grows well at this time of year"—she smiled—"but I'm sure you and Johnny will."

Turning, she surveyed the presently bare beds. "Now, how soon do you think that can be done?"

"Mmm. I know where we can get the pines . . . I suppose we'd have it done in a week." Edwards glanced at her. "Be faster if we didn't have to do those troughs—"

"The troughs and trees all at once, please."

"Well, then, a week."

"Excellent." Francesca nodded, then smiled confidingly. "My uncle and his family will be arriving in a week's time, and I would like the house to look well."

The faintest tinge of color showed under Edwards's weathered skin. "Aye, well," he said gruffly. "We'll have the place all right and special for ye in a week then, p'raps sooner. Now—" Stepping back, he looked around.

"Now you must return to your trees." Francesca nodded a dismissal.

Gyles had been watching from the shadows of the porch. Seeing Edwards lumber off, he strolled out and down the steps. Francesca saw him. Smiling, she came to meet him.

"Did you succeed?" Taking her hand, he drew it through his arm, covering her hand with his.

"Edwards and I have come to an understanding."

"I never doubted it could be otherwise."

They turned toward the bluff, strolling around the Castle to where Edwards's beloved trees gave way to shrubs and the occasional rose.

"I received a packet from Devil this morning." Gyles broke the companionable silence as they reached the old ramparts and the wide vista of his lands opened before them. "He and Honoria are back in London. He sent the latest parliamentary deliberations of note."

"Is Parliament sitting at present?"

"Yes—the autumn session is under way."

Gyles thought of it—his normal life until now, the ton largely back in residence, the usual round of balls, parties, and the even more important dinners, the jostling of the hostesses for prominence and the more serious discussions that took place behind the glittering facade. For years, that had been the focus of his life.

They paused, looking out over the land, ablaze in autumn's glory.

"Do we need to go to London—for Parliament?"

"No."

He'd thought of it, but not as *we*. He glanced at her, met her eyes briefly, tucked a whipping lock of her hair behind her ear, then looked back at the view.

His aversion to the idea of returning to London alone should have surprised him, yet it hadn't. He was, it seemed, getting used to the fact that, when it came to all matters pertaining to her, his barbarian self ruled. His true self would not be parted from her, would not even consider it.

They stood side by side and he surveyed his domain, then he lowered his arm, closing his hand about hers. "Come. Let's go down to the folly."

*   *   *

Folly indeed.

Later that night, Gyles lay on his back in the dark warmth, and listened to the soft sigh of his wife's breathing.

Hands behind his head, he stared up at the canopy, and wondered what the hell he was doing. Where he thought he was going.

Where *they* were going.

The correction summed up his problem. He could no longer consider the future from his standpoint alone. No matter what tack he took, what frame of reference, she was always in the picture.

In truth, her happiness was now more relevant than his, because his depended on hers.

Was it any wonder he was struggling?

It would have been easier if she'd made demands. Instead, she'd left the choice to him, avoiding the pitfall of setting her will against his. He was conditioned and prepared for such battles; the outcome would have been swift and certain.

And he wouldn't now be lying here, engulfed in uncertainty.

She'd made her position clear. He ruled, he made the decisions—and if she didn't like them, she would go her own way.

He didn't doubt she would. At her core lay a stubborness he recognized, an unswerving devotion to her cause.

A devotion he coveted for himself. Not just for his political ambitions, not just for his marriage, not even for the effect such a devotion would have on his life.

He wanted her devoted to *him*.

Wanted to see it in her eyes as she took him in, feel it in her lips as she kissed him, in her touch as she caressed him. All she gave him now, he wanted—forever.

He glanced at her dark head, felt the warmth of her body, relaxed and boneless against him. Felt an immediate urge to seize, to lock her to him.

Looking back at the canopy, he wrenched his thoughts back to his problem.

He wanted her love, her devotion, wanted her exclusively focused on him. She was prepared to offer him that. In return, she wanted one thing.

He wanted to give it to her—wanted to love her—but . . . that, in and of itself, was the very last thing he wanted to do.

The ultimate contradiction.

There had to be a way around it. For his sanity's sake, he had to find it. Had to find an option that would satisfy her, but still leave him unexposed, emotionally invulnerable.

The alternative was unthinkable. Still was and always would be.

Chapter 13

"*Well, my dear!* Married life clearly agrees with you."

Francesca beamed. On tiptoe, she kissed Charles's cheek, then turned to greet Ester. "I'm so glad you could come. It hasn't been long, I know, but I've missed you."

"And we've missed you, dear." Ester brushed cheeks, then gave way to Franni.

Francesca searched Franni's pale blue eyes; her cousin smiled blithely, stepped forward, and kissed her. Then she looked around. "It's a very big house, isn't it? I didn't see much of it, last time."

They were on the front porch. Charles's traveling coach was being unloaded in the forecourt.

"I'll take you on a tour, if you like." Francesca looked at Ester and Charles, extending the invitation to them all.

"Why not?" Charles turned from shaking hands with Gyles. "I'd enjoy a guided tour about the ancestral home."

"Let's go upstairs and get you settled, then it'll be time for lunch. After that, I'll show you the Castle."

Francesca started to gather Ester and Franni, but Franni slipped aside and went to stand before Gyles. She curtsied deeply. Gyles hesitated, then took her hand and raised her.

Franni looked into his face, and smiled. "Hello, Cousin Gyles."

Gyles nodded. "Cousin Frances." He released her and waved them all inside. Franni joined Francesca and Ester, eagerly looking around her as they traversed the huge hall.

"A *big* house," Franni echoed, as they climbed the stairs.

"So we'll only be here three nights." Charles smiled at Francesca. It was evening, and they were all gathered in the family parlor, waiting for dinner to be announced. "Thank you for being so understanding."

They were standing by the *chaise*. Before the hearth, Gyles was chatting to Ester, with Franni hanging on his every word.

"Nonsense." Francesca squeezed Charles's arm. "If the waters at Bath really do help Franni, then of course you must seize the chance and take her there again." Charles had warned her in a last-minute letter that their visit would be curtailed; he'd just explained why. Bath's sulphurous springs had given Franni more energy, but while Charles and Ester were keen to travel there again, they'd only been able to get Franni to agree by linking the trip to their visit to Lambourn.

"Indeed," Francesca continued, "if you wish to take her there in the future, you must write and let me know. You'll always be welcome here." She smiled. "For however many nights."

"Thank you, my dear." Charles's gaze rested on Franni. "I confess we're more hopeful than previously. Both Ester and I were worried that your leaving and the excitement of the wedding might prove too much, might even precipitate some worsening of Franni's condition. Instead, since recovering from the laudanum the day after the wedding, she seems only to have improved. It's been a relief."

Francesca nodded. She'd never understood the basis of

Franni's "condition," but if Charles and Ester were relieved and hopeful, she could only be glad.

Irving entered and announced that dinner was served, much to Franni's delight. Gyles very correctly offered both her and Ester an arm; Charles and Francesca followed.

They settled about the table in the family dining room. Francesca watched as Irving and the footmen served. Franni seemed delighted with everything. She held forth to Gyles on all she'd seen during their extended excursion around the Castle. Gyles had lunched with them, then retreated to his study; Franni had been unconcerned. Now, beneath her cousin's artlessness, Francesca could detect no sign of unease, sorrow, or upset.

She must have misinterpreted, and Gyles was not Franni's gentleman caller after all.

Charles, on her right, asked about a dish; Francesca replied. She chatted with her uncle and Ester, on her left. Franni sat beyond Charles, to Gyles's left, an arrangement dictated by custom rather than Francesca's wish. But it seemed her worry over her cousin's possible sensibility had been misplaced. If that were so, she was grateful, yet . . .

She turned to Ester. "Does Franni still rise very early?"

Ester nodded. "You might want to warn your staff."

Francesca made a mental note to mention the fact to Wallace.

"My dear, you must give me this recipe so I can take it home for Cook."

"Of course." Francesca wondered if Ferdinand could write in English.

"Good morning, Franni."

At the end of the terrace, Franni whirled, mouth gaping, then she relaxed and smiled as Francesca joined her.

"It's a lovely morning, isn't it?" Francesca said.

"Yes." Franni turned back to the view. "Although it's such a *large* house, it's quiet. I thought it would be noisy."

"There's only the staff and Gyles and me living here at present. Last time, there were all the wedding guests." Francesca leaned against the balustrade, unsurprised when Franni said no more. She let the silence stretch, aware it would help given she wanted to nudge Franni's mind onto a different tack.

Minutes later, she asked, "Franni, do you remember telling me about your gentleman—the gentleman who walked with you twice?"

Franni frowned, puzzled rather than defensive. "Did I?"

"Yes, at the inn. I wondered . . . do you know who he is?"

Her gaze on the horizon, Franni just smiled.

Accepting she wasn't going to get that answer, Francesca tried her next question. "Has he visited you recently—since you last came here?"

Franni shook her head almost violently, but she was grinning; Francesca thought she giggled.

Steeling herself, she spoke slowly and evenly, as they all did when speaking to Franni. "Franni, I just want to make sure you haven't confused your gentleman with Chillingworth. I—"

She broke off as Franni shook her head again, still grinning fit to burst. "No, no, *no!*" Franni swung to face Francesca; her eyes danced—she was almost laughing. "I have it all straight—yes, I do! *My* gentleman has a different name. He comes and walks with me, and listens to me and talks to me. And he's not Chillingworth. No, no, no. Chillingworth's an *earl*. He married you for your land."

A somewhat malicious gleam shone in Franni's blue eyes. "I'm not like you. The earl married you for your land. I don't have the right sort of land, but my gentleman wants to marry me—I'm sure he does."

She swung away and all but skipped along the terrace. "He'll marry me—you'll see. In the end."

Francesca watched her go, then turned inside.

The gentleman wasn't—had never been—Chillingworth. So who was he?

* * *

After breakfast, Franni went walking in the park, a footman trailing after her. After dealing with her household duties, Francesca joined Ester in the family parlor.

Ester looked up from her embroidery with a smile.

Francesca returned it. "I'm glad to have a moment alone with you, Aunt Ester." Crossing to the chair beside the hearth, she sank into it. Ester watched her, brows rising.

"Are you having any problems—"

"No—it's not me." Francesca studied Ester's blue eyes, like Franni's yet so different. "This is difficult, because Franni told me in what might be classed as confidence, except that Franni doesn't think in terms like that."

"No, dear, she doesn't. And if this is something to do with Franni, then yes, you should definitely tell me, confidence or not."

There was such resolve in Ester's voice that Francesca set aside all hesitation. "At the inn on our way to Lambourn . . ."

She recounted all Franni had told her, both at the inn and on the terrace that morning. "I'd worried that it was Chillingworth—he did walk with her twice. But he says he barely spoke a word to her, so it seemed odd she would have made anything of it, but . . ."

"But one never does know with Franni." Ester nodded. "I can see why you thought that, especially with her reaction during the ceremony. But if she says it wasn't him, then . . ."

"Precisely. It could be someone else—someone who's been meeting her when she walks about at Rawlings Hall. It wouldn't be hard to do without being seen. And she will inherit Uncle Charles's property, after all."

"Indeed." Ester's lips had firmed. "My dear, thank you for telling me—you've done exactly right. Leave the matter with me. I'll speak with Charles, and we'll deal with it."

Francesca smiled, sincerely relieved. "Thank you. And I do hope it all turns out well."

Ester made no reply. Frowning, she returned to her embroidery.

"Is this where you hide?"

Startled, Gyles turned. He'd been standing by the window in the library gallery, consulting a list of trials. In the doorway from the inner gallery, Francesca's cousin stood, smiling smugly.

Her gaze had already left him to travel the shelves.

"You have a lot of books."

He watched as she advanced, pirouetting to scan the room.

"There must be thousands and thousands."

"Yes. There are."

She stopped, facing him, head tilted, her gaze distant. After a moment, she said, "It's very quiet up here."

"Yes." When she said nothing more, simply stood gazing vaguely at him, he asked, "Did you enjoy your walk?"

"Yes, but I liked seeing the Castle more. Francesca was naughty—she didn't bring us here."

"There are some places Francesca would consider private."

He might as well have saved his breath; Gyles seriously doubted Frances took in anything she didn't wish to hear.

She stood silently staring straight ahead. Wracking his memory, he recalled their conversations at Rawlings Hall. "We have many trees here."

Her gaze focused on the window. She stepped closer to look. "Are they birches?"

"No. Most are oaks."

"No birches?"

"None close. There are some farther into the park."

"I'll look when I go for my walks."

Clasping her hands behind her back, she settled before the window as if intending to study the treetops. Gyles glanced at the journal in his hands.

"I'm afraid I must leave you—there's work I need to do."
He'd intended doing it here, but his study suddenly seemed a
wiser choice. There were always footmen in the hall; he
made a mental note to tell Wallace he did not wish to be disturbed by their female guests.

Franni nodded, then turned abruptly to face him, meeting
his eyes for the first time.

"Yes," she said, "that might be a good idea." She smiled;
her pale eyes glowed. "It wouldn't do for Francesca to come
up and find us together."

She continued to smile. Gyles studied her for a moment,
then, his expression impassive, stepped back, bowed, and
left her.

The clocks struck four as Francesca reached her bedroom
door—too early to dress for dinner, but she could indulge in
a long soak first. Opening the door, she stepped inside—

Someone was on her bed, sitting in the emerald-draped
shadows.

Then the figure turned, and she recognized the pale hair,
the pale face.

Exhaling, Francesca closed the door and crossed to the
bed. "What are you doing here, Franni?"

She was sitting on the bed, more or less in the middle. She
bounced. "I came in to see. The servants told me I couldn't
come up here, but I knew you wouldn't mind." Lifting the
coverlet, Franni rubbed her cheek against it, then reached
out and trailed her fingers down the silk curtains tied back
about the posts. Then she frowned. "It's so *luxurious.*"

"Chillingworth's mama had it done for me." Francesca sat
on the bed. "Remember? I read her letters to you back at
Rawlings Hall before we came for the wedding."

Franni frowned harder, staring at the emerald coverlet,
then her brows lowered even farther. She glanced at
Francesca. "Does he sleep here with you? In this bed?"

Francesca hesitated, then nodded. "Yes. Of course."

"Why 'of course'? Why does he?"

"Well . . ." She didn't know how much Franni understood, but her pugnacious expression confirmed she wasn't going to let the point slide. "It's necessary for him to sleep with me to beget children."

Franni blinked; the intense expression drained from her face, leaving it even more blank than usual. "Oh."

Another something to mention to Ester. Francesca stood; with an apologetic smile, she gestured to the door. "I'm going to have a bath now, Franni, so you must go."

Franni blinked again, then looked at the door, then she scrambled from the bed.

"Come," Francesca said. "I'll walk you back to the main wing."

Francesca had arranged a small dinner party for that evening, seizing the opportunity to begin entertaining locally, entertaining Charles and Ester in the process.

They gathered in the drawing room to await their guests. Lord and Lady Gilmartin and their offspring arrived first, with Sir Henry and Lady Middlesham close behind. Francesca made the introductions, then left Charles and Ester with the Middleshams while she sat beside Lady Gilmartin and listened to a catalogue of Clarissa's accomplishments. Gyles was chatting to Lord Gilmartin. Franni, meanwhile, had taken an instant interest in Clarissa and was talking at her, rather than with her, nonstop; Clarissa was looking a trifle dazed. Lancelot retired to stand before one window, striking a dramatic pose which singularly failed to attract any attention, everyone else being otherwise engaged.

Lady Elizabeth and Henni, accompanied by Horace in expansive mood, arrived before Francesca wilted under Lady Gilmartin's onslaught; with the round of introductions, the groupings changed.

Sir Henry and Horace, old friends, drew Lord Gilmartin into their circle. Gyles left them to their discussion of coverts. He surveyed the room. His mother had engaged Charles and Ester while Henni had taken Francesca's place beside Lady Gilmartin. Francesca was chatting with Lady Middlesham; as he watched, Clarrisa joined them. Lancelot was brooding by the window. That left . . .

Instinctive self-protection reared its head—

"Good evening, Cousin Gyles. Do you like my gown?"

Franni had circled the room to come up beside him. Gyles turned and briefly scanned her blue muslin gown. "Very nice."

"Yes, it is. Of course, I'll eventually have gowns like Francesca's, all silks and satins—gowns your countess would wear."

"Indeed." Why was it that one minute in Franni's company was enough to make him long to shake free of her and escape?

"I like this house—it's big, but it's comfortable, and your staff seem well trained."

Gyles nodded distantly. She was neither cloying nor snide; she displayed none of the usual behaviors he deplored. His aversion was primitive, instinctive—not easy to explain.

"However, there is one little man I don't like. He wears black, not livery—he wouldn't let me go into your rooms."

"Wallace." Gyles stared at Franni. "No one goes into my rooms except those who have a right to be there."

He spoke slowly, clearly—just like Francesca and Charles did when speaking to this strange young woman.

Her expression turned mutinous. "Is Francesca allowed in?"

"If she wishes, naturally. But I don't think she's been in."

"Well, her room is *beautiful,* all in emerald silk and satin." Franni shot him an unreadable look. "But you'd know that because you sleep in her bed."

This was without question the strangest conversation he'd ever had with a young lady. "Yes." He kept his tone calm and low. "Francesca's my wife, so I sleep in her bed." Looking up, about to search for help, he saw Irving enter the room. "Ah—I believe dinner is served."

She looked and smiled. "Oh, good!" She turned to him, clearly expecting him to offer his arm.

"If you'll excuse me, I must take my aunt in to dinner. Lancelot will lead you in." Gyles beckoned the young man over. He came readily enough, clearly prepared, after his moments of isolation, to be passably agreeable.

Franni's blanked face—so utterly without expression— remained in Gyles's mind as, with Henni on his arm, he led the procession into the dining room. Inwardly, he heaped praises on his wife's dark head. With the extra guests at table, Franni would be seated somewhere in the middle, well away from him.

As he handed Henni to the chair beside his, he murmured, "Charles's daughter, Frances—what do you make of her?"

"Haven't had much chance to form an opinion." Henni glanced down the table to where Franni sat.

"When you do, let me know."

Henni raised a brow at him.

Gyles shook his head and turned to greet Lady Middlesham on his other side.

The ritual of the port which he deliberately prolonged, not a difficult feat given the conversational abilities of Horace, Sir Henry, and even Lord Gilmartin in such an amiable setting, saved Gyles from having to deal with Francesca's cousin in the drawing room. Even so, he wasn't blind to the eager look in Franni's eye when he led the gentlemen back in just ahead of the tea trolley. Nor to the fact that her look turned to one of confusion, then frustration as the disparate groups gathered to chat over the teacups.

When their guests rose to take their leave, he held to

Francesca's side, taking refuge in the dictates of formality. As they moved into the hall, Ester paused beside Francesca and whispered in her ear. Francesca nodded and smiled. Over the melee as Irving and the footmen brought coats and scarves, Gyles saw Ester draw Franni up the stairs.

He was conscious of relaxing his guard, smiling as he shook hands and exchanged farewells, eventually braving the chill outside with Francesca to wave the carriages off.

Charles was waiting when they reentered the hall. He took Francesca's hands. "That was a most enjoyable evening. Thank you." He kissed her cheek. "It's been such a long time since we've entertained . . . well." He stepped back, and they turned and started up the stairs. "I'd almost forgotten what it was like. How pleasant such an evening can be."

Francesca's smile was radiant. "There's no reason you couldn't entertain on a similar scale at Rawlings Hall. Franni seemed to enjoy it."

Charles nodded. "Indeed. I'll speak to Ester about it." He halted at the top of the stairs. "Who knows? It might be a good thing all around."

With a nod and a "good night," he left them.

His hand at her back, Gyles steered Francesca to their private wing, listening to her happy chatter.

Francesca slipped from the warmth of Gyles's arms as early as she could the next morning, but she wasn't early enough to catch up with Franni before she left the house.

Tugging her shawl about her shoulders, Francesca stepped onto the terrace overlooking the Castle's gardens. The air was crisp and chilly, but the sun shone and the birds sang; the day beckoned.

Strolling to the steps, she descended to the lawns. Searching for Franni, she walked to the rampart, then descended to the lower level and her favorite seat. She didn't sit, but lingered long enough to drink in the view, drink in the fact that this land—his land—now felt like home to her.

Pondering that, she returned to the lawns and started walking a wide circle around the house. Wallace had said Franni had gone walking; she would be somewhere close.

Reaching the lawns before the stables, Francesca saw a figure in cambric striding along under the trees. Franni's carriage was distinctive, stiff, slightly jerky. She had a thick shawl wrapped about her, making her appear peculiarly bulky above the waist. Francesca set out on an intersecting course. Franni saw her as she drew near.

"Are you enjoying the morning?" she called.

Franni smiled with her usual hint of secretiveness. "Yes. It's been a lovely morning so far."

"Have you been looking at the horses?"

Joining her, Francesca walked beside her.

"They're big—bigger than Papa's. Do you ride them?"

"No. Gyles gave me an Arab mare for a wedding gift. I ride her, now."

"Did he?" Franni's expression blanked, then she murmured, "Do you?" A slow smile suffused her face. "That's good. I expect she gallops fast."

"Yes, she does." Francesca was inured to Franni's fluctuating moods.

"So you ride every day?"

"Most days. Not necessarily every day."

"Good. Good." Nodding, Franni paced beside Francesca, her strides longer, rather mannish.

They walked on in silence until they reached the boundary where the park met the nearest fields. Francesca turned back.

Franni kept walking, veering toward the track that led between the fields.

Francesca halted. "Franni?" With an impatient shake of her head, Franni kept walking. "Franni, there's nothing but fields that way." When Franni didn't slow, she added, "Breakfast will be served soon."

Without looking back, Franni waved. "I want to walk up

here a little way. I want to walk alone. I'll come back soon."

Nothing of any possible danger lay between the house and the escarpment. Francesca doubted Franni would go far up the steep track.

Turning, she started back to the house. Franni would be safe enough—and if she hadn't returned within the hour, she'd send a groom after her. Meanwhile, thanks to her husband's penchant for games at dawn, her stomach was growling. Breakfast sounded like a very good idea.

Over breakfast, Francesca, Charles, and Ester agreed to walk across the park to visit at the Dower House. Lady Elizabeth had issued the invitation last night.

Francesca looked up the table and raised a brow at Gyles. He shook his head. He needed to get on with his researching—what better time than with the house to himself?

Ester turned to Franni, who had recently joined them. "You'll like to see the Dower House. Remember? We passed it when we drove through the gates."

Franni's expression was blank, as if she'd gone within in search of the memory. Slowly, she shook her head. "I don't want to go. I'll stay here."

Charles leaned across and laid his hand over Franni's. "You'll enjoy the walk across the park under the trees."

Franni shook her head. Her face took on a mulish cast Charles, Ester, and Francesca knew well. "No. I'll stay here."

Charles eased back, glancing at Ester and Francesca. Francesca smiled reassuringly. She looked at Franni. "That's quite all right. You can stay here by all means, but if you should go walking, do remember to take a footman, just in case you get lost."

Franni blinked at her, then nodded and went back to her kedgeree.

Ester sighed. Francesca turned to her. "How soon shall we leave?"

Charles drained his coffee cup. "Give me five minutes to change my coat."

"You may take ten." Ester pushed back her chair. "I must change into a walking dress, and Francesca will want to do the same."

The three of them rose and left the breakfast parlor. Gyles strolled out with them. Reaching the top of the stairs, Francesca glanced back and saw Gyles hesitating in the hall, looking back at the breakfast parlor. Then he swung on his heel and walked to his study.

Ten minutes later, she, Charles, and Ester descended the front steps and strolled onto the forecourt.

"What a lovely arrangement of trees." Ester studied the six pencil pines set in mirror image on either side of the drive. "And those troughs set the whole off wonderfully. Such lovely old things."

Francesca's inner smile was wider than the one on her lips. The troughs had been disinterred without mishap and had cleaned up remarkably well. "Autumn crocuses are so pretty massed like that."

Behind them, the front door opened, then shut. They all looked around.

Gyles came down the steps, then strode up.

Francesca blinked. "I thought you were busy."

Gyles smiled charmingly, knowing that while he would fool Charles and Ester, his wife was immune to his wiles. "It's such a glorious day, and we won't have many more. The chance of a walk was too good to pass up, and there's one or two points I want to check with Horace, so duty can, in this instance, justifiably bow to inclination."

Charles and Ester accepted his excuse readily. Francesca studied his eyes, but refrained from asking the questions he could see forming in hers. He offered his arm, and she took it. Charles offered his to Ester, and they headed off beneath the nearly bare branches.

They passed a comfortable morning with Lady Elizabeth,

Henni, and Horace, then returned through the park in time for lunch. Franni didn't join them.

"She's sleeping," Ester reported as she took her seat at the table.

"Just as well," Charles returned. "She's been walking here even more than she does at home. Although she enjoys it, we'll be leaving tomorrow, so it's all to the good if she rests."

During the meal, Charles and Gyles discussed estate matters while Francesca caught up with the news from Rawlings Hall.

"I could do with a nap myself," Ester confided to Francesca as they left the dining room. "I find it hard to sleep in a rocking coach, and it'll be a long drive to Bath tomorrow."

Francesca watched Ester climb the stairs. In the hall behind her, she heard Gyles giving instructions to Edwards, who had presented himself at Gyles's request. Charles wished to view the succession houses. Francesca turned to see her uncle stride off with Edwards. She met her husband's eye as he turned her way. She smiled, then turned toward the family parlor.

His hand closed about her arm and she halted. His grip eased; his fingers trailed down to tangle with hers. Surprised, she turned to face him.

His eyes held hers, then he said, "I wondered . . . if you haven't anything pressing, would you help me with my research?"

She tried to keep her heart from leaping, or at least keep the fact from showing. "Your parliamentary research?"

"There's a hundred references to check and cross-check. If you're not busy . . . ?"

She smiled, aware that his fingers had already closed firmly about hers. "I'm not busy. I'll be happy to help."

She spent the entire afternoon with him. He had a list of books with notes on what he needed from each one. They worked down the list, book by book, Gyles at his desk, reading and taking notes, while she searched for the next volume or, having found it, sat in a chair beside the desk and located the information he was after.

When he finished a book, she'd exchange it for the next, pointing out the relevant text. He'd accept the new book and start reading while she returned the previous volume to its shelf. In the first few exchanges, he read the entire section, but thereafter she noted he focused only on the passage she indicated. She inwardly smiled. Their researching went faster.

Charles looked in a few hours later. He saw what they were about and asked after Gyles's interest. An amicable discussion ensued, which lasted until Ester, fresh from her nap, joined them, and it was time for afternoon tea.

Francesca rang and instructed Wallace to serve them in the library.

"Franni?" she asked, looking at Ester.

"She's awake but dozy—you know how she gets. Happy as a lark, but she wants nothing more than to loll in her bed. Ginny's with her, and knows to get her ready for dinner, so all's well."

Ginny was Franni's old maid. She'd been Franni's nurse and was devoted to her charge. Given Francesca had not been with them in the coach this time, Ginny had been brought to help with Franni, who was not easy over having maids she didn't know attend her.

Francesca poured the tea. They all sat and sipped. The afternoon passed in easy contentment.

"Maria vergine! Impossibile!"

Gyles was in his room dressing for dinner; he heard the exclamations and the spate of frenzied Italian that followed them, delivered in a definitely masculine voice.

Wallace, holding Gyles's cravat, stilled. "Ferdinand." He laid aside the linen band. "I'll remove him immediately."

"No." Gyles stayed Wallace with an upraised hand; although he couldn't hear her words, he could hear Francesca speaking. "Stay here."

Gyles crossed to the door leading to Francesca's bedchamber. Opening it, he saw Millie standing in the middle of the room, staring at the open door leading to Francesca's sitting room, through which another tirade of frantic Italian rolled forth.

Millie started as Gyles entered the room. He ignored her and crossed to the open door.

In the middle of her sitting room, Francesca stood wrapped in a dressing robe, arms folded, and waited for Ferdinand to run out of breath.

When he did, and paused, she spoke in a tone that effectively put an end to his hopes. "You're supposedly an experienced chef. It's beyond my comprehension that you are, so you say, unable to place a meal of any merit on the table before eight o'clock, despite having been warned this morning that dinner tonight will be at seven."

He answered with another torrent of Italian; once she caught his gist, she silenced him with an upraised hand.

Her expression severe, she studied him, then nodded. "Very well, if you are unable to perform your duties, Cook will take charge. I'm sure she'll manage to feed your master in appropriate fashion at seven o'clock."

"*No!* You *cannot*—" Ferdinand choked back the words. "*Bellisima,* I beg . . ."

Francesca let him prattle a little more, then cut him off with a slash of her hand. "Enough! If you're half the chef you believe yourself, you'll have a magnificent meal ready to serve"—she glanced at the clock on the mantelshelf—"in one hour." Looking back at Ferdinand, she waved to the door. "Now go! And one thing. Do not again seek me out here. If you wish to speak with me, you will consult with Wallace, as is proper. I will not have you disrupting my husband's household in any way—you are living in England

and must abide by English ways. Now, go. Go!" With an intensely Italian gesture, she shooed him away.

Cast down, Ferdinand slunk off, closing the door behind him.

Francesca regarded the door, then nodded. Swinging around, she headed back to her bedchamber, loosening her robe as she went. She approached the doorway—only then did she realize Gyles was standing in it.

Rapidly replaying Ferdinand's more impassioned passages, Francesca inwardly winced. No need to look too far for the reason behind her husband's stony countenance. He understood Italian well enough to have translated the worst of Ferdinand's histrionics.

Gyles's gaze, hard as granite, had moved past her.

"I could send him back to London." His gaze returned to her face. "If you wish . . ."

She tilted her head and considered. Considered the fact Ferdinand had unknowingly put his continued employment in jeopardy. Considered the revelation that her husband was an exceedingly jealous man. His gaze hadn't even lowered despite the fact her robe had slithered open and she was wearing only a thin chemise beneath.

She shook her head. "No. If you're to wield influence in political circles, then we'll need to host dinners and for that, Ferdinand's skills will be helpful. It's best he gets used to us making unexpected demands now, here, rather than later in London."

Gyles's gaze remained on her face. His expression softened not at all, but she got the impression she'd said something right—enough to appease the possessiveness prowling behind his eyes. Then he inclined his head. "If you believe he's capable of adapting, he may stay."

She stepped forward. His gaze drifted lower, a warm caress over her breasts, stomach and bare legs.

He stepped back and let her walk past him. His gaze flicked to Millie. "One thing." His voice was pitched so only she could hear. He met her gaze as she turned. "He is not again to come into this wing."

"You heard all I said?"

He nodded.

"Then you know he will not."

He held her gaze for an instant longer, then nodded curtly. He looked at Millie. "I'll let you finish dressing."

Gyles sat at the head of his dining table, Henni on his left, Ester on his right, and tried to keep his mind on their conversation. Tried to keep his gaze from straying to his wife, glorious in teal silk at the table's other end. Tried to keep his mind from dwelling on the scene he'd witnessed in her sitting room.

He'd been unprepared for the possessiveness that had roared through him, powerful, forceful, and unsettling. Equally unprepared for her calmness, her cool head in dealing with the Italian, for the rock-solid, unwavering loyalty he'd sensed behind her words.

Was that what love meant? What having her love would mean—never having to worry, to wonder, to consider where her loyalties might lie?

He tried to wrench his mind away but couldn't. He answered a question from Henni absentmindedly, unable to take his mental eyes from the prize.

She'd talked in terms of "we" and "us." She'd done so instinctively, without calculation—that was how she truly thought, how she saw them, their lives.

The barbarian within wanted that, wanted to seize the prize and gloat, while the gentleman had convinced himself he'd never desire any such thing at all.

"Gyles, stop woolgathering."

He focused, and quickly came to his feet as Henni and Ester, along with the other ladies, rose.

Henni grinned. She patted his arm as she turned away. "Don't dally so long over the port this time. I have an answer to your question."

* * *

The only question Gyles could recall was his wish to know Henni's opinion of Franni. That wasn't incentive enough to make him cut short his time in the comfortable company of Charles and Horace and rush to the drawing room, where he would once gain be exposed to Franni's disturbing presence.

No one else seemed to find her disturbing—odd and awkward, yes, but not unsettling.

After forty minutes, he drained his glass and bowed to the inevitable.

From the drawing room's threshold, he scanned the assembled ladies and located Francesca talking to Henni by the hearth. Charles and Horace ambled over to join Lady Elizabeth and Ester who were sitting on the *chaise*.

Franni was in an armchair beside Ester; Gyles felt her pale blue gaze as he strolled to Francesca's side but gave no sign he was aware of her.

"Well! There you are!" Henni turned to Francesca. "You'll have to take him in hand, my dear—that was far too long over the port for just a family gathering." Henni shook her head disapprovingly. "We can't have him developing bad habits." She patted Francesca's hand and moved to join those about the *chaise*.

Gyles watched her go, then met Francesca's emerald eyes. "Do you intend taking me in hand, madam?"

She held his gaze, then her lips curved. Her lashes fell as she leaned closer, her voice lowering to the smoky, sultry sound that shot heat straight to his loins. "I take you in hand every night, my lord." She looked into his eyes, then arched a brow. "But perhaps, tonight, you should remind me. I wouldn't want you developing bad habits."

His fingers had found hers, stroking across her palm. He raised her hand to his lips. "Rest assured I'll remind you. There's a habit or two you might like to try."

Her brows rose in artful consideration, then she turned as Horace joined them. Gyles learned it was Horace who'd told

Francesca where the urns and troughs from the forecourt had been hidden. Watching her charm his uncle, he had to admire her skill—Horace was not at all susceptible, yet he was very willing to extend himself for Francesca.

The action of glancing about the room, scanning his guests, was purely reflexive. Everyone was chatting, all except Franni. Gyles's gaze stopped on her; he'd expected her to be bored, possibly frowning. Instead . . .

She was smug, there was no other word for it. She was all but hugging herself with smirking satisfaction. Her gaze was on him and Francesca, but she wasn't really seeing—she hadn't realized he was watching her. Her lips were curved in a peculiar, distant smile. Her whole expression spoke of far-away thoughts and pleasurable imaginings.

Gyles stepped closer to Francesca. Franni's smugness increased. She was, very definitely, watching them.

Frances Rawlings was an exceedingly strange woman.

Horace turned to Gyles. "How's the bridge going?"

Francesca listened to Gyles's reply, then squeezed his fingers, slid her hand free, and strolled over to Franni.

"Are you all right?" With a swish of silk skirts, she sat on the arm of Franni's chair.

"Yes!" Franni sat back, smiling. "I've had a lovely visit. I'm sure we'll come more often, now."

Francesa smiled back. She turned the conversation to Rawlings Hall, avoiding all mention of Bath.

Charles and Ester joined them; Francesca stood so they could speak more easily. Then Ester sat on the chair arm the better to talk to Franni. Charles laid a hand on Francesca's arm. She turned to him.

"My dear, it's been such an enjoyable stay. I have to say it's made me feel thoroughly vindicated in urging you to accept Chillingworth's offer. Seeing you so settled has set my mind at rest."

Francesca smiled. "I'm happy, and very glad you came

and got to know Lady Elizabeth, Henni, and Horace—we're all related, after all."

"Indeed. It's a pity we're so out of touch."

Francesca said nothing of her plans, her familial aims. Time enough when she'd set them in train. But she was sincerely happy and relieved by how well the visit had gone. It was, in a way, the first feather in her social cap.

Ester stood, and the conversation veered to their journey the next day. Franni made a querulous comment over the detour to Bath; Charles sat on the end of the *chaise* to reassure her.

Ester raised a brow at Francesca, then murmured, "I do hope she won't refuse to drink the waters when we get there."

"Do they really help her?"

Ester regarded Franni, then quietly said, "Franni's very like her mother . . . as you know, Elise died. We can't be sure, yet, but Charles lives in hope."

Before Francesca could frame her next question, Ester said, "I haven't yet told Charles about Franni's gentleman. I will once we reach home. No need to worry before that. But I did speak with Franni, and she told me he exists, but he's definitely not Chillingworth." Ester met Francesca's eyes. "That must have been so unsettling for you—I'm glad we've sorted that much out."

Francesca nodded. "You'll write and let me know. . . ."

"Of course." Ester looked again at Franni, at Charles leaning close, speaking slowly and evenly. "She has improved, you know." After another moment, she softly said, "Who can say? Perhaps the cloud will pass."

The tone of Ester's voice, vulnerability mixed with sadness, made Francesca swallow her questions.

At the other end of the *chaise*, Gyles drew Henni aside. "Now, cut line. What answer do you have for me."

Henni glanced to where Franni sat slumped in the armchair, Charles hovering over her. "She's odd."

"I know," Gyles replied pointedly.

"I'd be tempted to say she's softheaded, or to use a vulgar but appropriate term, dicked in the nob, yet that's not quite it. She's perfectly lucid if a little simple, yet, after talking to her for a while, you look into those eyes and wonder if she's truly there, and who it is you've been talking to."

"She seems . . . innocuous enough."

"Oh, entirely—not *dangerous* in any way. It's more a case of not being at home." Henni looked at Francesca. "There's nothing like it on the Rawlings side—Frances must have got it from her mother, although Ester is as rational as you please." Henni glanced at Gyles. "We've never been any-thing but *hard*headed on our side of the family, and from all I ever heard of Francesca's mother, she was a strong-willed woman—too strong-willed for old Francis Rawlings to cow. No need to think any of Frances's traits will come into this arm of the family via Francesca."

Gyles blinked. He looked at Francesca, now exchanging gossip with his mother. "That never occurred to me." After a moment, his gaze still on Francesca, he murmured, "There's no element of her behavior I wish to change."

From the corner of his eye, he saw Henni grin. She patted his arm and gruffly said, "Horace keeps on about you being a lucky dog—for what it's worth, I agree with him."

Gyles looked down at her. "Thank you for your opinion."

Henni opened her eyes at him. "Which one?"

Gyles smiled. He stepped forward, drawing Henni with him, returning to the general conversations. He moved to Charles's side, to share a few companionable words, ignor-ing Franni's wide gaze.

They were leaving tomorrow morning; for Francesca's sake, he would bear with Franni's oddity for one last hour.

Chapter 14

The next morning, they waved their guests away. As Charles's carriage rounded the bend in the drive, Francesca sighed. Gyles glanced at her, pleased the sigh had been a contented one.

"I was thinking of riding out to check on the bridge." He waited until she looked up and met his eyes to ask, "Would you like to come?"

He'd wanted to see anticipation flare in her eyes; he wasn't disappointed. But then she grimaced; the light faded. "No—not today. I've accomplished so little in the last three days, I need to catch up. The Harvest Festival's only a week away, and I do so want everything to be perfect."

He hesitated, then said, "I don't need to check the bridge today—is there anything I can do to help?"

Disappointment vanished from her eyes. Smiling, she linked her arm through his, looking down as they turned back into the house. "If you would exercise your memory and tell me all you can remember of the day—what happened, when, and so on—it would be a great help. Cook knows some things, Mrs. Cantle knows others, and your mother and aunt remember still other bits, but I can't find anyone who remembers the day as a child." She glanced at him. "But you must. We have so many children on the estate, I want the day to be filled for them, too."

"If it's not, we'll be fishing them out of the pond and the fountain. That's what always happened when the younger crew got bored."

"Being wet at this time of year isn't wise, so we must ensure the younger ones aren't bored."

"Being wet never hurt me." Gyles steered her to his study.

"That," she declared as she swept over the threshold, "is not what your mother said."

They spent the rest of the day organizing their Harvest Festival—the first for twenty-eight years. Gyles recounted his memories, then they added the events mentioned by Lady Elizabeth, Henni, and Horace.

After lunch, they called in Wallace and Irving, Mrs. Cantle and Cook. By late afternoon, they had a battle plan.

Gyles sat in an armchair and watched Francesca, the general, seated behind his desk, outline her campaign. Their troops were ranged about the room on chairs, nodding, occasionally putting in a suggestion or correction. The enthusiasm swirling about the room was palpable.

"I know where we can get the right-size barrels for the bobbing," Irving volunteered.

Wallace nodded. "And we'll need to speak with Harris about the ale."

"Yes indeed." Francesca scribbled a note. "Now, Cook— you advise we get pasties from Mrs. Duckett?"

"Aye—my bread's as good as hers, but no one hereabouts has a hand for pastry like Duckett. And she'll be thrilled to be doing it again, too."

"Very good." Francesca scribbled on, then looked up. "Now, is there anything we've forgotten?"

They all shook their heads. Lips twisting, Gyles volunteered, "Edwards."

They all stilled, all exchanged glances, then Wallace

cleared his throat. "If you would leave Edwards to me and Mrs. Cantle, ma'am, I believe we can sort out all the arrangements without creating any undue disturbance."

Francesca looked down to hide her smile. "Indeed, that might be best. Very well." Laying down her pen, she looked at them all. "That's it—if we all do our parts, I'm sure it will be a wonderful, most memorable day."

"Wake up, sleepyhead."

Francesca snuggled deeper under her satin covers and tried to will away the hand curving about her shoulder, gently shaking her.

"It's past eight and the morning's clear," a familiar voice murmured in her ear. "Come riding with me."

She frowned. "We already did—didn't we?"

He laughed, his chest to her back, rocking her. "I mean on the downs, on Regina. She must be missing your runs."

"Oh." Wriggling up, Francesca pushed her hair back. Gyles was lounging on her bed, already dressed but without cravat or coat. Sitting straighter, she peered past him to the window. "Is it really fine?"

"As fine as we're going to get at this time of year." Rising and heading for his room, he threw her a challenging look. "Come on."

Francesca struggled out of bed. By the time Millie had appeared with her water and she'd washed and climbed into her habit, the anticipation of a rousing gallop had stirred her blood. Millie had left her crop and gloves on the bed; she swiped them up and looked about. "My cap?"

Millie's head was buried in the wardrobe. "I *know* it was here with the whip and gloves, but I can't find it."

Francesca heard striding footsteps in the corridor, then a tap sounded on her door. "Never mind. You can hunt it out later."

Gyles was waiting in the corridor. His gaze raked her as she emerged, then returned to her hair.

"We can't find it at the moment."

He waved her on, then fell in beside her, his gaze drifting again to her uncovered head. "I have to admit I've got used to that flirting feather."

She threw him a grin and started down the stairs. "I don't need a feather."

He caught her gaze, and stepped down in her wake. "Neither do I."

They reached the stable yard to find Gyles's grey saddled and held waiting, but no sign of Regina. They entered the stable and headed for the mare's stall, from which Jacob's voice could be heard, crooning.

He heard them coming and stepped out. "Don't ask me how it happened, but she picked up a stone. Wedged tight in her rear hoof it was, poor lamb. I just got it out." He showed them the small, sharp rock.

Gyles frowned. "How could that happen? She couldn't have been put into the stall without someone noticing."

"Aye—but there it is, plain as day." Jacobs shook his head. "All I can think is some rascally lad didn't take enough care and a stone got lobbed in with the straw. I'll be speaking with them, you may be sure, but for now, I'm right sorry, ma'am, but the mare's not for riding."

Francesca had gone into the stall to inspect her darling; she nodded and came out again. "No—you're quite right. That hoof's obviously tender."

Jacobs looked uncomfortable; he glanced from her to Gyles. "I'm not sure we've another mount suitable, ma'am."

Francesca scanned the huge hunters, then arched a brow at Gyles.

He sighed. "If you promise not to go tearing off, faster than the wind over the downs, then I suppose, seeing I'll be with you—"

"Thank you." Francesca gifted him with a glorious smile, then turned it on Jacobs. "That one, I think."

Gyles glanced at the black she'd selected, then nodded,

ignoring Jacobs's stunned look. "Wizard's at least reasonably biddable."

Francesca pulled a face at him. They walked back out to the yard. In a minute, Jacobs, still looking unsure, walked the black out.

His hand at her waist, Gyles urged Francesca forward. She stopped by the black's side and he lifted her to the saddle. Jacobs held the horse steady while she got settled. Gyles mounted and picked up his reins, glanced at the small figure perched atop the massive hunter, then wheeled. She brought the black alongside as they trotted out of the yard.

"Is it possible to ride through the village, then up to the downs that way?"

"Yes." He glanced at her. "Why?"

"We need to speak with Mrs. Duckett and Harris about the supplies for the Festival—I thought we might kill two birds with one stone."

He nodded. Instead of taking the track to the escarpment, he led the way along a ride that circled the house, running under the trees of the park to eventually join the main drive.

When they slowed and clattered through the main gates, Francesca laughed. "That's a lovely gallop."

They trotted on to the village.

Francesca went into the bakery to speak with Mrs. Duckett. Gyles strode down to the Red Pigeon, arranged the supply of ale with Harris, then returned to liberate Francesca from Mrs. Duckett's clutches, that lady having been as honored and delighted as Cook had predicted.

Both once more in the saddle, Gyles led the way up the street to the church. A path to the downs lay beyond it. Five minutes later, they crested the escarpment, the horses stepping into the wide, treeless expanse with evident anticipation.

The black pranced; Francesca held the big gelding back, waiting, watching for Gyles's direction. He glanced her way. "Any preference?"

A fleeting recollection popped into her head. "What about those barrows Lancelot Gilmartin mentioned? They must be close."

"A few miles." Gyles studied her, then added, "I wouldn't, myself, term them romantic."

"Well, you may take me there and let me see for myself." Francesca looked around as the black jigged impatiently. "Which way?"

"North."

Gyles sprang the grey and she went with him. Shoulder to shoulder, the huge hunters thundered across the rolling green. The wind of their passing whipped back Francesca's curls; exhilaration sang in her veins.

The sky was slate grey and no sun shone, yet there was a glow in her heart as they swept on. Again and again, she felt Gyles's gaze, on her face, her hands, checking her posture. This was no race; although they rode hard, the gallop was severely controlled, judged to a whisker so as not to feel restricted—an indulgence, yes, one held just within the limits of safety.

It was comforting to feel so watched over, to know that he was there, with her.

They gained the top of a low rise and he slowed. She followed suit, drawing the black in. The gelding was still frisky, still wanting to run. She patted his glossy neck as she trotted up to Gyles.

He nodded ahead. "See those mounds?"

She saw a cluster of earth mounds about a mile further on. "Is that it?"

"I'm afraid so."

His tone alerted her; she looked and found him gazing at a point much nearer to hand. Another rider, previously hidden in a dip, came riding toward them.

"Lancelot Gilmartin?"

"Indeed."

Lancelot had seen them. They waited. Gyles steadied his

grey as Lancelot came pounding up. Pounding too furiously. He hauled his bay to a too-precipitous halt. It snorted, backed, reared.

The black jerked and sidled; Francesca's arms were tugged sharply as he shook his head.

Gyles angled the grey closer. The presence of the more experienced horse calmed the black.

By then, Lancelot had his showy bay under control. "Lady Chillingworth." He swept her a bow, then nodded at Gyles. "My lord." Before either could reply, his glowing gaze locked on Francesca's face. "I knew you wouldn't resist the lure of the Barrows. I was on my way there when I saw you and turned back." He glanced at Gyles. "My lord, I would be happy to escort her ladyship farther. No doubt you have much business to attend to."

Francesca jumped in before Gyles could annihilate Lancelot. "Mr. Gilmartin, you misunderstand. I really couldn't presume—"

"Oh, nonsense. I insist. Tell you what, I'll race you."

Lancelot wheeled the fractious bay to come alongside— the horse stumbled sideways. Rumps bumped, Lancelot's mount jarring the increasingly nervous black, bumping it into Gyles's grey.

"No!" Francesca felt a tremor of panic rush through the black, felt the bunching of powerful muscles beneath her. "Hold steady," she snapped at Lancelot.

The bay had other ideas. It reared and lashed out. Lancelot was nearly unseated. His left arm flailed—his crop came down hard on the black's rump.

The black shot into a gallop.

Gyles lunged for the reins and missed. One glance at Francesca bobbing awkwardly on the black's back was enough. She was unbalanced and heading for a fall.

Cursing freely, he flicked a scorching glance at Lancelot. "You *blasted fool!*" He set the grey after the black, leaving Lancelot still struggling with his mount.

Gyles didn't spare another thought for Lancelot, not even for retribution, not for anything beyond the small figure bouncing as she struggled to retain her seat. Sidesaddle, she had no room for error on a hunter. Jouncing as she was, she had no hope of controlling such a strong beast. The downs thereabouts were uneven—the horse's pounding strides would jar all the way through her, wrenching her arms, weakening her hold on the reins.

Until she fell.

Gyles refused to think of it—to think of the occasional rock embedded in the sward. Refused to remember his father, lying so still on the ground.

Shutting his mind, he gave chase. And prayed she'd have the wit and the strength to hang on.

Francesca gritted her teeth, vainly trying to stop her breath being slammed out of her with every stride the black took. She'd had a plan in case one of Charles's hunters ever did run away with her: hang on until the horse tired. All very well in the forest, where the paths were flat but twisting, slowing a horse, tiring it quickly. Here on the open downs, the black was just getting into his stride—he could run without restriction.

The dips and folds meant little to the horse; they meant much more to her. Her arms felt like they were being wrenched from their sockets and still the horse flew. Only her boot firm in the stirrup and her leg locked around the saddlebow allowed her to keep her seat.

She wouldn't be able to do so much longer.

The thought crystallized in her mind. In that instant, she heard the heavy thud of hooves behind her, closing, slowly closing.

Gyles.

She locked her fingers more firmly on the reins, tried to balance her weight, to ease the jolts that with every stride were shaking her like a rag doll.

She could no longer draw a full breath—her lungs had forgotten how. Panic clawed at the back of her throat. Heat rushed up her nape.

Glancing ahead, she saw a series of folds lying like shadows over the green. Up and down, up and down—she'd never make it. Never retain her seat through that.

The grey was still closing. She couldn't risk a glance back to see.

Dragging in a breath, she threw what little strength she had left into hauling back on the reins. In vain. The black had his head down, and she didn't have the strength to fight him.

The grey's head drew alongside.

"Kick your feet free—*now!*"

She heard Gyles's command—pushed aside the thought that with her feet free, she'd surely fall—and did as he said.

In the instant her boots cleared the leather, she felt his arm around her waist, felt him seize her. She dropped the reins and pushed away from the saddle. Reached for him.

He lifted her, swung her over, pulled her to him.

She grabbed, clung, sobbed as she held fast, hands fisting in his shirt. She curled herself into him, pressed herself to him, her cheek to his chest, her boots and skirts flowing over one hard thigh.

Safe.

Gyles slowed the grey gradually—no showy abrupt halt that might dislodge Francesca. All he wanted was to hold her and let the reality of her safety sink into his bones. Let his panic and fear subside and sink back behind his defenses again.

Again. Only this time had been much worse.

She was still breathing brokenly when he halted the grey; she was shaking with shock, as was he. He wrapped his arms around her, set his cheek to her hair, and held her, then he tightened his arms briefly before easing his hold and trying to look into her face—

"I say!" Lancelot skidded his horse to a halt beside them. "Is everything all right?"

Gyles lifted his head. "*You witless oaf!* If you had an ounce of brain to your name—"

Francesca listened. Gyles's tone scorned, his words lashed. She agreed with every one. She was grateful he was there to deliver them, because she didn't have the strength, the breath, to do the occasion justice. She concentrated on breathing, on listening to her heart, and his, slow. Concentrated on the fact that they were both still whole. Still together.

As the tremors racking her faded, she shifted her head, registering the drift of Gyles's tirade, approving his tack—that of the sense and responsibility Lancelot should have shown, that instead he'd been grossly irresponsible, that through silly, childish behavior, he'd placed her at considerable risk.

She glanced at Lancelot—and realized Gyles's comments, pointed though they were, were glancing off Lancelot's self-conceit.

He waited for Gyles to cease speaking, then contemptuously waved. "Yes, very well, but I didn't mean it to happen. Lady Chillingworth knows I didn't. And it's not as if she got hurt."

Francesca raised her head. "I'm unhurt because Lord Chillingworth was with me. If he hadn't been, courtesy of your stupidity, I might well be *dead!*"

Lancelot paled. Francesca continued, "You're a *child*, Lancelot—you play at being an adult, but it's all a mask, a pose." She waved at the rise from which they'd come. "Back there, you heard only what you wanted to hear and behaved like the spoiled brat you are. Now, again, you're doing the same, thinking our words beneath your consideration.

"You're *wrong*. Behavior matters. Who you really are behind the mask *matters*. You will never succeed in life, let alone the ton, until you pay attention to what is, rather than playing an affected charade." She gestured dismissively. "Now begone! I do not wish to set eyes on you again, not until you gain in maturity."

His face another mask, this one more fragile than his usual Byronic imitation, Lancelot gathered his reins.

"One word of warning." Gyles's tone was a warning in it-self. "Do not attempt to call at the Castle until I, or my wife, give you leave."

Lancelot glanced at Gyles. And blanched. He bowed, wheeled his horse circumspectly, and cantered off.

Francesca blew out a breath and dropped her head back against Gyles's chest. "He is brainless, that one."

"I fear so." For a long moment, they simply sat and let time pass. Then Gyles said, "Incidentally, you will not again ride one of my hunters."

Francesca leaned back to look into his face. "I have no wish to ride any of your hunters *ever again*."

Gyles humphed. "We'll have to get you a second mount."

"No—Regina is enough. I'll likely ride less than every day, so if we have another horse just for me, someone else will have to exercise her." She wriggled around to sit facing forward between Gyles's thighs.

"Are you sure?"

"Yes. Now what do we do about the black?"

"He'll come in by himself. If he hasn't returned in an hour, Jacobs'll send out a groom." One arm locked about Francesca's waist, Gyles set the grey cantering back to the escarpment.

They said nothing as they crossed the rolling downs, then headed down a track that joined the road close by the Castle's gates. When they turned into the park and the trees closed about them, Gyles let the grey walk. Leaves crunched under its heavy hooves. Above them, bare branches formed a skeletal canopy against the grey sky.

He should have felt shaken to his core. Instead, he felt

victorious, deeply content with his wife safe and warm in his arms. He glanced down at her face, studied her profile. "Are you sure you're all right?"

She glanced up, emerald eyes wide, then she smiled. "I was frightened and shaken, but now . . ." Her smile deepened. Lifting a hand to his cheek, she turned in his arms and drew his lips to hers. She kissed him, gently, long and lingeringly. Then she drew back and looked into his eyes. "Thank you for saving me."

He smiled. Looking ahead, he steered the grey toward the stable.

The next morning, Gyles went riding alone, leaving Francesca asleep, warm and sated in her bed. He rode along the river to the bridge, inspected the new trusses, then rode up to the downs.

Some called the landscape bleak, mile upon mile of emptiness with only the call of larks high above to puncture its loneliness. Today, that suited him—he needed time to think. Time to reflect on the changes in his life, to try to understand them.

He hadn't imagined marriage would cause such change, such inner upheaval. Marriage to Francesca had. He'd known from first sight that she was potentially unsettling, yet unsettled was not what he felt. She spoke to him—the man not the earl, the barbarian not the gentleman—and he, most unexpectedly, had become accustomed to that. He wasn't sure what having her in his life was doing to his wilder self. Perhaps she was taming the barbarian.

He inwardly snorted, and thought of the day before.

Thought of all he'd felt when he'd seen her bobbing wildly on the back of the runaway black. His old fear had risen, sharp, intense—the fear of having her fall and die like his father. Yet, along with the fear, this time had come resolution, the determination to save her, the conviction that he could, and would.

And he had.

Yesterday he'd lived the difference between being thirty-five and powerful, not seven and helpless. He felt as if old demons had been vanquished. Ironic that he owed Lancelot Gilmartin's foolishness for that.

He slowed the grey as the escarpment drew near. He set the huge horse down the track to the Castle, cantering down the slope. Almost immediately he sensed an odd kick in the horse's gait. Reining in, he dismounted. A quick inspection confirmed one rear shoe was loose.

Patting the horse's neck, Gyles drew the reins over his head. "Come on, old son—let's walk." It wasn't that far to the stables, and he still had plenty to ponder.

Like love, and loving.

Yesterday had demonstrated how deep were the waters into which he'd drifted, yet he still had his head above the waves. He cared for her, of course, and she seemed content with that, with the concessions he'd made. He'd let her into his life—he paused and reconsidered: bit by bit she'd won her way into his life, if truth be told. They'd come to an amicable arrangement, one that fell short of him committing to love.

Was that enough? Enough to keep her loving him?

Eyes on the ground, he walked down the track, and admitted he didn't know. Her resolution on the battlements on the morning after their wedding still rang in his mind.

One thing he did know—he wanted her love, wanted her loving him, now and forever. The barbarian within had seized that prize and was not about to let go.

The image of the first time he'd seen her, the fact that he'd wanted her from that moment, led his mind to his mistake, to his initial perception of Franni—to the fact he'd been idiot enough to imagine she would make him a suitable wife to the point he'd thought it was she he was marrying.

God forbid. Thankfully, fate had.

He'd been as arrogantly foolish as Lancelot in his approach to finding his bride, but fate had taken pity on him, overriding his machinations to plant the right candidate at the altar beside him. And arrange matters so that, despite her temper, she'd been agreeable to marrying him. Agreeable to loving him.

He'd been so wrong about his bride—was he also wrong in refusing to love her? In not allowing what could be between them, what she wanted to be between them, to grow?

Fate had been so right over the matter of his wife. Did he dare to trust in fate again over the nature of their marriage?

Blowing out a long breath, he turned down the last stretch of track. Beside him, the grey slowed. Gyles looked up.

A yard ahead, a leather strap was stretched across the path just above knee height, secured around tree trunks on either side.

It was a leather rein from some carriage harness. Gyles halted before it. He tugged—it wasn't taut, but didn't have much give. He looked at the grey, judging where the strap would hit. He tested the leather, tested the knots securing it. Thought of what would have happened if he'd come down the path at a canter.

Or up the path at a gallop.

Frowning, he untied the strap from one tree trunk, rolling it in his hand as he crossed to the other tree.

He was the principal user of the path. Other than him, only Francesca rode this way. When exercising his horses, his grooms used the track along the river where they cantered under Jacobs's watchful eye.

The implication was obvious. "Who?" and "Why?" were less so.

He had no local enemies that he knew of . . . except, perhaps, Lancelot Gilmartin. Glancing at the leather rolled in his hand, Gyles stuffed it into his pocket, then caught the grey's reins and continued down the track.

Despite the boy's foolishness, he couldn't believe it of Lancelot. Such cold-bloodedness seemed unlikely—and he'd certainly have considered that Francesca might be the one caught, and surely he wouldn't want that. Then again, given her verbal dissection of his character . . . could youthful adoration turn so quickly to hate?

But if not Lancelot, then who? He was involved in political schemes which others vehemently opposed, yet he couldn't imagine any of the opposing camp employing such tactics. That was too fanciful for words.

He pulled the rein out of his pocket and examined it again. It was damp. It had rained last night but not since dawn. The rein had been strung there at least overnight. Possibly for longer. He thought back to the last time anyone had used the path. He and Charles had gone riding the first morning of their visit. After that, he and Francesca had gone by other ways.

Gyles reached the stable yard. "Jacobs!"

Jacobs came running. Gyles waited until he'd handed the grey to a stableboy before showing Jacobs the rein.

"It could be one of ours—heaven knows we've heaps lying about." Jacobs strung the leather between his hands. "I really couldn't be sure. Where was it?"

Gyles told him.

Jacobs looked grim. "I'll have the lads keep a lookout. Whoever put it there might come back to check."

"Possibly, but I doubt it. Let me know immediately if you or the lads see anyone or anything unusual."

"Aye, m'lord."

"And during the Harvest Festival, I want the stables closed off, and watched."

"Aye—I'll see to it."

Gyles headed for the house, trying to dismiss the notion that had popped into his head. The conundrum of how a stone had become embedded in his wife's mount's hoof when the horse hadn't been out. So the next time she'd been out, Francesca had ridden one of his hunters, a horse she couldn't easily manage.

He'd been with her and they'd ridden out by a different

route, but the scenario could so easily have been different. She could have gone riding by herself and taken the path up the escarpment.

Flexing his shoulders, he tried to push the resulting vision aside. It hadn't happened, and all was still well.

That, he tried to tell himself, was all that mattered.

Striding up to the side door, he hauled it open and went inside.

Chapter 15

The days leading to their Harvest Festival were filled with activity. Gyles spent much of the time within sight of Francesca, more to appease the brooding barbarian than from any conviction she was in danger. But while in his sight, she was safe—and keeping her in sight was no hardship.

His house came alive, filled with frenzied footmen; he was entertained to see Irving succumb to the pleasant panic. Even Wallace was seen hurrying, an unprecedented sight. Yet most of his mind remained on Francesca, his senses attuned to every nuance of her voice, to the tilt of her head as she considered some point, to the swish of her skirts as she hurried past. She was everywhere—in the kitchens one minute, in the forecourt the next.

And every night she came to his arms, happy and content and very willing to share all she was with him.

He tried, once, to settle with a news sheet. After reading the same paragraph five times and not taking in one word, he surrendered and went to see what Francesca was up to in the conservatory.

His mother, Henni, and Horace had arrived; he heard their voices as he strolled into the glass and stone edifice built out from the house beyond the library. With Francesca, they were sitting about a wrought-iron table positioned to make the most of the morning light.

His mother saw him.

"There you are, dear." She held up her face; he bent and kissed her cheek. "Francesca has been telling us of all that's planned."

"I've volunteered to oversee the archery contests." Horace squared his shoulders. "Did that years ago for your father. Quite enjoyed it."

Gyles nodded and looked at Henni.

"Your mother and I will be roaming the crowd, making sure all is as it should be."

"There'll be so many here"—Francesca glanced up at him—"you and I won't be able to be everywhere."

"True." He stood by Francesca's chair, his hand on its back, and listened to her plans. He'd heard then before and approved them all; he listened not to her words but the eagerness in her voice as she recited the day's schedule.

"By tomorrow evening, all should be in readiness."

Henni set down her cup. "A pity you'll have to wait until the morning to put out the trestles and boards, but it was ever the same. A Festival at this time of year can't expect to be other than damp."

"With luck, the day'll be fine." Horace stood. "Usually was, as I recall."

"Indeed. The whole estate will be praying for a fine day— I haven't seen such excitement for years." Lady Elizabeth rose and kissed Francesca's cheek. "We'll leave you to your preparations."

Francesca and Henni rose, too.

"Don't forget—if you need any help, you have only to send a footman across the park." Henni squeezed Francesca's hand, then turned to the door leading outside just as a large shadow filled the doorway.

"Ahem!" Edwards shuffled, then raised a hand to the frame and lightly knocked.

Francesca recovered first. "Yes, Edwards?"

He gripped his cap between his hands. "I was wondering if I might have a word, ma'am."

"Yes?"

He drew breath, glanced at Gyles, then looked at Francesca. "It's the plums, ma'am. They need to be harvested tomorrow."

"Tomorrow? But tomorrow's the last day before the Festival."

"Aye, well, trees and fruit and weather don't allow for festivals, like. The season's been late, and the fruit's just ripe—we need to get it in as soon as we have a dry patch long enough so it won't be damp." He glanced at the sky. "It's been clear for the last few days. By tomorrow, the fruit'll be right to pick—we daren't risk the crop by waiting till after the Festival."

Francesca had learned that the plum crop and the jam it produced was almost as old a Castle tradition as the Festival.

"So you'll need all the gardeners and stablelads?"

"Aye, and the footmen, too. Even then, it'll take the whole day."

Francesca frowned. They would never manage the preparations for the festival without all those hands.

Lady Elizabeth turned to her. "You can have the staff from the Dower House, if that would help."

Francesca nodded, then refocused on Edwards. "What if all of us pick? How long would it take then?"

"All?"

"The entire staff—everyone in the house. And the staff from the Dower House. Every pair of hands. That's more than double the number you need to do it in a day. If you have that many, how many hours will it take?"

Edwards cogitated. "A few. . . ." He nodded. "Aye—three hours would do it if we had that many. We've plenty of ladders and such."

Francesca almost sighed with relief. "Tomorrow afternoon. We'll complete all the preparations for the Festival, then have a late luncheon—then we'll *all* gather in the orchard and bring in the crop."

"That's an excellent idea." Henni nodded approvingly.

"I'll spread the word and speak to my lads." Edwards bowed and strode off.

"I must come over," Horace said as they moved to the now vacant doorway. "Sounds quite an event in itself."

"Do come," Francesca said. "We can have tea and scones as a celebratory picnic at the end."

"What a delightful idea!" Lady Elizabeth declared.

Gyles noted the look in Francesca's eyes—the look she got when she was busily scheming.

She flashed them all a smile. "If you'll excuse me, I must speak with Wallace immediately."

"Of course! We'll see you tomorrow afternoon." They waved as she disappeared back into the house, then Henni took Horace's arm and they stepped out onto the path.

Gyles gave his mother his arm. He helped her out onto the flags, conscious of her gaze on his face. She didn't move to join Henni and Horace, strolling slowly toward the park. Resigned, he met her gaze, then arched a brow.

She smiled. "You've been unbelievably lucky, you know."

He held her gaze. "I know."

Her smile deepened. She patted his arm, then set out in Henni and Horace's wake.

He knew very well how lucky he was.

The next afternoon, Gyles walked beneath the plum trees, surrounded by every last member of the Castle staff as well as those from the Dower House, and drank in the music of their chatter. His mother, Horace, and Henni had arrived—Francesca had presented them with baskets and directed them to a section of low-hanging branches. Henni had plum stains on her old dimity gown; both she and his mother were giggling as they picked.

Ladders were set up around six trees; there were two pick-
ers on every ladder and four gatherers beneath waiting to
place the fruit in the big wicker baskets. The orchard was a
hive of activity, powered by a celebratory air.

The preparations for the Festival were complete. Everything was ready; the staff had thrown themselves into
Francesca's revised plans with single-minded determination—the present exercise was their reward.

A time to play after all their work. Francesca had turned
what was usually viewed as a chore into an entertainment.
As he searched for her, Gyles felt sure he was witnessing a
tradition in the making.

"We'll just take this basket to the dray, ma'am."

"Be careful."

Gyles looked up. His exquisite wife, dressed in a simple
apple green day gown, was perched high on a ladder. She
reached for two plums, deftly plucked them, then cradled
them to her bosom and waited for her helpers to return.

Gyles moved into her line of vision.

She smiled gloriously. "I wondered where you were."

"I've been chasing you." He reached up, and she handed
him the plums.

Then she opened her arms wide. "Here I am."

Their eyes met. "So I see."

One hand on a rung, she reached out and picked another
plum, then carried it to her mouth and took a bite. Red juice
stained her full lips as she chewed, then swallowed.

"They're luscious." She took another bite, then held the
fruit out to him. "Try it."

He hesitated, then reached up and took the plum, turned it
and bit, drew in a mouthful. His gaze never left her. The fruit
was as luscious as she'd said. He savored the taste as he
watched her tongue slide out and around her lips.

"My lord?"

Gyles looked down. Francesca's assistants had returned

with a fresh basket. "Leave it there." He nodded at the ground beside him. "I'll gather for her ladyship. There's others who need help."

The boys grinned and dashed off, eager to check on their friends.

Gyles finished the plum, then looked up at his wife. "Shall we?"

She laughed and reached for more plums.

There was a competition running to see which group could denude the first tree. Edwards was the judge. When whoops announced one group thought they'd finished, he stumped up, scrutinized the tree for any missed plums, then declared the competition won.

The successful group whooped and danced. The others cheered, then quickly returned to finish their trees, then move the ladders to the next row.

There were twenty-four plum trees in the orchard, all gnarled veterans kept in excellent condition by Edwards's focused attention. The dray was sent rolling, groaning under the weight, to the kitchens twice before they reached the final trees.

The sun peeked out from under grey clouds, sending golden beams slanting through the trees as first one group, then another, finished their last tree. The ladders were carted away. Cook and Mrs. Cantle gathered the kitchen maids and hurried off to the house. Anticipating the fare to come, those already finished crowded around, helping those still picking.

Ten minutes later, just as the final plum was picked, Cook and Mrs. Cantle reappeared, leading a procession of maids each bearing a tray loaded with scones, freshly churned butter, and the last of the previous year's plum jam. Four footmen followed, carting two huge urns of tea.

A cheer went up, then rose even higher as Cook led the way into the orchard. Francesca stepped off her ladder. Gyles took her hand, and they walked to meet Cook.

She bobbed a curtsy and served them. They both took a

scone, buttered it, and piled it high with jam. Then Francesca turned to the waiting multitude.

Smiling, she raised the scone to them. "Thank you all—for today and tomorrow."

"And my thanks, too." Gyles raised his scone high. "To Lambourn!"

The rousing cheers raised the birds from the branches. With a wave, Gyles directed everyone to the trays. Exchanging a glance, he and Francesca retreated to where Mrs. Cantle was serving his mother, Henni, and Horace.

All three were liberally stained with plum juice. They were beaming.

"My dear, this has been a wonderful event."

"We'll have to do it next year."

"Every year."

Gyles checked; other than a few splatters, he'd escaped lightly. Francesca's gown was smeared at hip and breast, where she'd forgotten and wiped her sticky fingers.

Two grooms produced flutes. As the scones were washed down, a party atmosphere took hold. Gyles and Francesca, side by side, passed through their people, thanking and being thanked.

"No need to rush in again," Gyles told Wallace, ignoring the red juice running down the side of his dapper majordomo's face. "Everything's done. They deserve to enjoy themselves."

"The evening will bring a natural end to things." Francesca leaned on Gyles's arm and smiled at Wallace.

He smiled back. "Indeed, ma'am. We're on top of everything and can rest on our laurels, so to speak."

"Enjoy our laurels," Gyles murmured as they moved on. "Tomorrow's for the estate, but the plums are the Castle's harvest. This is the Castle's celebration." His arm slid around Francesca's waist and tightened—he swung her into the country dance just beginning, much to the delight of the staff.

Francesca laughed and danced, following his lead, his directions. People clapped and cheered them on; they whirled until she was giddy and breathless, drunk on happiness.

"Oh!" She collapsed against Gyles when he finally drew her from the throng.

"Mama's leaving."

They waved to Lady Elizabeth, Henni, and Horace, then watched the three stroll away across the park. The sunlight was dimming, the last westering rays fading, yet the party in the orchard was still in full spate.

Gyles bent his head and murmured in Francesca's ear. "I think we should leave them to it. If we stay, we'll remind them of their duties."

Francesca leaned back against him, folding her hands over his at her waist. "If they see us leaving, they'll feel compelled to come inside, too."

"In that case, it behooves us to slip away without them seeing, somewhere other than inside."

The seductive murmur tickled her ear. She smiled. "Where do you suggest?"

They slipped away through the trees, and only Wallace saw them go. Gyles signaled him not to notice. Francesca was not surprised when, her hand in his, Gyles headed down the path zigzagging down the bluff. Down to the ledge on which the folly stood.

Her heart was light; she laughed and let him pull her along. Her world was as rosy as the western sky. She'd been right to keep a rein on her temper, to muzzle her impatience, to mute all demands—to resist the urge to push and let him come to love her in his own way, in his own time.

She'd exercised more discipline than ever in her life before, and was reaping her reward. Poised to gather in the only harvest she'd ever wanted. He was so strong, so controlled, so resistant, yet he was almost persuaded. Soon, he would be, and her dream would become reality.

There was not a single dark cloud left on her horizon.

They reached the ledge as the sun dipped and the strip of sky between the clouds and the horizon burned a hot cerise. They paused to watch; she slipped her fingers from his, slid her arm about his waist and leaned against him. His gaze left the sunset and touched her face, then lowered. His head bent; his lips grazed the whorl of her ear.

She turned. Eyes met, then she lowered her lids and stretched upward as his lips covered hers. They kissed, long, lingeringly, fighting to keep the building urgency at bay.

And not entirely succeeding.

"Come to the folly."

His words, his arm around her, urged her feet to follow his. Their lips touched again, brushed again; they stopped again to feast.

By the time they finally reached the folly and he opened the door, desire had them firmly in its grip. Francesca smiled, feeling like a cat with a bowl of cream set before it; she led the way in, crossing to the middle of the room.

She'd been here often, drawn by the privacy and the silence, by the lingering scent of emotion. This was a place of quiet joys and shared pleasures; the past had made it so; now it was theirs. She turned and held out her arms. He closed the door, studied her, then paced slowly toward her.

His eyes were very dark; she smiled into them and reached for his cravat. His gaze lowered to her breasts; his fingers found the laces on either side of her gown.

"You've reorganized."

"A little." She'd moved his mother's abandoned tapestry into a corner. It belonged here, but not at center stage where he would always see it. "I had Irving bring the daybed down." With her head, she directed his attention to the large daybed beside them, placed to catch the view. "It'll be pleasant to lie here in summer and relax."

She let her voice convey her real meaning. His eyes lifted to hers briefly; they were turbulent, stormy. She caught only the barest flash of intention—lightning against the grey—

before his fingers slipped through her open laces and skittered along her ribs.

She shrieked. Laughing, she flung away—she was ticklish, and he knew it. He stayed with her, the knowing trail of his fingers quickly reducing her to a giggling wreck. She tried to escape but found herself trapped against the daybed. "Oh, stop!" She clutched the daybed's back for support, half–doubled over the cushions as she tried to catch her breath.

He stopped. From behind her, he closed his arms around her, pressing close, holding her against him. Still laughing, almost sobbing, she let him draw her upright, let him mold her hips against his thighs. Let him press closer still so she could feel the strength of his erection.

"What about autumn?" The deep whisper feathered her ear. "Do you think it would be pleasant to lie here now"—he shifted his hips against her—"and relax?"

He invested the word with far more sexual nuance than she had.

"Yes." From all she could feel, she would shortly be sobbing from quite a different cause. Anticipation streaked like silver fire down her veins. She licked her lips. "We could watch the sunset."

She felt him look up, then he murmured, in the same devilishly dark tone, "So we could."

He had her trapped between him and the daybed. Her gown was already loose. She felt him shrug. Turning her head, she saw his coat land on a nearby chair.

Arms clothed in soft linen closed around her, hard hands splayed across her curves. "I thought you were going to watch the sky change."

She shifted her gaze to the horizon. He bent his head and his lips brushed her nape. Then his lips and teeth grazed the long line of her throat, and his hands moved over her.

They knew her well, those wicked, wanton hands, knew

how to make her shiver, shudder, knew how to make her flower for him beneath her skirts. His touch was not delicate but possessive, each caress tending to the primitive. He made her hunger for more, made her want with a level of desperation that strangled her breath in her throat.

Her breasts were swollen and aching although he'd yet to lower the gaping gown and take them in his hands. Her nipples tingled; her stomach was a tight knot of need. He seemed to know; one hand closed possessively over her stomach, kneaded provocatively. Head back against his shoulder, she moaned and shifted her hips against him. The hand slid down; pressing her skirts between her thighs, he rubbed the side of his hand against her, slowly, deliberately, until she thought she'd go mad.

"I've"—she had to stop to swallow—"I've had enough of the sunset."

"But it's not dark yet."

She lifted her heavy lids. A pale wash of color was rapidly fading into the blue of the night. "It's dark enough."

"Are you sure?"

There was no humor in the question. If she'd had any doubt who it was who stood behind her, rapacious lord or smoothly elegant lover, his tone made it clear. The steely arms that held her, the hard body behind her, were in no mood to be gentle. Their coupling would be heated, furious—primal. The prospect—the promise in his voice, in his body—sent excitement lancing through her. "Yes."

His hands closed about her waist and he lifted her forward.

"On your knees, my lady."

His gravelly purr sent heat curling through her. He set her on the daybed, her knees close to its edge. He straddled her calves, keeping her knees more or less together.

"Bend forward. Hold on to the back of the bed."

She did. The daybed was wider than a *chaise*, but she could reach.

He flipped her skirts up, pushing them and her chemise over her waist, baring her bottom and legs. The cool air feathered over her fevered flesh; anticipation seared her. Then his palms curved almost reverently about her bottom, lightly caressing before trailing down the backs of her bare thighs. One left her; she imagined him unbuttoning his trousers while his other hand slowly slid upward, long fingers tracing the inner face of her thighs, higher and higher— he stopped before he touched her.

Her body reacted as if he had.

He shifted, moved closer. His hands gripped her hips.

The blunt head of his erection pressed between her thighs, probed her swollen flesh.

She would have wriggled and taken him in, but he anchored her hips, held her steady as he searched and found her entrance, then pressed inside.

He held her still. Inexorably he pushed into her, filling her inch by inch, stretching her softness, claiming it as his. She thought he'd gone as far as he could when his hips met her bottom, then he thrust and she gasped.

He drew back and filled her slowly again, again thrust at the last, jolting her breathing. Then he settled to a slow rhythm of thrust and withdrawl; within a minute she was melting.

Her body rocked with each thrust, each possessive claiming.

She tried to ease her knees apart, to gain some purchase in the dance. The rigid columns of his legs gave not an inch. He kept her knees trapped together as he plumbed her, entirely at his whim. As if to confirm that, he increased the pace, then, just as she thought the inferno would ignite, he slowed again to that same steady, pleasant but unfulfilling rhythm.

She could do little to influence his script. Could do nothing other than close her body like a glove about him and give herself up to his possession.

She did, and sensed him draw in a huge breath, then he released her hips, pushed aside the neckline of her gaping gown, released her chemise, stripped it away, and closed his hands about her naked breasts.

Heat poured through her. His touch was commanding, covetous yet as one who had the right. Fire flowed from her breasts to her womb, to where they joined.

He filled her again and again, over and over, his hips rocking hers, his hands closing about her breasts.

The fire flamed, spread, then erupted in a spasm of heat and desire, white-hot sensation shooting down every vein, frazzling every nerve. She cried out, and heard it as a distant song, then all she knew, all she felt, coalesced into one exquisitely intense sensation.

He held her there, his hands firm about her breasts as he thrust harder, deeper, faster.

She felt the power shudder through him, felt him surrender, felt him join her in that place where lovers go.

Gyles's heart thundered as he wallowed in the indescribable sensation of his body emptying into hers, so tight, so hot, so welcoming. He supported her in his arms, his hands full of the bounty of her breasts, his loins flush against her naked bottom.

A shudder of primal triumph rocked him.

She was a harvest he'd just reaped. Nothing in his life had ever felt so good.

They did lie, relaxed, on the daybed, but it was now full dark outside. Neither felt any desire to move, content in the warmth of the other's embrace.

Francesca's dark head lay on Gyles's chest. He stroked, letting his fingers slide through the silky black locks. He smiled self-deprecatingly as he recalled his original view of her as a woman too dangerous to seduce. A woman he should fear, given her innate ability to reach behind his civilized mask and communicate directly with the barbarian behind it.

He'd been right. That was, indeed, precisely what she did. Yet he no longer feared her ability—he exulted in it.

Why fate had been so kind as to send him one of the few women—the only one he'd ever met—who seemed to think nothing of his baser instincts, indeed, seemed to delight in said instincts, he didn't know. He was only glad he hadn't been able to do anything other than marry her.

The thought of not having her as his wife was enough to make him tighten his arms; she murmured and wriggled; he eased his hold.

He glanced down at her, and could no longer recall why keeping his true self in check had once seemed so important. It had been his way for so long—as if keeping his true feelings, his true nature, suppressed was essential to functioning, to living his life.

Hiding that side of himself from her had never been an option; he'd stopped worrying about it on their wedding night. With her, being himself, his true self, simply didn't matter. . . .

He stared out at the night.

That was why, with her, he felt so complete. So whole. Being himself, with her, was permissible, even desirable. She delighted in calling the barbarian forth, delighted in throwing herself in his arms—delighted in giving herself to a maruading rapacious barbarian. And she couldn't care less if he was incoherent at the time.

His lips curved in a smirk. Her own lack of coherence was telling—attempting any degree of conversation during coitus was wasted effort. He only had to touch her, and she became a totally sensate being—the only avenue of communication she was interested in was by touch and feel.

His gaze steadied on her face.

She was a field he would willingly plow for the rest of his life.

He didn't think she'd mind.

Shifting his hand from her head to her breast, he continued stroking. She made a smoky, purring sound and shifted suggestively. He smiled and lifted her across him.

It was time to sow some more.

So he could reap the harvest of her loving again.

Chapter 16

"*My lord,* if I could have a moment of your time?"

Caught watching his wife, Gyles turned his head. Wallace had entered the breakfast parlor and stood by his side, a covered salver in one hand.

"Her ladyship's, too." Wallace directed a bow down the table.

The morning of the Festival had dawned misty but fine. The sun shone benignly on all those scurrying about the Castle grounds, setting up trestles and boards. Most of the staff were outside; only Irving and one footman were attending them. Wallace caught Irving's eye; Irving directed the footman to the door, then followed, closing the door behind him.

"What is it?"

"One of the maids was instructed to fill the vase on the stair landing with autumn branches, my lord. To brighten up the spot for the Festival. When she tried to insert the branches, she encountered some difficulty. When she investigated, she discovered . . ."— Wallace lifted the cover of the salver—"this."

Gyles stared at a crumpled scrap of green, sodden and darkened. He knew what it was before his fingers touched it.

He lifted the fragments. The bedraggled feather, shredded of its fronds, hung limply.

Francesca stared. "My riding cap."

"Indeed, ma'am. Millie mentioned to Mrs. Cantle that it was not in your room. Mrs. Cantle told the maids to keep an eye out in case it was elsewhere about the house. When Lizzie found it, she brought it straight to Mrs. Cantle."

Gyles turned the remains of the cap in his fingers. "It's been destroyed."

"So it appears, my lord."

Francesca gestured. "Let me see."

Gyles dropped the wet scrap back onto the salver. Wallace took it to Francesa. Gyles watched her pick it up, spread it in her hands. The material had been ripped, the feather broken and stripped.

She shook her head. "Who. . . . *Why?*"

"Indeed." Gyles heard the steel in his voice. He glanced at Wallace. His majordomo met his gaze, his expression impassive. Wallace knew no more than he.

Francesca's expression cleared. She dropped the cap on the salver. "It must have been an accident. Get rid of it, Wallace. We've more pressing matters to deal with today."

Replacing the salver's cover, Wallace glanced at Gyles.

Lips thinning, he looked at his wife. "Francesca—"

The door opened; Irving entered. "I'm sorry to interrupt, my lord, but Harris has arrived with the ale. You wished to be informed." He bowed to Francesca. "And Mrs. Cantle asked me to tell you, my lady, that Mrs. Duckett has arrived with her pasties."

"Thank you, Irving." Laying aside her napkin, Francesca rose. She flicked a hand at the salver. "Dispose of it, please, Wallace."

She glided up the table, heading for the door. Gyles reached out and shackled her wrist. "Francesca—"

"It's nothing but a ruined cap." Leaning closer, she twined her fingers with his and squeezed lightly. "Let be. We've so much to do, and I do so want everything to be perfect."

There was a plea in her eyes. Gyles knew how much she'd invested in the Festival, how much she needed the day to be a success. He held her gaze. "We'll talk about it later."

She smiled gloriously and slipped from his hold.

He rose and followed her—into the chaos of the day.

He followed her for most of the day, not on her heels, but she was rarely out of his sight. The more he considered her shredded cap, the less he liked it. He'd never played host at the Harvest Festival yet the role was second nature. He strolled the lawns, greeting his tenants and their families, stopping to chat with those who leased the village shops. He passed his mother and Henni doing likewise, then went down to the archery butts to check on Horace.

While there, he presented the prizes thus far won, promising to escort his countess thither to bestow the major prizes later on. Leaving the butts, he watched Francesca chatting animatedly with Gallagher's wife.

Informality was the order of the day. Today was the day when the lord and lady rubbed shoulders with their tenants, meeting them man to man, woman to woman. It was not a challenge every gently reared lady met well, but Francesca was enjoying it. Her hands danced as she talked; her eyes sparkled. Her face was alive with interest, her expression focused. Gyles wondered what topic she found so engaging, then she looked down and smiled. He shifted and saw Sally's youngest child clinging to the front of her skirt.

The little girl was fascinated by Francesca; smiling, Francesca bent down to talk to her.

In a walking dress in green-and-ivory stripes, Francesca was easy to spot among the crowd. As she laughed, straightened, and parted from Sally, others stepped forward to claim her attention. Gyles would have liked to claim it for himself; instead, he turned to greet the blacksmith.

Only those connected with the estate were present. Gyles

didn't, therefore, need to watch for Lancelot Gilmartin and his theatrical posturings. He did, however, wonder if Lancelot was in any way connected with Francesca's ruined cap.

Finally, Francesca was free. Gyles caught her hand, linked her arm with his.

She smiled up at him. "Everything's going perfectly."

"With you, Wallace, Irving, Cantle, Mama, and Henni supervising, I don't see how anything could go otherwise."

"You're doing your part admirably, too."

Gyles humphed. "Has Lancelot Gilmartin called since our excursion to the Barrows?"

"No—not since then."

Gyles stilled. "He'd called before?"

"Yes, but I'd instructed Irving to deny me, remember?"

Gyles drew her on; those waiting their turn with her could wait a moment longer. "Could Lancelot have had anything to do with your ruined cap?"

"How? The cap was in my room."

"You thought it was in your room, but you might have left it somewhere. The Castle may be fully staffed, but it's so huge it's easy for someone to slip in undetected."

Francesca shook her head. "I can't imagine it. He might have been angry, but attacking my cap seems such a silly—"

"Childish thing to do. Precisely why I thought of Lancelot."

"I think you're making too much of the incident."

"I don't think you're taking it seriously enough. But if not Lancelot . . ."

Gyles halted; Francesca glanced at him, then followed his gaze. He was looking at the pit where a whole ox was roasting under Ferdinand's exacting eye.

"It makes even less sense to suspect Ferdinand. He's not the least bit angry with me—or you."

Gyles glanced at her. "He wasn't annoyed that you weren't receptive to his impassioned pleas?"

"He's Italian—*all* his pleas are impassioned." She shook Gyles's arm. "You're worrying over nothing."

"Your riding cap—a favorite possession—was found deliberately ruined and hidden in a vase. Until I discover who did it, and why, I will not let the matter rest."

She exhaled through her teeth. A farmer and his wife were tentatively approaching. "You're so stubborn. It's nothing." Smiling brilliantly, she released Gyles's arm.

"It's very definitely not '*nothing.*' " Gyles nodded urbanely to the farmer and stepped forward to greet him.

They separated. Despite her intentions, Francesca found her thoughts returning to the mystery of her ruined cap. There had to be a simple explanation.

After fifteen minutes with a bevy of giggling housemaids, she was certain she'd found it. When Gyles came to escort her to the archery range, she smiled and took his arm. "I have it."

" 'It' what?"

"A sensible explanation for my cap."

His gaze sharpened. "Well?"

"For a start, if someone wanted to ruin my cap to make me sorry—to pay me back for something I'd done or not done—then they wouldn't have hidden it in that vase. It might not have been found for months, even years."

Gyles frowned.

"But," she continued, "what if I'd left it somewhere and it was accidentally damaged—say with furniture polish. Any maid would be horrified—she'd be certain she'd be dismissed even if you and I know that wouldn't happen. What would a maid do? She couldn't hide the cap and take it away—their dresses and aprons have no pockets. So she'd hide it where no one would find it."

"It was mangled and pulled apart."

"That might have happened when the maid tried to put the branches in the vase. I was just speaking with her. She said the cap was tangled in the ends of the branches when she pulled them out to see what the problem was."

Francesca smiled as they neared the crowd gathered about the improvised archery range. "I think we should forget about my cap. It was only a scrap of velvet, after all. I can always get another."

Gyles got no chance to reply; she slipped her hand from his arm and stepped forward to present the prizes for the men's archery competition. He stood back; his mind continued to dwell on her cap.

A scrap of velvet and a flirting feather. It might have had little real worth, but despite her comments, it had been a favorite possession of hers. He'd grown fond of it himself.

Propping his shoulders against a tree, he watched her, careful to keep his expression easy, impassive. Her explanation was possible—he had to concede that. Other than Lancelot and Ferdinand, he could conceive of no one who might want to upset her. Even imagining such a thing of them was extrapolating wildly.

According to the staff, Lancelot had not been sighted on the estate since being warned to keep away, and despite her strictures, Ferdinand seemed as worshipful of Francesca as he'd ever been. Even more telling, while Lancelot or Ferdinand might be enamored of dramatic gestures enough to destroy the cap, they wouldn't, as she'd pointed out, have hidden the result—where was the gesture in that?

So . . . the destruction of the cap was an unfortunate accident. All they could do was shrug and forget it.

That conclusion didn't ease the tightness about his chest, nor the compulsion to remain watchful and alert.

Amid laughter and cheering, Francesca turned away from the archery butts. He stepped to her side. She smiled and allowed him to take her hand, set it on his sleeve. Allowed him to keep her with him for the rest of the day.

The Harvest Festival was a resounding success. When the sun sank low and the tenants finally rolled home, Francesca and Gyles joined their staff, helping to strike the trestles and return the perishables inside before the river mists spread through the park. Lady Elizabeth, Henni, and Horace helped, too. When all was done, they stayed for supper—just soup followed by a cold collation.

Lady Elizabeth, Henni, and Horace were driven home by Jacobs, and the entire household fell exhausted into bed.

It was midday the next day before things got back to normal.

Gyles and Francesca were seated at the luncheon table, serving themselves from the dishes Irving and a footmen offered, when Cook popped her head around the door, then sidled in. Francesca saw her and smiled.

Cook bobbed a curtsy. "I was just bringing this to Irving." She held up a glass bottle with a silver top. "Your special dressing."

Francesca's eyes lit. "You found it!" She held out her hand.

Cook handed over the bottle. "It was stuck away on a shelf in the pantry. I came across it just this minute when I went to put some of the jam away."

"Thank you." Francesca smiled delightedly. Cook bobbed her head and retreated.

Gyles watched as Francesca shook the bottle vigorously, then sprinkled the liquid over her vegetables. "Here." He held out a hand when she finished. "Let me try it."

She handed the bottle over. It had a conical lid with a hole in the top.

"What's in it?"

She picked up her knife and fork. "A mixture of olive oil and vinegar, with various herbs and seasonings."

Gyles did as she'd done, dribbling the shaken liquid over his potatoes, carrots, and beans. He lowered his face and sniffed—he sat back.

He looked at the bottle, still clasped in his hand—looked at Francesca, raising a sliver of carrot to her lips—

He lunged over the table and grabbed her wrist. "Don't eat that!"

Eyes wide, she stared at him.

He was looking at the piece of carrot speared on her fork; it gleamed with a light coating of dressing. He forced her hand down. "Put it down."

She released the fork. It clattered on her plate.

"My lord?"

Irving was at his shoulder. Easing back, fingers still locked about Francesca's wrist, Gyles held the bottle out to his butler. "Smell that."

Irving took the bottle, sniffed. His eyes widened. He stared at the bottle. "Well, my word! Is that . . . ?"

"Bitter almonds." Gyles looked at Francesca. "Get Wallace in here. And Mrs. Cantle."

Irving sent the footman hurrying off. He himself whisked the plates from before them.

Francesca was staring at the bottle. "Let me smell it."

Irving gingerly brought it to her. She took it, sniffed, then met Gyles's gaze. He raised a brow.

"It smells like bitter almonds." She set the bottle down.

The door opened; Mrs. Cantle entered, followed by Wallace. "My lord?"

Gyles explained. The bottle was passed around. The verdict was unanimous—the dressing smelled of bitter almonds.

"I don't understand how . . ." Wallace looked at Mrs. Cantle.

Her color high, the housekeeper faced Gyles. "The bottle went missing—it's been gone at least a week. Cook found it just a few minutes ago."

Gyles motioned to Irving. "Fetch Mrs. Doherty." Irving left. Gyles turned to Mrs. Cantle. "Tell me about this dressing."

"I asked if it could be made." Francesca twisted her hand and gripped Gyles's fingers. "It's a habit I developed since coming to England—I find dishes here too bland. . . ."

Cook arrived, pale and shaken. "I had no idea. I saw the bottle there and grabbed it, and brought it straightaway—I knew m'lady had been missing it this past week."

"Who makes the dressing?" Gyles asked.

Mrs. Cantle and Cook exchanged glances. Mrs. Cantle answered. "Ferdinand, my lord. He knew what Lady Francesca was describing—he took great care—felt quite chuffed, he did—to be making it for her."

"Ferdinand?"

Gyles looked at Francesca. He could see in her eyes her wish to deny all he was thinking.

Cook shuffled her feet. "If you don't mind, m'lord, I'll get rid of this wicked stuff."

Gyles nodded. Cook picked up the bottle and left.

Wallace cleared his throat. "If you'll pardon the comment, my lord, I would argue that Ferdinand is the least likely person to have used the dressing to poison Lady Francesca. He's devoted to her ladyship, and despite his histrionics he's been unfailingly good at his job; he's ultimately done all we've asked of him. Ever since her ladyship arrived, he's got on a great deal better with Cook, which was really the only odd kick in his gallop."

Mrs. Cantle nodded in agreement. Gyles turned to find Irving nodding, too.

"And," Wallace went on, "if Ferdinand wanted to poison anyone, he could do so, very easily and with a great deal less chance of being detected, by introducing poison into the more highly flavored dishes he prepares than by putting bitter almonds into her ladyship's dressing."

Gyles looked at them all. Given what he was feeling, it was difficult to incline his head and accept their argument. Eventually, he did so. "Very well. But then who put the poison in that bottle? Who has access to bitter almonds?"

Mrs. Cantle grimaced. "All you need is a kernal, my lord, and the trees are common—there's three on the south lawn."

Gyles stared at her.

A knock sounded on the door. Cook looked in. "Your pardon, m'lord, but I thought you'd want to know." She came in, closed the door, then, drawing a deep breath, faced them all. "I was tipping the stuff down the drain when Ferdinand came up. He saw what I was doing and asked why. Well, he was about to fly into one of his Italian pelters, so I told him. He was shocked—well and truly shocked. Couldn't say a word, at first. *Then* he said, 'oh—but wait.' Seems he used the last of an old bottle of almond oil—I *do* remember he hadn't enough of the olive last time he made the dressing, and I told him where to find the almond. I use it in my sweet crusts, you see. And I remember him telling me he'd had to use the last bit." Cook clasped her hands tightly. "So you see, it might have been the almond oil going bad that you all smelled."

Gyles looked at Wallace, then at Mrs. Cantle. She nodded. "Could be."

Gyles grimaced. "Bring the stuff back . . ."

Cook blanched. "Can't, m'lord." She wrung her hands. "I tipped it all down the drain and put the bottle to soak."

Francesca was glad to spend the rest of the day quietly, catching up with the myriad decisions necessary to keep a house the size of Lambourn Castle functioning smoothly—decisions set aside while preparations for the Festival were under way. She and Wallace, Irving and Mrs. Cantle met late in the afternoon to make notes on what had worked well, and detail suggestions for next year. Gyles didn't join them, but retired to the library; Francesca assumed he was sunk in his research.

She woke the next day to discover the sun shining weakly. She summoned Millie and dressed in her riding habit, mourning the loss of her cap but determined to let the matter lie. On reaching the breakfast parlor, she learned Gyles had already gone out riding, as she'd supposed. Finishing her toast, she headed for the stables.

"Aye—she'll be eager for a run," Jacobs said when she inquired after Regina. "I'll have her saddled in a trice."

He was as good as his word, leading the mare out and holding her steady while Francesca climbed into the saddle. She was settling her feet when she heard the clop of other hooves. Two grooms, mounted on two of Gyles's hunters, ambled out of the stable.

She smiled, nodded, then, gathering Regina's reins turned the mare toward the stable arch.

"The lads'll hang back twenty yards or so, ma'am."

Francesca halted. She blinked at Jacobs. "I'm sorry . . . I don't understand." She glanced past him to the grooms; they were clearly intending to follow her.

She looked back at Jacobs. The head stableman had flushed. "Master's orders, ma'am." He stepped closer so only she could hear. "He said as how you was not allowed out alone. If you wasn't with him, I was to send two grooms with you."

"Two?" Francesca forced her lips to relax. Whatever was going on wasn't Jacobs's fault. She glanced again at the grooms, then nodded. "As he wishes."

With that, she tapped the mare's side. Regina clattered out of the yard.

Francesca heard the grooms following. She'd intended to go up to the downs, to ride free and fast until she met Gyles. He'd be up there somewhere. They could have ridden together. . . .

Frowning, she turned onto the track through the park.

She needed to think.

Gyles joined her at the luncheon table. Francesca smiled and chatted; he answered, but didn't smile. Not that he frowned, but his eyes remained hooded, difficult to read. His expression said nothing at all.

With Irving and his minions constantly about, she had to bide her time. At the end of the meal, she would ask to speak with him—

"If you'll excuse me, my dear, I've a lot to catch up with."

Francesca stared as Gyles waved aside the fruit platter, dropped his napkin by his plate, and stood.

He nodded her way, his gaze touching her face briefly. "I'll see you at dinner."

Before she could say a word, he walked from the room.

Francesca followed his broad shoulders, then set her knife down with a clack.

It was possible he truly was swamped with work. In the interests of domestic peace, Francesca called for her cloak and went out for a walk.

The clouds had closed in; the sun had disappeared. The leaves lay thick under the oaks, a dense carpet muffling her steps. The air beneath the bare branches was still and cool, waiting for winter.

She tried to decide if she was reading more into the day's events than they warranted. Was she overreacting? In her heart, she didn't think so. Logically, she wasn't sure.

She'd followed a line parallel to the drive, under the trees—where was she going? With a sigh, she stopped. Going to the ramparts might distract her—she could see what sort of view there was on such a cloudy day. She swung around and stopped, staring at the two footmen who'd been ambling in her wake.

They halted. Warily waited.

Lips thinning, she started walking again. They bowed as she passed; she nodded and swept on—she didn't trust herself to speak. If she opened her lips she would scream, but it wasn't the footmen she wanted to scream at.

What did he think he was doing?

He was jealous, but it couldn't be that. On what grounds could he excuse such draconian measures? He'd been bothered over her cap's demise, but she'd explained that. And the ruckus over the odd smell in the dressing had simply been a mistake.

Reaching the ramparts, she stalked along. She could understand he might harbor some nebulous concern, but did he think she was so helpless he needed to treat her like a child? To be watched over by nursemaids? *Two* nursemaids?

Leaves crunched beneath her soles. At the point where the river curved, she halted, looking out over a landscape wreathed in gauzy mist. Her eyes saw; her brain did not.

She had a good mind to walk down to the folly and lock herself in—and wait until he came before she opened the door. Then he'd have to talk to her.

That, of course, was what was so irritating—the point that so exercised her temper. He was avoiding her because he didn't wish to discuss this latest start. He'd decreed, and it was to be, regardless of what she thought or felt.

She gritted her teeth against a nearly overwhelming urge to shriek. Lips compressed, she swung on her heel and headed around the house, then on through the park.

She strode back from the Dower House two hours later. Lady Elizabeth and Henni had welcomed her with praise and congratulations over the success of the Festival and what they were calling the Great Plum Harvest. She'd had to smile, sip her tea, and listen. With barely a pause, they'd moved on to the family, showing her the additions they'd made to the copy of the family tree she'd left with them.

That had distracted her. She'd become absorbed with their explanations, the names, connections, recollections. They'd gone as far as they could. She'd rolled up the family tree with all its addendums and brought it away with her.

It would be up to her what she did with it next. She'd never been part of a large family; she was feeling her way, yet she could see the possibilities. The potential. Ideas, still amorphous, floated through her head but she couldn't concentrate, couldn't make any decision on such matters—not yet.

Not until she'd discovered what was going on in her marriage, and decided what to do about that.

Distracted by their own chatter, neither Lady Elizabeth nor Henni had noticed her initial abstraction. She'd left without mentioning her sudden, unwelcome uncertainties. She hadn't asked why Gyles's reasonable concern should suddenly erupt into such overprotectiveness. The answer was one she needed to learn for herself—the matter lay between him and her.

That overprotectiveness irked—the two footman crunching in her wake were a constant reminder. She felt caged, but it wasn't that that hurt.

Gyles was avoiding her, refusing to reveal whatever the problem that had caused this reaction was.

He'd withdrawn from her, drawn back from her. . . .

She paused and forced herself to take a breath.

She'd thought they'd drawn close, but he'd stepped away, turned away. Had she imagined it—all that had gone before? She'd been so certain he was close to loving her as she wished . . . and now this. In a matter of hours, he'd cut himself off from her and retreated to a formal, conventional distance. He'd put up walls against her.

She didn't feel just caged, she felt shut out.

Drawing another breath, she set off again. The house stood amid its trees; she made for the front steps.

With every stride she took, her determination welled.

He'd said he would see her at dinner. Reaching the porch, she flung open the front door, strode into the hall and headed for the stairs.

She'd make sure he did.

Frustrated fury bubbled within her; she had to rein it in, had to wait. She swung into the gallery, making for the private wing.

A figure stepped out and bowed deeply. Ferdinand.

She halted before him. "Yes?"

"My lady." He straightened. He was only just taller than she was. Despite his olive skin, he looked wan.

When he simply stared at her, looking tortured, Francesca frowned. "What is it?"

Ferdinand swallowed, then blurted out, "I would *never*

have tried to harm you, my lady—you *must* believe that!" A
torrent of Italian, impassioned and more, followed.

Conscious of the two footmen ten yards behind her,
Francesca reached out, grasped Ferdinand's sleeve, and
shook hard. "Stop this! No one imagined you'd tried to harm
me, or, indeed, done anything wrong."

Ferdinand looked sceptical. "The master?"

Francesca caught his gaze. "If your master believed you
harbored any intention to harm me, you would no longer be
at Lambourn." She could taste the truth in the words. "Now
go back to your duties, and stop imagining anyone blames
you."

Ferdinand bowed low. Francesca walked on, her mind
whirling. Gyles knew—accepted—that the dressing hadn't
been poisoned. So why had the incident acted as a catalyst
for such change?

More questions only her husband could answer. Would
answer—tonight.

She picked up her pace. The footmen didn't follow her
into the private wing. They weren't needed there because
there were already two footmen, one stationed at either end
of the corridor, keeping watch over her rooms.

Teeth clenched, she flung open her door before either
footman could reach it.

"Millie?" Her little maid jumped up from a straight-
backed chair. Francesca closed the door. "I . . ." *Haven't
rung for you yet.* "What are you doing here?"

Millie bobbed. "Wallace said as how I should wait here,
ma'am."

Francesca stared. "When was this?"

"This afternoon, ma'am. After you went for your walk."
Millie came to take Francesca's cloak.

"You've been up here, waiting, all afternoon?"

Millie shrugged; she shook out the cloak. "I had your
things to tidy. Tomorrow, I'll bring up the mending."

Francesca watched her hang up the cloak, then turned away. "Call for water. I wish to bathe."

A long soak in hot water did not improve her temper. It did, however, give her time to plan her strategy, organize her arguments, and rehearse what she would later say.

To her husband, face-to-face.

The sooner such an interview was brought about, the better. Wrapped in a silk robe, her hair curling wildly from the steam, Francesca waved Millie to the two large wardrobes that held her clothes. "Open them both—I wish to select a special gown for this evening."

Gyles knew what he was facing the instant he set eyes on his wife that evening. He entered the family parlor with Irving on his heels. She looked up from the chair beside the fireplace, and smiled.

He stopped. Watched her while Irving announced that dinner was served.

She waited, patently expecting him to come nearer, to take her hand and raise her.

When he didn't, she arched one brow.

He waved to the door. "Shall we?"

She met his gaze, then rose and came to him. One part of him wanted to turn, walk away—run away—and take refuge in his study. Most of him wanted—

He wrenched his gaze from the creamy expanse of her breasts exposed by the magnificent bronze-silk gown. The gown was simple; in it, she was stunning. He couldn't stop his senses from drinking in the sight, from skating over her face, her hair, her lips.

He met her gaze briefly, then offered his arm. She placed her hand on his sleeve; soft and supple she glided beside him as they headed for the dining room—he felt as stiff as a board.

The meal provided a welcome diversion. He knew it wouldn't last.

"The Festival went well, don't you think?"

He inclined his head and nodded to a footman to serve him more beans. "Indeed."

"Was there anything you noted, anything that might have been better done otherwise?" She gestured with her fork. "Any complaints?"

He met her gaze briefly. "No. None."

He'd assumed the presence of Irving and the footmen would spike her guns temporarily; suddenly he wasn't so sure.

As if she'd read his mind, she smiled, slipped a piece of pumpkin between her lips, and looked down.

Despite the determination he'd glimpsed in her eyes, she made no further reference to recent events, but asked instead about London. He appreciated her acquiescence to his wishes. He would have to speak with her—her dress declared her stance on that—but any such exchange would be at a time of his choosing and, most importantly, in her bedroom, a venue in which he could end all discussion whenever he wished.

"Have you heard from St. Ives?"

He answered briefly, revealing as little as possible. Lines would need to be drawn; he'd already drawn some but hadn't yet decided where others would lie.

The meal ended. They rose and walked into the corridor. Pausing, she half turned and met his gaze.

He could feel her warmth, not just of her flesh but a deeper, womanly warmth, infinitely more tempting. The green of her eyes called him; the promise of her body showcased in bronze silk tugged at his senses. Drew him to her.

Her hand was rising to touch his arm when he stepped back.

Lids lowered, he inclined his head. "There's much I have to attend to. I suggest you don't wait up."

He turned and strode for his study. He didn't need to see her face.

Outwardly calm, Francesca retired to the family parlor. She sat by the fire for an hour, then Wallace pushed in the tea trolley. She allowed him to pour for her, then dismissed him. She sat beside the fire for another hour, then set aside her cup, rose, and went upstairs.

She changed, setting the bronze dress aside. Then she dismissed Millie.

In a fine silk nightgown beneath a peignoir of heavier silk, she stood by one window in the darkened room and gazed out at the moon-drenched night.

And waited.

Another hour passed before she heard the door to the room next to hers open, then close. She heard Gyles's footsteps cross the floor. Heard him speak to Wallace.

She imagined Gyles undressing. . . .

She turned her head, stared at the connecting door. Then she was crossing to it, reaching for the handle. If they were going to discuss anything, she wanted her husband fully clothed.

She flung open the door and walked through. "I wish to speak with you."

Coatless, his cravat loose about his neck, Gyles paused, then he drew the linen free. "I'll join you in a moment."

She halted ten feet away, crossed her arms beneath her breasts, and looked him in the eye. "I see no reason to wait."

Gyles took in the seething emotion in her eyes. He glanced down the room. Wallace was easing out of the door. Jaw setting, he looked at Francesca. "Very well." His tones were clipped, cold. "What is it?"

Unwise words; her eyes flared. But the fact she reined her temper in left him even more uneasy. He'd seen her furious before; this time, she was burning with a cold flame—one to cut, rather than scorch.

"I am not a child."

She enunciated the words clearly. His eyes on hers, he raised his brows, then let his gaze slide over her lush figure. "I wasn't aware I had treated you—"

He shut up.

She laughed coldly. "Like an infant incapable of any degree of self-preservation? A lackwit unable to walk through the park without falling and causing herself some hurt? Or was it that you imagined I'd be attacked and ravished under the trees"—she flung out an arm—"there, in your own park?"

She wrapped her arms about her again, as if she was chilled by her own fury. Her eyes locked with his. "You have given orders that have made me a prisoner in this house— this house that is supposedly my home. Why?"

The simple question slipped under his guard and rocked him. He'd expected her to rail against his restrictions, not cut straight to his heart and ask why. He let seconds tick by, let his breathing slow, steeled himself before stating, "Because I wish it."

She didn't react—didn't fling her hands to the sky and berate him. She studied him, her gaze steady and direct. Then, slowly, she shook her head. "That, my lord, is not answer enough."

"It is, however, all the answer you will get."

Again, she didn't react as he expected. Her eyes widened; her gaze raced over his face, then she swung on her heel and walked back to her room.

The door closed, softly, behind her.

Gyles stared at the closed door. The coldness inside him deepened, intensified to pain. He'd thought he couldn't get any colder; he'd been wrong about that, too.

He'd been wrong about so much.

So wrong in thinking that to love was a decision that was his to make. Yes, or no. It hadn't been like that.

A sound at the main door made him glance that way. With a curt gesture, he waved Wallace away. He needed a few moments to get his armor back in place, to gird himself to suffer the cold. He'd felt fear before, but it had never been like this. Never this deep, this black, this icy. Every time she caused it to rise, it grew more powerful, more profound. He thought he'd vanquished it, or at least come of an age where he could manage it and triumph. The moment in the forest, replayed with greater intensity on the downs, had left him feeling victorious.

A hollow victory. If he was with her when danger threatened, all was well. He still felt the fear, but he wasn't helpless against it, and he knew it. He'd proved it. He was who he was, in his prime; there were few dangers from which he couldn't defend her. Protecting her encouraged the barbarian, fed his baser self.

But his true self had no armor against invisible foes, no ability to protect her from them.

Against all conscious direction, his true self had fallen deeply in love with his wife.

Dropping the cravat, he started loosening his cuffs. He'd felt the first chill touch when he'd lifted her mangled hat from Wallace's salver. He'd tried not to notice, to pay it no heed, as if by doing so he could deny its existence. Then had come the incident of the dressing.

He been helpless to deny his fear. Ever since, it had ruled him.

Knowing that the dressing had not been poisoned made no difference; it changed nothing.

He was irrevocably in love with his wife. His world had come to revolve about her smile, and he could not face even the faintest possibility that she might be taken from him.

Wallace had returned. Gyles heard the quiet sounds of his valet-cum-majordomo hanging his discarded coat in the wardrobe.

The door to Francesca's room opened. She came in, agitation flowing about her, whipping the skirts of her peignoir. Her hair looked wild, as if she'd run her hands through it.

Gyles flicked a glance at Wallace to see his majordomo sliding once more from the room. Inwardly bracing, he faced Francesca. "What now?"

Her face was pale. He didn't want to meet her eyes, didn't want to see the bruising in the green.

"Why are you doing this?"

Her voice was low, not sultry but shaking with suppressed emotion.

"Because I have to."

"Why?" Francesca waited, her heart a leaden fist in her chest.

"Francesca . . ." Gyles sighed through his teeth, then he met her gaze, his eyes stormy, impossible to read. "You married me." His voice was as low as hers but much harder, more forceful. "Even after that last meeting in the forest, you married me. You knew very well *what* you were marrying— you, of all women, knew that."

"Yes. But I still don't understand." When he turned, she shifted so she could still see his face. She wasn't going to retreat, to let him shut her out. Drawing in a strangled breath, she spread her arms wide. "What have I done to deserve this? Why are you treating me like a felon in your house?" That struck a nerve. He flicked her a sharp glance. "Yes," she went on, "like a would-be thief, someone to be watched over at all times."

"Everything here is yours—"

"No!" Her eyes clashed with his. "Everything here is *not* mine!"

Sudden silence enveloped them; they both stilled. Teetered on a precipice. Their gazes were locked. Neither breathed. She felt his will reach her, press her to draw back . . .

Into that stillness, with great deliberation, she let her

words fall, "The one thing I want—the one thing I ever wanted from this marriage—is not mine."

His face closed. He straightened. "I told you from the first what I would give you—have I reneged on anything I promised?"

"No. But I offered you more, more than we had bargained—and you took. Gladly."

He couldn't deny it. His jaw hardened but he said nothing.

"I've given you more than we spoke of. I've tried hard to be all you wanted in a wife—I've managed this house, acted as your hostess, done all I promised. And I've done more, given more, been more."

She held his gaze, then more softly asked, "Now tell me, please—what have I done to deserve your distance?"

It was pointless to pretend he didn't understand, that he didn't know what she wanted, what she'd hoped. What she'd dreamed. Gyles held her darkened gaze and wished he could, but they'd gone too far for that. From the first they'd dealt directly, at a level of communication he'd shared with no one else, albeit a communication without words. They were attuned—aware of the other's moods, of the subtleties in their thinking. She'd been transparent from the first. And he'd let her believe that she could see into his heart, into his soul, when in reality his heart was forever shielded and his soul was locked away where no one could reach.

For that—for all she had been and was—he owed her his honesty. "I never promised to love you."

The emerald of her eyes darkened. She looked at him for a long moment, then, swallowing, she lifted her chin. "Love is not something one can promise."

She turned and left him, the skirts of her peignoir trailing behind her.

Chapter 17

Love was something that came slowly, on silent feet. Something that crept up on a man unawares and took him prisoner. She'd said she felt like a prisoner now—she was a captive, did she but know it, to the love that had him in its grip. Neither he nor she could break free. Not now.

It was too late for second thoughts. Too late to take evasive action. Once love struck, it was an incurable disease. Ineradicable.

He'd accepted that, finally, not without a fight, but the long hours of the previous night when he'd held her tight against him had revealed a reality far more absolute than he'd believed could be.

Love simply was. It asked no permissions, required no decisions. It lived. It lived in him.

Gyles's thoughts ran on as he stood beside his tallboy and unbuttoned his shirt. Wallace came back in; sitting in a chair, he allowed him to pull off his boots. Gyles remained in the chair, his gaze fixed, unseeing, across the room.

What to do? The memory of her eyes just before she'd turned and left him was etched in his mind. He could eradicate that look with three little words, reinstate her glorious smile. He could tell her, and then try to work out some framework of existence, together. Was that wise? Could he trust her?

One small corner of his mind whispered yes, the rest of him ran screaming at the thought. Trust a woman with his heart, with the key to his defenses? Give her the ability to destroy him? The concept ran deeply against his grain; if the barbarian was absolute in protecting her, he was equally committed to protecting himself.

There had to be some other way. He rose. Dragging his shirt from his waistband, he continued unbuttoning it.

The terms of their marriage—the terms he'd specified—rang in his mind. She'd given him all he'd wanted. All except . . .

The truth hit him, rocked him.

His gaze shifted to, then focused on the connecting door. Muttering a curse, he strode across, opened it, stepped through. Remembering Wallace, he shut it behind him.

It took a moment to locate her in the moon-streaked dimness. She was on the other side of the bed, in an armchair pulled to face the window. She flicked him a glance. As he rounded the bed, he saw her surreptiously dab at her eyes.

He stopped behind the chair. "Why didn't you tell me?"

She glanced back and up at him. "Tell you what?"

Her voice was thick, her puzzlement genuine.

He set his jaw. "You're pregnant."

Her wide-eyed look told him she'd known, but had, at least momentarily, forgotten. She twisted to partially face him. "I . . . wasn't sure. It's only been a few weeks. . . ."

They'd been married seven weeks.

The clash of his emotions was so powerful he swayed, physically shaken, emotionally at sea. The future had just become so much more dangerous—so much more precious. To him.

What did it mean to her?

The huge eyes that stared up at him, green even in the

poor light, were overbright. She was watching him, waiting . . .

He couldn't think. His mind was streaking in a dozen directions, panicked, reeling. He had to keep her safe, had to take her out of danger. He looked into her eyes. He couldn't explain—couldn't find the words, couldn't force them past the vise locked about his heart. Couldn't face his vulnerability. He'd let her think he was rejecting her. If he now asked for her company, would she reject him? Possibly. If he ordered her, would she go? No. Yet he had to get her away. Had to.

He drew in a huge breath, mentally girded his loins. Curtly, he nodded. "I'll be leaving for London in the morning."

Her lips parted in shock. Then her breasts swelled; her gaze kindled. "Indeed? Am I to take it you're invoking our agreement?"

"Yes." The shadows hid his deception. "We go our separate ways." He turned as if to recross to his room.

"Wait!" The word resonated with fury, hot now, not cold. He turned back as she scrambled from the chair. "If you're going to London, then so am I!"

He held his breath, searched for the right tone. "I wasn't aware you had any acquaintances in town."

"I'm looking forward to making some." Her voice purred with anger. She tilted her chin. "I'm sure there'll be many eager to befriend your countess."

He managed not to react. Managed to coldly incline his head. "As you say."

He thought he heard her teeth grind. "I *do* say!" She flung her hands in the air. "I've offered you more than you required, more than you looked for in our marriage. I've been understanding and patient—how *patient* I've been!"

She started to pace, flinging words at him. "I have *not* made demands, I have *not* pressed you—I've waited, self-effacing, for you to come to your senses! And have you?

No! You set your path—designed our marriage—before you even met me. Yet although the potential's far greater than you imagined, will you rescript your views? No! You're too *pigheaded* to change your mind, even when it's in your best interests!"

Her skirts whirled as she rounded on him, eyes afire, hands dramatically flying. "Very well! If you're so *insensible* as to turn your back on what might be, so be it! Go back to London and your scintillating mistresses! But I won't be left here, immured in your castle. I'm coming to London, too—and I fully intend to enjoy myself as I please." She narrowed her eyes at him. "What's sauce for the gander is sauce for the goose."

She didn't wait for an answer but swung away. Fury shimmered in the air about her. She halted, her back to him. Folding her arms, she stared at the window.

Gyles let a moment pass—it would be unwise to agree too quickly—then said, coldly and evenly, "As you wish. I'll give orders that you'll accompany me tomorrow."

Throughout her tirade, he'd held to the shadows. He'd schemed and got what he wanted, what he needed—and rather more besides. The story of their marriage.

He heard her sniff. Without turning, she inclined her head in haughty agreement. Face set, he crossed to the door to his room. Opening it, he saw Wallace, waiting patiently.

"Her ladyship and I will leave for London as early as possible tomorrow. We anticipate taking up residence in the capital for the immediate future. See to it."

Wallace bowed. "Indeed, sir." He considered for only a moment. "I believe we can be ready to depart by eleven o'clock."

Gyles nodded. "You may go—I won't need you again tonight."

Wallace bowed again. Gyles watched him go, then turned—and discovered Francesca close beside him. He shut the door. "Satisfied?"

They were close, face-to-face in the dimness. She rose on her toes, bringing their faces closer still. Her expression was belligerent; banked anger lit her eyes. "Rawlingses are so *very* stubborn."

Her eyes, narrowed, held his for an instant, then she flung away, crossing the room in a glide of swishing silk.

His own eyes narrowing, Gyles watched her go, replaying her words, then he realized.

She was a Rawlings, had been born a Rawlings, too.

Releasing the doorknob, he followed her to her bed.

She'd risked a lot on a stubborn man changing his mind.

As she sat in the swaying carriage the next day, Francesca had ample time to dwell on that fact. To consider all she'd risked—her future happiness, indeed her life, for she was too deeply committed, now, to draw back. She'd placed her heart on the scales in allowing herself to fall in love with him; that was done and could not be undone.

It wasn't just her future, either, but his, too, if only he would acknowledge it. She was sure he saw the truth, but getting him to admit it, act on it? There lay the rub.

How to get him to change his mind? The question fully absorbed her as the miles rolled past. It all seemed to hinge on who was the more stubborn—on whether she was willing to risk all to gain her dream.

She tried to see forward, to think ahead, imagining the possibilities. Thoughts of the past night kept intruding. She didn't want to think about that.

About the way he'd closed a hand in the hair at her nape and swung her to him, tipped her head back, and kissed her as if he'd been starving. About the way his hands had raced over her, stripping the silk from her, greedy for her skin, her flesh, her body. The feel of him over her, around her, inside her, hard and commanding, demanding. He'd wanted and taken with the ruthlessness of a conqueror, and she'd been with him every step of the way. Taunting, defiant, taking her own pleasure in his possessiveness, recklessly urging him on.

Holding him to her long after, when the tempest had passed and left them drained.

She flicked a glance sideways, briefly studied his profile. One elbow propped on the window ledge, his chin supported in that hand, he was watching the streetscape of London roll by.

She'd woken in the night to find him curled around her, his chest to her back, one hand splayed protectively over her stomach. When she'd woken in the morning—been woken by the maids scurrying furiously—he'd been gone. The chaos of the morning had left her no time to think, let alone reflect, not until they'd rolled out of the park and Jacobs had turned his team toward the capital.

They'd stopped at the Dower House, but Lady Elizabeth and Henni had been out walking. Horace had received them, jovial as ever, unsurprised that they might indulge in "a bolt to the capital." They'd left messages of farewell with him.

It had been Horace who'd been the focus of her thoughts as they'd bowled through Berkshire. Horace who'd been Gyles's father figure through his formative years—the years in which a boy learned by observation the ways in which men behaved to women. It was obvious that Horace was sincerely devoted to Henni, but that perception owed more to Henni's calm happiness than any overt behavior on Horace's part.

Horace had taught Gyles to be a gentleman, and Horace eschewed all outward shows of affection, of love, toward his wife, regardless of his true feelings.

Eyeing Gyles, Francesca mentally ran through the catalogue she'd assembled of the actions, the small gestures all but buried beneath the activities of their lives, that had left her hope intact.

He'd tried, deliberately, to dash that hope, to lead her to believe he was denying her absolutely, denying any chance of her dream transmuting to reality, yet all the while his actions spoke differently.

Not just his actions in their bed, although their tenor certainly did not support the facade he'd tried to project—that of an expert lover who nevertheless remained emotionally indifferent to her. She suppressed a dismissive humph: he had *never* been emotionally indifferent to her—the idea!

How he could expect her to believe it she didn't know.

Especially when there were a thousand other things that gave him away. Like his fussing when they'd stopped for lunch at an inn. Was she well wrapped and warm enough? The bricks at her feet hot enough? Was the food to her liking?

Did he think she was blind?

He knew she wasn't. That puzzled her. It was as if he'd accepted that she'd know or at least suspect that he felt more for her, but that he was hoping, if not expecting, that she'd pretend she didn't know.

That didn't, to her mind, make sense, yet it wasn't, she was sure, an inaccurate summation of their present state.

He said one thing but meant, and wanted, another. He'd said they would go their separate ways—she'd be greatly surprised if that came to pass.

Did he want some sort of facade in place, like Horace and Henni? Was he hoping she'd agree to that? Could she?

In all honesty, she doubted she could. Her temperament was not amenable to hiding her emotions.

Was that the direction he wished to steer them in?

If so, why?

She'd asked him last night, and he'd refused to answer. There was no point asking again, even if the context was somewhat altered. At base, it was the same question—the question she kept tripping over, again and again.

So she'd have to forge on, try to find a way forward, without the answer. It was as if she were doing battle on a field obscured by mist—fighting for her future, and his, without knowing where or what obstacles were in her path. If he thought she'd grow discouraged, give in, and settle for less than the enduring, open love she'd always wanted, especially now she knew it could exist if he would allow it to be, he would need to think again. Resigning battles was not her forte.

Unfortunately, it wasn't his either.

She slanted an assessing glance at him. They would see.

The coach slowed, then turned a corner. A huge park appeared on the right.

Gyles glanced at her. "Hyde Park. Where the fashionable go to be seen."

She leaned closer to look past him. "And should I be seen there?"

He hesitated, then said, "I'll take you for a drive around the Avenue one day."

She sat back as the carriage rounded another corner. Almost immediately, it slowed.

"We've arrived."

Francesca glanced out at a row of elegant mansions. The carriage halted before one; the number 17 glowed against the stonework flanking the door.

The carriage door was opened. Gyles moved past her and descended, then handed her down to the pavement. She looked up at the green-painted door, at the gleaming brass knocker.

Behind her, Gyles murmured, "Our London home."

He led her up the steps and into the blaze of the hall. The servants were waiting, lined up to greet her, Wallace at their head, Ferdinand farther down the row. They'd traveled up in Gyles's curricle ahead of the main carriage. Wallace introduced her to Irving the Younger, then stood back while Irving introduced her to Mrs. Hart, the housekeeper, a thin, somewhat ascetic woman, a Londoner from her speech. Between them, Irving and Mrs. Hart introduced all the others, then Mrs. Hart murmured, "I daresay you're eager to rest, my lady. I'll show you to your room."

Francesca glanced about. Gyles was standing under the chandelier, watching her.

She started toward him, glancing back at Mrs. Hart. "I'm not tired, but I would love some tea. Please bring it to the library."

"At once, ma'am."

Reaching Gyles, she slid her arm through his. "Come, my lord. Show me your lair."

He should have put his foot down and ushered her into the drawing room. Two days later, Gyles could see his mistake clearly. Now the library, which in this house doubled as his study, was as much her lair as his.

He quelled a sigh and frowned at the letter spread on his blotter. It was from Gallagher. He glanced to where Francesca sat reading in an armchair before the hearth. "The Wenlows' cottage—do you remember it?"

She looked up. "In that hollow south of the river?"

"The roof's leaking."

"It's one of three, isn't it?"

He nodded. "They're all the same, built at the same time. I'm wondering if I should order all three roofs replaced."

He looked at her, watched consideration flow across her face.

"Winter's nearly here—if one of the other roofs spring a leak, it'll be hard to fix if it's snowing."

"Even if it isn't. Those old roofs get so iced, even without snow it's too dangerous to send men up." Setting a fresh sheet on the blotter, Gyles reached for a pen. "I'll tell Gallagher to replace all three."

She read while he wrote, but looked up as he sealed the letter. "Is there any other news?"

He recounted all Gallagher had told him. From there, they got onto the subject of the bills he was researching. They were deep in a discussion of demographics relating to the voting franchise when Irving entered. "Mr. Osbert Rawlings has called, my lord. Are you receiving?"

Gyles bit back a "no." Osbert wasn't in the habit of calling for no reason. "Show him in here."

Irving bowed and departed; a minute later he returned, Osbert in tow. Announced, Osbert nodded to Gyles, who rose. "Cousin." His gaze swung to Francesca; Osbert beamed. "Dear cousin Francesca—" He broke off, glanced at Gyles, then back at her. "I may call you that, may I not?"

"Of course." Francesca smiled and held out her hand. Osbert took it and bowed over it. "Pray be seated, or is your business with Gyles?"

"No, no!" Osbert eagerly sank into the other armchair. "I heard you were in town and felt I must call to welcome you to the capital."

"How kind," Francesca replied.

Suppressing a humph, Gyles sank back into the chair behind his desk.

"And"—Osbert searched his pockets—"I do hope you don't consider it impertinent, but I've written an ode—to your eyes. Ah, here it is!" He brandished a parchment. "Would you like me to read it?"

Gyles smothered a groan and took refuge behind a news sheet. Still, he couldn't help but hear Osbert's verse. It wasn't, in fact, bad—merely uninspired. He could have thought of ten better phrases to more adequately convey the fascinating allure of his wife's emerald eyes.

Francesca politely thanked Osbert and said various encouraging things, which led Osbert to fill her ears with predictions of how much she would enjoy the ton, and how much the ton would enjoy her. That last had Gyles compressing his lips, but then Francesca appealed to him over some point and he had to lower the news sheet and answer, *sans* scowl.

He bore with Osbert's prattle for five minutes more before

desperation gave birth to inspiration. Rising, he crossed to where Francesca and Osbert sat. Francesca looked up.

"If you recall, my dear, I'd mentioned taking you for a drive in the park." Gyles turned his easy expression on Osbert. "I'm afraid, cousin, that if I'm to give Francesca a taste of all you've been describing so eloquently, we'll need to go now."

"Oh, yes! Of course!" Osbert unraveled his long legs and stood. He took Francesca's hand. "You'll enjoy it, I'm sure."

Francesca said her farewells. Osbert took his leave of Gyles and quite happily departed.

Gyles watched his retreating back through narrowed eyes. "Well, my lord."

He turned to see Francesca, head tilted, regarding him with a smile.

"If we're to go driving in the park, I'd better go and change."

A pity—she looked delectable as she was, the scooped neckline of her day gown drawing his eyes, the soft material, clinging to her curves, drawing his senses. But she'd be too cold in his curricle. Catching her hand, he carried it to his lips. "I'll order the carriage. Fifteen minutes, in the hall."

She left him with a laugh and one of her glorious smiles.

It was the fashionable hour, and the Avenue was packed with carriages of every description. The larger, more staid broughams and landaus were pulled up along the verge, while the smaller, racier curricles and phaetons tacked along between. Speed was not of the essence—no one was in any rush; the whole purpose of the exercise was to see and be seen.

"There's so many here!" From her perch on the box seat, Francesca looked around. "I'd thought at this time of year, the town would be half-empty."

"This is half-empty." Gyles divided his attention between

the carriage in front and the occupants of the carriages beside them. "During the Season, the lawns are half-covered, and there're more horsemen about. What you're seeing is primarily the elite of the ton, those who have business, usually politics, that brings them up for the autumn session."

Francesca surveyed the ranks. "So these are the ladies I most need to get to know."

Gyles's brows rose, but he inclined his head.

Then he slowed his horses, drawing the curricle closer to a carriage on the verge. Francesca looked, then beamed. "Honoria!"

"Francesca! How delightful!" Honoria looked at Gyles and, still smiling, nodded. "My lord. I can't tell you how delighted I am to see you here."

Gyles's answering smile was chilly. Francesca raised her brows fleetingly at Honoria—the swift look she received in reply clearly stated: *I'll explain later.*

Honoria gestured to the three other ladies sharing the barouche. "Allow me to introduce you to Devil's aunt, Lady Louise Cynster, and her daughters, Amanda and Amelia."

Francesca exchanged greetings, smiling as she recognized the thoughts behind the girls' wide eyes. Each was the epitome of a fair English beauty, with golden ringlets, cornflower blue eyes, and delicate, milky complexions. "You're twins?"

"Yes." Amanda's gaze was still skating over her.

Amelia sighed. "You're most amazingly lovely, Lady Francesca."

Francesca smiled. "You're very lovely yourselves."

A thought popped into her head; her eyes widened, and she smothered a laugh. "Oh—excuse me!" She shot a wicked glance at Honoria and Louise. "It just occurred to me that if we made an entrance, all three together—Amelia on one side, me in the middle and Amanda on my other side, it would look quite extraordinary."

The contrast between their fairness and her exotic coloring was marked.

Louise grinned. The twins looked intrigued.

Honoria laughed. "It would cause a sensation."

Gyles caught Honoria's eye and glared.

Honoria's smile deepened; she turned to Francesca. "We must have you around for dinner—Devil will want to meet you again, and we must introduce you to the others. For how long are you down?"

Gyles left Francesca to answer. Perched beside her on the curricle's box seat, he felt increasingly exposed. He was pleased when, all relevant details exchanged, they took their leave of Honoria and her companions and he could drive on.

They didn't get far.

"Chillingworth!"

He knew the voice. It took a moment to locate the turban, perched above a pair of obsidian eyes that were the terror of the ton. Lady Osbaldestone beckoned imperiously. Seated beside her in her old brougham, watching with a too-knowing smile, was the Dowager Duchess of St. Ives.

Gyles swallowed his curse—Francesca would only wonder, and he had no choice anyway. Angling the curricle into the verge, he drew up beside the brougham.

Lady Osbaldestone smiled widely, leaned over and introduced herself. "I knew your parents, my dear—visited with them in Italy—you were only three at the time." She sat back and nodded benignly, her black eyes gleaming with deep satisfaction. "I was *exceedingly pleased* to hear of your marriage."

Gyles knew the comment was directed at him.

Francesca smiled. "Thank you."

"And I, my dear, must also add my congratulations." The Dowager, her pale green eyes warm, took Francesca's hand. "And yes," she said, smiling in response to the question dawning in Francesca's face, "you have met my son and he spoke highly of you and, of course, Honoria told me all."

"I'm delighted to meet you, Your Grace."

"And you will be seeing more of us, my dear, I have no doubt, so we will not keep you and Chillingworth any longer. It will soon grow chilly, and I'm sure your husband will want to whisk you away."

The twinkle in her eyes was not lost on Gyles, but retaliation was out of the question—it was far too dangerous. Both he and Francesca bowed; he escaped as fast as he dared.

"Are they—how is it described? *Grandes dames?*"

"The grandest. Do not be fooled. They wield considerable power despite their age."

"They're rather formidable, but I liked them. Don't you?"

Gyles snorted and drove on.

"Gyles! Yoo-*hoo!*"

Gyles slowed his horses. "Mama?" Both he and Francesca searched, then he saw Henni waving from a carriage farther up the line. "Good Lord." He drove up and reined in. "What on earth are you doing here?"

His mother opened her eyes at him. "You're not the only ones who might fancy a bolt to the capital." She released Francesca's hand. "And of course, Henni and I wanted to be here to support Francesca. It's a good opportunity to get to know the major hostess without the distraction of the Season."

"We've already met Honoria and Lady Louise Cynster, and the Dowager Duchess of St. Ives and Lady Osbaldestone," Francesca said.

"A very good start." Henni nodded determinedly. "Tomorrow we'll take you up with us, and we'll visit a few more."

Gyles hid a frown.

"But where are you staying?" Francesca asked.

"Walpole House," Lady Elizabeth answered. "It's just around the corner in North Audley Street, so we're close."

Gyles let his horses prance. "Mama—my horses. It's getting cold . . ."

"Oh, indeed you must get on, but no matter—we'll see you tonight at the Stanleys.' "

He felt Francesca's glance but didn't meet it. They made their farewells and parted. He took the shortest route away from the Avenue, then headed out of the park.

Francesca sat back and considered him. "Are we going to the Stanleys' tonight?"

Gyles shrugged. "We have an invitation. I suppose it's as good a place as any to start."

"Start what?"

Features grim, he guided his pair out of the gates. "Your emergence into the ton."

He'd wanted to put it off for as long as he could—he realized that now. And he knew why. His wife would exert the same visceral tug on the ton's rakes as honey exerted on bees. At this time of year, those present were of the most dangerous variety, undiluted by the more innocuous bucks up from the country for the Season. Those at the Stanleys' would be the London wolves, those who, as he had done, rarely hunted outside the capital with its alluringly scented prey.

He'd made up his mind that he wouldn't leave Francesca's side before they'd even greeted their hostess.

She, predictably, was thrilled.

"A great pleasure to see you here, my lord." Lady Stanley nodded approvingly, then shifted her gaze to Francesca. Her expression warmed. "And I'm delighted to be one of the first to welcome you to the capital, Lady Francesca."

Francesca and her ladyship exchanged the customary phrases. Gyles noted her ladyship's transparent friendliness, not something to be taken for granted in the cut and thrust of the ton. Then again, the ton had been back in London for some weeks; the news that he'd married and that his marriage had been an arranged one would have circulated widely.

That news would gain Francesca greater sympathy and

acceptance than would otherwise have been the case. She'd never been in competition with the ton's ladies or their daughters given that the position of his countess had never been put on the marriage mart.

That was the good news. As they parted from their hosts, and he steered Francesca into the crowd, Gyles took in the creamy mounds of her breasts revealed by the neckline of her teal-silk evening gown, and wished he could retreat. Take her home to his library and lock her in, so that only those men he approved of would see her.

None knew better than he that the news that their marriage had been arranged would expose her to the immediate scrutiny of those who'd recently been his peers. One look, and any rake worthy of the name would come running. She exuded the air of a woman of sensual appetites, one who would never be content with the mild attentions of an indifferent husband.

The thought was laughable. He shook his head. She noticed and raised a brow.

"Nothing." Inwardly, he shook his head again. He must have been mad to have set himself up for this.

"Lady Chillingworth?" Lord Pendleton bowed elegantly before them; straightening, he glanced at Gyles. "Come, my lord—do introduce us."

Mentally gritting his teeth, Gyles did. He couldn't very well do otherwise. And so it began—within ten minutes, they were surrounded by a pack of politely slavering wolves, all waiting for him to excuse himself and leave her to them.

Hell would freeze before he did.

Francesca chatted easily. Her social confidence increased her attractiveness to this particular audience. He knew them all, knew the question he was raising in their minds by remaining anchored by her side. How to escape before one of his ex-peers guessed his true position and decided to make hay of it was the primary question exercising his mind.

Relief appeared in an unexpected guise. A tall, fair-haired gentleman shouldered his way through the crowd.

Francesca was surprised when, apparently without exerting himself, the newcomer won through to her side. Intrigued, she offered her hand. He took it and bowed.

"Harry Cynster, Lady Francesca. As your husband has been elected an honorary Cynster, that makes you one of the clan, too, so I'll claim the prerogative of a relative to dispense with formal introductions." Harry exchanged a glance with Gyles over her head, then concluded, his blue eyes wickedly alight, "I'm honored to meet you. I always did wonder who would trip Gyles up."

Francesca returned his smile.

"I'm exceedingly surprised to see you here."

She turned at Gyles's drawl; he was looking over the heads, scanning the room.

"She's not here." Harry met Francesca's gaze. "My wife, Felicity. She's expecting our first child." He glanced at Gyles. "She's at home in Newmarket. I had to come up for the sales at Tattersalls."

"Ah—the mystery's explained."

Harry grinned, tightly. "Indeed." He paused for a heartbeat, then looked at Francesca. "But I would have thought you'd guess." He again smiled his winning smile. "I'm here on a mission. My mama would like to meet you." He glanced again at Gyles. "She's sitting with Lady Osbaldestone."

Gyles caught Demon's glance, recognized the ploy, recognized the fellow feeling that had prompted it. He hesitated for only an instant before asking, "Where, precisely?"

"The other end of the room."

To the bewildered disappointment of the gentlemen about them, Gyles excused himself and Francesca. Her hand anchored on his sleeve, he led her through the crowd, Demon equally large and discouraging on her other side.

Francesca glanced from one hard male face to the other—both were scanning the crowd as they strolled, watching for any gentleman who might attempt to accost her. She had to hide a smile as they delivered her to the *chaise* where Lady Osbaldestone sat, resplendent in puce trimmed with feathers. Alongside her sat another *grande dame*.

"Lady Horatia Cynster, my dear." The lady pressed her hand. "I'm very glad to meet you." She shifted her gaze to Gyles. "Chillingworth." She gave him her hand and watched as he bowed. "You're an exceedingly lucky man—I do hope you appreciate that?"

Gyles arched a brow. "Naturally."

"Good. Then you may fetch me some orgeat, and her ladyship would like a glass, too. You may take Harry with you." She waved them away.

Francesca was intrigued when, after an instant's hesitation, Gyles inclined his head, collected Harry Cynster with a glance, and left them.

"Here—sit down, gel." Lady Osbaldestone shifted, as did Lady Horatia. Francesca sat between them.

"You needn't worry about all those others." Lady Horatia waved in the direction from which they'd come. "They'll melt into the woodwork once they realize you're not for them."

"Good thing, too." Lady Osbaldestone thumped her cane and turned gleaming black eyes on Francesca. "If the rumors are even half-true, you'll have enough on your plate with that husband of yours."

Francesca felt heat rise in her cheeks. She quickly turned, as Lady Horatia said, "Indeed, in such situations, it's wise to keep your husband occupied—busy. No need to let him work himself into a lather over nothing, if you take my meaning."

Francesca blinked, then nodded, rather weakly.

"No saying what he might do if he got overly exercised on that point." Lady Osbaldestone nodded sagely. "One of the difficulties when marrying Cynsters—one has to draw a very firm line. Too prone to revert to their ancestral selves if rubbed the wrong way."

"But . . . I don't understand." Francesca glanced from one to the other. "Gyles isn't a Cynster."

Lady Osbaldestone snorted.

Lady Horatia grinned. "They made him one by decree—unusually farsighted of them, but it was doubtless Devil's idea." She patted Francesca's hand. "What we're saying is that there's not a whisker to chose between them—what applies to the Cynsters applies equally to Chillingworth."

"Come to that," Lady Osbaldestone opined, "the same applies to most of the Rawlingses, but the others are generally milder sorts."

"Do you know them? The other Rawlingses?"

"A good few," Lady Osbaldestone admitted. "Why?"

Francesca told her.

Gyles and Harry returned with two glasses of orgeat and one of champagne for Francesca, to find all three ladies with their heads together, discussing the Rawlings family tree. Harry exchanged a glance with Gyles, then strolled off. Fifteen minutes passed before Gyles was able to extract Francesca from the discussion.

"I'll see you at my at-home next week," Lady Horatia said, as he finally drew Francesca to her feet.

"I'll be there, too," Lady Osbaldestone said. "I'll let you know what I've learned then."

Gyles gave mute thanks that the old tartar wasn't planning on calling in Green Street. "Mama and Henni are near the main door." He steered Francesca through the crowd.

After another fifteen minutes, during which his mother, Henni, and Francesca made numerous social plans, he dragged Francesca away.

"It sounds like you'll have barely a moment to yourself."

Francesca glanced at him—mentally replayed his words, analyzed their tone—then she smiled and pressed his arm. "Nonsense." She glanced around, then sighed. "Nevertheless, I do think I've made enough plans for one night." She turned to him. "Perhaps we should go home."

"Home?"

"Hmm—home, and to bed." She tilted her head. "Of course, if you wished, we could stop by the library."

"The library?"

"Wallace will have built up the fire—it should be rather cozy."

"Cozy."

"Mmm—warm." She rolled the word on her tongue. "Pleasant and . . . relaxing."

The sultry promise in her voice sent heat pouring through him. Gyles stopped, changed tack, and headed for the door.

Chapter 18

Two weeks later, Gyles stood by the side of Lady Matheson's ballroom, reconsidering the madness that had made him bring Francesca to London. His need to protect her had forced his hand; she was safer here, away from the strange happenings at Lambourn, in a smaller, more secure house, yet her emergence into the ton had brought dangers of a different sort.

The sort that ate away his civilized facade and left his true self much too close to his surface.

"Gyles?"

He turned, smiled and bent to kiss Henni's cheek. "I didn't realize you'd be here."

"Well of *course* we're here, dear. The Mathesons are connections of Horace's, don't you remember?"

These days he thought of little beyond his wife.

"Where's Francesca?" Henni looked inquiringly at him, obviously expecting him to know.

"Sitting with Her Grace of St. Ives." He directed Henni's gaze across the room.

"Ah. Thank you, dear. Incidentally, that was an excellent dinner the other night, and the little gathering the week before went very well, I thought."

Gyles nodded. Henni left him, wending her way through the crowd toward Francesca. The dinner had been their first—Francesca's first in London, his first as a married man. The anticipation had drawn them together, had had them working together even more closely than before.

It had been a triumph; the sharing had added an extra dimension. When Henni had labeled the dinner "excellent," she hadn't been referring to the quality of the dishes, although with Ferdinand seeking to please, that had been exceptional. It had been Francesca who'd sparkled and fascinated; he'd found it easy to enact the role of proud husband and do his part to carry the evening.

The small party they'd hosted the week before had been Francesca's first foray into the wider arena of tonnish entertaining—that had been an outright success, too.

She was a success, and she was taking it in her stride. The support of his mother, Henni, and the Cynster ladies helped. He was grateful for their interest, but he knew very well to whom he owed the bulk of his gratitude.

He watched as Francesca, deep in a dramatic discussion with Honoria, looked up as Henni approached. Her smile—that glorious, heartwarming smile—wreathed her face, and she stood to kiss his aunt's cheek. Then she turned back to Honoria, drawing Henni into their conversation.

Gyles couldn't help a small smile. She threw herself into things wholeheartedly; she'd done the same with the ton, honestly intrigued, enjoying the offered entertainments. Her delight, not that of an innocent but a newcomer, had shown him his old, worn world in a new light.

Settling his shoulders against the wall, he continued to watch her, keeping watch over her.

On the *chaise* beside Honoria, Francesca was aware of her husband's regard. She'd grown used to it; indeed, she found it comforting knowing that if anyone less than desirable approached her, he would be there, at her side, in a heartbeat. The ton was large, and while she now knew some of the right faces and names, there were many she didn't know—and some of those she didn't need to know.

One such was Lord Carnegie, but his lordship was too wise to approach—not yet. But she knew what he was, what he was thinking; every time his gaze touched her, she had to quell a shiver as if some slimy slithering thing had touched her bare arm. His lordship hove into view and bowed. Francesca pointedly looked away.

Honoria glared. "Disreputable popinjay!" She lowered her voice. "They say he killed his first wife, and two mistresses, too."

Francesca pulled a face, then switched to a smile as Osbert Rawlings approached and bowed before them.

"Cousin Francesca." Hand over his heart, Osbert shook her hand, then bowed and shook Honoria's.

"Just saw Carnegie move off." Osbert glanced back, then stepped closer. "Not a nice man."

"No, indeed," Honoria agreed. "I was just telling Francesca . . ." She gestured vaguely.

"Quite." Osbert nodded, then decided Carnegie was too dark a subject for discussion in such company; the way his face suddenly lit made that clear. "I say! I've just been hearing about the latest production at the Theatre Royal."

Osbert was never vague about anything to do with verbal performance. He kept them entertained for the next ten minutes with a vivid account of Mrs. Siddons's latest triumph. Amused, Francesca listened, aware Gyles was watching, aware of what he would be thinking, yet despite his dismissiveness, he didn't disapprove of Osbert.

Indeed, Osbert had become her cavalier. He attended the majority of functions they did and was always ready to put himself out to amuse and entertain her. If she ever needed an escort, and Gyles was not to hand, she would take Osbert's arm without a qualm. And if she was starting to suspect that Osbert claimed her company at least in part as a defense against the mothers who still had him in their sights, she was happy to keep that suspicion to herself.

Osbert was too much of a dear to throw to the lions.

"Well, well—how the mighty have fallen."

Gyles drew his gaze from his wife, and fastened it on Devil as he lounged beside him. "You can talk."

Devil glanced across the room at Honoria, and shrugged. "It comes to us all." He grinned wickedly. "Am I allowed to say 'I told you so'?"

"No."

"Still in denial, are we?"

"One can but try."

"Give it up. It's hopeless."

"Not yet."

Devil snorted. "So—what's the real reason you're standing here propping up the wall?"

Gyles made no attempt to answer.

Devil shot him a measuring glance. "Actually, I wanted to ask—what are the chances of your cousin Osbert inheriting these days?"

"Few and diminishing."

"And when might those chances vanish?"

Gyles frowned. "Midsummer. Why?"

"Hmm—so you'll be up for the Season?"

"I expect so."

"Good." Devil met Gyles's gaze. "We're going to need to push harder with those bills if we're to succeed."

Gyles nodded. He looked at their wives. "It's occurred to me that we might be missing an opportunity to persuade some of our peers to our cause."

Devil followed his gaze. "You think so?"

"Francesca understands the salient points as well as I."

"So does Honoria."

"Well, why not? While in town, they spend the better half

of their days talking with the other wives. Why shouldn't they steer the conversation—introduce the notion, plant seeds and nurture them—all in a good cause?"

After a moment, Devil grinned. "I'll suggest it to Honoria." Glancing at Gyles, he straightened, an unholy gleam in his eyes. "Of course, you realize that in making such a suggestion, you're going to encourage Francesca to invest even more time in the social whirl." With spurious concern, Devil frowned. "I'll understand if you can't bring yourself to do it—it must be frustrating, recently married as you are, to find your wife in such demand."

Gyles scowled before he could stop himself, then scowled even more when Devil grinned devilishly and, with a salute, stepped out of reach.

He was not that transparent. Devil had been able to put his finger on the one sore point created by Francesca's social success only because he'd felt, or perhaps still did feel, the same way. The social whirl of the ton had not been created to foster marriage. Weddings, yes, but not what came after. And it was that—the after-the-wedding stage—that now consumed him.

And Francesca. It wasn't as if the difficulty was his alone, and for that, he was thankful. She, too, clung to the few hours they could spend together, in his library, comfortably reading, sometimes discussing, exchanging views—learning more about each other.

But as the ton discovered her, those private hours had shrunk. Then disappeared.

Her mornings were consumed with visits—at-homes, morning teas—usually in the company of his mother and Henni, Honoria, or one of the other ladies with whom she'd become friends. All right and proper.

She was rarely in for luncheon, but neither was he. While she spent her afternoons making further connections and strengthening those already made, he waded through the myriad administrative demands made by the estate, or met his friends at their clubs. He and she met again for dinner but never dined alone—they were now in constant demand as more and more hostesses discovered her.

After dinner, there were balls and parties to attend; they always returned home late. And if she still came to his arms eager and wanting, while they loved as passionately as ever, there yet remained a sense of deprivation, a lack.

He was an earl—he shouldn't have to lack.

"A message from North Audley Street, ma'am."

Francesca set aside her toast and lifted the folded note from Wallace's salver. "Thank you." Opening the note, she read it, then glanced at Gyles. "Your mama and Henni are both feeling under the weather, but they say I shouldn't stop by to visit them. They say it's just the sniffles."

"No need to risk catching them, too." Gyles looked at her over the top of that morning's *Gazette*. "Does their indisposition affect your plans?"

"We were going to attend a morning tea with the Misses Berry, but I really don't feel like going alone."

"Indeed not. You'd be the youngest present by a decade." Gyles laid aside the *Gazette*. "I have a suggestion."

"Oh?" Francesca looked up.

"Come walking with me. There's something I want to show you."

She was intrigued. "Where?"

"You'll see when we get there."

To Francesca's astonishment, "there" proved to be Asprey, the jewelers, in Bond Street. The "something" was an emerald necklace.

The assistant snibbed the catch at her nape. Wonderingly, she raised a hand to touch the large, oval-cut emeralds that hung from the collar, itself made of oval-cut stones. Gyles had insisted she remain in her morning gown with its scooped neckline; she now understood why. The emeralds flared, green fire against her skin.

She shifted this way, then that, watching the light play in the stones, noting how her eyes deepened, as if reflecting the emerald's fire. The necklace was neither too heavy nor too ornate. Neither was it so delicate that it risked being overwhelmed by her own dramatic coloring.

It could have been made just for her. . . .

She looked past her own reflection and saw Gyles, behind her, exchange an approving glance with the old jeweler who'd come from the back of the shop to watch.

Francesca turned and caught Gyles's hand. "You had this made for me?"

He looked down at her. "They had nothing quite right." He held her gaze for a moment, then squeezed her fingers before sliding his hand free. "Leave it on."

While he complimented the jeweler, the assistant helped her into her pelisse. Francesca buttoned it up to her throat. It was chilly outside, but that wasn't the reason. She suspected the necklace would be worth a small fortune. Over the past weeks, she'd seen many jewels, but nothing of such simple, dramatic worth.

Gyles slid the necklace's velvet case into his pocket, then collected her, and they left the shop. On the pavement, he noted her pelisse's high collar and smiled. Taking her arm, he led her farther up the street.

"Where are we going now?" Francesca asked. They'd left the carriage in Piccadilly—in the opposite direction.

"Now you have the necklace, you need something to go with it."

What he had in mind was a gown, another item created to his specifications. He'd commanded the services of one of the ton's most exclusive modistes; Francesca stood before the long mirror in the private room off the Bruton Street salon; all she could do was stare.

The gown was simple, reserved in its lines, yet on her, it became a statement of sensual confidence. In heavy emerald silk, the bodice fitted her like a second skin, the triangular neckline neither high nor low, yet because of the gown's fit, her breasts would draw all eyes—if it wasn't for the necklace. Gown and necklace complemented each other perfectly, neither detracting from the other. From the raised waist, the silk fell sleekly, flaring over her hips into a stylish layered skirt.

Francesca stared at the lady in the mirror, watched her breasts rise and fall, watched the emeralds wink green fire. Her eyes appeared enormous, her hair a froth of black curls anchored atop her head.

She glanced at Gyles, sitting relaxed in an armchair to one side. He caught her gaze, then turned his head and said something in French to the modiste—Francesca didn't catch it. The modiste slipped out, closing the door.

Gyles rose; he came to stand behind her. He looked at her reflection. "Do you like it?"

His gaze roamed over her. Francesca considered her answer, considered what she could see in his face, unmasked in that instant.

"The gown, the necklace." She held out her arms, palms up. "They're beautiful. Thank you."

For what he'd allowed her to become. He'd made her his countess in name and in fact. She was now his. His to bejewel, his to gown. His.

She'd wanted that, dreamed of it, accepted it. She'd prayed he would, too. She turned her head, laid a hand along his cheek, and guided his lips to hers. His hands, warm through the silk, closed about her waist as their lips met, brushed, then settled. But only for a heartbeat.

The sudden rush of heat, of desire, had them both reining quickly back. Their eyes met; their lips curved in identical, knowing smiles.

He held her gaze, then raised a hand and lightly brushed the tight peak of one breast.

"You can thank me later."

* * *

She did, spending the better part of the night in that endeavor. Throughout the following day, while she chatted and visited, drank tea and listened, Francesca's mind constantly slid away, seduced by her memories. At one point Honoria arched a knowing brow and left her blushing. She wondered who else saw through her social veil and correctly guessed the cause of her distraction.

The following morning, she breakfasted with Gyles, as was becoming their invariable habit. He questioned her about her day's engagements, then suggested she don her pelisse and come for a short drive with him in his curricle to try out the paces of his new team of bays.

He kidnapped her for the entire day.

Deaf to her protests, he bowled through the streets, taking her into the City, to St. Paul's, where they walked hand in hand, gazing at the brasses and monuments, to the Tower and London Bridge, then off to see Cleopatra's Needle, then on to the Museum.

It was, in many ways, a journey of joint discovery; when she peppered him with questions, he admitted he hadn't visited the sights recently, not since he'd been ten.

That made her laugh—he retaliated by subjecting her to an inquisition on her life in Italy.

Indeed, his questions came so readily, rolled so easily from one point to the next, that she started to suspect that the purpose behind the outing was at least in part so he could learn more of her.

She answered his queries with a light and joyous heart.

Gyles caught her shrewd glances, saw the light dancing in her eyes. She would have been even more thrilled had she known his principal motivation. True, he did want to know more about her, but his deepest, most compelling reason for spending the entire day with her was simply because he needed to.

Needed the time with her to soothe an odd uneasiness, to reassure the barbarian that she was still his during the day as much as she was during the night. Needed the time to draw her to him with more than just his arms, his kisses. Needed to prove to himself that he could.

When he turned the bays for home, Francesca sighed; smiling softly, she leaned her head against his shoulder. He bent his head and dropped a quick kiss on her forehead. Her smile deepened, and she snuggled closer. It occurred to him that he was wooing her, although not in the accepted sense. He wasn't wooing her to make her fall in love with him. He was wooing his wife to keep her loving him.

He would do it until he died.

Almack's. Francesca had heard of it, of course, but she hadn't imagined it would be so plain, so . . . boring. Tonight was not one of the usual subscription balls—it was too late in the year for that. Instead, the hostesses had graciously invited those of their accepted circle still in town for one last evening within the hallowed halls.

Casting a critical glance around as she strolled the main room on Osbert's arm, Francesca felt that the hallowed halls could do with redecorating. Then again, the throng that filled them was glittering and glamorous enough to deflect attention from the dull, rather shabby decor.

Lady Elizabeth and Henni had encouraged her to accompany them; they'd explained it was an occasion at which a new countess could not afford not to be seen. On learning of her plans over the breakfast table, Gyles had suggested she wear her new gown and her emeralds.

Encountering her in the hall as she was leaving, he'd paused, hesitated. Shadows had hidden his face, then he'd taken her hand, carried it to his lips, and told her she looked ravishing.

The gown and necklace bolstered her confidence. They felt like armor, so carefully scrutinized had they been. Knowing she looked well had allowed her to meet the sharp eyes with unimpaired serenity. Under the auspices of Lady

Elizabeth and Lady Henrietta, as Henni was more properly known, she'd been introduced to all the hostesses. All had signified their approval; all had expressed the wish that she would be a frequent visitor in the years to come.

"Why?" Francesca shook Osbert's sleeve. He'd arrived shortly after they had, and had made a beeline for her side. "Why would I wish to attend here often?"

"Well," Osbert temporized, "in your case, I suppose there isn't any great need. You'll want to look in every so often to keep in touch—find out who the favored of the latest crop of young ladies are, which gentlemen are looking to take the plunge, and so on. But until you have a daughter to establish, I can't see that this place will help you. *Except* on occasions like this, of course."

"Even then." Francesca waved at the crowd. "Where are the gentlemen? Most of those here are so young, and they look like they've been dragged along by their mamas. Half of them are sulking." They reminded her forcibly of Lancelot Gilmartin. "There are only a few like you who've braved the dangers." She patted his arm. "I'm grateful."

Osbert colored and looked exceedingly conscious; Francesca smiled. Scanning the throng, she sighed. "There are no gentlemen like Gyles here."

Osbert cleared his throat. "Gentlemen like Gyles usually . . . er, stick to their clubs."

"After spending all day in their clubs, I would have thought they'd prefer to spend their evenings with feminine company."

Osbert swallowed. "Cousin Gyles and his sort aren't exactly encouraged to cross the threshold here. Well, they're not likely to want a young bride, are they?"

Francesca caught Osbert's eye. "Are you sure," she murmured, "that it isn't a case of the hostesses avoiding guests they can't control?"

Osbert's brows rose; he appeared much struck. "You know, I never thought of it quite like that, but . . ."

A stir about the main entry arch drew their attention. Francesca couldn't see through the crowd; Osbert craned his neck, looked, then turned back to Francesca, his expression amazed. "*Well!* What a turn up."

"What?" Francesca tugged his sleeve, but Osbert was looking again. He raised his hand in a salute.

An instant later, the crowd before them thinned, then parted. Gyles came stalking through.

"Madam." He nodded curtly, taking her hand, ignoring her stunned expression.

He glanced at Osbert, who was struggling to hide a grin. Gyles caught his eye; Osbert abruptly took refuge behind his habitual vague mask. He nodded. "Cousin."

Gyles returned the nod, then looked at Francesca.

Smiling delightedly, she slid her fingers from his grasp only to place them on his sleeve, slipping into her usual position at his side where she felt so comfortable. "I thought gentlemen like you weren't encouraged to attend?"

Hard grey eyes met hers. "You're here."

Gyles skated his gaze over her shoulders, over the emeralds winking against her fine skin. The rustle of approaching skirts had him turning, saving him from saying something even more revealing.

"Gyles, dear—*what* a surprise!" His mother quizzed him with her eyes. He kissed her cheek and glanced at Henni.

With her head, Henni indicated the main archway. "You certainly made an entrance. Countess Lieven's still standing there, shocked to her toes."

"It'll do her good." Gyles glanced over the crowd. Not as many gentleman as he'd expected. Better than he'd hoped. "Come." He glanced at Francesca. "Now I've made the supreme sacrifice of donning knee breeches, we may as well stroll."

"Yes, do." His mother caught his eye. "Go that way." She pointed to an arch that led into a succession of anterooms. Gyles inclined his head and turned Francesca in that direction. Presumably there was someone that way who needed to know that he was protective of his wife.

His stunning, ravishing, too-delectable-to-take-his-eyes-off wife. His arrant stupidity in suggesting she wear her new gown had rebounded with a vengeance. He'd only done so because he'd been dying to see her in it, and Almack's was surely the most innocuous of venues—that had been his rapid reasoning. The truth had hit him between the eyes when, smugly expectant, he'd come out of the library having heard her footsteps on the stairs, and seen her, gowned and jeweled, a hundred times more sensually evocative than his imagination had painted her.

The company at Almack's was largely innocuous. Any gentlemen present would not be of his ilk. Few wolves would bother poking their noses in there. He'd told himself all that and more while struggling to concentrate on a legislative draft.

Hopeless. He'd tossed aside his papers and gone up to change—he'd caught Wallace grinning when he'd asked for his knee breeches.

If it hadn't been for the effect Francesca had on him, dressed as she was, so close beside him, he'd be scowling. Instead . . . he wasn't all that averse to spending an hour strolling in her company.

He was known to most of the matrons. He and Francesca were stopped frequently; some dared to quiz him, but most were genuinely intrigued—entertained—by his presence. Francesca chatted with her usual assurance. He had all but relaxed when, turning from Lady Chatham, they found themselves facing a large, rather portly gentleman with florid features.

"Chillingworth." With a genial nod, Lord Albemarle shifted his gaze to Francesca. "And this, I take it, is your new countess who I've heard so much about."

Gyles gritted his teeth and made the introduction. His

hand lay over Francesca's on his sleeve; he squeezed her fingers warningly.

"My lord." Francesca acknowledged the introduction haughtily and made no move to slide her fingers from beneath the comfort of Gyles's warm hand. Lord Albemarle's eyes were too cool, his gaze too assessing.

His lordship smiled, fascinated, clearly intent on satisfying his curiosity, apparently unaware of the danger he was courting. She felt Gyles stiffen; she tensed herself, expecting him to excuse them with some cold remark—

"Gyles! How good to see you again." A lady, tall and imposing, appeared at Gyles's side. She was handsome in a hard, glittering way. Her gaze locked with Francesca's. "I did hear that you'd gone down to the country to get yourself a wife—I take it this is she?"

Silence stretched. Tense before, Gyles was now rigid; Francesca sank her fingers warningly into his arm. She held the woman's gaze.

Eventually, Gyles drawled, glancing briefly her way, "My dear, allow me to present Lady Herron."

Francesca waited, her expression serene, her head high. After a moment, two flags of color appeared in Lady Herron's cheeks. Less than cordially, she curtsied. "Lady Chillingworth."

Francesca smiled coolly, inclined her head, and looked away.

Unfortunately, toward Lord Albemarle.

"My dear Lady Chillingworth, I believe the musicians are going to favor us with a waltz. If you would—"

"Sorry, Albemarle." Gyles caught his lordship's surprised glance. "This waltz"—he put emphasis on the word so Albemarle would understand—"is mine."

With a curt nod to his lordship, another to Lady Herron, he stepped back. With a haughty nod for his lordship, Francesca followed. She ignored Lady Herron completely.

The instant Gyles drew Francesca into his arms, he knew they were in trouble. Thanks to Lord Albemarle, he was feeling too much like his barbarian self, his civilized mask thinned to a veneer. On top of that, one glance at Francesca's face, at the contemptuous light in her eyes, was enough to tell him that she'd guessed the connection between himself and Louise Herron. Through his hand at her back, he felt the tension vibrating through her, felt the ripple as her temper unfurled.

He steeled himself, inwardly swearing that whatever she said, he would not let her down; he would not, in this arena, react—

She looked up; the expression in her eyes was one of haughty disgust. "That woman is ill-mannered." Her gaze dropped to his lips; a moment passed, then her eyes rose to meet his again. The disgust was gone—something else, something very like possessiveness, flared in the green. "Don't you think so?"

Gyles found himself scrambling—mentally jettisoning the notion she was about to enact him a scene over his past liaisons, trying to grasp the fact that she was angry, yes, but not with him. And that anger, in this case, had given rise to . . . intent of a different sort.

The sudden surge of his reaction caught him; he tightened his hold on her. Without a blink, she stepped nearer. Her breasts brushed his coat, and she shivered and pressed closer yet.

He should have been praying all those watching would be struck blind; instead, he whirled her slowly down the floor, caught, willingly trapped, in the fire of her eyes.

Francesca understood—suddenly, blindingly—and instinctively reached for what she needed. Possessiveness, jealousy—she'd seen both in him, but never thought to find the same clawing need eating her from inside out. Tension held them, swelled and grew, like to like, reflected and intensified between them. It was she who shifted her hand to his nape, scored her nails lightly through the short hairs, he who held her so tight through a turn that their bodies sensuously rubbed, locked for one instant, then parted.

The tight sheath of emerald satin was suddenly constricting, a skin she needed to shed. They were both breathing shallowly, too quickly, when the music died.

"Come." Face graven, he kept hold of her hand, turned, and towed her toward the door.

"Wait." Francesca glanced back. "I came with your mother and Henni."

Halting under the archway, he looked down at her. "They'll guess you've left with me."

There was no question in his eyes, only a challenge. Francesca didn't hesitate—with a nod, she stepped past him.

He'd brought the town carriage. He handed her up, called a terse, "Home!" then followed her in. The instant the door shut, in the instant the carriage lurched and rolled forward, she turned to him, reached for him.

He reached for her.

She framed his face and their lips met, fused. She parted her lips, drew him in, invited, incited him to take. And he took. Greedy as she, as hungry, as urgent. Their tongues touched, tangled, dueled. She pressed closer, spread her hands over his chest, then found a stud and slid it free.

He pulled back, chest heaving, and caught her hands. "No. Not here."

"Why not?" She shifted against him, one knee over his.

"Because we're nearly home." He paused, then added, his voice gravelly and low, "And I want to peel this gown from you." He grazed one palm over the peak of her breast; they both watched the nipple pebble under the tight silk. "Inch by slow inch, and I want to watch as I do it." He raised his hand, speared his fingers through her hair, tipped her face up to his. Bent his head. His breath washed over her lips as he murmured, "I want to watch you. Your eyes. Your body."

His lips closed over hers, and she let him sweep her away, into a sea of hot desire.

The carriage slowed. He glanced out, then set her back on the seat. The carriage halted; they straightened their clothes. She felt as if her dress was barely on, barely capable of containing her. He descended and handed her out. Head high, she preceded him into the hall. She could barely breathe. With a nod to Irving, she headed on up the stairs. Gyles paused to speak with Wallace, then followed.

His fingers twined with hers as they walked down the corridor. By unspoken agreement, they touched no more than that—didn't dare.

"Get rid of your maid—you won't need her tonight."

Francesca slipped her fingers from his and opened her door while he walked on to his.

"Are you sure, ma'am?"

"Quite sure." Francesca shooed Millie to the door. The little maid went, reluctantly closing the door behind her.

The click of the latch echoed from the other side of the room. Francesca turned; she watched as, already coatless, Gyles pushed away from the shadows cloaking the connecting door. Their gazes locked as he approached.

Closed the distance, lifted his hands to frame her face, tipped it to his, then devoured.

They'd made love so many times, yet it had never been like this. She'd never been so greedy. So determined, so demanding. She taunted, teased—wanted more. Wanted him. He'd claimed her, branded her as his so many times. Tonight it was her turn. His turn to be possessed, to be the one taken—she would settle for nothing less.

She was prepared to settle for more.

Prepared to let him take the reins at the start, to acquiesce when, with their blood already up, pounding in their veins, he roughly drew back, turned her, positioned her so, bathed in the glow of the lamps burning on her dresser and the table by the door, she stood before him, facing her reflection in the long mirror.

"Inch by slow inch."

He'd warned her; now she watched, waited, as he unhooked her gown. His hands rose, pressing the back opening of the gown wide, then sliding the silk from her shoulders. The bodice fitted her well; he peeled the fabric from her curves. Her breasts suddenly felt cool, deprived of the heated silk, covered only by her fine chemise. He knew but only smiled at her quiver, leaving the gown in folds about her waist, urging her to lift her arms free.

She did, then didn't know what to do with her hands. Watching their reflection, she leaned her shoulders, now bare, back against his shirt-clad chest, then reached back and set her palms to his hard thighs, fingers gripping.

His expression hardened, but his gaze was fixed on her body, on her hips as he eased the gown lower. She kept expecting him to touch her, to set his hands to her chemise-clad skin to ease the nerves quivering beneath, afire with anticipation. Instead, he touched her not at all as, inch by deliberate inch, he pushed the gown lower, over her thighs.

Until, with a silken swoosh, it slid to the floor.

For one instant, they both gazed at the pool of emerald about her feet. Then, slowly, she lifted her gaze and took in the tableau he'd created. Her hair was still up, startlingly black against the white of his shirt, a mass of curls cascading down to just brush her shoulders. Her arms were bare; from mid-thigh, her legs were, too. In between, the ripe curves of her body were veiled and mysterious beneath her thin chemise. Her skin glowed in the lamplight, its honeyed tones definite against his shirt, soft and feminine against the black of his knee breeches.

With her hands on his thighs, balanced before him, she felt like a prize, one he'd won.

As she watched, his face hardened. His hands closed about her waist.

She lifted her arms, reached back, up, to rest her hands on his shoulders. His lips curved as he bent his head and touched his lips to her temple.

His hands closed about her breasts. She gasped and arched more definitely. He kneaded knowingly, avoiding the tight peaks, then his hands drifted, wandered, curving over her hips, over her stomach. His touch was not gentle but possessive, a conqueror mapping his domain.

Watching from beneath her lashes, she deliberately shifted against him, rolling her hips against his thighs, wordlessly taunting.

He reached out, grasped the back of a nearby chair, and swung it to stand with the seat beside her.

"Take off your stockings."

For me. The words were unsaid; their meaning hung in the air. Without hesitation, she rebalanced, kicked off her slippers, then bent one knee and placed her foot on the seat. And gave all her attention to performing the simple act of sliding her garter down her leg, then removing her silk stocking. She let her hands linger, smoothing over the sleek curves of her leg as she eased the stocking down. Then she shook out the wisp of silk, draped it over the chair back, and repeated the exercise.

Every iota of his concentration was locked on her, on her legs, on each deliberately sensuous movement of her arms and hands. She knew without looking; she could feel his desire like a warm weight on her skin.

Finally, it was done; she pushed the chair away, then straightened, leaned back against him, against his chest, against his thighs—and met his gaze in the mirror.

His face was set, the stamp of passion naked upon it. His chest swelled, then he lifted his hands to the ribbons anchoring her chemise. Two tugs and the ribbons slithered free; he stripped the chemise from her in a single stroke.

And she stood naked before him, breasts high and peaked, full and lightly rosy, her stomach taut, the curves of her hips and thighs creating a frame for the dark curls that drew his eyes. Francesca savored the moment, drank in the blank lust that, for one instant, dominated his expression, then she turned and surprised him.

He blinked, looking over her head at the reflection in the mirror. It distracted him long enough for her to unbutton his shirt and slip free the hooks at his waistband.

He glanced down as she pressed her palms to his chest, then slid them outward, spreading the shirt wide. He reached for her; she quickly whipped the shirt back over his shoulders, trapping his arms.

"It's hardly any fun if I'm the only one naked."

His gaze fixed on the mirror. "I'm not sure about that."

She left his arms trapped and concentrated on easing his breeches down, avoiding touching his rampant erection. While she bent and dealt with the closures below his knees, he watched, unlacing his cuffs as he did. She felt his gaze; she would have only one chance to seize the initiative and push their interaction in the direction she wished.

Crouching, she drew down both breeches and hose; he freed one foot, then the other, then flung his shirt aside—

She went to her knees before him, sank her fingers into the backs of his thighs, then smiled, wickedly, up at him.

Gyles read her intention in her eyes. He scrambled to protest, to say "No!" but the word lodged in his suddenly dry throat. Her smile deepened; her lashes lowered. Knees between his feet, she rose, leaned closer. The silken caress of her hair, swinging forward to brush his taut thighs, distracted him. He glanced at the mirror, caught his breath at the sight, then watched as her head bent.

He felt the touch of her breath like a brand on that most sensitive part of his body. Then her lips touched, kissed, lingered teasingly, then they parted and she took him into the hot haven of her mouth.

His eyes closed, his spine tensed, then tensed again as she caressed him. His fingers found her head, speared through the lush locks to close about her skull. He cracked open his lids, stared into the mirror, watched her shift and press closer, then he saw her take him deeper. The heat in his loins exploded; his eyes closed. He heard a moan.

So did Francesca. The sound delighted her. She'd wanted to do this for weeks, but while he'd allowed her to caress him thus, he invariably cut short the moment. Not this time. She was determined to do it her way, to take her time and give him all he deserved. To take him, possess him, as she wished. The constrast of strength and exquisite softness had always fascinated her; his body was so strong, so invincible, yet this one part was so sensitive.

With her hands locked about the backs of his thighs, fingers sunk deep, with her on her knees before him, her mouth locked about him, he couldn't easily break free.

She gave herself up to the moment, to her task, aware that every second of her devotions drained his resolve and made it less likely that he'd interfere. This time, it was he who would have to endure, to let his senses dance to her command, to let her brand him with her loving.

The salty tang of him filled her senses. Releasing one thigh, she cradled the tight balls in their pouches, then stroked the base of his shaft.

Felt his reaction. Felt the tension coil, felt him lock his spine, felt his hands close hard about her head, holding her still. . . .

"Enough!"

She heard the hoarse command; releasing him, she looked up.

He brushed her hands aside, swooped, locked his hands about her waist, and lifted her. Lifted her high—she grabbed his arms for balance—then he swung her to him.

She locked her legs about his hips. In the same instant, he entered her. Hands locked about her waist, he steadied her and thrust in, deeper, then deeper still. She tightened her legs and pressed closer, pressed down, until their bodies were locked, fused, joined.

They were both gasping.

Running her hands over his shoulders, she wound her arms about his neck, hauled his face to hers, and kissed him. He kissed her back—ravaging and voracious. She met every challenge and hurled it back, took as much as she gave. Using her legs for leverage, she eased up upon him, then slid down. Hands spread, curved around her bottom, he supported and guided her. Used her body as she used his, pressing pleasure on her, taking it in.

Their joining became, not a battle of wills, but a battle of hearts—who could take more, give more. There was no answer. No winner, no loser. Just them, together, wrapped in sensual pleasure.

Held by a sensual need only the other could fulfill.

Time suspended as they let their bodies couple unrestrained. Their eyes met in heated glances, lips met in heated kisses while their bodies met in growing urgency.

It wasn't enough, not for either of them. Gyles carried her to the bed.

"Don't you dare lay me down." It took all the breath she had to gasp the words.

The look he cast her was inexpressibly masculine. "Damn difficult woman," he ground out. But he sat, then swung his legs up on the bed, then juggled her and came up on his knees. Spreading them wide, he settled her so she was still wrapped about him, her thighs riding his hips.

He met her eyes. "Satisfied?"

She smiled, closed her hands in his hair, and kissed him.

It was the same position in which they'd first made love, yet so much had changed since then. Not them, themselves, but what lay between them, the flame, the fire, the commitment, the devotion.

The acceptance.

As they continued to love and the lamps burned low, Francesca sensed the last barriers fade. Not only in him, but in her, too, until there was just them, together, facing the reality of what that truly meant. Coping with it.

Her gaze was locked with his when she finally crested the bright peak; as her lids lowered and fell, he joined her. They held still for a long minute, struggling to breathe, waiting for their whirling senses to slow, then she tightened her arms about his neck and laid her head on his shoulder. And felt his arms tighten about her, holding her to him.

She smiled. He was hers just as much as she was his.

Chapter 19

"*Have you received* any news from the Castle?"

Seated at his desk in the library, Gyles looked up and watched Francesca walk toward him. "Not since Monday."

It was raining outside, a steady downpour. Francesca went to the window and stood looking out.

Gyles forced himself to look back at the letter on his blotter. After a moment, he glanced up—and found Francesca gazing at him. Her eyes lit with a soft glow, and she smiled. He focused on her lips—remembered all too vividly what they'd felt like closed about him, remembered all that had transpired throughout the past night.

He wrenched his gaze back to her eyes. She read his, tentatively tilted her head. "I won't be going out in this. Do you have anything—any legal cases or information—you'd like me to find?"

The purr of her voice was like a caress, a gentle, understanding one. Gyles held her gaze, then looked back at his desk. He searched and drew out a list. "If you could find these references . . . ?"

Taking the list, she perused it, then moved down the room. Under cover of replying to a letter, Gyles watched her, studied her—looked within and studied himself. After last night, she had every reason to hope, yet she wasn't pushing, wasn't presuming, even though he knew that in her heart, she knew. As did he.

How to cope? After last night, when they'd both knowingly, deliberately, allowed passion to strip their souls bare, that seemed the only question left.

She returned carrying a large tome. As she set it on the desk, he reached out and snagged her wrist. She looked up, brows rising. He laid down his pen—the ink had dried on the nib—and tugged; she let him draw her around the desk.

"Are you happy here in London, going about within the ton?" Reluctantly releasing her, he sat back.

She leaned against the desk and looked at him, eyes clear, gaze direct—wondering what tack he was taking. "It's been entertaining—a novel experience."

"You've become very popular."

Her lips curved lightly. "Any lady who was your countess would attract a certain amount of attention."

"But the sort of attention *you* attract . . ."

There it was—that much admitted, brought into the light. She held his gaze, then looked away. Moments ticked by, then she said, "I cannot choose whom I attract, nor can I dictate the nature of their attentions. However"—she again met his eyes—"that doesn't mean that I return or value such attentions."

He inclined his head, accepting that. "What elements"— he paused, then continued—"would cause you to smile upon, to hold dear, a particular gentleman's attention?"

She hadn't expected that question; her eyes darkened, turned distant as she searched for the answer.

"Honesty. Loyalty. Devotion." She refocused and met his gaze. "What does anyone—man or woman, lady or gentleman—desire in such a sphere?"

He hadn't expected such simple truths, hadn't counted on

her courage, her propensity to follow, reckless and regardless, wherever he led.

Gazes locked, they both considered, wondered . . . hoped.

Gyles knew very well where they stood. Teettering on the brink. "There's a Madame Tulane, an Italian soprano, performing at the final gala at Vauxhall tonight." He drew a playbill from beneath his blotter,

Francesca's face lit; he handed her the playbill and watched her devour the details. "She's from Florence! Oh, it's been so long since I heard—" She glanced up. "Vauxhall—is it a place I can go?"

"Yes and no. You can only go if I take you." Not precisely true, yet not a lie.

"Will you take me?"

Her excitement was palpable. He waved at the shelves. "If you help me with these references, we can leave immediately after dinner."

"Oh, *thank you!*" The playbill went fluttering; she flung her arms about his neck and kissed him.

It was the first time they'd touched since last night, or, more precisely, that morning.

She drew back. Their gazes locked. Green and grey without any masks, any veils. Then she smiled, sank onto his lap, and thanked him properly.

The rain stopped at noon; by eight o'clock that evening, Vauxhall Gardens was packed with revelers, all eager to enjoy one last fling. A chill dampness hung in the air; the minor avenues were dark and gloomy yet still crowded, occasional feminine shrieks attesting to their attraction.

Gyles inwardly cursed as he steered Francesca through the throng. Who would have believed half of London would turn out on such an evening? The jostling hordes included every class of Londoner, from ladies like Francesca wrapped in velvet cloaks, to shopkeepers' wives, primly neat, looking around curiously, to whores, painted, feathered, bawdily trying to catch gentlemen's eyes.

"If we go through the Colonnades, we'll come out close to our booth."

Francesca could see the square outline of what must be the Colonnades ahead. The crowd was so thick, they kept halting, pausing. In one such interval, she looked around, and saw, not ten feet away, Lord Carnegie.

His lordship saw her. His gaze flicked to Gyles, then returned to her. He smiled, bowed.

The crowd shifted, blocking him from view. Francesca looked ahead and quelled a shiver.

They reached the Colonnades. Gyles turned under the first arch—just as a tide of revelers rolled out in the opposite direction. Francesca was caught, wrenched from Gyles's side and pushed back along the path.

She thought she'd lose her footing and fall. Regaining her balance, she struggled to break free of the melee. Her voluminous cloak was pulled this way, then that.

Hands grabbed at her arms—even through her cloak, she knew it wasn't Gyles. She jerked free, turned, but in the jostling crowd she couldn't see who'd grabbed her.

Dragging in a breath, she tried to forge her way back to the Colonnades. The crowd parted, and Gyles was there.

"Thank heavens!" He hauled her to him, locked her close. "Are you all right?"

She nodded, closing her fist in his coat.

"Come on."

Gyles tried to ignore the primitive uneasiness rippling through him. He held her close as they made their way through the Colonnades. They reached the Rotunda. From there, the way was easier, the crowd composed primarily of gentlefolk less inclined to jostle.

As he'd arranged, their guests were waiting in the booth he'd hired. Francesca was disarmed and delighted.

"Thank you," she said when, radiant, she returned to his side. "I didn't expect this. You've been busy."

"It seemed a good idea."

Devil and Honoria were there, as were his mother, Henni, and Horace. The Markhams and Sir Mark and Lady Griswold, old acquaintances who'd grown closer with Francesca's entrance into his life, rounded out the party.

The evening passed pleasantly. The booth was in a prime position; they had an easy stroll to the Rotunda, where seats had been reserved for the ladies for the performance. The gentlemen seated their wives, then retreated to a safe distance to discuss the bills they'd been working on and other important matters, such as the hunting and shooting they might have during the winter.

At the end of the performance, Francesca rose, delighted. With Honoria, she headed to where their husbands stood.

"Well!" A crabbed hand shot out and snagged her wrist.

Francesca turned, then smiled. "Good evening."

"And a very good one it is for you, quite clearly." Lady Osbaldestone turned to Helena, Dowager Duchess of St. Ives, seated beside her. "Told you it'd happen sooner rather than later." Turning back to Francesca, she released her hand and struck it admonishingly. "Now you've got him in harness, just make sure you keep him right up to the bit, gel! Understand?"

Struggling to hide a grin, Francesca didn't attempt a reply.

"If you don't, just ask Honoria there. She hasn't done too badly at all."

Lady Osbaldestone grinned wickedly. Honoria bobbed a curtsy. "Thank you."

Smiling, the Dowager touched Francesca's hand. "It's a great joy to see Gyles suitably settled at last, but it is true— you will have to make sure he doesn't slide. At least until the role becomes second nature. Then . . ." She gave a Gallic shrug signifying that then, all would take care of itself.

Parting from the older ladies, Francesca whispered to Honoria, "How do they know?"

Honoria glanced at her, then whispered back, "It's written all over your face, and his."

Her nod directed Francesca's gaze ahead, to where their husbands stood waiting. Two tall, strikingly handsome, broad-shouldered men with eyes just for them.

Honoria flicked her an understanding glance as they neared. "It feels good, doesn't it?"

"Mmm" was Francesa's reply. Smiling, she took Gyles's arm, and they turned toward their booth.

"Mmm, what?"

"Mmm-hmm." Francesca dimpled up at him. "Are we dancing, my lord?"

Gyles looked to where couples were waltzing in the area before the booths. "Why not?"

So they whirled. Gyles was aware of the admiring male glances they drew; he could hardly complain. She was happy so she glowed, her eyes sparkling, her lips curved. That smile and the light in her eyes were all for him.

The dance ended; as they headed back to the booth, they came upon another area of congestion. Gyles held Francesca's hand firmly and led her through; she walked behind him, sheltered by his body.

They turned the corner toward the booth door, and the crowd eased.

A lady halted directly in front of Gyles, startling him into halting, too. She smiled like a cat and stepped closer.

"My lord—what a surprise."

Gyles blinked. Her tone was a poor imitation of Francesca's seductive purr. That instant's hesitation encouraged the woman. Smile widening, she pressed close.

"I had heard you were no longer *receiving*, but that can't be right, *surely*. Just because you're married . . . well, a leopard doesn't lose his spots overnight, *does he?*"

Who the devil is she? Gyles couldn't recall.

"*This* leopard," came a voice from beside him, "is spoken for."

The madam's eyes flew wide; to Gyles's surprise, she took an involuntary step back as Francesca stepped between them.

She looked the woman down, then up, then tipped up her nose haughtily. "You may be interested to know that I take an active interest in my husband's social life—all requests for his company on any but business matters should henceforth be addressed to me. And as for his spots, you may be sure I appreciate them and have every intention of enjoying their benefits for many years to come."

The woman blinked. So did Gyles.

Francesca's head rose another notch; he would have given a great deal to see her face as she imperiously, asked, "I trust I have made myself clear?"

The unknown lady cast him a very fleeting glance, then— and he would have sworn to her own surprise—bobbed a curtsy. "Indeed, my lady."

"Good." Francesca waved. "You may leave us."

Blushing vividly, the woman did.

Gyles shook his head. Curving a hand about Francesca's waist, he urged her on. "Remind me to send any further importuning ladies your way."

"Do." On the threshold of the booth, she whirled and faced him. Her eyes burned with green fire—not the warm sort. With her chin set the way it was, he could understand why the lady had retreated.

"I'll be happy to deal with them." Her expression stated she would relish the dealing. Her eyes met his, then haughtily, she turned into the box. "I am, I believe, more than a match for them."

Gyles wasn't about to argue. She was more, much more, than any who had gone before. Aside from all else, she was a Rawlings—they shared, it seemed, quite a few character traits.

Smiling, he stepped into the booth, sliding one hand about her waist to draw her to him.

In the aftermath of that scene, in light of the thanks Francesca spent the night bestowing on him, Gyles found it impossible to deny her her wish to visit her old governess in Muswell Hill. She left immediately after luncheon. He retired to the library, confident that with two extra grooms riding with John Coachman, he had no need to fret.

Three hours later, a commotion erupted in the hall. He rose—before he could take a step, Wallace threw open the door. "There's been an incident, my lord."

Before his heart could plummet, Francesca swept in. "No one was hurt."

Tugging off her gloves, she crossed toward him. Gyles took in her frown, took in the fact she was clearly unharmed. "What happened?"

A cough drew his attention. John Coachman stood on the threshold beside Wallace. "Highwaymen, m'lord. But what with the lads on top—they were carrying their pistols like you ordered—we came to no harm."

Gyles waved him in and beckoned Wallace as well. "Sit down. I want to hear exactly what happened."

Francesca subsided into the armchair beside his desk, the armchair that had become hers. Gyles sat as Wallace and John drew up straight-backed chairs.

John sat. "It was on our way home, m'lord, as we were coming down the hill to Highgate. They was lying in wait in Highgate Wood—three of 'em. Two burly louts and one skinny one. They'd mufflers 'bout their faces and the usual sort o'coats. Run-of-the-mill highwaymen."

"Shots were fired?"

"By our lot, yes. They turned tail and ran."

"Were they armed?"

"I 'spect so, m'lord, but I didn't see any pistols."

Gyles frowned. "Check with the grooms. If they were highwaymen, they would have been armed."

"Aye." John eased to his feet. "If you've finished with me, m'lord, I need to check the horses."

"Yes, and well done, John. Please convey my thanks"— Gyles glanced at Francesca and saw her summon a smile for the coachman—"*our* thanks to both grooms."

John bobbed to Gyles, then Francesca. "I'll tell 'em, you may be sure."

Wallace rose and repositioned the chairs. Gyles flicked him a glance: *Find out what you can and tell me later.* Wallace bowed and followed John out, shutting the door.

Gyles considered Francesca. Her frown, more in her eyes than her expression, had returned. She glanced at him. He raised a brow.

"I just never imagined being set upon by highwaymen so close to town. It was not pleasant."

Gyles rose, crossed to her chair, drew her to her feet, then closed his arms around her. "Were you frightened?"

She clung. "No—well, a little. I didn't know what was going on—I didn't know our grooms were armed or that it was they who had shot. I thought *we* were being shot at!"

Gyles tightened his hold, rocked her slightly, laid his cheek against her hair. "It's all right. Nothing came of it." *Thank God.* "I'm afraid such occurrences are not unheard of, which is why I ordered John to take two grooms. At this time of year with the wealthy leaving London, the outskirts of the capital provide the richest pickings."

But highwaymen usually waylaid travelers at night, or at least in the evening. Broad daylight was too risky.

Francesca eased back. "I must go and change. I think I'll take a long bath."

Her liking for relaxing baths had not escaped Gyles. He released her. "We're dining in tonight, aren't we?"

"Yes. The roundabout is slowing, so it'll just be the two of us." She opened her eyes at him. "Will you be bored?"

Gyles raised a brow. "You'll have to see to it I'm not."

"Ah—the duties of your countess." With a die-away air, she curtsied and turned to the door. "I'll go and fortify myself."

Gyles laughed. The door closed behind her; his laughter faded. He returned to his desk.

She'd said she valued honesty—that she wanted honesty from him. When, after dinner, they entered the library, Gyles considered the truth, considered how much he could bring himself to reveal. Considered why it was necessary.

Francesca headed for the desk and his latest list of references. He caught her hand. "No."

She turned to him, brows rising. He gestured to the *chaise*. "Let's sit. I want to talk to you."

Intrigued, she sat nearer the fire. He sat beside her. The fire was roaring; Wallace had built it up while they'd dined.

Better not to think too much. Better just to ride into battle like his forebears and expect to win.

He shifted his gaze from the fire to her eyes, from crackling flames to vibrant green. "We appear to have a problem. Things—odd things—have been happening. I accept that there's no reason to imagine they're intentional"—he blocked out the vision of the rein tied across the track—"yet . . . I can't help but be concerned."

Silk shushed as she faced him. "You mean the highwaymen? But you said such things are expected."

"Not quite expected, and not occurring like that. In daylight, no pistols waving, and"—his gaze locked with hers—"the carriage was driving *into* London, not out."

"But it must have been . . . well, an accident that my carriage was attacked."

"Must have been." Gyles felt his face harden. "Like that incident with your special dressing—it *must have been* an accident. Yet . . ."

She tilted her head, her eyes steady on his. "Yet what?"

"What if it wasn't." He took her hand, simply held it, felt its warmth in his. "What if, for some reason we can't at present fathom, someone has designs on your life?"

If it hadn't been for his tone and the expression in his eyes, Francesca might have smiled. Instead, remembering the father he'd lost, imagining what she hoped she now meant to him, she curled her fingers and gripped his. "No one has designs on my life. There's no reason anyone would seek to harm me. As far as I know, I have no enemies."

He looked down at their twined hands. After a moment, he returned the pressure of her fingers. "Be that as it may, that's not, of itself, the problem I alluded to."

She tried to see his eyes, but he continued to look at their linked hands.

"Our problem, one we need to discuss and come to some agreement over"—he glanced up—"is my concern."

The veils started to shimmer, to lift. It wasn't, she'd discovered, normal practice for John Coachman to take one groom, let alone two fully armed. She held Gyles's gaze. "Tell me of this concern."

Not a demand, an encouragement.

He exhaled. "It's not . . . comfortable." His gaze shifted to the fire. A moment passed, then he looked into her eyes. "Since we first met, whenever you're in danger—whatever sort of danger, imagined or real, whether I'm with you or not—I feel . . ." He looked inward, then refocused on her eyes. "I can't describe it—black, icy cold, painful but not physically. A different sort of pain." He hesitated, then added, "A hellish fear."

She returned his gaze, gripped his fingers more tightly.

"If I'm with you, it's not so bad—I can do something— save you, and all ends well. But if I'm not there, yet believe you're in danger—" He looked away. After a moment, he drew in a long breath and turned back to her. "Can you understand?"

She comforted him with her eyes, pressed his hand. "Is

that why you placed so many guards on me at the Castle?"

He laughed, short and harsh. "Yes." He rose, and she let him draw his hand from hers, watched as he paced to the hearth, braced one clenched fist on the mantelpiece and stared down at the flames. "If I can't be with you, then I feel *compelled* to do everything I can, to give you every guard I can—to protect you in any way I can." An instant later, he added, "It's not something I can make a rational decision about. It's something I *must* do."

She rose, went to him. "If that's so, then . . ." She shrugged and touched his arm. "I will bear with the guards—it's no great matter."

He shot her a hard glance. "You don't like footmen dogging your every step."

"Nor do I like my maid spending half her day in my room, simply to watch over my things. *However*, if it will bring you ease, then"—she stepped closer, raising her face to his, speaking directly to his cloudy grey eyes—"I won't let it annoy me. I won't like it, but I don't care about such things—" She paused, held his gaze. "As much as I care for you."

Exultation clashed with something more primitive, with the fear that lingered never far from his mind. For one instant, Gyles felt giddy, then he straightened. "You'll accept whatever guards I assign?"

"As long as you tell me of them, so I'm not surprised to see them." Green eyes met his; her brows rose.

He grimaced. "A maid will always be in your room, and a footman will always be with you—in sight of you within the house, within reach outside it."

"Unless I'm with you."

He inclined his head. "And if you go walking anywhere, two footmen will accompany you."

"Anything else?"

"John will take an extra groom when he drives you."

Francesca waited, then asked, "Nothing more?"

He thought before shaking his head.

"Very well." She drew his head down and kissed him. "I will bear with your guards, my lord. And now"—she turned and headed for the door—"I'm going upstairs to dismiss any maids hovering in my room." She glanced back at him. "Will you be long?"

He hesitated, but didn't look at his desk. "No. I'll be up shortly."

Smiling, she opened the door and left him.

As she climbed the stairs, she thought over all he'd said, over all the incidents he might construe as dangerous.

The memory of hands grabbing at her in the crowd last night returned. She was almost sure there'd been more than one set—more than one man. Man? Yes, she was sure of that—the hands had been large and clumsy. And rough—not the smooth hands of a gentleman.

Should she mention it? To what purpose, other than to prod an emotion Gyles clearly didn't appreciate feeling?

She didn't believe there was any danger—accidents happened. People in crowds grabbed at each other to steady themselves. No one wished her ill. But she'd seen how deeply the very notion affected Gyles. Real or imagined—he'd admitted it made no odds.

Bearing with guards was a small thing to do; she would do it gladly. It was impossible not to feel touched by his concern, impossible not to feel cherished, no matter the price.

Impossible not to see what drove him, what gave birth to his uncomfortable concern.

Was it too early to celebrate victory?

Pondering that point, she entered her room.

Late the next morning, Francesca paused in the front hall, surveying the two footmen wrapped in their coats, ready to accompany her on her walk.

She turned to Gyles as he came out of the library—to check on her reaction, she had not a doubt. "I'm only going around the corner to Walpole House. I'll sit with your mother and Henni for a while, then I'll return." She smiled at him. "Don't worry."

He grunted, threw an unsmiling glance at the footmen, then turned back to the library.

Unconcerned, she swept to the door, waited for Irving to open it, then sallied forth—aware that Gyles had stopped by the library door, aware to the last of his lingering gaze.

"And the rein was tied securely?"

Grimly pacing, Gyles nodded. "Around boles on either side of the track."

Devil grunted. "Difficult to see how that could be an accident."

"The other incidents, yes, possibly. But not that."

They were in a private room at White's. Gyles had remembered the difficulty Devil had faced soon after his marriage to Honoria. Odd, potentially fatal accidents, just like those happening to him and Francesca. In Devil's case, the accidents had, with Gyles's help, been laid at the door of Devil's then heir. In the present case, however . . .

"I really cannot see Osbert being in any way involved." Gyles shook his head. "It's laughable."

"I might once have said it was laughable for a Cynster to try to kill another Cynster, too."

Gyles shook his head again. "I don't mean because we're related. I mean because he honestly has never wanted the title because the estate goes with it. He was so grateful to Francesca and he likes her—worships her. Within reason."

Devil's lips twitched. "Of course."

"He's made himself her principal cavalier. I've gone along with it because I trust him, and he's with Francesca at times I'm not." Gyles hesitated, then added, "And because he's using her as a shield."

"The matchmaking mamas are still after him?"

"Presumably while evaluating him as a possible future earl, someone realized he's comfortably plump in the pocket quite aside from what he gets from the estate, and, as a poet, he doesn't indulge in wasteful habits. He doesn't gamble or keep mistresses, or run through his blunt in any other tonnish way. Which brings me back to my point. Osbert doesn't want the title. Killing me or Francesca simply would not be in his best interests."

"All right. Why not one step away? In reality, Charles was one step away from the title. Who's after Osbert?"

Gyles halted. Frowned. "I don't know."

"You don't know?"

He waved aside Devil's incredulity. "The Rawlingses are not like the Cynsters. The family's as large, but it's fragmented—one branch doesn't talk to another, news of marriages isn't widely disseminated. After Osbert . . . we'd need to go back at least two generations, and then see which branch had precedence, then follow it down . . ." Gyles grimaced. "I'll get Waring onto it."

"Do," Devil stood. He met Gyles's gaze. "It's the most logical, most likely explanation, you know."

Gyles turned to the door. "I know."

Francesca fervently hoped Gyles was at White's. She'd heard it was located in St. James. If her husband was there, safe within its portals, he wouldn't be around to see her jauntering about town in the carriage, when she'd told him she was only walking to North Audley Street and back.

What he didn't know wouldn't hurt him. On the contrary—it would save him unnecessary worry. She'd *had* to get a new pair of gloves and sending Millie was impossible as Millie had hands twice the size of hers. Perfectly justifiable, yet who knew how Gyles might react?

But she'd be home soon. She glanced out of the window at the passing buildings. And saw Charles and Ester going up the steps of one.

Francesca leapt up and opened the hatch. "John—stop!"

Two minutes later, she entered the building, a liveried

footman behind her, a groom trailing a few yards farther back. Ignoring both, she looked around. The building housed an emporium offering numerous wares for sale. An apothecary shop took up the back counter; it was there she found Charles and Ester.

"My dear!" Ester's eyes widened; she moved to hug Francesca. "Oh, it's good to see you." Ester held her at arm's length, studying her face, then her carriage dress. "You look wonderful! Are you enjoying the capital?"

"Very much." Francesca cast a puzzled glance at Charles. "But I had no idea you were here. Franni?"

"She's here, too." Charles exchanged a glance with Ester, then took Francesca's arm and steered her to the counter's end. "She's at the house we've rented, along with Ginny. We had to come here for more laudanum. They're making up the dose."

Francesca took in the strain in his face. "Is Franni being difficult?" She looked from Charles to Ester.

Ester grimaced. "At times. We got your letter that you were here in town—I read it to Franni. She's always shown such interest in your doings. Well, after that, nothing would do but we had to come to London, too. She was so eager— we were going to write, but then we thought we'd just come. It's not difficult finding lodgings at this time of year. But when we got here . . ." Ester glanced at Charles.

"Franni's been unpredictable. Even-tempered one minute, quite difficult the next." Charles took Francesca's hand. "We wanted to call on you, but it seemed unwise, even though Franni's been so insistent she wants to see you. It would be irresponsible to expose her to the social activities I'm sure you're involved in." Charles's lips twisted. "We thought of writing and inviting you to call on us, but Franni got quite wild. She's been insisting we call at Chillingworth's house, but we didn't feel we could."

Francesca opened her mouth to assure him otherwise; Ester put her hand on her arm.

"My dear, you need to understand that it's not simply a

matter of the effect socializing might have on Franni, although we're certainly exercised by that thought. The truth is, we couldn't guarantee Franni's behavior. She's unpredictable, rebellious and, I'm afraid, secretive, too."

Ester exchanged a glance with Charles, then continued, "Franni's slipped out alone, without Ginny, twice. And you know how watchful Ginny is. Charles and I are afraid to leave Franni, but sometimes we must. We're very concerned." Ester lowered her voice. "We're sure something's afoot, but we've no idea what. It may be something to do with Franni's gentleman visitor."

"Did you ever learn who he was?"

Ester shook her head. "You know how difficult it is to talk sensibly with Franni when she doesn't wish it."

Charles had noticed the footman. "I'm glad to see you're not going about alone."

Francesca didn't mention the groom, who was pretending to look at mufflers. "Chillingworth insists." She waved the point aside. "But I have a suggestion, one that might help with Franni. You say she's been pressing to come to Green Street—she may have convinced herself that was what would happen when you got to London, and she's reacting because it hasn't. So why not visit—why not bring her to dinner tonight?" She held up a hand. "Before you say anything, this would be a quiet family dinner, just the three of you and Gyles and myself."

Ester and Charles exchanged a glance. "But," Ester said, "surely you have plans—"

"No, none. This week it's grown quiet—many have already left town. There'll be a few parties next week to celebrate the year's end, then we'll retire to the country."

Francesca was looking forward to it, to seeing the folly in the snow. "Tonight, there's nothing, so we'll be at home. If you bring Franni to dinner, there'll be no social whirl to unnerve her, but she can see the house and visit as she's wished. Maybe that will calm her."

Ester and Charles exchanged a long look.

Francesca suddenly recollected that Gyles would return to Green Street soon, and he'd expect her to be there. "I must go." She grasped Charles's hand. "Say you'll come."

Charles smiled. "You're very persuasive, my dear."

Francesca beamed. "Seven, then. I know Franni doesn't like waiting."

"If it's not too much trouble, dear."

"No, no—seven." Making a mental note to tell Ferdinand, Francesca waved and hurried to the door.

She was in the hall letting Irving take her pelisse when the front door opened and Gyles strolled in.

He considered her, then raised a brow. "Was that our carriage just rounding the corner?"

"Yes." She swept up to him, stretched up to kiss his cheek, then slid an arm through his. "I had to get new gloves. I took a groom and a footman, and they were with me all the time, so there was no possibility of danger." She glanced at him. "Are you satisfied?"

He sighed and steered her into the library. "I suppose I'll have to be." He hesitated, then added, "I don't want you to feel caged."

She smiled, telling him with her eyes that his protectiveness no longer bothered her, then she crossed to the *chaise*. "I met Charles and Ester while I was out. I invited them to dine with us tonight—you don't mind, do you?"

Pausing before his desk, Gyles took in the happiness shining in her face. "No—of course not."

Francesca held her fingers out to the fire. "Franni's here, too, of course, so there'll be five at table."

Gyles was grateful she was warming her hands and not looking at him. Rounding the desk, he sat and reached for the pile of correspondence awaiting his attention.

Francesca leaned back. "I said seven—I told Irving to tell Ferdinand."

Gyles's lips twitched. "I wonder—"

A knock fell on the door; Wallace entered and bowed. "Ferdinand wishes to know if he might speak with you, my lady. About dinner tonight."

Gyles looked down at his papers.

Francesca sighed. "I will see him in the parlor. Wallace, you will attend this meeting, too."

Wallace bowed. "I'll fetch him, my lady."

Wallace withdrew. Francesca stood and stretched. "At least dealing with Ferdinand keeps my Italian from growing rusty."

Gyles looked up. "Before you go—"

She turned; he laid aside the letter he'd been perusing. "You made a copy of the family tree—what did you do with it?"

Something—consciousness?—flashed through her eyes; it was immediately overlaid by curiosity. "We—your mother, Henni, and I—elaborated. Added on all the branches and connections we could. Why?"

"I need to assess the relationship of some of the connections. Can I see your effort?"

"Of course." She hesitated. "But I would like it back, please."

"I only need to look at it to see if your combined wisdom knows more than I."

She smiled gloriously; her dimple winked. "I'll fetch it for you in a moment."

"After you've dealt with Ferdinand." Gyles waved her to the door. "Perhaps I should brush up my Italian."

At the door, she arched a brow. "I've taught you some new words with which you're becoming quite proficient, but perhaps you're right and it's time for another lesson."

With a sultry glance, she left him.

Gyles stared at the door, his mind formulating visions of such a lesson, then he frowned, shifted, grabbed the next letter, plonked it before him, and forced himself to read.

Chapter 20

Charles, Ester, and Franni did not stay late. After seeing their guests to the door, Gyles and Francesca retreated to the library. As usual, Wallace had left the fire blazing. Francesca sank into an armchair with a contented sigh.

"That went well, I thought."

Gyles glanced at her but made no reply. He looked at his desk, then back at her, then crossed to the *chaise*. Sitting, he stretched out his legs. "Charles seemed very grateful. Was there some reason for that?"

He'd noticed the shared glances, the satisfied looks.

"Franni's been pestering them to visit here."

"I see." Gyles watched Francesca. Staring at the flames, she idly twirled one black curl. He let a moment pass, then asked, "Tell me about Franni."

Francesca looked at him. "Franni?"

"She's . . ." Gyles struggled to find a word that conveyed the reality. "Odd."

The way Franni's eyes had gleamed when he'd spoken to her, the way her fingers had fluttered when he'd taken her hand, the way she'd pressed too close as he'd escorted her and Ester to the table—all these were indelibly imprinted on his mind. Throughout, she'd watched him like a hawk, but a cagey hawk—whenever one of the others had glanced her way, she'd been staring at something else.

He'd felt hunted, and felt ridiculous for it. Franni was precisely the cipher he'd first thought her, only more disturbed. Weak and ineffectual, she was a nonentity—certainly no threat. Nevertheless, he'd clung to Francesca's side as much as possible.

But Franni had caught him when they were leaving. The intensity of her regard, the light in her pale blue eyes, had sent a shiver down his spine. Luckily, Ester had noticed and rescued him, giving him a small, helpless smile. As if asking for understanding, forgiveness.

Gyles frowned. "Franni's not normal. What's wrong with her?"

Francesca sighed; she looked into the flames. "I don't know—I've never known. She's been like that, a bit better, a bit worse, since I met her. I've always thought of her as childish, and while that fits in some ways, she's quite forward in others."

She glanced at Gyles. "Neither Charles nor Ester ever said, but I gather her condition has something to do with her mother's death. She died when Franni was very young. I heard from the servants that she—Franni's mother—threw herself from the tower. It's been boarded up ever since. I wondered if Franni had witnessed it, and if it had turned her mind in some way."

Gyles looked into the heart of the fire, staring at the leaping flames. He knew what effect witnessing a parent's violent death could have on a child. He could imagine all sorts of reactions, could still feel the roil of remembered emotion about his own heart. Yet in all that he couldn't see what emotional reaction could explain all he'd sensed in Franni.

He glanced at Francesca and found her watching him. "Enough of our guests." He sat up. A muted crackle reminded him; he reached into his coat pocket. "I forgot to give this back to you."

He held out her annotated copy of the family tree.

She took it. "Did you find what you wanted?"

"Yes." He'd spent the hour before dinner making his own copy. "You and your helpers are to be commended—you've done an excellent job."

Francesca hesitated, then lifted her eyes to Gyles's face. "I've been meaning to ask, apropos of this." She lifted the paper. "The reason we did it was to get an idea of the extent of the family. I wondered . . . would you be agreeable to us hosting a party? Just for the family, a few close friends and connections. Maybe some dancing, but more an evening to mingle and chat, to get to know each other better."

He held her gaze. "The year's almost done."

"It would be an informal affair. I thought perhaps late next week?"

Gyles read her wish in her eyes and saw no reason to deny her. He suspected she'd get few acceptances, given the season, given the family, but if, as his countess, she wished to play the matriarch . . . "Thursday?"

She smiled her wonderful, heart-stopping smile. "Thursday. Your mother and Henni will help with the invitations."

He drank in her smile, then let his gaze drift down, over her slenderness to the slight bulge below her waist. It was barely visible, even when she was naked, yet when she lay beneath him and he joined with her, he could tell.

She carried his child—even if it was a girl, he didn't care. Just thinking of it sent a surge of feelings through him, emotions he'd never felt before.

He lifted his gaze to her face, and knew his shields were down, that she could read him like a book. He no longer cared. "Come." Rising, he held out his hand. "Let's go upstairs."

She smiled—a knowing, understanding smile—put her hand in his, and let him draw her to her feet. "As I recall, my lord, I need to teach you more Italian."

* * *

Two days later, Gyles convened another meeting in a private room at White's. Devil was there, as were Horace and Waring.

"It's Walwyn." Gyles closed the door and waved them to the chairs.

Devil sat. "Your heir once removed?"

Gyles nodded. "Walwyn Rawlings—a cousin some number of times removed. We share a great-grandfather." Fishing his copy of the family tree from his pocket, he handed it to Devil.

Devil studied it, then frowned. "You'll need to do something about this principal line—you were an only child, and your father was one of two. And the other was a female."

"Never mind that. Go back to the next generation."

"Eight. And before that another eight." Devil's frown deepened. "I see what you mean. Branches everywhere."

Devil handed the paper to Horace. Horace squinted at it. "This is what Henni and your mother have been helping Francesca with."

Gyles nodded. "And they received help from Lady Osbaldestone and others. I doubt we'd get anything more accurate."

Horace passed the paper to Waring. "Seems clear enough. Osbert's your heir, and after him, Walwyn. But why did you want to know that?"

Waring, likewise, looked up inquiringly.

Gyles told them.

"That's . . . not comforting." Horace looked deeply troubled.

"Indeed not." Waring had taken notes. "It appears that the first attempt was on your life, but subsequently, once the possibility of an heir more definitely arose, the would-be murderer turned his sights on Lady Francesca."

"Blackguard!" Horace thumped the table. "But it would make sense, I suppose, to remove her first."

"Indeed." Gyles cut the thought off. "But now we're

alerted and she's well guarded, we need to focus on laying this would-be murderer by the heels."

Devil sat up. "So what do we know of Walwyn Rawlings?"

"He must be about fifty," Gyles said. "I can only recall meeting him once, about the time of my father's death."

Horace nodded. "I remember. He was the black sheep no one wanted to acknowledge, a thoroughly disreputable sort. He'd been shipped off to the Indies. The family thought they'd seen the last of him, but like a bad penny, Walwyn turned up just after your father died." Consulting the family tree, Horace pointed. "His father, old Gisborne, was still alive then—he sent Walwyn to the right-about. Gisborne sent me a letter warning me to have no truck with Walwyn, that he wasn't to be trusted."

Waring wrote steadily. "This Walwyn seems a more likely villain than Mr. Osbert Rawlings, I must say. Do we have a description of Walwyn, any idea where he might be found? Is he married?"

Horace snorted. "Unlikely. According to Gisborne, tavern wenches were more Walwyn's style."

"Walwyn," Gyles said, "used to hobnob with those on the fringes of society. He developed a penchant for the company of sailors and, last I heard, he was living above some tavern in Wapping."

"Wapping." The fastidious look on Waring's face elucidated his opinion on that.

The thought that the earldom and Lambourn Castle were a considerable step up from a tavern in Wapping resonated in all their minds.

"With your permission, my lord, I'll set some men onto locating Mr. Walwyn Rawlings immediately."

Gyles nodded. "And while you're scouring Wapping and the docks, we"—his gaze took in Devil and Horace—"had better scout out nearer pastures. If he so chose, Walwyn could, I suspect, still pass for a gentleman."

"Hmm—while helping Gabriel earlier in the year, I had

reason to chat with the owners of the major shipping lines. If Walwyn's haunting shipping, then he might have come to their attention." Devil cocked a brow at Gyles. "I could ask if they'd heard of him."

"Do." After a moment, Gyles said, "I'll place a notice in whatever handbills circulate on the docks. There's no reason we can't ask outright for information on Walwyn's whereabouts, not in that quarter. The offer of a reward might locate him faster than anything else."

"Good idea."

Waring nodded. "I'll have my men look for suitable handbills."

"Think I'll visit some of the older Rawlingses," Horace said. "Long-lived folks. It's possible they may have heard something about Walwyn."

"So we've all got something to do." Gyles rose. Devil did, too.

Frowning, Horace lumbered to his feet. "But, I say, no need to tell the ladies, what? It'll only frighten them."

Gyles and Devil looked at Horace, then exchanged a glance.

"As Francesca's already under constant guard, and she's aware of a possible threat, there seems little point in belaboring the matter and raising what might be an unnecessary fuss." Gyles glanced at Waring. "I think, for the moment, all inquiries should remain confidential."

"Indeed, my lord."

"Indeed." Horace turned to the door. "No need for the Rawlingses to provide the ton with the last scandal of the year. Aside from anything else, our ladies wouldn't thank us for that."

"Chillingworth."

Gyles halted and turned. He'd left Devil with friends in the gaming room but had yet to quit White's; he'd been strolling absentmindedly toward the door. He hadn't recognized the voice that had hailed him, and had to dredge his memory to locate the name of the portly gentleman stumping his way.

Lord Carsden eventually halted before him; leaning on his cane, he looked up at him from under scraggy brows. "Hear you, St. Ives, Kingsley and some others are thinking of proposing a few amendments in the spring session."

Gyles nodded, his mind racing. Carsden rarely concerned himself with politics, but he did have a vote.

"Mind if I inquire what the substance of your amendments might be? I've heard they might be worth supporting."

Hiding his surprise, Gyles waved to an anteroom. "I'll be happy to explain."

He led the way into the room, and was immediately collared by Lord Malmsey.

"Just the fellow I was after," his lordship declared. "Heard a whisper there's some amendments in the wind that perhaps I ought to take note of, what?"

Gyles ended holding court to four peers, all with a new-found interest in the political sphere. He outlined the basics of what their group intended to propose; all four gentlemen frowned, nodded, and, ultimately, stated their interest in supporting the cause.

None mentioned who had activated their heretofore dormant political consciences and steered them in the group's direction; Gyles was too wise to ask. But when he reached home later that afternoon and headed upstairs to dress for the evening, he paused outside Francesca's door.

He hesitated, then tapped.

Light footsteps approached. The door opened, and Millie looked out.

Her eyes grew round when she saw him.

Gyles put his finger to his lips, then beckoned her out. She stepped over the threshold; he put out a hand to stop her closing the door. With his other hand, he gestured down the corridor. "I wish to speak with your mistress—she'll ring when she needs you."

The little maid looked scandalized. "But, m'lord—she's in her bath."

Gyles looked down at her. "I know." It was where Francesca usually was at this time of day, relaxing prior to donning her evening gown.

"Off you go." He waved Millie away.

Looking positively horrified, the maid backed, then turned tail and went.

Gyles grinned and slipped through the door.

A hip bath stood on a rug facing the fire; Francesca, black curls piled high on her head, was sitting facing the flames. Wisps of steam rose, wreathing about her as she smoothed a soapy sponge down one gracefully extended arm while softly crooning what sounded like an Italian lullaby. Gyles listened for a moment, then closed the door.

"Who was it, Millie?"

He strolled forward. "Not Millie."

She tipped her head back against the rim and watched as he neared. Smiled delightedly. "Good evening, my lord. And to what do I owe the pleasure of your company?"

He halted by the bath's side and smiled down at her. Let his gaze roam the curves of her breasts, sheening wet and laced with suds. "I believe my pleasure is rather greater than yours."

She arched a brow; he reached for her hand, lifted it, bent and pressed a kiss to her wet knuckles, then turned her hand and ran his tongue over her palm, then sucked lightly at the pulse point at her wrist.

He raised his head reluctantly. "You taste good enough to eat."

Their gazes met, held; she raised both brows in question. After a moment, he smiled, squeezed her hand and released it. "We have to be at the Godsleys by eight."

Drawing up a chair, he sat. "I wanted to ask if you're acquainted with Lady Carsden."

Francesca nodded. "We meet quite frequently. She moves in the same circles."

"And Lady Mitchell?"

"Indeed, but Honoria knows her better than I." Drawing her knees up, wrapping her arms about them, she searched his face. "Have their husbands spoken to you?"

"Much to my amazement. I don't think Mitchell or Carsden has been in the House since their investiture."

Francesca grinned. "Well their wives felt it was time they said something—did something—useful. Will it help?"

"Every vote helps. But I wanted to ask—how many have you and Honoria spoken to? Do you have any idea which others might be inclined to support us?"

Eyes sparkling, Francesca leaned forward. "Well . . ."

They traded names and opinions; from there it was a short step to the overall numbers, the increasing possibilities of success. They lost track of the time, only remembered it when Francesca suddenly shivered and looked down at the cooling water.

Gyles frowned. "Damn—I forgot." He stood. "I'll ring for more hot water."

"No—don't bother. I was finished anyway." She pointed at a towel.

Gyles turned to pick it up as she rose. He turned back—and stopped, his mind wiped clean.

Dropping her sponge in the water, Francesca straightened and looked up, instantly noted the stillness that had claimed him, his fixed gaze—the flames flickering behind the grey of his eyes. She let her gaze roam swiftly, then she smiled, reached for the towel, tugged it from his slack grasp.

Dropped it on the floor and reached out her arms to him.

"I'll write to Lady Godsley that I was in fear of taking a chill. And now, my lord, you had better warm me up."

Gyles met her gaze, then reached for her, locked his hands about her slender waist, and lifted her from the tub.

Five days later, their select band of searchers still hadn't found Walwyn, hadn't unearthed the slightest trace of him, which only made them even more wary, more suspicious. According to Walwyn's sister's husband, "the old reprobate" was definitely in London, but where and in what guise they had no idea.

Leaving yet another meeting at White's, Gyles returned home in time to dress for dinner. Tonight was Francesca's family party, her attempt to gather the clan. He hoped for her sake the family would rally and enough would attend for the event to be deemed a success. She, his mother, and Henni had had their heads together for the past week, organizing and ordering. Although Francesca had regaled him with their preparations, distracted by his search for Walwyn, Gyles hadn't taken much in.

He did know tonight's dinner was to be a small affair with, aside from Francesca, only his mother, Henni, and Horace present.

"There were simply too many to invite," his mother told him when he joined them in the drawing room.

"Indeed." Henni took up the tale as he moved to greet her. "Even restricting the list to the heads of the different branches—why, there were over fifty, plus spouses—and if we'd selected amongst them, well—that would have caused ructions, which is precisely what we're attempting to heal." She frowned up at him as he straightened. "You're looking a trifle peaked, dear. Have you been busy with your parliamentary business?"

"Among other things." Gyles turned as Francesca slipped her hand through his arm. He smiled. As she exchanged some comment with Henni, he took in her appearance.

Tonight, she'd chosen to wear old gold. Her gown was of lush silk in that deep, rich shade that invoked the idea of treasure, the silk shawl draped over her elbows a medley of subtly contrasting hues, all golds and soft browns. Her hair was piled high, artfully cascading to brush her shoulders, the black locks a dramatic contrast against her ivory skin. From her ears, gold earrings dangled; a simple gold chain encircled her throat. And in the midst of the gold, her eyes glowed, intense as any emerald.

She glanced at him.

"You look exquisite." Gyles raised her hand to his lips, let his gaze touch hers.

"Dinner is served, my lord."

As one they turned. Joined by Lady Elizabeth, Henni, and Horace, they moved into the small dining room.

By eight-thirty that evening, Gyles was more distracted than he'd been all week. From his position beside Francesca at the top of the stairs leading down to their ballroom, he craned his neck, looking back along the row of guests waiting to greet them.

He couldn't see the end of the line.

Francesca nudged him. He hauled his gaze back to the elderly lady waiting to speak with him. He took her wizened hand, racking his brain for her name.

"Cousin Helen has traveled up from Merton to be with us tonight."

Gyles shot a grateful glance at Francesca, then murmured polite phrases to Cousin Helen, who then informed him, in a voice that would have done credit to a sergeant major, that she was deaf as a post.

Patting his hand, she moved on down the stairs. Gyles caught Francesca's fleeting grin as she turned to greet their next guests.

There had to be three hundred of them—three hundred Rawlingses, plus an assortment of others. Gyles was relieved to welcome Devil and Honoria.

Honoria nodded regally, the twinkle in her eye telling him there was no point trying to hide his astonishment.

"I never imagined there would be this many."

"You underestimated the power of curiosity—what lady in her right mind would turn down an invitation from your new countess?"

"I've never claimed to comprehend the minds of ladies."

"Very wise." Honoria cast a glance over the now teeming ballroom. "From what Devil told me of your family tree, there might well be more Rawlingses than Cynsters."

Devil turned from Francesca in time to catch that; he looked around and nodded. "It's possible."

"Heaven forbid!" Gyles muttered *sotto voce*.

Honoria threw him a disapproving look; Devil grinned, then, sobering, caught Gyles's eye. "Seems an excellent opportunity to further our recent activities."

The thought had occurred to Gyles. Surely someone present would know where Walwyn was. "You start. I'll join you when I'm free."

Devil nodded.

"What activities?" Honoria asked.

"I told you we're looking for supporters for our bills." Devil steered her down to the ballroom's floor.

Gyles turned to greet the next guests—cousins and connections even more distant, they'd all answered Francesca's call with an alacrity he found both disarming and disconcerting. As if they'd been waiting for the opportunity to replace the distance developed over recent decades with a more cohesive framework, a stronger sense of shared purpose based on familial ties.

Quite aside from their number, that sense of togetherness distracted him.

The line was thinning when a typically tall and lanky male Rawlings, his face lined and weather-beaten, his clothes sober and unfashionable, approached, a tall, plainly dressed lady on his arm. The man smiled at Francesca and bowed stiffly, but it was the stiffness of disuse rather than haughtiness.

"Walwyn Rawlings, my dear."

Francesca smiled and gave him her hand.

Gyles only just stopped himself from grabbing her and thrusting her behind him.

Walwyn continued, "Allow me to present my wife, Hettie.

We married over a year ago, but I confess I've yet to spread the news through the family." He nodded to Gyles, smiling pleasantly, then glanced at the throng in the ballroom. "It looks like tonight will do the job for me."

"I'm so pleased you could join us." Francesca smiled at Hettie and shook hands. "You live in Greenwich, I believe?"

"Yes." Rising from her curtsy, Hettie glanced at Walwyn. Her voice was soft and sweet. "Walwyn's the curator of the new museum there."

Walwyn offered Gyles his hand. "Maritime stuff, you know."

Gyles grasped Walwyn's hand and shook it. "Indeed?"

They'd been wrong—on a number of counts. Gyles spent a few minutes chatting with Walwyn—enough to convince himself beyond reasonable doubt. Walwyn had nothing to do with the attacks on Francesca. The years of hard living had stripped Walwyn of any ability to dissemble—the man was as open as the day. And besotted with his wife. Gyles recognized the signs. Where neither his family nor society had held the power to reform Walwyn, love in the guise of gentle Hettie had triumphed.

Guilt—or was it fellow feeling?—prompted Gyles to beckon Osbert over. He introduced Walwyn and his wife and charged Osbert to take them about and introduce them to his mother and others of the clan.

Osbert was pleased to be of use. As he tucked his wife's hand protectively in his arm, Walwyn caught Gyles's eye and inclined his head, his gratitude plain to see.

Watching them go down the steps, Gyles inwardly shook his head. How foolish they'd been not to mention their search to their wives. A simple question to Francesca, Henni, or even Honoria would have got them a result a week ago.

"Gyles?"

He turned, smiled and greeted another Rawlings.

Beside him, Francesca smiled and charmed, inwardly

amazed. Intrigued. She'd embarked on her plans to draw the Rawlings family together out of a sense of duty, a feeling that, as Gyles's countess, it was what she should do. Now she'd succeeded, it was patently apparent that the evening was giving rise to something considerably more powerful and profound than social discourse.

The rush of family feeling, rediscovered for some, novel to others, including herself, was a tangible tide flowing through the room. A tide their guests dived into and contributed to with an eagerness that was itself a reward.

"Come. Let's go down."

The end of the long line had finally arrived. She glanced at Gyles, handsome as sin beside her. With a smile, she laid her hand on his sleeve; together they descended to join their guests—their family.

Some saw and turned; others followed suit. She saw their smiles, saw them raise their hands.

Had to blink back tears when spontaneous applause rolled through the room.

She smiled, graciously joyous, upon them all, then glanced at Gyles, and saw pride, undisguised, in his eyes.

They reached the ballroom floor and he lifted her hand, touched his lips to her fingers.

"They're yours." He held her gaze. "As am I."

Others approached, and they had to turn aside. Later, with a shared glance and a nod, Gyles drifted from her side. But the triumph remained; it grew as the evening progressed precisely as she, Lady Elizabeth, and Henni had hoped, with a light and festive air.

Gyles moved through the crowd, chatting easily, receiving compliments innumerable on his exquisite wife. Eventually, he found Horace, then Devil, alerting them to Walwyn's presence and his exoneration.

Devil grimaced. "So now the question is: if not Walwyn, then who?"

"Precisely." Gyles looked around. "Try as I might, I cannot bring myself to believe that any here tonight wish either Francesca or me harm."

"No sly glances, no hard looks?"

"Nary a one. Everyone seemed honestly pleased to meet us."

Devil nodded. "I've been listening and watching, and I agree—I haven't picked up the slightest sign of discontent, let alone malevolent intent."

"That's what's missing. There's not the smallest whiff of malignancy."

Devil went to nod, then laughed and clapped Gyles on the shoulder. "We're hardened cases. Here we are, put out because there's no dragon present to vanquish."

Gyles grinned. "True." He glanced at Devil. "I suspect that, as far as tonight goes, we'd be wiser to set the problem aside and enjoy ourselves."

Devil had found Honoria. She was watching them through the crowd. "And if we don't, we'll only bring an inquisition down on our heads."

"There is that. We'll meet tomorrow and see where we stand."

They parted, Devil to cross the room to Honoria, Gyles to circulate until he found his way to Francesca's side. He was standing beside her, conscious of pride and something more primal, when Charles, a late arrival, came to make his bow.

"Only me." He smiled at Francesca. "This wouldn't do for Franni, as you know, but I couldn't miss the occasion."

"I'm very glad you came." Francesca pressed his hands. "Is Ester well?"

"Indeed—she's sitting with Franni."

"And Franni?"

Charles's eyes dimmed. "She's . . . well, it's hard to say. Her behavior's erratic . . . difficult." He forced a smile. "But in general terms, yes, she's well."

A lady approached Francesca—with a last smile for Charles, she had to turn away.

Charles shifted to Gyles's side. "This is a remarkable turnout. You must be pleased."

"Indeed—Francesca's worked wonders."

"I always knew she would."

"I do recall you being very certain of her abilities. For that, and your wise counsel last August, you have my undying gratitude."

"Ah, well." Charles looked at Francesca. "It seems to me the right choice was made all around."

Gyles was sure he heard Fate chuckling.

Charles turned back to him. "You'll understand if I don't remain long. We're returning to Hampshire the day after tomorrow, so tomorrow will be busy."

Gyles felt a pang of relief. He held out his hand. "I'll wish you and Ester and Franni a good journey now, in case I don't see you before you leave. But now you're here, do take the opportunity to meet some of the others."

"I will." Charles released his hand, took his leave of Francesca, then wandered into the crowd.

Gyles watched him go. He liked Charles, had from the first, but he was glad to know Franni would soon be leaving London, would, within days, be hidden away once again in deepest Hampshire. He now understood Charles's wish to live quietly, removed from the eyes of the polite world. Protected from that world, from the whispers, the pointing fingers.

Society was not kind to those like Franni. Gyles understood Charles's stance and respected him for it.

He glanced at Francesca. He understood her, too, enough to know that loyalty and devotion came naturally, a part of her she wouldn't deny. A part he couldn't ask her to deny. Explaining his nebulous unease over Franni was something he'd rather not attempt, given Francesca saw Franni as merely childish, backward, disturbed because of her mother's death.

There was more to Franni's strangeness than that—he would take his oath on it—yet she was such a helpless soul, how could he speak against her?

Over the past week, the plans for tonight had taken all Francesca's time; he hadn't had to worry she'd try to visit Franni. Given Francesca's character, forbidding her to see her cousin was out of the question, persuading her to that end wasted breath. But if Franni would soon be gone, he wouldn't need to speak, to steer Francesca from her company purely to ease his very likely unjustified, totally amorphous concern.

He remembered Franni as he'd last seen her—remembered the burning look in her pale eyes—and uttered a heartfelt silent "thank-you" to Charles for resolving his problem for him.

Francesca turned to him. He smiled as she introduced a young cousin shortly to make her come-out.

For Francesca, the evening was perfect and more, a triumph unmarred by any infelicitous occurrence. All proceeded exactly as planned, and the turn out of Rawlingses exceeded her wildest expectations.

"I never imagined so many would come." Tired but inexpressibly happy, she leaned against Gyles as, with the house at last quiet about them, the very last guests gone, they strolled toward their apartments.

"I never imagined there *were* so many." Gyles's arm about her waist tightened briefly. "You performed a miracle."

She laughed, shook her head. "No—I merely gave the miracle the opportunity to be. They came, they made it— *they* were the miracle." She understood that now; she squeezed the hand at her waist. "You've no idea of the plans being made—for family celebrations, for balls next Season. Why, two of the families discovered their daughters, both to be presented next year, were born on the same day, so they're now planning a huge event."

"I can imagine."

At his dry tone, she paused before her door and looked up

at him. "But it's good, isn't it? Good that the family's together again, no longer fragmented and apart?"

Gyles studied her eyes, then raised a hand and traced her cheek. "Yes. It's good." He hadn't thought it important until she'd made him see. He glanced at her door. "Now get rid of Millie so we can celebrate your success as you deserve."

Her brows rose; her green eyes glowed. "Indeed?" The glance she threw him as she opened her door was provocation incarnate. "As you will, my lord."

It wasn't as he willed but as they willed.

They came together in the dimness of her room, earl and countess, lover and loved, partners in life. They were partners in truth, bound by a power nothing on earth could break; Gyles no longer saw any point in denying it, in trying to hide it. Saying the words, out aloud, might still be difficult—might always be beyond him—but living their truth was not. Not with her.

She was life and love—his future life, his only love. They came together with the ease of practice, and the power of their own passionate natures, reflected between them, intensified almost beyond bearing now there were no barriers between. He let the last down, deliberately, intentionally—let it sink without a qualm, without regrets. Fate—and she—had shown him, taught him that love was a force beyond his control, a force whose power he coveted and craved. A force that, having once experienced its majesty, its enthralling allure, he could not exist without.

It was a part of him now and forever. As was she. And if there was still an element of his nature that shook with fear at the realization, at the unequivocal knowledge of how much she meant to him, and how much his life now depended on her, she knew and applied the only balm that could ease him, could soothe the soul of the barbarian he was.

She loved him back—with a powerful passion that burned like a flame in the warm darkness of her bed. A flame that joined with his own and heated them, set them afire, consumed them.

Wrapped in her arms, sheathed in her body, he drove into her and drove them on. Their lips met, fused, tongues tangled. Their hearts thundered and rejoiced.

There were moments in life when simplicity held more power than elaborate gestures. When a direct, undisguised act shattered perceptions and cut to the heart of the truth. So it was that they loved—directly, simply, with no guile to shield their hearts, no remnant of separateness to keep their souls apart.

When, locked together, they tumbled into the void, into the abyss of creation, the only sound either could hear was the beat of the other's heart.

Later they stirred, parted, then slumped together in the darkness. Gyles reached down and drew the satin comforter up, over their cooling bodies. He collapsed back on the mounded pillows and drew Francesca into his arms, settled her warm curves against him.

After a while, she stretched, languid as a cat and equally boneless, then she wriggled around and draped her arms about his neck. "I'm so pleased."

Her purr warmed him. He recognized the ambiguity for what it was. "So you should be."

She wasn't talking about the party; her soft chuckle confirmed that. "I suppose we should sleep."

"We should." She was increasing—she needed her rest. "No need to be greedy. We've all our lives ahead of us."

"Mmm." She nestled her head on his shoulder.

Within minutes, she was asleep.

All their lives. Gyles listened to the soft huff of her breathing. Then he closed his eyes and dreamed.

Chapter 21

"*Do come along!* We'll be late."

"Nonsense." Francesca smiled placatingly at Osbert as Irving helped her into her pelisse. "It's only just three. Lady Carlisle won't be expecting us so early."

"Oh, won't she?" Osbert cast a knowledgeable glance over Francesca's new green wool coat with its velvet collar and matching velvet muff. "That suits you. Where was I? Oh, yes. Her ladyship and every single one of her guests will be waiting to hear about last night. How the Great Rawlings Experiment went."

"Experiment?" A sharp rap on the door had Francesca glancing around. She watched as Irving accepted a note.

Laying the note on a salver, Irving brought it to her.

"A young lad said it was from your cousin, ma'am. He expected no reply."

"Franni?" Francesca unfolded the note. She read it; her emotions swung sharply from the inner joy that had warmed her all day—the joy of knowing that the love she'd always wanted, a love to last a lifetime, was hers—to plunge into worrying concern. The change was abrupt, cold reality slicing keenly into her warm world of earthly bliss.

The short note was in Franni's unformed hand. Lowering

the single sheet, Francesca focused on Osbert. "I won't be attending Lady Carlisle's afternoon tea. Please convey my apologies to her ladyship."

Her voice growing brisk, she turned to Irving. "Have the carriage brought around. Two footmen, as usual."

"*Wait* a minute!" Osbert replaced Irving as he bowed and withdrew. "Where are you off to?"

Francesca glanced at the note. "St. Margaret's Church, Cheapside."

"*What?*"

"Osbert, I *must* go—Franni says to come immediately. She won't be able to wait long. I can understand that. She and Ginny must be out walking—"

"*Not* in Cheapside. Not the sort of place ladies go for walks."

"Regardless, that's where Franni is, and she'll have her maid with her, and it's a church, after all. We'll be perfectly safe. And I'll be taking my escort with me."

"You're taking *me* with you."

"No." Francesca laid her hand on his arm. "I don't dare. Franni says she must tell me something about Ester, that she's ill but concealing it—I have to find out what Franni knows. And she won't tell me if you're with me."

Wallace approached. "The carriage is on its way, ma'am. If I might make so bold, it would be best to take Mr. Rawlings with you."

Francesca shook her head. "That's impossible and unnecessary. I'm going to visit a church, meet my cousin, and exchange a few words. I won't be going anywhere else, I promise you." Hooves clopped beyond the front door; she whirled. "I'll return as soon as I can."

"Francesca!"

"Ma'am, if I could suggest—"

Francesca swept out of the house. Osbert and Wallace followed. Wallace halted at the top of the steps, watching with open concern as Francesca was handed into the carriage. Osbert was not so constrained; he followed Francesca to the carriage, lecturing all the way.

When the door shut and he was still on the pavement, he glared. "Gyles *won't* like it."

"Probably not," Francesca replied, "but I'll be back before he knows."

The carriage lurched, then rumbled off. Osbert watched it go through narrowed eyes. *"Women!"*

A discreet cough at his elbow had him turning. Wallace met his gaze. "If I could suggest, sir . . . the master's quite experienced in managing females."

"Yes, I know. Devilish clever in the saddle and all that, but what's that got to say . . . oh."

"Indeed, sir. I believe his lordship is presently at White's. You, of course, could gain instant access, and you could explain the intricacies of the situation."

Osbert scowled at the corner around which the carriage had disappeared. "I'll do it. White's, you say?"

"Indeed, sir." Wallace waved imperiously. "Here's a hackney."

Osbert turned from tossing the jarvey his fare, and saw Gyles framed in the doorway of White's. "Hoi!"

Pushing through the crowd thronging the pavement, he reached Gyles as he came down the steps.

Gyles frowned. "I thought you were escorting Francesca this afternoon."

"So did I." With a curt nod to Devil, one step behind Gyles, Osbert complained, "She's gone off to some deuced church in Cheapside."

"What?"

"That's what I said. Told her it was no place for the likes of her. So did Wallace—or he tried to, anyway—"

"Why did she go?"

"She got a note from her cousin. She—the cousin—said she had something to tell Francesca about someone called

Ester. Francesca seemed to think it perfectly normal for this cousin to have set up a meeting in St. Margaret's Church in Cheapside. She wouldn't let me go with her—said the cousin would balk or some such thing—"

Gyles grabbed Osbert's arms; he only just refrained from shaking him. The familiar black fear was roiling inside him, tentacles tightening about his chest. "Did she take the carriage?"

Osbert nodded. "And two footmen. And there was an extra groom on top, too."

"Good." Gyles released Osbert. Devil stepped down, joining them. Gyles looked at Devil, then shook his head. "She's well guarded, but . . ." He knew she was in danger. Real danger. He thought of Franni, and his blood ran cold. "I don't like this."

"I don't either. Nor did Wallace," Osbert averred.

"I don't like the sound of Cheapside either." Devil raised a brow at Gyles. "Your call."

Gyles considered. "Osbert—grab a hackney. You and I are going to Cheapside."

"Excellent!" Osbert strode off.

Devil raised both brows. "And me?"

"I need someone to take a clear and concise message to Francesca's uncle."

"Ah, I see." Devil's gaze followed Osbert down the steps. "Charles Rawlings?"

"Yes. He and his party are staying at Bertram's in Duke Street. He said he'd be busy getting ready to leave tomorrow, but I need him to come to St. Margaret's in Cheapside. Tell him Franni's there."

"Francesca's cousin?"

"Yes. I don't know what's going on—what Franni's up to—but . . ." Every instinct was screaming. Gyles met Devil's green gaze. "Can you make sure Charles gets the message?"

"Of course. And then?"

"Just that." Gyles hesitated, then added, "Whatever comes after, I suspect it'll be best kept within the family."

Devil held his gaze, then nodded and clapped Gyles on the shoulder. "I'll make sure the message gets through with all speed."

Devil strode off toward Duke Street, two blocks away. Gyles made for the hackney Osbert had waiting.

"St. Margaret's in Cheapside," Gyles ordered the jarvey. "Fast as you can."

Francesca sat on the leather seat of her carriage, swaying as it rolled through the streets. Beyond the windows, the day slowly faded. She recognized the great houses along the Strand, then the road narrowed through the Fleet. At one point, John Coachman pulled up and the groom scurried around, lighting the carriage lamps. Then the carriage rocked on, slowing as the horses climbed the hill to St. Paul's, then, the clop of their hooves echoing from the stone facades, started down the farther slope, into a part of London Francesca had never seen.

Soon, wisps of fog laid pale fingers across the windows. The road angled nearer the river; the fog grew denser, shops and taverns shrouded in the sulfurous murk.

Francesca frowned; the pricklings of unease, the stirrings of presentiment, were growing too strong to ignore. Why had Franni chosen such a place? Osbert had been right—Ginny would never have taken Franni walking here. The chill outside penetrated the carriage; a shiver slithered down Francesca's spine.

Something was dreadfully wrong.

She would only find out what was going on if she went on and met Franni. Even here, the environs of a church would be safe, and she had four burly men with her.

The road grew narrower. As the surface grew rougher and the carriage jolted along, she tried to think how to manage the coming meeting, how best to ensure their safety—Franni's, Ginny's, and her own—without throwing Franni off her stride.

The city's bells tolled four o'clock as the carriage slowed, then halted. The carriage dipped as the groom and footmen descended, then the carriage door was opened.

"Ma'am?"

John had halted the carriage beside the church's lych-gate. Francesca held out her hand; one of the footmen helped her down. Steps led to a path through the church's graveyard. Francesca studied the dark bulk of the church, barely visible through the gloom, then glanced back.

"You." She waved at the groom. "Stay here with John. You two"—she gestured to the footmen, both thickset and reassuringly solid—"come with me."

They didn't question her dispositions. One footman opened the lych-gate and stepped through. "Your pardon, ma'am, but I think I should lead the way."

Francesca nodded. What had Franni been thinking of?

Was she really here?

That, at least, was answered as they approached the church. Most of the building was dark but light shone from the nearer end of the transept. Flickering lamplight illuminated a chapel; Francesca glimpsed a figure pacing. The windows were stained and ornate; she couldn't see through them, but the figure's stiff gait left no doubt in her mind.

"That's my cousin." She looked around. "How do I get in?"

There was no direct access to the chapel; they followed the massive walls of grey stone to the church's main door. It was ajar. Francesca retreated, waving the footmen back. She halted along the wall, ten paces from the door. "You'll need to wait here. My cousin is simpleminded. She won't speak if she sees strange men with me."

The footmen exchanged glances. The one who'd led the way shifted. "It's just that, ma'am, we've orders to keep you always in sight." He glanced at the fog-shrouded night. "In such places, within reach."

Francesca shook her head. "I'm going in, and you are not, but you can see the door from here, so you can watch and make sure no one else goes in. I'll leave the door open, so if anything goes amiss, I can call and you'll hear." She held up a hand to stay any protests. "*That* is what we are going to do. Remain here."

She marched to the church door, sure they wouldn't disobey her direct orders. A quick glance as she reached the door confirmed that; the pair stood watching, fog draping their shoulders. Francesca stepped into the church.

It was old—ancient. And the cold was intense, as if it seeped from the very stones. Francesca quelled a shiver, glad of her pelisse and muff. There was no light beyond the distant glow shed from the chapel.

Ruts had been worn in the flags. To conceal this, threadbare runners had been laid over rush matting. Francesca's feet sank into the padding as she walked down the darkened nave, then turned left. A heavily carved screen hung with shadows partly hid the chapel. There were two archways, one on either side, worked into the screen. Francesca made for the one on the left through which the lamplight beckoned most strongly.

She halted in the archway. Before the altar on which a single lamp stood, Franni paced.

Relief swept Francesca. Franni wore a heavy cloak, the skirts jerking as she walked, the hood back so the lamplight sheened her fair hair, drawn back into the usual loose knot at her nape. Francesca stepped forward. "Franni?"

Franni whirled, pale blue eyes wide, then she recovered, straightened, and smiled. "I knew you'd come."

"Of course." Five rows of short pews flanked a central aisle. All empty. As she started up the aisle, Francesca scanned the area around the altar. "Where's Ginny?"

"I didn't need her—I left her at the hotel."

Francesca halted. "You came alone?"

Franni giggled, ducked her head, then shook it, her gaze locked on Francesca. "No. Oh, no."

Francesca remained where she was, level with the second pew. She stared at Franni, at the glow that lit her eyes, and listened to her high-pitched giggling. Fear slithered, ice-cold, down her spine. "Franni, we should leave. My carriage is waiting." She held out a hand, beckoned. "Come. You like driving in carriages."

Franni grinned. "I do. Yes, I do. And I'll be driving around in carriages a lot more soon." From the folds of her cloak, she raised a pistol and pointed it at Francesca. "When you're gone."

Francesca stared at the pistol, at the round black mouth. Fear locked about her heart. She knew nothing about guns, but firearms fascinated Franni; she loved the bang. Francesca had no idea if Franni knew how to load and prime a pistol, or if she could shoot one, yet the long barrel was pointed directly at her chest. Supporting it with both hands, Franni held the pistol steady.

A faint sound broke the spell, eased the icy grip of shock. Francesca realized she'd stopped breathing. Dragging in a breath, she lifted her gaze to Franni's face.

Her breath caught again. Franni's expression was triumphant, her eyes afire with undisguised intent.

"I figured it out, you see."

"Figured out what?" Francesca forced the words out. If she screamed, she'd be dead before the footmen reached her. Turning and running would end the same way. "I don't understand."

Talking—spinning out the time. That was her only option. While she lived, there was hope—she could see no further than that. She could hardly believe she was here, talking to Franni over the yawning mouth of a pistol. "What are you talking about?"

Franni's expression turned smugly condescending. "It was obvious but *you* didn't see it, and there was no need to tell you—not before. He married you for your land, you see. I didn't have the right land, and he had to have it—I quite see that. But he met me and fell in love with me—why else did he come back to speak with me a second time? He didn't even want to see *you*."

Francesca stared. "Gyles?"

Franni nodded, still smug, increasingly superior. "Gyles Rawlings. That's his name. Not Chillingworth—he's the earl."

"Franni, they're one and the same."

"No, they're not!" A frown leaped into Franni's eyes. Her hands tightened about the pistol—it hadn't wavered in the least. But the feel of the wooden butt between her hands seemed to reassure her. The tension gradually lessened; Franni's shoulders lowered. "You just don't understand. Gyles wants to marry me—there's no point you trying to say that isn't so, because I *know*! I know how such things are done—I've read about it in books. He walked with me and listened politely—that's how gentlemen show their interest." Her expression stern, Franni frowned at Francesca. "You can stop trying to tell me I'm wrong. *You* didn't see Gyles's face when he turned and looked at me just before you joined him at the altar."

No, but Francesca could imagine it—could imagine the draining of expression, the momentary blankness, the dawning horror. Gyles had thought he was marrying Franni—she could recall the moment when he'd stared at her cousin, then his gaze had whipped around to her.

Franni nodded. "*Gyles* wanted to marry *me*, but the *earl* had to marry you, because *you* had the land."

Her jaw set; her pale eyes blazed. "Grandpa was a *fool!* He told me I was just like him and he was going to make sure *I* got the best inheritance, not you, because you were devil's spawn. So he changed his will, and my papa inherited Rawlings Hall. But Grandpa was *stupid*—the best inheritance was that silly piece of land *you* got!" Her eyes were twin flames. "It *should have been mine!*" Franni leaned forward. "It would have been mine but for *you*."

Francesca said nothing. Despite Franni's rantings, the pistol barrel remained pointed at her chest. She felt faint, the cold and shock draining life from her; she was suddenly very aware of that other life—such a precious life—she carried within her. Slowly reaching with one hand, she gripped the back of the pew beside her.

"It's all *Grandpa's* fault, but he's dead so I can't even tell him—"

Franni raged on, heaping scorn on Francis Rawlings, the man in whose honor they both were named.

It was the longest journey Gyles had ever taken. Francesca was in danger; he knew it with a certainty he couldn't deny. He might be generations removed from his barbarian ancestors, but some instincts remained, dormant but not dead.

As the hackney raced through the City, then out past St. Paul's, he struggled to keep his mind focused, to ignore any thought of Francesca coming to harm. If he thought of that, acknowledged the reason for that roiling black fear and thus gave it credence, gave it purchase in his mind, he, and therefore she, would be doomed. The barbarian within couldn't face, couldn't endure, that.

He concentrated on the fact that once he was with her, she'd be safe. He could and would rescue her. He had twice before. There was no question—not in his mind, not in his heart, not even in his soul—that he would save her. Whatever it took, he would do. Whatever was demanded, he would give.

They rattled into Cheapside. The jarvey had proved a demon driver, swearing and cursing his way through the tangled thoroughfares. They'd covered the distance in record time; although the road had narrowed to a single lane, the jarvey cracked his whip and they raced on.

"Tip him well and tell him to wait," Gyles said, as the reckless pace slowed. Osbert had remained silent all the way; he only nodded now as, grim-faced, Gyles reached for the door. He was out on the cobbles before the hackney halted.

John Coachman was waiting beside the town carriage.

"Thank God, m'lord. Her ladyship went up to the church twenty minutes ago. She told us to wait here. She took two footmen with her—Cole and Niles. I think they're up there"—John gestured to the fog-shrouded church yard— "but I can't be sure, and we didn't like to yell."

Gyles nodded. "Osbert, come with me. John—wait here. Mr. Charles Rawlings will be along soon—send him straight up to the church."

Gyles opened the lych-gate and strode up the path, Osbert at his heels. They both slowed as some way to the left through the thickening fog they saw a light glimmering through the transept windows. Gyles halted. A single figure was outlined, but he couldn't make out details.

"Francesca?" Osbert whispered.

It was the hair that decided it. "No. I think that's Franni." She seemed to be stationary. Gyles strode on.

Alerted by their footsteps, Cole and Niles materialized from the gloom.

"Her ladyship's in there, m'lord—she told us to wait here. The door's open so we can hear if she calls."

"Have you heard anything?"

"Just some distant talking—can't make anything out."

Gyles nodded. "Remain here. When Mr. Charles Rawlings arrives, direct him inside. Tell him to be as quiet as he can, at least until we learn what's going on."

The men stepped back. Beckoning Osbert to follow, Gyles entered the church. The padded carpet muffling their steps was a boon. Quickly, he made his way to where flickering light shone from the side chapel.

Gyles heard Franni's voice as he neared.

"I thought he loved *me*, but he couldn't have! He gave you the best inheritance even though he'd never *seen* you!"

"Franni—"

"*No*—don't try to argue! People always tell me I don't understand but I do! I *do*!"

Still in the shadows, Gyles stepped to where he could see through the archway—and froze. He put out a hand to stop Osbert following. "Franni's there, with Francesca." His voice was a thread, carrying no further than Osbert. "Franni's standing before the altar, one step up. Francesca's by the second pew in the central aisle." Gyles drew a tight breath, let it out with the words, "Franni's holding a pistol aimed at Francesca."

Osbert did nothing. His gaze locked on the tableau before him, Gyles murmured, "Stay here and keep out of sight. Franni's high-strung—she'll get a shock if she sees you— she doesn't know you. We don't want to alarm her and have her pull the trigger." Gyles paused to moisten his dry lips. "In a moment I'm going in. Stay out here, out of sight, but get into a position where you can watch and witness whatever happens. Just don't let her see you."

He sensed Osbert's nod. Osbert wasn't his ideal as a second, but thus far Osbert was managing well. Still as a statue, Gyles listened once more to Franni's ranting.

"I *know* the truth. Gyles's loves me—*me!*—but he had to marry you to get the land. Now he's got it, he would marry me if he could, but he can't." Franni paused; her gaze had never left Francesca. "Not while you live."

Franni's voice lowered. "Of course, he should kill you— that's what he should do—anyone can see that. But he's too noble, too softhearted." Franni straightened and lifted her chin. "So I'm going to kill you for him, and then he and I will marry, just as we've always wanted."

Her voice had taken on the singsong cadence of one reciting a bedtime story.

"Franni." Francesca held out a hand. "This won't work."

"It will, it will, it *will!*" Franni stamped her foot. Francesca flinched. The pistol didn't waver as Franni launched into another diatribe about how everyone thought she was helpless.

Gyles didn't think they'd make that mistake again. He saw Francesca raise her hand and speak—the torrent of Franni's words swept her appeal aside.

He wanted to let Francesca know he was there, reassure her so she didn't do anything rash. It wasn't easy to force his attention from Franni—instinct as old as time had him focused on her—but he shifted his gaze to his wife, kept it there. He knew when Francesca realized. She lifted her head a little, to the side, as if searching for him with her senses, then she straightened and drew her hand from the pew.

"So I'm going to take care of things *my* way." Franni waved the pistol, but immediately brought it to bear again, aimed at Francesca.

Francesca folded her arms over her waist—with a pang, Gyles recognized the instinctive action, the innate urge to protect their unborn child.

"So." His wife's usual warm tones were strained. "What are you going to do? Are you going to shoot me here—in a church?"

Franni's slow smile was taunting, cruel. "No—this is Papa's pistol and I have to take it back. I'd rather it wasn't smelling of powder. I'll use it if I have to, but I've thought of a better plan." Her smile grew colder, her eyes emptier. "A *much* better plan. You're going to disappear."

Abruptly, Franni refocused and flicked a glance to Francesca's right, to the side of the chapel draped in shadow. "These men will take you away."

Francesca looked. Three men stepped forward; she'd been so intent on Franni she hadn't noticed them at all. John Coachman's words rang in her head: two burly men and one scrawny one. John had been describing the highwaymen who'd attacked her carriage. Was it coincidence these three fitted the description?

All three stared at her; one licked his lips. Francesca felt her eyes flare; she fought an urge to step back. The men saw her reaction; they leered and shuffled to the other end of the pew, meaty hands hanging at their sides, opening and closing as if impatient to get hold of her.

Fear rushed over Francesca's skin and left it crawling. Her breath was trapped in her chest. She thought Gyles was close, but was he? She had footmen outside . . . with the thought came the realization that this was a church. There'd be a door leading out of the vestry, most likely on the other side of the church from where her footmen waited. The church stood on a corner—she'd been vaguely aware of the lane beyond the graveyard. In this fog, she could be whisked away and none of her husband's servants would know.

"No. That won't work." It was all she could think of to say.

"Yes, it will." Franni nodded continually; the pistol remained steady in her hands. "The men will keep you, then when you have the baby, they'll bring it to me, then they can dispose of you however they want. That seemed only fair. After all, Gyles won't want you—he'll have me. He'll have forgotten about you by then."

Francesca swung to face Franni, instinctively tightening her arms about their baby. How had Franni known? Then she realized. Franni didn't know—having babies after being married was what happened in books.

"I have it all worked out. Ester told me it would be best if I don't have babies of my own, so instead, I'll have your baby to raise, and you'll be gone, so Gyles will marry me and I'll be Lady Chillingworth."

"No, Franni—it won't happen like that."

Franni gasped and looked up. The pistol wobbled, but she immediately steadied it. Then she smiled, so sweetly, so happily, Francesca could have wept.

"You've come."

The warmth in Franni's voice was unmistakable, the change in her demeanor equally so. Satisfied she'd accepted his appearance, Gyles walked forward. His gaze raked the three men—that was enough to make them step back.

"Yes, Franni. I'm here." He met Francesca's eyes briefly. "Sit down." She did, sinking onto the pew. Stepping past, he halted in front of Franni, directly between her and Francesca. "Give me the pistol." Gyles held out his hand commandingly.

Dazzled, delighted to see him, Franni eased her grip—then her gaze suddenly sharpened. She clutched the pistol and abruptly stepped back, to the side, bringing Francesca once more into sight. Her eyes narrowed as she stared at Gyles, struggling to read his face. "No-oo!" The word was low, rumbling, defiant. Her gaze flicked from him to Francesca. The pistol was once more trained on Francesca's chest. "You're being noble. Chivalrous. You men—come here and tie him up!"

"I wouldn't advise you to try that."

"Don't listen to him!" Franni's eyes snapped; her jaw set. "He's just being noble and chivalrous. He's an earl—they're supposed to be like that. He has to say he doesn't want her dead because she's his wife. He'd feel guilty if he told the truth, but the truth is, he wants her dead so he can marry me, because he loves me. *Me!*" She flicked a wild-eyed glance at the men. "Now come and tie him up!"

The men shifted uneasily. The scrawny one cleared his throat. "You say the pretty lady's his wife—and he's an earl?"

Gyles looked at the men. "How much is she paying you?"

The men eyed him warily. "Promised us a hunnerd, she did," the scrawny one said. "But she only paid a guinea down."

Gyles reached into his pocket, drew out his card case, extracted a card and pencil, then scribbled on the back of the card. "Here." He slipped case and pencil away and held the card out at arm's length. "Take this to the address written on the card and Mr. Waring will give *each of you* one hundred pounds."

"No!" Franni cried.

The men glanced at her, then at Gyles. "How'd we know that's what'll happen?"

"You don't, but if you don't take the card and go now, I can guarantee you'll get nothing—and if you're still around by the time I'm free, I'll hand you over to the watch for questioning about a carriage that was recently attacked in Highgate Wood."

One of the beefy men stirred, glanced at his companions, then lumbered along between the pews. He took the card, frowned at the writing, then glanced at his fellows. " 'Carn—let's go."

The three turned and tramped out of the chapel via the second archway.

"No, no, no, no, *nooooo!*" Franni wailed. She gnashed her teeth, stamped her feet, and backed until she met the altar. Her head swung wildly; the pistol waved, too, but she corrected it, brought it to bear on Francesca, sighting—

Gyles pushed the front pew forward and stepped across Francesca. "Franni! Enough. Things are not going to happen the way you thought."

"Yes, they are! Yes, they are!"

Her heart in her mouth, Francesca stood. "Franni—"

Gyles turned his head. *"Sit down!"*

Francesca did. Forced herself to do it. Franni only had one pistol, one shot. Better he faced that one shot than her—she knew that was how he felt. It wasn't how she felt, but . . . she was no longer in a position to think only of herself. She made herself sit still, fists clenched in her lap. She listened to Gyles talk calmly, as if Franni wasn't bordering on hysteria with a loaded pistol in her hands.

"Listen to me, Franni." Gyles cut off Franni's wailing assertions. "I know you've been trying to make things happen. I want you to tell me all the things you've done. Was it you who stretched the rein across the path up to the downs at Lambourn?"

Francesca frowned.

"Yes, but it didn't work. It didn't make her fall from her horse and die."

"No." Gyles trapped Franni's gaze and grimly held it. "But Franni—I use that track more than Francesca. I was the one who found the rein stretched across the path. It was pure luck I wasn't riding at the time, or *I* might have fallen and died."

Franni's jaw slowly fell. Her mouth worked weakly as she sought for words. "I didn't mean that to happen—it wasn't supposed to be you. It was supposed to be *her*. I put a stone in her little mare's hoof so she'd ride one of the big horses and fall for certain." She blinked blankly. "I did everything right, but it didn't work."

"No, it didn't. Was it you who tore up Francesca's riding cap and stuffed it in the vase?"

"Yes." Franni nodded; the movement rocked her whole body. "It was a silly hat—it made her look nice. Interesting. I didn't want you seeing her in it."

"And was it you who put the poison in Francesca's dressing?"

Franni frowned. "Why didn't that work? It's hers—no one else uses it."

"I did—and I smelled the poison."

"Oh." Franni looked crestfallen, but she'd yet to lower the pistol. She stared at Gyles. "I always tried to do things that would hurt only her—I didn't want to harm anyone else. I didn't even want to harm her, but she has to die—you do see that, don't you?"

The sincerely beseeching look in her eyes made Gyles feel ill. Poor Franni. He understood Francesca's protectiveness, and Charles's and Ester's. . . . "How did you hire the men?"

Smugness returned to Franni's eyes. "Ginny's old. She sleeps a lot. Especially when I slip some of my laudanum into her tea."

"So you drugged your maid and slipped out. What did you do then?"

"I asked a coachman to take me to a place where I could find men who would kill others for money."

Gyles blinked. "Did any of these men harm you?"

Franni looked at him blankly. "No."

Gyles didn't know whether to believe her or not.

He felt a tug on the back of his coat. Francesca whispered, very low, "She answers direct questions literally—honestly."

Small mercies. "Very well." He captured Franni's gaze again. "Now, you don't want to hurt me, do you?"

"Of course not."

"You want to make me happy?"

She smiled. "Yes, that's right."

"Then give me the pistol."

Franni considered, then nodded. "I'll give it to you after I've shot her."

She moved to sight Francesca; Gyles moved, too, blocking her view. Franni frowned at him. "Why are you stopping me? We have to get rid of her—you know that. I'll do it—you don't have to."

Gyles inwardly sighed. "Franni, I'm prepared to swear on that Bible behind you that I'll only be happy if Francesca is my wife, alive and by my side. If you want to make me happy, then shooting Francesca isn't the right thing to do."

Franni's face blanked; Gyles could almost see her mind working. Fingers touched his, slipped into his hand. He briefly squeezed—Francesca squeezed back, clung. He inwardly frowned. Was she trying to warn him?

"No!"

The negative thundered about them. He refocused on Franni to see her transformed. Her head was high, her eyes blazed; her spine was rigid. Her grip on the pistol had tightened.

"I won't have it! That's *not* how it will be. I want you to marry me, *and you shall*. I want it to happen so it *will*. I'm going to shoot her—"

Franni ducked to the side, trying to see Francesca. Closing his hand hard on Francesca's fingers, Gyles held her down, kept her behind him.

"I'm going to shoot her, yes I am—I want, I want and *I shall have*! You don't need her now—you have her land. There's no reason for you to want her now. I want you to want me instead. You *must*!"

Franni's stamp echoed through the chapel.

Francesca struggled to free her hand; Gyles crushed her fingers unmercifully. He shifted this way and that, constantly blocking Franni's attempts to sight her. With his arm braced, she couldn't stand, couldn't try to distract Franni. Her cousin was mad—in her heart, she'd suspected it but had never let the thought form—but now Franni was close to threatening Gyles—didn't he understand how the stories went? If she couldn't have him for herself, then Franni would play out her plot to the end—she'd kill Gyles rather than let Francesca have him.

It was her grandfather all over again but worse. Francis hadn't been insane; Franni was. Francis had been stubborn enough to cut off his nose to spite his face. Franni was capable of worse.

"Let me up!" she hissed.

"No!" Gyles hissed back.

He didn't even look around. Francesca felt frantic. Franni would shoot—

"Franni—*stop!*" There was enough command in Gyles's voice to stop everyone. Behind him, Francesca froze, quivering, waiting. . . .

"Franni, I want you to listen to me—listen very carefully—because I want you to understand all that I say. I want you to look into my eyes so you'll know I'm speaking the truth." Gyles paused. "All right?"

Francesca waited, then she felt a slight relaxing in Gyles's grip and assumed Franni had nodded.

"Very well—listen carefully. I love Francesca. I always have, from the first moment I laid eyes on her. I love her completely, unreservedly—do you know what that means, Franni?"

Bowing her head until her forehead touched their clasped hands, Francesca listened, then she heard Franni say, softly, weakly, "You *love* her?"

"Yes." There could be no question that one word was the

truth—it rang with a conviction no power but one could give. Gyles paused, then said, "You were at our wedding—you heard the words of the service. 'With my body I thee worship. With my soul I thee adore.' I said those words, Franni, and they're true—every one."

Silence followed, cool, still. Minutes ticked past, then into that stillness, Francesca heard, as if from a great distance, a soft sobbing, falling like rain. . . . Lifting her head, she drew in a deep breath and stood. Gyles's arm eased and he let her come to her feet by his side, just behind his shoulder.

Franni still held the pistol, but as her sobs grew, the barrel wavered, then sank. Franni lowered her arms, doubling over in unrestrained grief—

"*Franni!*"

"*Aaaah!*" Franni shrieked, jumped, jerked the pistol up—

Gyles cursed, half turned, flung himself at Francesca—just as she grabbed wildly at him.

The pistol's report shattered the stillness and sent echoes crashing about the church.

They fell. In a wild tangle of arms, legs and grabbing hands, they hit the flags between the pews.

Francesca lost her breath. Immediately, she sucked air in. "My God! Are you hurt? Did you get shot?" She tugged and reached around Gyles, hands spread, searching, trying to find out—

"No, dammit! Did you?"

She met Gyles's gaze, grey and furious. Relief poured through her, and more besides. She smiled. "No."

He frowned at her. "For the Lord's sake! Here—sit up." He struggled to get up but his shoulders had wedged between the pews. He wriggled but couldn't get free. "You landed beneath me—the floor's stone, for heaven's sake! Are you sure—"

Francesca framed his face. Pandemonium raged about them; she ignored it, shut it out, looked deep into his eyes. "What you just said—you meant it, didn't you?"

Charles and Ester were there, struggling with a now hysterical Franni. Osbert waded in, trying to help. Every sound faded to stillness as Gyles looked down at her. "Every word."

He found her hand, raised it, and pressed a kiss to her palm. "I never wanted to love—and especially not you. Now I wouldn't have it any other way." He looked into her eyes; she saw the change in his—the hesitation, the uncertainty. "And you?"

She smiled beatifically, then lifted her head and touched her lips to his. "You know very well I love you . . ."—she searched for words, then simply said—"as you love me."

He bent his head and kissed her, gently, lingeringly—she kissed him back, letting the moment sink into her memories, and his.

When he drew back, she smiled through happy tears. "I knew from the moment I saw you that you would never be dull or boring."

"Dull or boring?" He shoved the front pew forward, then grabbed the back to lever himself from her so he didn't crush her further against the floor. "Are those the criteria on which you judge my performance?"

He stood and held out a hand. She let him pull her to her feet. "Among others. But now I know so much more, I have even higher standards."

He met her gaze. "I'll bear that in mind."

The wailing and admonitions had gained in volume. They turned to see Franni threshing furiously, sobbing, eyes shut, mouth wide. Osbert and the two footmen were holding her, trying not to hurt her and getting hurt for their pains. Ester, disheveled, having clearly grappled with Franni herself, was trying to frame her niece's face, speaking soothingly, trying to reach Franni and calm her.

Charles stood before them, facing Franni, the pistol hanging limply in one hand. As they watched, he drew in a huge breath, then turned and saw them. His face was ashen. He looked at the pistol, then stepped down and laid it on the front pew. Approaching them, he lifted his head; bracing himself, he stopped before them.

"I am so sorry." The words seemed to sap all his strength. He ran a hand through his hair, glanced back at Franni.

He was more shaken than they were. Francesca exchanged a glance with Gyles. "It's all right." She took Charles's hands in hers.

He returned the pressure of her fingers, attempted a smile, but shook his head. "No, my dear. I wish it were, but it's not all right." He glanced again at Franni; her sobs were gradually abating. "Ester and I have been afraid something like this would happen. We've been watching Franni for years, wondering, hoping . . ." He sighed, then looked at Francesca and released her hands. "But it wasn't to be." Straightening, he glanced at Gyles. "I owe you an explanation." Francesca and Gyles opened their mouths; Charles held up his hand. "No—please, let me say it. Let me tell you so you can decide for yourselves. So you can understand."

Francesca and Gyles exchanged a glance. Gyles nodded. "As you wish."

Charles hauled in a huge breath. "You'll have heard that Elise, my wife, Franni's mother, threw herself to her death from the tower at Rawlings Hall. That's not precisely true. I was with her. She didn't throw herself." Charles's face grew bleak. "She fell while trying to push me over the edge."

"She tried to kill you?"

"Yes." The word was a long, painful sigh. "And don't ask me why—I never knew. But that's not the whole story. It doesn't start there. Elise's mother, Ester's mother, too, also . . . went mad. She was incarcerated for a time, but eventually died. I don't know the details. I wasn't told, never knew, not until Ester came to live with us a year or so after Franni was born. After Elise started . . . changing." Charles dragged in a breath. "It runs in the women of that family, but not all of them are affected. Ester isn't. The trouble starts, if it's going to start, sometime after twenty years of age. Elise . . ." His daze grew distant. "She was so lovely—we were so happy. Then it turned into a nightmare. Delusions that gradually escalated to derangement. Then to violence. Then it ended."

Francesca reached for Gyles's hand, grateful for the warmth when his hand enveloped hers.

Charles exhaled, shook his head. "Ester knew about her mother. She didn't think it wise for Elise to marry—it's the reason Ester never has. But our fathers, mine and Elise's, were set on the match. I'm sure Papa didn't know at the time. He did afterward, of course. As always, such happenings are hidden away. Ester was sent to an aunt in Yorkshire until after Elise and I were married, and Franni was born."

His gaze exhausted and bleak, Charles looked at Francesca. "I'm so sorry, my dear, that you were caught up in this—we'd been hoping for so long that Franni would be spared . . . we just kept hoping. We didn't realize until we were here, in London, that she was truly deteriorating. You have to believe me—we never imagined she'd go . . . so fast."

Visibly steeling himself, Charles faced Gyles. "What will you do?"

Gyles looked at Charles and felt nothing but compassion, saw nothing but a man who had loved his wife and sought to protect his only daughter. Raising a hand, he gripped Charles's shoulder. "I assume you'll want to take Franni back to Rawlings Hall without delay. Can you manage? What can we do to help?"

Charles blinked. He searched Gyles's eyes. "You won't press charges?"

Gyles held his gaze. "Franni's a Rawlings. Despite her illness, she's family, and she can't help how she is."

Charles looked down. Francesca squeezed his arm. His throat worked, then he whispered, "Thank you."

Gyles dragged in a breath, and looked again at Franni,

now slumped, exhausted, supported by Ester and one of the footmen. "I'd offer to help carry her to the carriage, but I think it might be best if Francesca and I left. Franni will be more docile with us gone."

Charles nodded.

"If you can manage it, call at the house before you leave London. We'd like to know all's well." Gyles held out his hand.

Charles gripped it. "I will—and again, thank you."

"Take care." Francesca stretched up to kiss her uncle's cheek. "*All* of you."

Charles's lips twisted. He turned away as Osbert came up, looking more serious than Francesca had ever seen him. "I'll stay with Charles—help get the girl into the hackney."

Gyles clapped him on the shoulder. "Drop by tomorrow and fill us in."

Osbert nodded and turned back to the group before the altar. Francesca took one last look at Franni, eyes closed, head back, mouth agape, sagging against Ester, who was gently brushing back her wispy hair.

"Come." Gyles turned Francesca. His arm about her, he guided her from the chapel.

"I want, I want, and *I shall have.*" In the dark warmth of the carriage, wrapped in Gyles's arms, Francesca repeated the litany. "That Franni got from our grandfather. It was one of his favorite sayings."

Gyles held her close. She'd made no demur when he'd lifted her into his lap the instant they'd started off. He needed to hold her, to reassure the barbarian that all was well and she was here, still with him, safe and unhurt. She seemed equally content to rest against him, her head on his shoulder, one hand splayed on his chest, over his heart. "I thought you never met old Francis."

"I didn't. Papa told me—he explained about Grandfather, about how stubborn he was. He wanted me to know just in case. . . ."

Gyles thought of a man farsighted enough to protect his daughter into any possible future. "I'm sorry I never met your father."

"He'd have liked you—approved of you."

Never had Gyles felt more conscious of his own happiness, his own good fortune. He thought of all he had—all Charles had not had a true chance to enjoy. "Poor Franni. Not only did she inherit madness from her mother, but she also absorbed old Francis's peculiar madness."

"I didn't say anything before—to Charles. It would only upset him more. Ester told me Francis spent a great deal of time with Franni, and that that had pleased Charles."

Gyles pressed a kiss to Francesca's curls. "Best leave him with that memory."

The carriage rattled on. They'd pulled the leather flaps down over the windows, shutting out the chilly night, creating a dark, companionable cave.

"Thank you for not pressing charges."

"I meant what I said about Franni being family."

She'd taught him, made him see, what family in the wider sense was about—the support, the net of caring. After a moment, he added, "In a way, we're indebted to Franni. If she hadn't been there to appear as the cipher I thought I wanted to wed, then I would have realized who Francesca Rawlings was before we sealed the matter, and then it wouldn't have been sealed at all."

"Would you really not have married me if you'd known who I was? Known that Francesca Rawlings was me?"

Gyles laughed. "I knew the instant I set eyes on you that you were the *last* woman I should marry if I wanted a meek, mild-mannered cipher as wife. And I was right."

At her soft humph he smiled, but then sobered. "If Franni hadn't been there, we wouldn't be here now, married, in love, expecting our first child. My only regret is that my appearing at Rawlings Hall seems to have acted as a catalyst for her delusions."

"If not you, then some other." Francesca was silent for some time, then murmured, "Fate moves in mysterious ways."

Gyles stroked her hair. "We won't be able to visit Rawlings Hall. Franni will do better without seeing us again."

"I feel for Charles and Ester. To have watched and waited all Franni's life, only to have their worst dreams come true."

"We can still help—make sure Charles can hire the best carers for Franni. And we can make sure Charles and Ester get away every now and then—we can invite them to Lambourn in summer."

"We could make it an annual arrangement that they visit, so they don't get shut away, and the family don't lose track of them."

Francesca wriggled in his arms so she could look into his face. The carriage had reached the City; courtesy of the streetlamps, more light was seeping past the flaps, enough to see. "I was thinking . . . Honoria told me about the gathering the Cynsters have at Somersham. I think we should do something similar at Lambourn, don't you?"

Gyles looked into her face and smiled. "Whatever pleases you, my lady. You may create whatever traditions you please—I and all I have are yours to command."

Delighted, not so much by the words as by the expression in his eyes, in his face presently devoid of any fashionable mask, Francesca smiled back. Inside, her heart rejoiced.

All she'd ever wanted, all she would ever need, was here, and hers. After last night, she'd been prepared to accept the reality without any declaration. Now she had it all—an enduring love and the words that acknowledged it clearly stated between them.

She studied his eyes, his face—the angular planes that gave so little away. Perhaps they owed Franni one thing more. "Why was it so difficult for you to say it—to utter such a small, simple word?"

He laughed, but not in amusement. "A small, simple word—only a woman would describe it as that."

He hadn't answered her question. Her eyes on his, Francesca waited.

He sighed and let his head fall back against the squabs. "It's hard to explain, but as long as I didn't say it aloud, didn't openly admit it, then enough doubt existed so I could pretend I wasn't taking a chance, that I wasn't risking misery and destruction by being so foolish as to love you."

Francesca frowned. Why . . . ? Then she realized. Reaching up, she framed his face, made him meet her eyes. "I will always be here—I will always be with you. You may put as many guards about me as you wish, for however long it takes for you to accept that."

Gyles read her eyes, then forced himself to say, "I learned very young that when you love, you leave yourself open to unimaginable hurt."

"I know—but it's still worth it."

Gyles studied her eyes, then kissed her lightly, drew her back into his arms and rested his cheek against her hair. She was right. Nothing was more contrary than love. Nothing left a man more vulnerable, yet nothing could bring him such joy. In order to reap the harvest of love, it was necessary to accept the risk of losing that same love. Love was a coin with two sides, gain and loss. To secure the gain, one had to embrace the risk of loss.

How much he'd changed since the day he'd set out for Rawlings Hall. His home had been cold, lacking warmth, lacking life—he'd set out to find a wife to rectify the deficiency. He'd found her, and now she was his. His sun, warming his house, nurturing his family, giving meaning to his life. She was literally the center of his universe.

He decided he might as well tell her. After a moment, he murmured, "It didn't all happen at once, you know."

"Oh?" She wriggled and he let her turn once again so she could see his face, and he could see hers.

Taking her hand, he raised it to his lips. "Body, mind, heart, and soul." His eyes on hers, he pressed a kiss to her palm. "My body was yours from the first instant I saw you—you claimed it as yours on our wedding night. My mind and heart you fought for and won—they're now yours for all eternity." He paused, sobering as he looked into her emerald eyes. "And as for my soul, it's yours, freely offered—yours to take and chain as you choose."

Francesca held his gaze and thought her heart would burst, with joy, with a happiness too profound to contain. Freeing her arms, she slid her hands over his shoulders, skating one to his nape as she raised her face to his. "Thank you, my lord. I accept."

She sealed the bargain with a kiss—a kiss that promised a lifetime of bliss in the shackles of an enduring love.

They had only one formal engagement remaining before leaving for Lambourn—Lady Dalrymple's Christmas dinner. It was early December, weeks before Christmas, but the last of the ton would soon depart the capital and return to their estates. Gyles would have given a great deal to escape earlier to Lambourn and escape the inevitable roasting from one of the few of his kind who would also be at the dinner.

There was to be no escape.

Francesca, superb in a gown of sea-green silk, drew all eyes, not just because of her lush curves but more so because of the radiant happiness glowing in her eyes, coloring her voice, implicit in her every gesture. To the irritation of his rakish self, he seemed incapable of doing anything other than beam with proprietorial pride.

Devil, of course, saw and understood, as few others would. From across the table set with silver and glittering crystal and the rich tones of Limoges dishes, Devil grinned—devilishly—and raised his glass in a private toast.

Gyles had no difficulty making out his words.

"Welcome to the club."

Author's Note

Dear Reader,

So at last you've learned of Chillingworth's fate. We can now leave him and Francesca to get on with their well-rounded and passionate lives, and turn our attention to the next Cynsters to fall.

It's the twins' turn to find love in the next two Cynster volumes. The years have rolled by and although they've been searching constantly and diligently, they've yet to find any suitable men—gentlemen of rank who measure up to their high standards, men who can hold their own when compared to their Cynster cousins. They have, they decide, reached the end of their tether—they're no longer willing to wait on fate to turn her attention their way. So they each devise a campaign—a strategy to find and win the man of their dreams. To Amanda, the matter's obvious—as they've failed to flush out any suitable prey in the conventional hunting fields of ballrooms and drawing rooms, then they need to look elsewhere. She turns her determined sights on venues where more dangerously exciting gentlemen—gentlemen like her cousins before they were wed—are to be found.

In waltzing into their lairs, she discovers it's not at all difficult to attract attention; unfortunately, not all is of the type she welcomes. In weathering an unexpected storm, she finds herself indebted to the most fascinatingly elusive gentleman, a devastatingly handsome earl who prefers the shadows to the glittering lights of the ton. Amanda decides he's the lion she wishes to tame, but first she must snare him. In the game that ensues, pursuit and passion go hand in hand, first driving one, then the other, until the love that grows from it is strong enough to demand the resolution of a long-ago mystery, paving the way for Amanda's earl to return to the light by her side.

Read of Amanda's pursuit of love in the next volume of the Cynster series, to be released by Avon Books in April 2002. Amelia's tale will follow in October 2002, followed by the story of Simon, the youngest male of the Bar Cynster generation.

AND NOW FOR A SPECIAL ANNOUNCEMENT:

Watch out for a Cynster special Christmas volume Avon Books and I have dreamed up just for you. On sale in December 2001 and throughout the festive season, *The Promise in a Kiss* takes us back in time to witness the first meeting between Devil Cynster's parents, Sebastian, 5th Duke of St. Ives, and Helena, Comtesse de Stansion. That first magical meeting sows the seeds of the passionate liaison that, over time, lays the foundation for the wonderful world of the Cynsters, and the Cynster generation whose tales you've enjoyed reading.

Experience *The Promise in a Kiss*—and enjoy!

Stephanie Laurens